TOFFY'S DIVIDE

TOFFY'S DIVIDE

NIFEMI ALUKO

NEW DEGREE PRESS

COPYRIGHT © 2021 NIFEMI ALUKO

All rights reserved.

TOFFY'S DIVIDE

ISBN   978-1-63730-365-8   *Paperback*

         978-1-63730-366-5   *Kindle Ebook*

         978-1-63730-367-2   *Ebook*

This one is for Eghe

CONTENTS

———

AUTHOR'S NOTE

I am a storyteller, music lover, and entrepreneur, and I make beats.

Communication through words, language, rhythms, and visual cues is the fabric that weaves our human experiences together, builds empathy, and provides the springboard from which innovation emerges.

With my passion for music, I see music all around me: the beats of hearts, the unsteady tempo of footsteps, the timpani of traffic, the crashing of cymbals, the whistling of wind, and pockets of vibrations that travel through the medium of air that surrounds us all. That's where the story of Toffy begins.

I didn't initially set out to write this novel. All I needed was a story prompt that I could use for a music project. In the absence of having the right prompt, I decided to write a story about "a guy writing a story" with hopes of borrowing from my experiences and observations. This took me on a journey to explore myself and the world around me, through the lens of Toffy and the residents of the technology-consumed and highly divided J City in the year 2049.

As an engineer who spent years deploying model-predictive control technology to optimize manufacturing plants, I had a glimpse of the promise artificial intelligence (AI) held before the buzz and mainstream applications of AI. I moved on to business school at Stanford University in California, where this buzz was reinforced. I departed Silicon Valley to head back home and start a business in Nigeria. Spending my time between Nigeria and California exposed me to the growing inequality, across and within both regions.

Toffy's Divide explores these themes—inequality, capitalism, consolidated power, and technological advancements—and how they impact the everyday person in an increasingly connected automated age.

Our cognitive ability to generate original thought sets us apart from other species. The creativity to solve problems gives us the ability to utilize our resources more efficiently. Building new tools and technologies has become an inseparable part of our existence. Technology enables us to do so much. It allows us to build giant architectural structures quickly, move tons of goods and services across oceans, explore other planets, and communicate with loved ones thousands of miles apart within seconds. Technology has truly enhanced our experience and existence as human beings.

Technology is a good thing, a great thing in fact; however, technology can also be detrimental to society. It can be used to control, exploited to oppress, and manipulated to distract us from the present, from each other, or even from creative production, the very things that make us human.

To prevent the negative effects of technology, we have to tap into our cognitive and creative energy. We have to become more aware of our space and time. We have to create space to *create*. That's what Toffy fights to do, battling internal and external forces just to tell his own story in a city where residents are essentially controlled and overwhelmed with distracting content on screens plastered all over.

In thirty years, technology will be more refined in terms of applications in artificial intelligence and biotechnology, both of which could be used in positive or negative ways. A heightened level of responsibility will be placed on corporations, governments, institutions, and individual consumers to use this technology positively, and for the greater good. We explore this in Toffy's story as well as his employment at J Enterprise—a corporation that owns almost everything, including the government and institutions.

No one can predict the future, but it's fun to try.

The futuristic setting of Toffy's world explores the possible implications from our continuous advancements in technology. It's connected to the question that I believe a lot of people have on their minds.

How will we use these tools that are supposed to make our lives better?

Will we use technology to accumulate power in a few hands, worsen our widening inequality, damage our environment further, negatively disrupt the labor markets, and incite damaging narratives?

Or will we use technology to empower more global citizens, promote self-awareness, and foster communal collaboration that brings communities and the world together while aiding new levels of training for the expertise needed to keep people gainfully employed in the automation age?

Curiosity drove me to write this story. Along my journey, I continued to feed my passion for creativity by making beats and writing lyrics, which eventually developed into a creative practice. Combining my love for music, technology, and business took me down the path of writing *Toffy's Divide* over the last five years.

Along the way, I published *Press Play: Music as a Catalyst for Change*, a nonfiction book about music and how it can be channeled to galvanize social change and global empowerment. I learned much from that experience and applied it to finishing *this* book. I sampled ideas from major influences such as *Fahrenheit 451*, extrapolating the concept of authoritarian rule that wants to rid people of new knowledge, but instead of burned books we have deleted memories and erased hard drives.

I borrowed concepts from the conformist order in another favorite of mine, *1984*, painting the picture of Toffy's internal struggle between maintaining the status quo and having the courage to break away to find purpose, with a humble attempt to predict the future just like George Orwell did when he published *1984* in 1949.

The role of mass media in the market-driven world of J City was informed by *Manufacturing Consent* while the dangers that arise from a lack of self-awareness within leadership both in corporations and government was inspired by another amazing read—*The Wizard of the Crow*. All these books touch on a possible reality where accumulated power and institutions are used to divide and disempower the people.

Just like I do with my music, I sampled these ideas and combined them with mine to create something new and original.

Toffy's Divide is a story about courage, a story for people who love stories about self-discovery. It's for professionals looking for motivation to act on their creative outlets; people looking for inspiration to break from meaningless routines; technologists, futurists, and people interested in what the world could look like in the year 2049.

This is a story to remind us that we can all forge our own paths. We can manifest our destinies and transform our realities.

My hope is that this book opens up the possibilities of increased self-awareness, empowerment, a yearning to collaborate with like-minded people, and ultimately the ability share your own story (in whatever medium the reader prefers). Everyone has a unique story to tell, and our world is shaped by storytellers.

What started as a thought to write a story prompt for a mixtape ended up as a full story that's now a published book.

This is a reminder to myself, and hopefully to others, that we have the power to create the space to create. We can follow our curiosity and enjoy the journey as it takes us to unexpected and beautiful places. We have the power to reconnect with ourselves and what it means to be human.

We can create, and we can build more responsibly.

CHAPTER 1

———

Toffy sat cross-legged in the backseat as his automobile propelled itself seamlessly over the silky streets of J City. It picked up speed at the green light and halted at stop signs and pedestrian crossings, all on its own.

Automation at its finest. *J City engineering in the house.* That's how the ads went. Just like everything else in High Town, Toffy's car answered the calls of the automation gods and no one else.

Although Toffy had been in his vehicle driving away from his office for precisely thirteen minutes and twenty-one seconds, according to the car's dashboard, his office building was still as visible as it was when he just stepped out. A towering emblem of capitalist strength, the building was intentionally constructed so it appeared the same size wherever one was in the city.

"Onyx. Play relaxing music." Toffy took a deep breath and sighed.

"Here's some relaxing music for you, Toffy," the female voice of his vehicle replied. The tunes played out. Toffy swiveled his chair around.

As the J Building stalked Toffy and all other residents through the glitter-littered streets, Toffy could not get his mind off work. The building, from the distance, was a constant reminder that he had not done enough for the day. *Did I leave too early today? I maxed out on my utilization, but there's still so much to do if we're going to meet the deadlines for release date.* Toffy could not stop thinking about the product he and his team had been working so hard on. Release date was only a few weeks ahead.

His vehicle buzzed at fifteen minutes—a timer he had set to avoid sitting in the vehicle aimlessly for hours. A month ago, at the height of development of "Project D," Toffy had sat and worked in his vehicle as it drove him around the city for exactly six hours and thirty minutes. Absorbed in his work, he had forgotten to input his destination, and the vehicle had driven him around, winding endlessly in the several spiraled streets of the city until sunrise, and then back to where he had started—in front of J Enterprise. He never made it home that night. He changed his clothes at his desk and had an early start at work. Ever since that day, Toffy had set a buzzing reminder every fifteen minutes to make sure his AV was on track toward a prescribed destination of his choosing.

"Onyx. Play the latest city updates." The music had made him more tense.

Toffy gazed out the window as Onyx weaved through the different layers of the city. The streets were tarred jet black. People walked along the side of the street in uniformed consistency. There were no visible drainage holes, the street itself made out of porous material that allowed water to pass through. No pavements or sidewalks. The vehicles knew their place, and the people knew their place on the streets—as close to the shining screened-covered buildings as possible.

Flashy shows and adverts transfixed the people as they passed.

A young child threw an uncontrollable tantrum at the helm of one of the buildings. The child, who must have only started walking recently, had his bulging eyes glued to pulsating primary colors. The mother struggled to peel him off the screen. The child kicked and screamed as the mom swept him off his feet, threw him across her shoulder, and walked away swiftly. She knew she could have easily been persuaded by her tempered child.

If only children understood the concept of conserving money, Toffy thought, peeling his face away from the mother and son.

From the backseat view in his autonomous vehicle, he saw endless diminishing rows of screened buildings.

Onyx buzzed at thirty minutes. Two minutes afterward, the announcement came in from the transparent megaphones placed around the city: "You are safe. Everything is all right. Have no worries. You are safe," the daily 11 p.m. safety announcement.

Toffy closed his eyes and repeated: "Everything is all right. Everything is all right. Everything is all right."

All the buildings had switched, showing the same thing. In bold black letters on a white screen, the words moved from left to right, matching the deep voice that authoritatively propelled out of the speakers. "You are safe. Enjoy your night. You are safe," the megaphones continued.

Toffy sat back in his seat, his shoulders slumped, reminded that they were all being watched and monitored. Every act, every step, every movement of the eye, every undress, every zipped-up skirt, every buttoned shirt, every kiss, every punch, every birth, every death, it was all being monitored by the screens.

But who watched from the other side?

No one could escape the gaze of the all-seeing screens.

The screens and the buildings were all owned by a few. Control consolidated in the hands of not two, but one. All owned by the company Toffy worked for.

Onyx slowed to the right of the road, closer to a line of people looping around a gold, egg-shaped structure.

"You have now arrived at your destination," Onyx said. It beeped and silently went on snooze.

The car door opened, and Toffy stepped out. The gold building was the latest addition to the skyline. It was opening day for the structure that had taken a long four months to build. The design was the brainchild of the infamous architect Vanch, who coined himself "the most revolutionary architect ever."

The screens, curved on the egg-shaped building, looped replays of the speech Vanch had given earlier in the afternoon at the opening ceremony.

Toffy stopped to watch the replays of Vanch working up the eager crowd. "It's all about being a genius these days. The most genius thing you can do is *not* be a genius."

The recorded crowd around Vanch erupted in delirious applause.

"Oh, Vanch," shouted a man from the audience on the screen, "that's the most genius thing you've ever said." The man rounded out his comment with an edited belly laugh.

"The thing that makes this building so different," Vanch continued, "besides the fact that it's only partially covered by screens, is that unlike other buildings, this is a pigeon-egg-shaped building." Vanch paused. "Come on. There have been turkey-egg-shaped buildings and ostrich egg shaped domes, but this will be the first pigeon-egg-inspired building."

The crowd erupted in cheers.

"We love you, Vanch," yelled a woman from the audience.

Hmmm, that's true. This building is not fully covered by screens. Toffy examined the top half of the new building. He moved his gaze back to the screen on the bottom half of the building. The replay continued.

Vanch raised his hands as a signal for the audience to stop clapping. He grasped for the appropriate silence he needed to dazzle them with his next statement.

"It does not end there," Vanch shouted with his eyes closed. "This is the first building of its kind that's gold with a touch of salmon and a hint of stained brownish-red, like the soil of the old days."

He opened his eyes, displeased with the lack of eardrum-rupturing applause.

"There have been similar buildings," he continued. His eyes wide open now, "but this is the *first* that's gold with a touch of salmon and a hint of stained brownish—"

The crowd erupted again before Vanch finished.

"You are not a genius, and that's what makes you a genius, Vanch," a young lady yelled out. She had a shiny white silk glove on one hand.

So much praise. Pleasant building, yes, sure. But all the adulation. Every time I think we've taken it too far, something pops up to show me we haven't taken it far enough.

Toffy walked toward his destination. At the corner of the new building, close to the intersection, was a pulsing red balloon opening that led to the most recent addition to J City nightlife. A multitude of people lined up waiting to enter the new spot. Ladies in long and short dresses. Men in suits and

T-shirts. Different outfits with prints all recently downloaded specifically to be seen at LOW BAR's opening week festivities.

"Hi, Toffy. Fancy seeing you here," Clarika said.

Toffy was not too delighted to see his neighbor. "Yeah, just meeting up with a friend," he responded reluctantly.

"It's awesome here. Isn't it?" Clarika continued. "Another highlight in the night life of the ever-evolving J City."

"Yeah," Toffy said. He walked faster. "See you later."

Toffy hurried off and passed the long line toward the front door. The petite lady in a flowing blue dress at the door recognized him. She played with her glasses.

"We only accept reservations," she said with a mischievous grin, pretending to be lost in the guest list, "but I'll make an exception because it's you."

"Thanks." Toffy blushed. "I'm actually meeting up with Sarni."

"Oh yeah, he's right there." She pointed down the rows of lit chairs. Sarni gestured for Toffy to join them.

"What's up?" Toffy asked, excited to see his friend.

"Here you go," Sarni exclaimed. "You need to catch up." He handed Toffy a shot glass of clear liquor. Sweat touched his gold wristwatch.

"Ah, man. It's that type of night, huh?" Toffy said. He took off his jacket and slid into the chair across from Sarni.

Two women in their early twenties joined them at the table.

"Let me do the introduction here," Sarni said. "Toffy, this is Fiona." He pointed to the young lady in a red dress. "And this is… please remind me of your name again." Sarni placed his hand below his chin to hold his head up. His wristwatch slid down his arm to the top of his shirt sleeve. "Just kidding. This is Danell."

"Nice to meet you, ladies," Toffy said.

"Sarni," Danell said, giggling with Fiona, "why didn't you tell us you had such a good-looking friend?"

"Ladies, please! Toffy here is in a committed relationship," Sarni said and gestured toward his three-person audience, "and I love Deja too much to be pawning him off to young tigers like you two."

The two ladies laughed as Fiona sat next to Sarni and Danell next to Toffy.

"The good news is," Sarni continued, "I can have the two of you beautiful ladies all to myself." Sarni stretched his hands out and gently held both their hands.

"Thanks, Sarni," Fiona said, "for getting us in here today."

"Yeah. Really. Thanks," Danell echoed.

"I still can't believe we got in here for opening week," Fiona said as she smiled and flipped her head backward. "The reservation list is about five months out. My friends will be *so* jealous."

"Five months?" Toffy said. "Really? Is that true? How is that even possible? This building was built in four. How is the reservation list that—"

"Don't ask *me*. I'm not a priest," Fiona interrupted and typed into her mobile device, dictating each word out. "Here at the Pigeno. First in. Last out," she continued. "For all of you still on the line outside, all the best trying to get in. Gaddam, ladder-climbers. For those of you watching those on the line, get a life. You don't even deserve a ladder. Lastly, and definitely the least, those of you at home looking at these fabulous pictures…"

Her device completed the sentence before she dictated it.

"Posted!" she yelled. She dropped her device on the table and took a swig of her drink. "And thank you for…" Fiona put her hand on Sarni's thigh and gestured toward the bathroom.

"Yeah. Don't mention it," Sarni responded. He looked at Toffy and back at Fiona. "I would have joined you guys, but I can't indulge too much tonight. We have a game tomorrow." He looked at Toffy again for confirmation. "Isn't that right, Toffy?"

"Yes. We need Sarni in top shape," Toffy responded.

"Exactly. Have to stay focused, because even when you're on the same team, you never know what side you're playing for." Sarni ended the conversation with a smile directed at Toffy. Toffy smiled back.

The red lights of the bar pulsated as music blasted through the speakers at a steady rate of 125 beats per minute, all night. *Boom. Boom. Boom. Boom.*

I have to get home soon. Work is calling. Toffy tapped on his device. His utilization bar for the day was at a 99.9 percent. *Good. But I can't let this slip.*

People on the dancehall swayed in an elongated trance. Laughter reverberated around the room. Clicks and clacks of bottles and glasses bounced off the inner walls of the egg-shaped room. The energy was alive. On tables, people clinked glasses and shared finger food. They all worked at J Enterprise, so they exchanged only inter-department cards. New romances, deals, and hookups were blooming.

Celebration in waves. Work hard today, celebrate tomorrow. But there's hardly a tomorrow to celebrate—just more work. Only a few nights like this. Excessive. What are we really celebrating? Maybe all these champagne bottles don't need to be opened, Toffy observed. Sweat dripped down Sarni's face as he danced with Danell and Fiona at the edge of the circular dance floor.

Vanch sat in the corner taking notes on his personal screen. He would iterate the internal design of the building based on the notes.

Toffy didn't expect to stay out so long, but the face within the bezel of his vintage Hag Teuer wristwatch revealed 3:11 a.m.

He grabbed his jacket, said bye to Sarni from a distance, and rushed home.

Toffy silently walked through the front door of his apartment. Only half tipsy, he silently dropped his device on the kitchen counter. In the darkness he unbuttoned his shirt as he walked toward the window to get the faintness of light that shone through from the city.

The flashing lights of High Town reflected on the glass. *That white cloud. The fog. That fluffy thing.*

The vast white cloud that laid at the edge of the town was visible from his apartment window. It had always been a great view until Toffy realized what lay beneath.

The fluff. A coverup? Behind it. I can't unsee it.

As he carefully slipped on his pajama pants, he caught a glimpse of a small black book in the corner of his apartment, as if perfectly placed in a spot to conceal its location. Toffy examined the little black book intently. Something about the way it was placed invited him closer.

Toffy remembered why he had put the little black book in the corner. He was not supposed to bring it home. He was going to write his thoughts in that book inconspicuously. Toffy shoved it further behind one of the latest sculptures he and Deja had won at an auction.

It would be better here, Toffy thought.

His eyes adjusted to the darkness enough to see the layout of every object in his apartment: the paintings on the wall, the high-design minimal furniture, the programmed automations all around.

Toffy walked to his room and slowly opened the door, glancing at the sculpture in the corner to make sure his little black book was not visible.

No one can see what I've written in that book, or I'll lose it all.

CHAPTER 2

———

Toffy woke up unusually early. His clock displayed 4:32 a.m. in bold green lines. He had only closed his eyes an hour ago. Toffy scanned the room. *The screens are off. I should write.* He reached behind the sculpture, grabbed the book, and sat on the floor in the corner. He dared not look at the things he had written. He turned to a blank page and picked up a pen hidden behind the flower vase.

Intimidated by the blank page, he started writing.

There's so much trouble in the world. They say.

SO MUCH TROUBLEEEE......

How is this allowed to happen?

Just the other day, a bomb dropped from the sky and killed a woman and four of her children. The husband was covered in blood and soot, pulling his wife and half his baby's body from the rubble. He cried. He asked God, "Why?" Bombs going off in forgotten corners of the world, and all we hear in J City is the muted aftershocks.

How can they let this happen?

It's like no one cares. I saw a video of a kid shooting another man, and then the police came and shot the kid. Then, the kid's sister came and shot the police officer's wife, and then the police officer's wife's brother shot the police officer and the kid's sister.

Why? Is that video real? I saw more strange things with my own eyes. The haze. The line.

There's so much violence. So many weapons.

How much longer can we go on like this? But this is not seen on the everyday screen. No one wants to see it. Especially not here in High Town. I don't want to see it. I want to unsee it. In Low Town, there's a load of it. How can I go back to a time when men and women were not fighting and killing one another?

The screens there are doing the opposite.

Who is to blame? Am I to blame? How have I helped?

All I do is create products and write mindless copy for the mindless. To get them to buy more. To make them happy. To tell them the world is good. That everything is going to be all right. All just to keep them in a buying mood so the corporation can take more of their money through advertising.

No one cares anymore.

The way earthly things are going, I swear to you, anything can surely happen.

Now we want to delete new thoughts. Nothing new will be able to—

"GOOD MORNING. HOUSEHOLD OF TOFFY," came splurging out from screen 2x5i, the main screen across from the couch. It doubled as a television in his living room.

Toffy looked up at the screen. "Five o'clock in the morning? Crap!" In a swift motion, he tossed the book behind the sculpture next to the couch and threw the pen in the other direction.

He stood up in a feigned stretch.

"Good morning, Fluence. You caught me in the middle of my early morning workout."

"That's a new workout," the screen said. "You are sitting on the bare floor. That's beyond your tactile comfort. Would you like me to order a floor mat?"

"No, no, no. I'm fine"

"As you wish. Here is your daily news, but let's start with the daily assessment."

Toffy walked closer to the middle of the room with the soft piercing sounds of the beeping apartment, a daily routine.

"Assessment complete. All good. Nothing strange," the screen said. The beeping stopped after only fifteen seconds.

"Everything is in order. You know what else is in order? The world. The world is such a beautiful place. You should try this new coffee brand. It can be here in less than four minutes. You will be walking out the door to the smell of mint and lavender in your coffee."

Toffy prepared his gym bag. He knew he would love to try the mint lavender in coffee.

They know me too well. Fluence's recommendations are always right. My years of training have deepened its personalization output for me.

"PLACING ORDER FOR MINT LAVENDER COFFEE," the screen continued. "How about new vacation spots to consider, Mr. Toffy? Look at all the beautiful places in the world you can go."

Toffy could not resist looking at the screen. The clear blue waters and white sands sent a mixed warm and cool feeling down his chest. The screen knew exactly what he wanted, even though he knew he wouldn't be able to enjoy it.

I would probably end up working on that beach. Unlimited vacation days, but no one really takes them, Toffy thought.

"THE WORLD IS IN PERFECT ORDER, MR. TOFFY. VACATION BOOKED," Fluence's steady voice continued from the screen. "Now, let's check on the status of your coffee and order a new pair of socks for your game this morning."

Toffy had forgotten about the book. The wars. The violence. He scrolled the morning news on the surface of the kitchen counter. He muted the toy promotion that played on the cereal box.

A note from Deja flashed on the fridge's silver screen. It read: "Dinner next week? Hopefully nothing comes up!" *Hopefully nothing comes up.* Toffy echoed the message in his mind. The same note had been flashing for three weeks.

He placed his used bowl in the designated "Dirty Dishes" section. Later in the afternoon, the cleaning robo-service would gain secure access to his apartment, place all the dishes in the washer, and rearrange them all neatly in a glassed counter above the washer.

Toffy was greeted by the scent of his coffee and the pleasant buzz of typical J City mornings as soon as he stepped out of his apartment building. A crew of men brought down a panel of screens on the building at the corner of the street adjacent to Toffy's apartment. A brand-new screen was unpacked at the bottom of the crane, which elevated the three men unscrewing the screen on the third floor of the glossy silver building.

He jumped into his vehicle. "Hello, Onyx. To the office," Toffy said.

It immediately turned on and hummed into the street.

The shiny white pyramid that was J Building gleamed in the close and intimate distance. It followed everyone around town, reaffirming its presence on the residents.

The sight of the pyramid immediately hit him with a wave of anxiety.

So much to be done. Toffy's heart raced. *The people will finally get a taste of Project D. Seven months. Nonstop development. Can't wait to be done with it. Reduce the pressure.*

Toffy and his team had built an automatic self-editing machine. The machine was built over rigorously trained neural networks, designed to "save people from themselves."

Project D, short for its full name—Deleteron, a product by J Enterprise—would positively save mankind from itself. It was initially cooked up by Chez, the Chief Initiator of All Initiatives (CIAI) of J Enterprise. On that dull morning, he had the bright idea of cutting down overhead in the revisionist department by making sure there was no history to revise in the first place.

"We spend so many hours each year revising what has happened in the past," Chez had proclaimed. "Changing stories and editing. All that is going to change in our very immediate future. I present to you Deleteron, the NI-based machine that edits unwanted words and stories as soon as they are typed, dictated, written, or reported. Long gone are the days of artificial intelligence, surreal and augmented intelligence. Now, we are leaning heavily into NI: *natural intelligence.*

"This will be on every computer," Chez had proclaimed. "On every mobile device. At every school. Every store. Every library. On every screen. We are at the cusp, once again, of changing the world. They will write about us in the history books. Well, we will write about ourselves."

Onyx slowly rolled toward the park that led toward J Enterprise. Toffy stepped out to a congregation of people gathered for a ceremony.

"What's going on there?" Toffy asked one of the security officers.

"They are breaking ground for the new structure that's about to be built," the security officer responded. "They are saying it's going to be a big one. Not quite sure what it's for."

A church? I haven't seen that in a while. Toffy looked back at the gathering. "Why are they on their knees bowing and raising their hands to the sky?"

"I heard it's a structure for the man at the top who shall not be mentioned but who's actually mentioned all the time," the security officer said and winked. "Hey, look at that." The security officer pointed to the shiny blue billboard across the street from where the crowd was gathered. "She did something very nice there," he continued. "Returning that lost key for the man's digital wallet. Did you see it? He had some decent assets in there. Surprising her score only went up by two points. Should be more, in my opinion."

Two points. I can use two points right about now. It would get me closer to the next level. That triple A priority. Toffy didn't let his thoughts slip out of his mouth.

"Yeah. She did well," Toffy said.

"Yup. I'm glad she got the spotlight."

As Toffy started walking toward the narrow automated path that led to the single door of the white pyramid, a man holding a large piece of paper came running down, hysterically yelling, "Food shortage. Long queues. Bad roads. Corruption. Mass manipulation. Corponilization. Read all about it. Get your own…"

The man was swept off his feet with a quick slap to the face and punch to his rib cage. His eye bulged out after the two hits to his body. He was rustled away as one of the security officers snatched the paper from his hand, rumpled it, and placed it inside his pocket. The yelling man with the paper disappeared like he had never existed.

"Lunatics. You can't get enough of them these days," the security guard said to Toffy, shaking his head. The BW emblem on his uniform glowed.

Immediately, the screens on the building changed and started flashing.

Great roads lead to paradise at your feet.
There, an abundance of food for all to eat.
Get it quick, as soon as you speak.
The truth's accounted for each and every week.

Colorful pictures of newly designed roads and gadgets flashed intermittently on the screen.

Lunatics? Are they?

Toffy stepped on the auto-path and was glided toward the front of J Enterprise, along with other employees on the metallic human carousel.

When he got to his desk to prep for his meeting with James, his mobile device flashed, a voice notification from Deja.

"I saw that you got home late last night," Deja said. "I hope you can still give your speech tonight."

"Come on, of course," he responded. His words appeared on all the screens and synced into his message with Deja.

Why wouldn't I?

"Are you sure you don't want some of your family there?"

"No. It's fine."

"Okay. Your suit is on the twenty-sixth floor."

"Thanks, baby."

Toffy and Deja had been dating for close to six years, social standings providing torque. It was almost forbidden for them to enjoy each other's company and have fun outside work. Without explicit statements about this restriction, it was against their culture, as established by the corporate gods.

"Stop it. Let's get serious. Remember—our social score!" Deja would always remind Toffy whenever they got a little carried away enjoying themselves.

That damn social score. The moving target of usefulness for us all.

Toffy read the last message he had sent and wondered if he should send another voice note.

Toffy watched his device hopefully, but no new message came in. *Okay. I think she's done. That's that then.*

Nobody took time off for the fear of joining the useless class. Even on vacations, they all worked. Anxiety filled the missing percentage when an individual's utilization fell below one hundred percent. Regular-life was work, and work-life balance was a perfect symphony of a life centered around work.

Vacations advertised but no time off. Work-life balance. WLB. WFH. WTF. Can't get relegated to the useless class. Useless. You-C-less. The new nickname. Once you become you-C-less, you actually see less. Not me. I need to see it all. Toffy quickly silenced his thoughts.

If I claimed to be sick, they'd say I'm too healthy in the mind to be fully sick. So, no sick time off. Only the triple A's get that health preference. We get more medication. I need to up my score. I should probably cancel that vacation. It would be nothing but stress. I'll just end up working. Yeah, I'll cancel it. It's probably the best thing for my productivity. I can't let it drop now. Not now. Low Town? No, that's not for me.

Most caught twenty-two hours of work and took two hours of sleep, aided by the Ultra-wake pills. Hardly any time for people to interact, to develop anything that was rich, or to be creators of relevant tools. No time to collaborate except to please the puppet-master at J Enterprise.

J Enterprise controlled all the resources. They owned all the land. They controlled all the labor.

The company's mission statement, plastered proudly on the walls:

Day 1—work for the next day.

Day 2—work for the next day.

Day 3—work for the next day.

Day 4—work for the next day.

Day 5—work for the next day.

Day 6—work for the next day.

Day 7—work for the next day.

Toffy dropped his phone to look through his emails. *Eighty-four unread messages. Damn!*

He went through as many as he could before his meeting with James. He had to speed through them if he was going to meet his utilization target for the day.

Just have to get through this. Toffy's stomach tightened with every second that passed. *Can I hit my goals today? Of course I can. No time for negative thoughts.*

Toffy had learned in school never to speak up about problems because that wrecked productivity. Pounded in his mind with the mantra plastered around his campus: *Negative thoughts produce ineffective bots.*

At the prescribed time, he dropped everything and went up to the fortieth floor to meet James. The entire floor was his office. The roof was a point that joined all four walls. The apex of the giant pyramid. James shared the top floor with his secretary, Tefa+.

Toffy waited to be called in and sat across from the only screen in the room, which displayed a series of short clips repeatedly in an endless loop. A shoeless man in a white flowing dress rang a small bell in his hand. "All hail James nooowww..." *Talam Taram*. The shoeless man swung the golden bell like a hammer. "All hail James nowwww," he yelled with spread-out hands. *Talam Taram* rang the bell.

The scene switched to a bright-colored picture of James and words written below it: "Long Live the James. Solver of all problems, answerer to all questions. Sponsored by the Association of Autonomous Vehicles and Roads (TAAV'R)."

"Heard you will be spearheading the J Event tonight." Tefa+, James's secretary, interrupted Toffy's attention. "Good for you. Toffy is all grown-up now." She returned to the screen on her desk in front of her.

Tefa+ was plugged in to her screen, her sixty-four-year-old self augmented by the translucent screen in front of her. Her best self cognified by interaction of bits to supplement her ability to serve the company's mission.

As Toffy waited, he heard rumblings from downstairs. The vibrations came from six floors below. He knew exactly what was happening. The voices were all too familiar. He knew what time it was.

"The J speech is intense today, huh?" Toffy said.

"What do you mean?" Tefa+ responded.

"The rehearsals going on. On the thirty-fourth floor. The rumblings are more intense today." Toffy smiled.

"You can hear that?" Tefa+ said with a curious face. "How can you hear that? I can't hear anything except my fingers typing across this keyboard as we speak. I can barely hear *you.* You are special, Toffy. Oh! You can go in now." She pointed at the large wooden double doors. "See you later tonight," she said and winked.

Toffy remembered the history of those doors, seared into the rugged contours of his brain membranes. James had bragged over and over about how the door was flown in from outside J City. "It's a one-of-a-kind, natural flyeness bamboo, engineered in Japan," he would say.

James had his two legs on the table, smoking his vape and drinking a brown-colored liquor.

"Your generation has the usual Fridays," James said as Toffy walked toward his desk, his voice a blend between raspy and forceful.

"I have scotch and cigar Friday," James continued. "These are the simple pleasures you get to appreciate when you get to this level in life. Sit down, Toffy." He pointed at the seat across his table. The bass in his voice intensified with every exhale of vaporized smoke. "When I was your age—and the world as we knew it back then was shifting—it was take or be taken, eat or be eaten!"

Toffy made sure not to blink. James would see that as a sign of weakness. Toffy had heard this same speech several times. He repeated each word James uttered verbatim under his breath.

"...and one day, it would be impossible for them to touch me at number one."

Top-notch expertise. Top of the class insights. That was James's way of "giving back."

A man sat quietly next to James, notepad open as usual. The flesh of his skin could hardly fill out the black-turned-gray suit he wore every day. The oversized suit would have looked out of place if not for the oversized glasses resting on his nose. James's biographer was always there and looked like he was about to faint from starvation.

"Did you get that?" James asked. "I said, 'and one day, it would be impossible for them to touch me at number one.'"

He waited.

The biographer hurriedly wrote it down and showed James what he had written.

Although the dictation application on the screen could take down notes even better than a human, having his biographer at his beck and call gave James a nostalgic sense of importance. Efficiency had become commoditized. Unique human experiences, the only luxury.

"Isn't that right, Toffy?" James asked after an intermission from his monologue.

"Yes," Toffy said.

"And you are a very important piece of that puzzle," James continued.

The biographer pushed his glasses closer toward his bulging eyes and wrote: *One of the employees is an important piece of the puzzle. James was very inclusive in his empire-building.*

"Did you get that?" James asked.

The biographer tilted the page to show him. In bold letters: *Guy across the table—one of his employees is an important piece of the puzzle.*

James gave a thumbs up. "Where was I?"

After three seconds had passed and Toffy had not responded, the biographer realized this would be a great opportunity for him to add more value. He said in a squeaky and faint voice, "You said to him, 'You are a very important piece of that puzzle.'"

"Ahh, that's right," James echoed.

The biographer sat back with a smile on his face. His breath clouded the lens of the leopard-patterned-framed glasses. He scribbled in his notepad: *Ideas for later: Promising future as a certified memory-jogger.*

"So yes, you are an important piece of the puzzle, Toffy," James said intimately.

Why am I an important part of the puzzle?

"What puzzle is this?" Toffy said and continued to examine James's face.

This wouldn't be the first time Toffy heard about being part of some puzzle.

Toffy's memory was sparked. *Puzzle? Musta. The council. Vibrations.*

It all started two weeks ago when Musta told him about "the project."

CHAPTER 3

Toffy couldn't get "the project" out of his head.

Not ever since he'd met up with Musta at Skreet's Café. They had rendezvous at the spot on two occasions, one week apart.

The first time they met at Skreet's Café was the same night after they made a special connection during the daily J speech at the corporation. On that blessed day, the J speech had gone on for the first thirty seconds as usual, a combination of memorized praises for James repeated as everyone gathered around the screens.

"James, you are the great," employees of J Enterprise said in perfect synchrony. "The one who says no to the wait. The one who has opened up the gates. James, you are the great."

The screen flashed models of the new structure across from the pyramid. The model showed, in quick succession, how the building was to be built from foundation to an apex that never seemed to come to a point. The building model soared higher and higher, past the clouds and into the infinity realm.

The screen flashed the title:

The three-step roadmap to J Infinity.
Get a copy of the model sent to your device.
BLINK IF INTERESTED.

Everybody blinked and soon afterward each person's mobile device received a notification.

The screens went pitch black. After a concerted gasp in the room, the cafeteria became uncomfortably silent, the smell of freshly minted vegetables more vivid for the three seconds the screens were off.

"Here it comes!" a voice said in the spaced-out room.

The screen came back on to full white, accompanied with a piercing beep. It switched to a recognizable face. Immediately, each employee scrunched their face and started spitting out air in short spurts toward the screen. *Spiiiih, spiiihh, spihhh, spiiih.* The sound reverberated around the room.

The screen flashed, alternating between the face and the white screen. The employees spat air out and stomped their right foot at the rhythm of the switching screen. *Spppiiihh, stomp, spiihh, stomp, spihhh, stomp,* growing louder.

Here we go again. Toffy looked around the room.

Pure disgust was written over the faces around him, all focused on the screen. The face on the screen was one they didn't want to see—a face of someone different they did not want to deal with.

Toffy spat and stomped along with everyone else. *Spiihhh, stomp, spiihhh, stomp.* He was in full rhythm with the alternating screen. He rolled his body into the motion, moving like a snake.

I have a lot of work to catch up on. I hope this is a quick one. Does he deserve this much of our time? Do they? Every time? What has he done this time? Sowing seeds of confusion?

Toffy looked at his utilization, blinking on the black band wrapped around his wrist. *Can we speed this up?*

The screen changed again. The spitting and stomping ceased.

A man in a red suit appeared. "We need to protect our society from men like that. Men like that go around confusing people with theories, telling our men, women, and children about things that would only cause them to question their certainty in life."

The man paused, the clicking sound of his golden shoes audible as he fidgeted with confident eagerness. His square face easily accommodated his thick eyebrows and protruding thin lips. His social score hovered above his head, a proud 112.

"Men like that," he continued, "get their joy in making people unsure in a world that is nothing but certain and safe. Spreading lies from unidentified sources. Providing a second side to a story when we all know there's only one side of a story, and that story can only be told by the experts and credible citizens—not crazed men and women. That's why I have a panel of experts here to discuss."

The screen zoomed out from the portrait of the red-suited man and focused on the multicolored oval desk. Four people sat behind it from left to right.

Toffy took stock of all their social scores: *112, 111, 109, 105, 108. The AAA priorities. The upper echelon.*

"I'm sure each of you don't need an introduction," the host said, addressing his guests. "Your expertise is well-known around town." His suit changed to a dark shade of pseudo-maroon. Pointing at the first man to his left: "Expert Number One, please go ahead."

"Yes, thank you. I'm Expert Number One." He wore a gray suit, his body stiff as an ice pick. "I don't need any further introduction. As you know, my expertise is around governance and rules. Yeah, I'm a government kind of guy. My expertise is government-related, never debated but highly regulated."

The crowd around the screens burst into cheers. Smiles all around.

"Great to have you here with us to keep us well-versed in popular opinion," the maroon-colored suit man said. "Let's hear from Expert Number Two. Please introduce yourself."

"Hi, as most already know, I'm Expert Number Two," the lady in the green money-colored jacket said. "I am a business expert. I involve myself in things related to business and economics and stuff that has to do with supply and demand and generally things like that. Price. Strategies. Dealerships. Someone buying stuff, another selling it. The rich getting rich and the poor staying poor kind of business. You know, that's where my expertise lies.

"As an authority figure," the lady inhaled as she pushed her chest out, balled up both her fists, and jammed them both at her waist, "my expertise in business is close to none. My social score speaks for itself. That's why some call me BEE. Biz. Expert. Extraordinaire, to the rescue. First *buzzzzness* tip of the day: they call this the 'power pose.' That's free expert advice for you." Expert Number Two sat back down.

Expert Number Three picked up where Number Two dropped off. "I'm the technology expert. You know, the tech guy. If it has anything to do with technology, I'm your guy. I'm an expert at all tech knicks and knacks. Me. *This guy.*" He pointed at himself and then adjusted his rumpled collar. "When you need—"

"I'm Expert Number Four, the expert of expertise," the lady at the end of the table sprang out, cutting off Expert

Number Three mid-sentence. "I'm the expert of expertise because I tremendously reduce the research cost an organization needs to get insights into any topic. My expertise comes at such a low price that you can pretty much pay me to say anything with expert verbiage."

Expert Number Three rolled his eyes.

Everyone watching the screen saw him. They knew he couldn't address what had just happened. He had the lowest score on the table. Even though his score was higher than all who watched the screen in the room, the power dynamics were still at play on the highest level.

"Great to have you all here," the moderator said. "Unfortunately, we are almost out of time and will not be able to dive deep into our topic for today—the rise of contrarian belief. But before we finish, just a sentence from each expert on this topic." The panel moderator paused and continued, "The rise of contrarian belief. What are your thoughts? Let's start with you, Expert Number One."

"Well, contrarian belief is something I don't believe in, and as a government expert, you know it goes against popular belief. That's why it's so unpopular, so stay away from it as much as you can."

Does anyone else really believe a word these experts are saying? Saying the same thing. Most times saying nothing. Maintaining and propping up their scores. Probably a heavy dose of J Aid today. That green juice of indoctrination. Toffy stood at the edge of the room.

Expert Number One sipped the J Aid mixture from its distinct luminous green can. He was recharged to continue his duties of comfortable data-spewing.

Building on one another's claims. Heaping one point after the other. An orchestrated triangulation of empty words. The

self-feeding biases of popular belief. They spew and pat them-
selves on the back. I shouldn't be having these thoughts. Toffy
straightened his posture. *The experts have played it properly.*
Just like they taught us all in school "When you get in, stay in.
By any means necessary." I need to get back to my desk soon
or I might be out. No more access.

"To all those points…" The camera zoomed to the moderator, whose suit had changed color again to dark brown. "J
City does not tolerate new ideas, contrarian beliefs, anything
unpopular. Why make this world more uncertain? Relish in
the certainty brought to you by the corporation."

"Yeah!" A concerted yell from the room.

"Make sure you go out and fund the BWs. The boogey-
woogeys," the host continued. "These Brain Watchmen and
women, along with their Baron Wards, are the ones who
sacrifice their lives to make sure unsolicited new ideas are
pounced on immediately. They are the ones around each
corner to straighten up the children, making sure we stick to
only what we know is good for us. Make sure you give them
your support by donating to their funds."

A number appeared on the screen and everyone in the
office cafeteria pulled out their mobile device to make a
donation.

Across the room, Toffy noticed that Musta had not
pulled out his device. He had both hands on his lower back,
an unimpressed look on his face as he stretched his waist
forward.

Toffy hesitated before hitting the donate button.

"After your donation, contribute some more," the man
on the screen continued. "Join the brotherhood of the BWs.
Boogeys for short. If you see anything new or strange, you

hiss, you *claw*, you *stomp*, you bounce on and strangle the life out of it. I'll leave you with this."

A reel of faces appeared on the screen.

"Yes, shame them all!" the lady behind Toffy yelled out. Her blue suit and trousers were pristine, her gaze intense.

"Look at their low scores and the offenses that got them there." She gestured for Toffy to look forward.

Numerous faces appeared on a scrolling reel on the screen. None of their scores went above fifty-nine.

"Years of reeducation and city inspections were not sufficient for these ones!" she yelled at the screen and then continued stomping and hissing.

Cussing in public. Late payments. Propaganda against the corp. The offenses were damaging. All of them on the city blacklist now. Toffy took in a deep breath.

The screen went white, and the initial face reappeared again. The air-spitting and stomping resumed, everyone in unison. *Spiihhh, stomp. Spihhh, stomp, spihhh, stomp.*

Toffy didn't join in this time. Musta had disappeared from the corner where he'd stood across the room. Toffy swung his head back, surprised to find Musta standing right next to him. He was chewing something. Toffy knew well enough that Musta was chewing the insides of his cheek. He had come so close that their shoulders were practically touching. It was strange enough the two men were not spitting and stomping, but to start a nonconfrontational conversation in the midst of a J speech would raise too many red flags.

Toffy kept his eyes focused on the screen. It showed the J City social rankings.

1) 105+ AAA (healthcare priority)
2) 96–104 A+ (schooling priority)
3) 85–95 B (two years—reeducation)
4) 60–84 C (three years—city inspections)
5) 0–59 D (five years—blacklist)
WHERE DO YOU STAND? WHERE WILL YOU BE TOMORROW?

Flashed at the bottom of the table.

Musta leaned in and whispered in Toffy's ear, "Meet us at the café on the corner of Action and Indifferent Street tonight," and walked away.

***

The day passed, and Onyx came to a halt on Indifferent Street, three cars away from the intersection with Action Street. Toffy stepped out and walked toward a building that spiraled around its center with a green trim, red base, and gold fittings.

The usual unusual crowd was at Skreet's Café, named after its owner—Namdy Skreet. He was an eccentric character in J City, well-known for his divergent thoughts about pretty much every topic that existed. His café-turned-bar-at-night carried the same eccentric gene as its owner.

Wild pictures on the wall. No screens at all. The place was poetic, bringing people from High Town and Low Town into one melting pot where everyone seemed to speak in stanza. Sirens sang songs for romancers. Drummers pounded rhythms for the dancers.

Most people in High Town loathed Skreet, at least that's how they signaled. The High Towners were driven there purely by intrigue. They appreciated its culture but hated its essence. The dark spot provided a brief respite from the monitoring gaze of the screens. Every second spent there had a negative impact on their transparency points. Only a few had enough points to sacrifice. A lot of the High Town patrons went there as a reminder of what they didn't want to become—the Low Towners.

Musta sat in the corner on a round table in his usual earthy-colored outfit. His legs fidgeted with controlled energetic excitement that was not obvious on his face.

"There you are," Musta said. "Let me grab a table for you." He pulled an unoccupied table from the right corner of the café, which still had only a few patrons. "Here you go, Toffy." He then pulled a chair in between the two tables on which they sat and placed upon it two little black books.

That's how it was at Skreet's Café; chairs were tables and tables were chairs.

"You must be crazy, coming to talk to me during the J speech," Toffy whispered. "I'm sure there could have been a more appropriate way to bring this up. Someone would have tagged us to be followed. We shouldn't even be here." Toffy checked his device, his utilization at a miserable eighty-six percent.

"Well, it seemed like a perfect opportunity, and I took it," Musta said with a smile. "The easiest way to go unnoticed is to make sure you do things precisely when people think they *should* notice things. Just as the best time to go undetected is exactly when scrutiny for detection is at its peak." Musta leaned in toward the chair to grab one of the books. "We are working on a project, and we need a good storyteller."

He did not disclose the full nature of the project.

"It will be the biggest project in the twenty-first century," Musta ended with excitement.

Toffy was used to Musta's grandiose statements, but he couldn't deny he always got it right. Musta followed his curiosity wherever it took him.

"To be truly happy in life, you have to be open to new opportunities." He repeated this phrase again as he talked about the big project. "Be open to new opportunities, Toffy. Don't you want to do more? You have always yearned for more than what your hands can grasp. Reach out and do more. You should actually *do* something, something real."

As the night progressed, Musta got more and more animated. He smoked. Rolled another one. Then puffed again. He stood and walked to the stage in the room as it continued to fill up and grabbed the microphone.

"Here's my out-spiration from my inspiration," Musta said as he grabbed the microphone tighter. "Smoke trees and low key, it's a daily vocation. Revolution calls on spheres forever rotating, power grabbed while intellectuals keep debating. *Braaahhh.*"

Musta put the microphone back on the stand, raised a clenched fist high in the air, and walked off stage. The crowd did not seem bothered. They remained indifferent. He stopped to shake a few hands on his way back.

"You see, Toffy, we just have to swing into action. Make it happen. You know?" Musta handed him one of the little black books from the chair. "When you are up for it. Just write something. Write *anything*. Get mad! Make a difference if you can."

They sat on their tables, smoked, and watched musical acts all night long as Skreet's Café filled up through the night with vibrating radiant energy. Toffy tapped on his device, providing one-word responses to office mail to keep his plummeting utilization buoyant.

***

"Oh, that's a great idea," Toffy said. He had given the same response to the last three statements from Musta.

He had indulged Musta and smoked the finest natural herb with him, his mind more open to ideas streaming in with no filter.

"Yup. Skreet's does have the best Mary Jay in town." Musta exhaled the smoke and examined the pipe in his hand. "Ever since they commercialized the perfect tree, the real herb has almost become extinct. Skreet's is the only place with the natural. That underground. The real. Well, one of the few places." Musta pulled on a few strands of his beard and smiled.

His pearly white smile, a perfect exclamation point to the preceding paragraphs that contained the enticing invitation. Toffy felt this one.

It seemed like a challenge, a quest, an adventure... a chance to do more or a chance to just do something that felt *real*.

All he had to do, as Musta put it, was just say, "I'm in."

"That's all you have to say. 'I'm in,'" Musta had said. "Just tap on the button whenever you are ready."

I wonder if the Benign-ware will be onto this, Toffy thought as he stared at the big blue button that read

"I'M IN"

boldly on his mobile screen.

***

What could it be? What will I be doing? How will I balance it with work? Would this even be tolerated by the screens? Equations that needed to be solved rotated in Toffy's mind for days after meeting with Musta.

He was apprehensive, maybe even fearful for his life without uninterrupted work.

No one has called the Brain Watch on me yet, though. The boogeys haven't pounced on me yet. Even though I'm entertaining more new and different thoughts. No one has smashed my head in. Toffy questioned his reality and had new questions for each thought that popped up.

Why are my coworkers and I the only ones useful enough to be gainfully employed?

Toffy thought about "Project D" and the effects it would have on the corporation and the city.

The technological initiatives being cooked up to keep the wealth aggregated in the hands of the few and separated right beneath the feet of the masses, the useless, which seemed not to exist anymore.

The effects of rapidly improved Benign-ware swept across his mind.

The cemented digital divide. The growth of the corporation fueled by the fossil decay of humanity.

He stewed on his daily chores at the pyramid. The repetitive cycle of it all.

Rise, ride, chat, ascend, chat, write, burn, chat, hype, delete, chat, descend, ride, lay.

Rise, ride, chat, ascend, chat, write, burn, chat, hype, delete, chat, descend, no time for play.

Notions of Musta's project had broken him out of flaccid numbness into an upright excitement.

But moments of excitement of the new was always short-lived. He quickly remembered his responsibilities and his score.

It will probably take me away from what I'm doing, Toffy reminded himself with comforting objectivity. *I have a lot on my plate with all the work I have to do.*

Have you made your decision? He would stare at these types of words on a signboard, thinking he had to give an answer, and then he'd quickly shrug it off with scientific reasoning.

A good marketing trick to keep the mind engaged. Or are they onto me and my thoughts?

These signs and adverts were everywhere. The world, constantly sending him a message he was not ready to accept.

On that late night, as he walked back home from the grocer in the shared space at the corner, a flyer that had been trampled on by the little feet of the children who attend the banking school across the street caught his attention. He straightened the roughed-up flyer out with his foot. Looking around to make sure he was not being watched, he tilted his head down.

"MASS MANIPULATION. SCARCITY. NOT ENOUGH TO GO AROUND—says anti-establishment group leader."

Toffy picked up and then crumpled the paper into his pocket and walked home.

The screens on the way back:

They want to paint us bad outside from within.
When the reality is—we are the victims.
We keep the order, so that no one scares.
Enough to go 'round, resource for the shares.

CHAPTER 4

——

Toffy had hidden the little black book in the bottom shelf next to his bed.

The first day he brought the book out and opened it, the screen in his apartment started beeping.

"Mr. Toffy, doing some writing?" Fluence's voice beeped out of screen 2x5i. "Need some help with that? Looking for related topics to research. Here are some topics for you: 'Ten ways to improve your writing,' 'seven skills every writer in engineering should have,' 'three vacation spots to write your best work.' Let's choose another vacation spot for you."

Fluence knew exactly how to impact Toffy's decisions. It had been trained for Toffy, by Toffy, but not with Toffy. Fluence was everywhere Toffy went. Active on every screen.

Fluence's voice from the screen that stretched from a few inches above the ground to a quarter way from the slick white ceiling continued, "Here are the lists of the top trending vacation destinations for people who have notebooks just like yours. If you open the notebook and show me the content, I can recommend the best location to finish your writing, Mr. Toffy."

"No, Fluence! No vacation for me. Actually, please cancel the last vacation I booked," Toffy said. "Well, you booked."

"No problem. No vacation. Cancel vacation," Fluence's voice ululated. "Vacation preferences recalibrated." The screen went silent.

Unlimited breaks that never get used, Toffy thought. *They know we won't use it. And they also want to see the content of my book? Why?* He hadn't written anything in the notebook since the last time.

How's my utilization looking this morning? The screen showed 100 percent. *Let's keep it that way today.* Toffy moved on to zoom off for work.

***

Four thirty in the morning. Toffy stopped the alarm on the clear interface on the frame of his bed the next day

Thirty minutes to write, Toffy thought after pushing himself off the bed onto his feet.

But I didn't finish the update last night. He remembered Deleteron. *Okay. I'll write for fifteen minutes and do the update later, just before go time.*

Each screen in all homes in High Town were on the same privacy schedule. The screens went off between one and five o'clock each morning. The little black book was exactly where Toffy had left it the day before.

He opened it and was immediately overwhelmed by the blank page. There were no suggestions about what to write. No recommendations from the screens this time. Just a white page with blue lines.

Toffy grabbed his pen and wrote:

Where do I start? What do I have to say? Just write. You might get somewhere at the end of the day. Write, write, write, write whatever comes to mind. Okay.

We are here in J City, a city that's completely run by J Enterprise. I am a writing engineer, or an engineered writer, whatever description fits. The words are engineered and delivered in zeros and ones, manipulated and delivered in bits. They want to get around and interact. More of them intersect in an era of collaborating metadata. Say "hi," passed on by cars, drive one around, no need to hold a wheel. I once had a driver who is now deemed useless. I sit in the backs of cars and chill. He chills too but has no ends to justify his means. I rise higher because I have friends who solidify my schemes. The orders come from the top. I just add words for the garnishment.

New thoughts rise, vibrating from afar that say, "Down with the establishment!"

Toffy threw his pen down, his eyes wide. He quickly closed the book, knowing he shouldn't have written those words. He looked at the screens, but they were still off. He opened the book again to confirm what he thought he had written.

In bold letters, "Down with the establishment!"

He paced up and down his room, went back to the book, and wrote:

Flip the system on its head, a gazelle can't scare lion

Man a trample through, man a chant down Babylon

He threw the pen down again.

"What am I writing?" he whispered. "That's so unusual."

The rumpled note picked up from the street now lies
safely under my pillow above the sheet...

On that day he and his team had tested an iteration of the Deleteron product. The beta testers had grown increasingly frustrated as she typed. Each word of her story typed, immediately erased. Deleted with no receipts nor anything to track, gone, never coming back.

Gone forever. Toffy shook his head. *Confusion on her face.* She had tried over and over again. Nothing. Silence. She looked around for assistance. No one was there to help.

Tears down her eyes. Toffy's eyes held back any change in their moisture level.

He knew what he saw. She knew it too. Everyone in the room knew. She would never be able to write her story. Her existence confined to her limited time on earth. No one would know of her existence once she returned to the dirt. Her story mistitled history.

Toffy blinked his eyes. Chez's reaction was expected.

"This initiative is taking off as planned." Chez was all smiles as he pumped on the shoulders of the engineers who adjusted the test variables on the screen in front of them. He wiped the sweat above his lip with the edge of his sleeve.

Toffy closed his eyes. Pixels continued developing and disintegrating behind shut lids. Numerous micro screens flashed as colors changed. The violet-to-red transition swerved in motion like a snake, sometimes spiraling. It had form.

The form only supports the function. Toffy remembered the day they perfected frictionless transactions. Bio-content matching. The ease came from the purpose it was serving. Accumulation.

You look. You like. You receive. Toffy smiled. *The value proposition was too easy to remember.*

"Forget your hand in a wallet." He remembered Chez talking about Pink Money vo.1 on the street where they erected the first iris-enabled screens across the buildings. "Now your money is stored in your eyes. People watch the content they like and pay for it directly without even clicking to play. You open your eyes, and you are already opted in. Amazing. This initiative might be my best." Chez was excited as he presented the success of the trial run to James. "Pink Money." He mentioned the product name after every slide he flicked through.

Toffy snapped out of memory lane. He realized it was 4:57 a.m., three minutes until the screens woke up. He sprang up, shoved the book behind the shelf, and ran into the bathroom.

He did not open the book again until the morning of the J Event.

***

J Enterprise controlled the narrative. Their media division was also in charge of infrastructure development. All the new buildings were integrated with their screens.

Ten years after it was institutionalized by the city council in the year 2039, the screen laws had every inch of every building covered with screens—both on the inside and outside.

The observers and distributors of information, those screens, Toffy thought. *Advertisement personalized to its "ever-evolving" and dynamic audience.*

With a new advertising model dreamt up by Chez, the friction between advertising expenditure and money made had been reduced to complete insignificance.

Direct-to-gaze, each sight commoditized, streams only fluttered with the blink of an eye.

From inception, J Media was launched to help other companies spend their advertising budget efficiently. They evolved quickly, making transactions so efficient that once residents laid eyes on adverts, money was immediately taken out of their integrated wallets and pockets.

The content was the product. Paid for with plasma-related currency. Internal preferences recorded to consistently serve the people exactly what they want. Pink Money. Regardless of decision to purchase or not, money deducted for watching. A refined filtering engine to give us only what we want. To the undiscerning eye, wealth cannot be built.

The residents got poorer and only got joy from watching senseless adverts that kept them hopeful about life while the same adverts took money from their pockets.

J Enterprise grew quickly. The habits of the residents evolved with the screens. Toffy's work ethic assisted J Enterprise's growths. It grew his excellent career and got him the opportunity to write some of those addicting ads. He was a natural, and he quickly learned all the tricks of the copy trade.

James often joked that Toffy could write copy that would warm the heart of a fisherman on a cold Alaskan morning.

He picked up this skill as he rose at the corporation. Although he had abandon writing the spoken word as a teenager, his chase of communicating efficiently, with written code in an increasingly digital world, led him down the path to wordsmithing—a digital native and scribe royalty.

The love for binary code was prioritized in an era where institutions were churning out desk-ridden keyboard-typing engineers. He knew how the economics would play out. *Software engineers got paid better than writers.* He cared about the status. He wanted to have a clear definition of value. *Everyone cares. That singular unit of importance. Everyone is watching. What's your social score? What's the social score?*

Measured between zero and the highest score, which belonged to James, it determined who the haves and have-nots were in J City. The highest score had been in James's family since the score became integral to life in the city. James consistently broke his own record every quarter over the last six years.

His score was at an all-time high—130.

Toffy's rise in the corporation was evident in his position to headline the speech at the J Event, an annual event on James's birthday. His social score was at its highest ever.

"It can always be better," Toffy's school counselor had once said. "Everyone's social score can always be better. You don't want it to drop too low, where you'd have to fight your way back from Low Town life. Not Low Town. At worst, stay afloat, keep your score steady. At best, keep swimming, keep rising."

Toffy had a mental tattoo of those words on his heart.

Only people who had risen to Toffy's level could give a speech at the event. Bragging about it, they considered themselves special. Fraternizing in smoky whisky-laden dim-lighted clandestine locations that signified the status band along the spectrum of privilege they abided in.

They were only a few. They exchanged business cards amongst themselves and stopped talking to people who had not given a speech. They ramped up their worship for James for fear they could get kicked out of the prestigious league of speech-givers. They gave one another awards, praised each other on the screens, congratulating every statement they collectively uttered in public. It was crowd-source self-fandom.

"We are the great. You are the skates" was a quote they yelled out with joy in their meetings, making sure the message stuck.

Toffy was honored by the selection to headline the event, but he was really only doing it because Deja had persuaded him to. Things were much rosier then. They were both a lot happier.

I'm really only doing this for her. She persuaded me. I could not resist. Her passion, hidden behind her drive to succeed, Toffy thought as he sat in James's office, watching him talk, overtaken by the thought of doing more.

He was still in James's office, but he was not really there.

Doing more. Maybe with Deja. Hopefully. Things were a lot rosier when she sold me on this speech. She. We were a lot happier. Even if it was for a short while.

The thoughts in his head were more interesting than the words coming out of James's mouth.

"...because of your leadership in engineering," James slammed his hand on the desk. Toffy snapped out of memory lane. He had seen the same vengeance in James's face when he had ordered for the social score of four chatty employees be reduced by ten points. Toffy sat up.

"We have taken forty percent market share, in the new region," James continued bragging, "and those assholes in

Fasian can kiss my big forty percent ass now. That's why you are an integral piece of this puzzle."

Toffy realized he had tuned out, thinking about his friend Musta for what must have been more than ten minutes.

James just kept talking.

Does he know I wasn't listening? Toffy sat nervously. *Pay attention. The least you can do is feign interest.*

"They can kiss my Black ass," James said as he laughed out loud. The biographer paused, and James said, "Of *course*, you can leave *that* in. On second thought, please take it out."

The biographer tore out the page. He had written something about how James motivated his staff at the top. Amused, he decided to put the paper back and left a note at the bottom, which read:

> *James finds a way to continue to inspire the youth, even those who have made it far in their career. He keeps filling their ears with countless knowledge. He is so selfless. He keeps talking even when the recipient seems to be staring blankly into space. The young man seems like he may be somewhere else. Like the gems of wisdom are going in one ear and out the other. He probably has no idea what is being said... maybe I can remind him what was said and jog his memory. This could really be a promising new career for me.*
>
> *Note to self: Explore career as memory jogger. (Memory Jogging as a Human Experience.) Check in with rhythm specialists.*

James was neither Black nor someone who cared if he was saying inappropriate things or not.

Men like James didn't get to where they were without doing whatever it took, not caring about who got stepped on along the way. The same traits were adored by the youth of J City.

Take what is yours! written boldly on the portrait behind him.

"I hope you like your new office," James said to Toffy without genuinely expecting a response. "You are only two floors below me now. Look out of this window. This could all be yours someday. I want you to know that my door is always open. Stop by any time."

Toffy thanked James, still unclear why he was in his office.

James said, "You can leave now." As Toffy walked out, James called his name out. Toffy looked back. "I'm proud of you. I'll be looking forward to your speech at the charity event tonight; I trust you'll say all the right things. Oh, and thanks for last week. Mission accomplished; your visit to the people in Low Town helped. I only send people I can trust on missions like that. It goes a long way, and as you have noticed, your effort does not go unappreciated."

Toffy already had his hand on the doorknob when he replied, "Sure."

The biographer looked ready to restate all he had written down.

The huge doors automatically shut behind him.

***

Toffy walked into the office. He wanted to forget what had happened the week before.

"Welcome back. How did the meeting with James go?" the voice from the screen asked.

"Good."

"You have a lot to do before the big J Event tonight, Mr. Toffy. Since you left you've received one hundred fifty messages, thirty percent of which are flagged as urgent, fifteen large code files for your review, and three copies that require your perfect touch. Not to mention, you still have not looked at my proposed speech."

The screen, which circled around him in his new office, showed the figures in a prioritized table. Toffy was immediately immersed in the circular and transient view around him that constantly updated. His office wasn't fixed. It continuously became different.

Toffy took a deep sigh as he approached his desk and squatted for his seat to adjust to his body. At the same time his phone went off, a text from Deja.

He swiveled around in his chair to look at all the pixels illustrated before him, wondering where to start. *Okay, the urgent messages,* he thought. *Ugh, I really don't want to deal with anything urgent right now.*

His mind swirled like a whirlwind as he scrolled through the one hundred and fifty new messages he received in the last two hours.

"Okay, screen, play some focus sound waves. You know the frequency that works for me."

A few minutes passed. *Okay, this isn't working.* Toffy was still on his message board, but no messages had been opened. He couldn't keep his mind from wandering to his thoughts, his meeting with Musta, and those words in his black book. He walked over to his window, peered toward the east, reflected on his visit to Low Town the week before, and let out a deep sigh. He couldn't let go. His utilization bar popped up shrinking and blinking orange:

2 percent... 2 percent... 2 percent...

Once he made eye contact with the utilization screen, Fluence took over the room. "You better get to it, Mr. Toffy, or you might not meet your utilization numbers for the day. Just for the record, your utilization has dropped significantly over the past week. Here are some openings with your HRT. Should I book an appointment?"

"No," Toffy said firmly.

Human resource therapist. No. I don't need motivation. He pulled out the hyperlinked library in his desk. The digital folder with the highest metadata interactions came in a brown leather-bound case.

Bits want to interact. Written on the book. Toffy opened it, overwhelmed by the commodifications of answers. He didn't know exactly what to ask.

"Close the door." The door to his office slowly swung closed.

He needed isolation from the chattering down the hallways. The praise for James was heightened that day, on his birthday.

"Increase noise reduction," Toffy yelled out as he stared at his book.

He was two pages in. Searching. Linking. Flowing. From unfinished thoughts to the greatest ideas, Toffy tapped away, his mind in a realm of brownian fluidity.

The noise from outside had been muted to a silent buzz, but Toffy could still feel the vibrations. The energy accompanied with the amplification of the discrete self. Especially the low frequencies. Some of which reverberated from down the hall. His utilization screen clinked:

12 percent... 12 percent... 12 percent...

The stumping footsteps hit like giant kick drums, shaking the building. Everything amplified for J Event.

Outside his glass door was James in an all-white suit walking with his hands stretched out. The baggy-suit biographer followed closely behind, and a crowd of workers followed.

A bell rang out from the screen in the right corner of the room, startling Toffy out of his brief moment of silence. The screen showed James and his followers downstairs. The cleaner on the ground floor had joined them, the only human cleaner left in the building. All others had been rendered useless by automation.

"What should we be prioritizing right now, Mr. Toffy?" Fluence asked in her fine-tuned voice.

Toffy could not detach from the show outside the building, amazed by the cleaner in the parade on the screen. She was old, but her movement was surprisingly youthful.

"James is cominnngggg," she cried out and rang the bell in her right hand, *challam, challam*. "James is here, ooooooh," she wailed, and rang the bell in her left hand, *challam, challam.*

The residents of J City lined the street, and James walked with his hands stretched out as he swiveled through the crowd. The Baron Wards lined the streets controlling the crowd.

I need to focus. Toffy struggled to keep his mind on his tasks with the show on his screen.

I would have turned the screens off, but that'll affect my transparency factor. I don't need an unnecessary dent on my social score. Every second it's off, the social scores just drops. Nope, not now. He stiffened his neck to focus on the transition screen between screen tag five and six.

Just keep going! You can do this. A mantra he repeated in his head as he focused. Forty-seven minutes later, his utilization had increased to 41 percent.

CHAPTER 5

———

Toffy went down to the tenth floor for lunch. The cafeteria was buzzing at a higher pitch than usual because of all the talk about the J Event later that evening.

His utility for the day was at 64 percent, so he was a little more relaxed than earlier in the day. If he spent another seven hours, he would hit his target of 100 percent utilization at precisely 7:30 p.m., enough time to get ready and be there promptly for the main event at 8:00 p.m.

He walked around the island of food, a variety of colors and shades. Each had a unique benefit, but Toffy was wise enough to know they were all the same. He was there when each lab-cultivated vegetable was given its unique value proposition.

It's all the same. Different day, different brand, different messaging. Food, clothes, medicine, instruments easily replicated and ready for download.

A neat row of boxed replicators was arranged in front of a neat row of screens waiting to produce food and pharmaceuticals from CO_2 and water. Each replicator was paired with a 3-D printer, once thought obsolete in the food industry, now found use as it recreated different forms and tastes from the powdered nutrients.

"What can I get you?" the screen above the replicator asked.

Toffy moved the tip of his black shoes to the line. The red light from the screen above the replicator scanned his eyes. "What I need to get!" he mumbled his words.

"Coming up!"

A customized plate emerged from the white chrome machine.

Why does it even ask when it already read me?

Toffy got a full scoop of mixed and mashed green, blue, yellow, and green number seven vegetables. He dashed to a table. Only fifteen minutes to spare. In the corner of his eye, he spotted Dafonzo.

Oh no! He immediately straightened his face.

Dafonzo was already talking his mouth off, vegetables stuck to his teeth as he spat across the table deliriously. Fera from HR moved her head with a constant circular motion to avoid Dafonzo's liquid projectiles. Toffy scanned around for the emptiest table. He zoomed in on one at the far-left corner of the white-walled lunch room. The fear of an unsolicited conversation gripped his belly.

It's only Tefa, unaugmented. She gets it, Toffy thought as he picked up his pace. *She wouldn't speak, and if she did, she would quickly get the message.*

Toffy silently sat down. Tefa raised her head in his direction. Toffy did not break eye contact with his multicolored plate of spiceless vegetables. She looked back at the screened book she was reading.

"Tooffffffyyyyyy," a voice spoke out.

All the fear in the world condensed in Toffy's face. He knew who it was.

Dafonzo stood in front of him, dropping his tray. "How are you going to slide past and not say hello? What are you now, antisocial? Or have you become one of those weird anti-establishment people who don't have a sense of what's perfect in this world?" Dafonzo pinned himself into the seat across from him.

"Can I join you?" he asked, as if he really cared about the answer. "Don't you just love it here? Huh, Toffy? I'm sure you're on top of the world right now. Congrats, man. You've made it."

Danfozo's head bopped while he grabbed Toffy's hand across the table and shook it vigorously.

"Thanks," Toffy said, unable to entertain the Dafonzo type. They were always trying to buy favors or position themselves in places where they believed power resided. Toffy looked at his watch and thought his silence would clue Dafonzo in to leave him be.

"Have you seen what's been happening on the screen these days? All this propaganda?" Dafonzo said, not taking the hint. "I tell you, the work we do here is so important. We are both designers and curators of perfection. Like, look around you, everything is perfect. No stress. The screens are personalized. You get exactly what you want pretty much before you can even think about it. I can't see how *anyone* would have a problem with what's going on."

He's heavy on the "greens" today. The G54-621 nutrient blend must be at work, Toffy thought as he looked down at Danfonzo's tray. Danfonzo took another generous swoop of the powder. His belief in the company's mission intensified, obvious in the renewed glisten in his eyes.

"And Project D. I can't wait for you all to finish and release that product. Let's see how the Antis deal with that." Dafonzo leaned in. "I wonder if they are already building a defense for it?" He paused, looking through Toffy's eyes. "Well, the boogeys would have jumped on that idea before it even progressed into a full thought. Why wouldn't anyone want the way the world is right now? Like, just shut up and maintain your social score. It works for everybody."

Toffy had lost interest in his food. If he continued eating, he would be eating vegetables covered in Dafonzo-saliva dressing.

"I have to head out, Dafonzo. Lots of work to do today. Catch you later," Toffy said as he stood.

"Already acting special, I see," Dafonzo said with an asymmetric smile. "Fingers crossed, I'll be in the running for a speech at a J Event soon."

Dafonzo crossed his fingers and squeezed his eyes shut. He mumbled a little prayer. Toffy took the opportunity to slide away.

Toffy walked past the table with the men in black jackets. Their broad-shouldered jackets had orange regalia around the left sleeve. The different shades signified their status in the fire crew. The men of J Fire were bulkier than most employees in J Enterprise. They regarded themselves as the custodians of humanity's peace of mind, a crucial segment of the Brain Watch. Their job was to burn down houses that contained books and artifacts that could confuse people about the order of the world. They took great pride in their jobs and boasted about their last burns over lunch. They hardly mixed with other employees. Once in a while they would sit with the Baron Wards.

Although they didn't have a heartbeat, the Baron Wards were the closest augmentation to the fire crew. In their white coats, their exterior was of smart material that signaled, bent, and adapted to its environments, constantly learning new tricks. A necessary complement to uncertain missions of the fire crew whose human skin had limited malleability. They had skin in the game. The Baron Wards didn't, but they were both optimized for the same thing—enforcement.

Sarni was the head of the fire department. He sat at the top of the long lunch table. Across the twenty men seated on both sides of Sarni, Toffy made eye contact with his friend. Sarni winked at him.

"Oh, I'm sorry," Toffy said. He wasn't looking and had bumped into Chez.

It was Chez's bright idea, a year ago, to integrate the media and fire department. When Chez sold the idea to James and the rest of the team, he was theatrical as usual. He had put his hands together and interlocked his fingers, saying, "It's called *synergy.*

"You see," Chez had continued, "the fire department burns the books, the media department deletes and rewrites. You tracking? We can consolidate resources. It's another brilliant idea that came to me as I hit my eleventh mile on my daily morning run."

Chez had busted into a stretch routine as he spoke. "We are the official censors, the judges, and the executors. We control what is seen, said, and done. No one wants to feel inferior, so we take anything out that makes anyone feel less than what they are. Discomfort, guilt, anguish, or any other form of psychological distress. None of that anymore. In fact, we douse them with overconfidence to make sure they remain in that mood. That *good* mood, here in High Town. That *buying* mood.

"Toffy, are you even listening?" Chez asked as Toffy snapped back to the vegetable-scented cafeteria. "Did you hear me? I said I have a new initiative. I'm thinking about revealing it later this evening, maybe at the event." Chez zoomed off.

Toffy walked back to his office, even less energetic. He looked at the screens in the hallway and in the elevator. It drained him. Every pixel linked to the air he breathed. The message was the same—everyone wanted attention. He had helped build this world.

It seems like the ones who made it to the screen were those who'd erred on the side of total outrage, Toffy thought. *The more outrageous, the more time and attention they received.*

Everyone wanted to have their own identity. They all had their separate communities, and they all yelled at one another whenever they met. All for attention.

Toffy had seven hours and three minutes to hit 100 percent utilization before the event.

***

The room slowly filled. For the first time since Deja asked him to give the speech, Toffy was nervous. Deja was close to the stage. He walked up to her.

"You need to be seated right away," Deja said. "The event starts in approximately four minutes."

"Okay. Hello. I just came to say hi," Toffy said with a smirk on his face.

She gave him a quick peck on the cheek. "Seriously, you need to get seated. There is too much going on, and I don't need you adding to my stress right now."

Toffy smiled. He knew there was a smile buried deep down beneath her worried face.

"Okay, okay. I'm going to sit down." Toffy hurried off and asked, "Where am I sitting?"

Deja flagged down one of the waiters and asked her to take Toffy to his seat.

"You look nice, by the way," Toffy said to Deja.

Toffy sighed deeply, disappointed by the interaction. *A growing distance beyond the surface.* Toffy felt Deja slipping away. *The rigors of the job. The constant justification of why we do what we do. The expectations and the stress.*

He sat and recognized the artifacts in the room this time. A week ago, he thought they were all created and framed by the corporation. His thinking was different now. It looked very familiar. It reminded him of a distant place he had only recently visited.

Replays of James walking among the residents of J City were up on the screen.

"Ayooo." A familiar voice rippled through Toffy's sound waves.

The lights dimmed to start the event.

"Man of the hour," Sarni tried to whisper as he excitedly approached Toffy from behind. "The man himself: Toffy! The golden child! The senior man of the moment! The most able of all bosses!"

Sarni had a huge smile on his face. He took his seat next to the one across from his name card. He continued teasing Toffy.

"You know, it could have been *me* giving that speech," Sarni said, "if not for the special treatment, and the fact that you share the same bed with the organizer. Cute ol' Deja and Toffy... awe."

Toffy laughed at the teasing, but there was a harder tone than usual in his friend's voice. *Were the jokes masking something else? Jealousy, maybe? He didn't really think Deja picked me for the speech because of our relationship instead of my obvious skill set. Did he? What if Deja did? Her bright round eyes are not as bold toward me anymore. Maybe someone else was more deserving of the spotlight. I wonder if I was an easy fill-in option...*

The commotion at the hall entrance interrupted Toffy and Sarni.

James was making his way into the building, but the city councilmen had to be present before he walked in. Gathered from High Town and Low Town, they wore all their recently applied garments.

The High Town council heads made it to the event on time. The Low Town councilmembers came from far away, and they had to make a show of it. They had their security push everyone out of the way. Never would they want to be seen as useless. They made sure everyone knew how useful they were.

"Out of the way, out of the way," shouted one of their security guards. "Can't you see the senior members are coming? There's no respect on this side of town. Everyone just thinks they are somebody because they have cars that drive them around." The man opened his eyes wider and shouted, "I said, move out of the way!"

Sarni didn't flinch, unfazed by their antics.

Toffy was puzzled and intrigued. "What is going on? These guys are just ridiculous. Right?"

"Yeah, nothing new," Sarni said. "The low to high trajectory can leave anyone confused with power in the hopes of retaining it."

"What do you mean?" Toffy asked. *What does he know that I don't?* That second question didn't escape his mouth.

The three councilmen from Low Town finally dropped into the room. They approached the three from High Town seated at the council table, and both groups exchanged brief glances of disdain.

These were the six councilmen for the whole of J City. There were actually five men and one woman, but to maintain the order, they were all referred to as councilmen.

Muidi, the only councilwoman, played her role well. A token of goodwill and corporate diversity.

"No respect in this town. Look at them, they can't even stand up to greet us," one of the Low Town councilmen whispered to the other.

Councilman Loya from Low Town reached out a shaky hand toward the High Town councilmembers. "Good to see you again, Council Ditty," Loya said.

Ditty shot out of his chair for the fear of being in a position of less power as Loya towered over him. "Good to see you too, Loya." Loya sat as fast as he could to complete the handshake seated—a blatant show of disrespect.

Ditty, recognizing what Loya had done, sat slowly. He didn't want to sprain his back. They both looked at one another, grasping each other's frail handshake with all the squeeze and intent their hands could muster.

The other two councilmen from Low Town, Council Bunajo and Obechat, remained standing. They looked down at High Town Council Bejaai and Muidi. The four of them had seen the power dynamics between Loya and Ditty. It was unclear who'd won that encounter. Silence was the next best strategy. They all remained silent.

"I see you Low Towners did not get the memo," Bejaai said to break the silence. "James is wearing white today."

Loya, Bunajo, and Obechat looked at one another, all in black garb.

"Take a look at the screens," Muidi said and smirked. "We know you don't have that where you are coming from."

Obechat grabbed a big red device from Loya's pocket, pushed a button and yelled into it, "Operation C-O. I repeat. Operation C-O. Code White. I repeat. Code White."

One of their security officers rushed in with a red device. "Sir, we heard your call but don't fully understand," the panicked officer said.

"We practiced this before we came here. You are the most unreliable force. Operation C-O. Operation *Change Outfits*. Code White. *Change outfits to white!*" Bunajo yelled at the man.

"Yes, sir." The officer bowed and ran to the door. "Bring the white outfits immediately."

Three men rushed in. The three councilmen from Low Town stood and stretched their hands to the sky as the white outfits were thrown up toward the ceiling. The garbs then slowly glided down onto each man.

"*Now* who needs a memo?" Obechat said.

Bejaai seemed impressed by the show but did his best to look unmoved.

"It's election, or rather, *selection* season. We are in top form." Loya smiled and looked at Ditty, still unsure who was holding onto power between the two of them at the table.

As the security officers from Low Town walked away, one of J Enterprise's security at the door blasted his voice to the air, "Activate Operation JIA—James Is Approaching." The Baron Wards got in sync and formed a parallel formation with a clear pathway between them leading from the entrance all the way to the ball room.

"Operation JIA," echoed around the room.

The crowd slowly filling up the room now dispersed. The attendees still at the door moved away from the entrance as the auto-path was activated, splitting the crowd in two.

Sarni and Toffy watched all the commotion from the front of the room.

"Anyway," Sarni said and laughed, tapping Toffy on the shoulder, "I won't be able to stay for your speech, but I know you will do as horribly as you usually do. I have another charity case that requires my full attention."

James glided in. Everyone stood in applause. His suit had changed back to his usual black.

The High Town councilmen pressed a button on their mobile devices, and the color of their clothes changed to black. Ditty gave Loya a look that said, "Look who's winning now."

Loya, Bunajo, and Obechat slowly pulled off their white clothes.

James glided to his seat in the center of the room. He welcomed the applause and cheers. With one hand he signaled "please sit," and with the other, "don't stop clapping."

The councilmen were confused, so they clapped halfway by using one hand to tap the table.

James stretched both hands out, looking pointedly down the middle of the room. With a stern face he closed both palms, waving them slowly. Everyone fell silent. He opened up his palms and slowly lowered them to his sides. Everyone sat down.

Silence in the room. Sarni leaned toward Toffy. "As I was saying, check out the latest charity case." Sarni laughed, protruding his lips toward the phone to direct Toffy's attention. "Look at her. Just *begging* for me to take care of her. And trust me, I'll be taking *care* of her, if you know what I mean." He winked and added, "Hey, man, don't judge. There are different forms of charity, and this is my way of giving back to the world. In fact, I just learned something new."

He pulled his personal screen closer. "Check this out. So, I just realized you could unlock a new league on this dating application. I was just playing around with it and figured it out. All you have to do is swipe: left, right, right, up, down, left, double-tap to like. *Boom!*" Sarni swiped with indiscriminate precision on his mobile device. "Look at that! A whole different secret league. That's how I found my lady in red, who I'll be keeping warm tonight." He stuck his tongue out, looped his waist around, and rubbed his belly. "It's a cold world, Toffy. And some people just need warmth. If you catch my drift. Oh, yeah. All righty… gotta roll. All the best with the speech. Peace, my guy."

As Sarni snuck out of the ballroom, he offered James an expression of confirmation. No one would have noticed the briefness of their eye contact except for the two of them, and Toffy. They communicated with no words. No sounds. If the message could be heard, it would be something of the sorts of, "Get the job done."

Toffy knew exactly what it meant. Sarni was on a mission for James. The same way he had gone on a mission for James just a week ago before his perception of blissful reality had been turned upside down.

The line below the fog, separating High and Low Town. The disparity, too much, too drastic. How can they coexist in this same city?

Toffy watched Sarni walk away. He had the steps of someone who knew the ins and outs of what made the entire system run. Sarni's calm but deliberate steps knew the wheels of the system needed spinning.

Benefit the few, reinforced by them too.

As Sarni confidently opened the doors out of the event, he knew how it all worked. He had power moves.

Why wouldn't he? He'd spent his last ten years working directly under James, the ultimate power guy, Toffy thought.

As the doors closed behind Sarni, a gust of wind hit Toffy's face that sparked his memory. The mental impression was vivid in Toffy's mind, and so was the discussion in James's office on that particular day.

Low Town! Toffy let out a faint whisper.

"You must go right away, Toffy," James had said, looking out the window. "They are trying to bring down what we are building here, with unnecessary smear campaigns."

"Okay. Okay. Hmm. Okay," Toffy had responded in a flustered state. "What about my utilization for the day? I'm also working with Chez to make sure we stay on schedule for—"

"They don't know that all I do is for them. This is more important, Toffy," James responded. "You keep allowing them to pull strings, and the ideals we've ingrained will be pulled apart."

The biographer had dozed off in his chair.

"And I can only rely on someone I can trust for this type of work. And I trust *you*, Toffy." James had handed Toffy a brown envelope. "Please see that it is taken care of immediately."

"Definitely," Toffy had said, happy to feel entrusted. He dictated toward his raised wrist to show diligence: "Tell Onyx to pull up to the front—"

"No. No. Nooo." James pulled Toffy's hand away from his face. "Take public transportation. We don't want this linked to us in any form or fashion. It's not worth switching off your vehicle tracking system."

"Public transportation? I haven't taken that in years. Don't you think it will be more efficient—"

"Take the public transport," James commanded.

CHAPTER 6

———

Toffy stepped off the auto-path.

That was as far as it could take him. He had first stepped on the path from the secret passage that James rushed him through from a back door in his office. He stayed on it all the way from the white pyramid, which still hovered in his rear view.

Things were quite different from when he had his vehicle driving him around. He saw, felt, smelled, and heard things he hadn't before. A man pulled a white bag out of the trash, peeled the bag open, and picked at the paper, throwing anything that stuck to his fingers into his mouth.

The red digital bubble floating above his head displayed his social score, a miserable forty-two.

Woah. That's low!

A man with a humpback approached. "Hey, my man, do you have something for me? I just want to get some screen time." The man rubbed his eyes until they went red. Huge dark circles, a sliver of color as his light brown iris disappeared in the darkness of his dilated pupils.

"I'll do anything for some screen time. I'll even—" He threw up on the floor. The floor absorbed the puddle of yellow chunks like nothing had fallen onto it.

A fog built up. Toffy hurried off to the train station.

"Just need some screen time," a woman with shut eyelids said, walking aimlessly around. "Can I get some screen time?" A gust of wind blew by.

It was like Toffy was seeing these people for the first time.

Who wouldn't have access to the screens? They are everywhere! We all went through the iris-integration.

He walked past a line of people. It swung around the corner, a line so long they had formed concentric circles looping around a building. The building's sign displayed: USEFUL EMPLOYMENT OFFICE.

The train map flashed on the screen. He pulled out the sheets from the envelope in his hand to read the instructions on the first page.

Meet Mr. and Mrs. Kransup, located at 54263 Plot 5, Building 3, Estate 7, Low Town.

Take the H-L train from Station First Stop to Station Last Stop.

Someone bumped into him, and the envelope fell to the ground. Toffy stomped on the envelope before it flew away and then bent to pick it up. When he stood upright a man in a blue shirt and green army backpack yelled at him. "Watch where you are standing, donkey!"

The slender figure was not a part of the J Corp Army. His attire must have been a pass-down. Torn at the armpit. His backpack was hanging on by the thread of its strap.

Toffy had never been called a *donkey* before. Emotions he had never felt rushed through him. In his mind, he imagined greeting the man with a kick to the face. He immediately felt ashamed for entertaining such thoughts.

"Jive, donkey," the man said, with utter disgust on his face. He spun around and hurried off to get on his way. His social score was reduced for the vocalized abuse.

The train would arrive in two minutes. Toffy was definitely out of his element. He twisted around, startled by the sharp sound that came from the screen behind him.

The profile of two residents.

NOW BLACKLISTED

in bold red letters. Right below it, two smaller text lines blinked:

Social Score < 59.
5 years in Level D.

Toffy gasped. *Level D.*

The man on the right wore a torn blue turtleneck sweater. The night before he lost a total of three points for tossing a cigarette butt while jay walking. Two offenses in one act.

Level D. He wouldn't be able to apply for a loan again.

To the right was a woman in a purple overall. It had yellow patterns around it.

Two points gone—for spreading false rumors.

Her face was rigid. In her eyes, the shame was obvious. She had let her children down. They might not be able to apply to the school of their choice again.

Getting a job, forget about it. Toffy shook his head. *Purchasing flight tickets will be close to impossible. I have to hurry up and deliver this letter so my social score doesn't drop like these people. I've heard it's in the air. Contagious low scores. I can't imagine letting my score drop below fifty-nine! What are they thinking? Blacklisted? For half a decade. How do you bounce back from that? So irresponsible.*

"Hey, you. Where are you going?" said a man with a black baseball cap bent at the rim.

Toffy looked around.

"You. Yes, that's right. I'm talking to *you.*" He removed his hat, wiped away sweat on his forehead, and put it back on. "You looked confused," he continued as he walked toward Toffy. "Let me ask you this. What is a brand-new cat like you doing around this way here?"

"I'm heading into Low Town," Toffy responded cautiously.

"Low Town, you say. Where the real ones play." The man had a smirk on his face. "If you don't mind me asking, what are you going to do in Low Town?"

The train swished to a stop.

Toffy stood and looked at the man, "Sorry, I have to get going."

"No problem, my friend."

As toffy was about to enter the train, the man yelled, "Don't forget, everything is either a *trip*, a *trick*, or a *trap.*" He laughed and kept on walking.

The train doors closed as it rushed out of First Stop station.

Toffy took a seat in a silent corner as the train went through the city. He checked the time and then his utilization; surprisingly, it hadn't dropped. With every stop, the train emptied, the outfits of passengers dustier, the faces more hollow. A family of four walked in and sat across from him at the eighth stop. As the train departed, the family huddled in a cramped circle and stayed in that position for the length of their journey. There was a young boy and his younger sister. Their outfits looked like they had not been re-downloaded for months, and the parents' not for years. The father must have been in his forties. They looked beaten down as they scurried off the train three stops later.

I download a new outfit daily. What was their *life like? What do they do? Where do they live? Why did they seem so scared?*

The train consistently got lighter on its approach to Last Stop. The screens on the train also started changing. Some went off entirely, others showed just static. The few working screens displayed things Toffy had never seen before.

Toffy looked around, tapping his feet with nervous energy. He looked at the envelope in his hand. He had considered getting off the train and going back home.

Why did James send me here? His face tensed as he pulled the first sheet of paper out of the envelope.

The sudden stop of the train jerked him forward.

The last few people on the train stepped out. Toffy was the only one left. He waited for the train doors to close, but they didn't, so he stayed seated.

***

Fifteen minutes passed and the train doors were still open. Toffy looked around the train. No one was in sight. He pulled out the map to make sure he was not mistaken and stepped out onto the platform. The sign outside the train read, "Second to the Last Stop," so he slowly walked back into the train.

"Sir. Sir," a man in a yellow jacket called out. "Did you leave something on the train?"

"No, I'm going to Last Stop."

"You are going to Last Stop?" He grabbed his mobile device and spoke into it, "We have a passenger here going to Last Stop."

From the mobile device: "*Last Stop? At this time? Are you sure?*"

"Boss, are you sure you're going to Last Stop?"

"Yes," Toffy replied.

"Yup. He's going to Last Stop," he said, looking at Toffy from head to his toes.

"*Dammit. At this time? Who's this person? Nobody goes to Last Stop at this time.*"

"Some recently downloaded-outfit type of dude." He looked at Toffy from head to toe.

"*You're gonna have to take him. I've got to catch up on some screen time. This is my only time to do that. I don't know. You are going to have to take him.*"

"All right, Mr. Fresh Download. Get back in the train. Let's get you to Last Stop. If you don't mind me asking, what is a brother like you going to do at Last Stop? I mean, it's—" He stopped abruptly. "Never mind. It's probably none of my business. Let me get you there A-S-A-P, sir."

Toffy held on tightly to his envelope and walked back into the train. The man in the yellow jacket and gray pants disappeared, his sharp whistling heard from a distance.

The train started up again. All the screens went off. The lights flickered.

"Fellow passengers," the familiar voice returned from the speakers. "Fellow passenger, *hooooold* on tight. We are on our way to—" the voice paused again "—*Last Stop, Last Stop,*

Last Stop!" The train jerked forward and sped off in rumbling fashion. The force jerked Toffy's head back.

Five minutes later, the train came to a screeching halt.

Toffy had been wrecked. He had no clue what had just happened. It was a whirlwind. The dusty windows of the train reflected the beaten look on his face which hid the delight he felt when the train had finally stopped. He bent down and tapped around for the envelope James had given him.

"My envelope!" Toffy exclaimed.

"My son. Listen closely. You are in Heaven. Welcome to the Promised Land," a bass-loaded voice came from above.

It sounds like a voice from the heavens. Toffy perked up, looked around, eyes wide.

The voice continued: "Step out of the doors to begin your journey. Once you are on your path, take the first right into the door that's open, and you shall find that which you seek."

Toffy cautiously walked out of the train with his eyes open wider. Past the blinding-white brightness was an open door to the right.

"What is to be found is right there on the ground," the voice spoke out again, this time with more bass.

Toffy looked down, a brown rectangle on the floor. He slowly reached down to pick it, hands on his waist as he came back up. He raised it high.

"Yes!" Toffy exclaimed.

On the brown rectangle, bold red letters: CONFIDENTIAL.

"As you picked that which was on the floor," the voice continued raining down, this time with intimate proximity, "take my scripture as your daily chore. Look clearly, in case you aren't sure. Open the envelope because it's yours."

A snicker turned into hysterical laughter. Toffy turned around to find the man in the yellow jacket holding his belly and laughing.

"Ha-ha-ha-ha. My man, welcome to Last Stop," the train driver said, sitting down to control his laughter.

He put his hands together over his mouth. He made his face stern, looking Toffy in the face. "My Son. Listen closely. You are in Heaven." He burst out laughing again. "That was fun. I'm not even going to lie. Why lie? Ehn?"

He wiped his watered eyes.

Toffy snapped to it.

Don't count me out. Don't take me for granted. Those were Toffy's thoughts. He looked at the envelope in his hand, held it tightly, and then dusted himself off. He began walking.

"Hey, bright clothes," the train conductor said, "you're gonna be eaten alive down here. Let me help you out. My name is Davo, a-k-a *God...* ha-ha-ha-ha. What's your name?" he asked with his hand stretched out. "My son. It's me, God, asking you. What's your name?" Davo wiped the tears from his eyes.

"Tof—I'm Toffy,"

"Where are you going?" Davo asked and grabbed the envelope.

Toffy snatched it back.

"Okay, okay. I'm just trying to help you out, Mr. Fresh," Davo responded. "Let me get you someone to drive you to your location."

Someone to drive me...

"Hand this card to the man upstairs, and he'll take you to your location,"

Toffy took the black card and walked off the train. Davo just kept shaking his head. Toffy went up the steps. It was desolate. Not a single soul was at the train station. The station looked deserted, run-down even.

The haziness in the air consumed Toffy. Dark, hazy, and brown, Toffy squinted to find his way through. He heard something scurry past him. Then, something zoomed by his ear, buzzing loudly. Toffy reacted, slapping at his own face.

Soon the haze cleared out. Toffy could finally see people at the corner of the street. Some sat, doing nothing. Just sitting and staring. He looked around for a taxi, but none was in sight. He turned to go around the corner and found a yellow car with a black line painted across the body of the vehicle.

"Hi, is this a—" Toffy said and then looked at his card to reconfirm, "a taxi?"

The man in a blue coat and black hat pointed at the side of the vehicle, to the bold letters: TAXI.

"Oh, okay. I got this black card." Toffy leaned in toward the driver. "The train guy told me to—"

"Told you to what?" The driver snatched the card out of his hands. "Geh in da car," the man snapped and sat upright as he turned the key.

Toffy got in the back, and the car started moving before he could fully close the door.

"So, I'd like to go to…" Toffy said and pulled out his envelope, "five-four-two-six-three plot five."

"Sharrit! I know where we are going." The driver stared Toffy down through the rearview mirror.

"H-how can you already know," Toffy stammered, "where… where I need to be going?"

"God told me," the driver responded sharply.

His face looked familiar.

"Do I know you?" Toffy asked. "Are you—"

"Sir, kindly sit back and let me concentrate on the road."

"Well, we are going to five-four-two-six-three plot five, building three, estate seven, Low Town," Toffy said and sat back into the musty car seat.

"Is that where we are going?" the driver responded. He mumbled a few words. "Just sit back, relazz, and let me get you to your location." His voice returned to normal levels.

Did he just say, "You too must be feeling like God now, huh?" No. Of course not. But— Toffy looked around.

The twenty minutes of driving passed as though they were at sea. The car went up and down, maneuvering around and through the bumps and the holes in the road. Toffy had not experienced anything like it before. Throughout the ride, he held on to the side rest and his tongue to stop himself from yelling a few times.

A lot of people were sitting and standing on the side of the road, doing nothing. Unlike where Toffy came from, there were no screens. People just gazed into the distance. The few vehicles that passed by were in horrible condition. Broken down vehicles were on the road, charred garages. Buildings abandoned. And no screens to watch.

No screens around on buildings. This place is void of light.

Every corner, there was hope of it getting brighter, but that hope was soon diminished after each turn. Toffy looked all around the driver. He squinted, hoping to learn more about him or squeeze out anything about the driver's quantified self.

Nothing. No social score on his outfit or above his head. Can I trust this person?

Toffy adjusted his lens. He scrutinized the man's character before switching his attention to the environment around him. Out of the window, no annotation of objects. Not a single number in the darkness to quantify his surroundings. Just the rawness of life.

He can he see where he's going? I can't even see my feet.

Toffy examined the internals of the car once more. The seat was a soft brown, made gray by the night. Outside his immediate sight, a multicolored heap moved closer as the car swiveled forward.

"Oh my god!" Toffy shouted and sat up in the car. "Is that... is that *plastic* growing out of the ground?"

Toffy stuck his face to the window, his mouth open in amazement. A mound of plastic bottles were piled up on the watery-hole on the side of the road.

"Wait, is that how plastic is made? It grows out of the ground?" Toffy asked.

"Yeah, sure," the driver said. "You see, that thing in the ground is a gutter. Irrigation technology at its finest. That's why we are the only ones in J City who can plant beautiful plastic trees that just keep growing out of the gutter. Maybe we can grab some plastic flowers for you to take to your special one back in High Town." The driver shook his head and stomped on the brakes.

Toffy was jerked forward and slammed back in his seat.

"We are here." The driver hopped out of the car.

Toffy looked around, waiting for his door to open; it didn't.

What's going on here? Toffy mumbled under his breath and pulled on the plastic lever sticking out. It opened.

He stepped out and stepped in.

"Looorddddd!" he yelled out. It felt like an eternity, how long he was falling. Toffy braced himself for impact before hitting a slushy bottom. It was a small hole in the ground, and he was already knee-deep in it.

"Watch where you're going," the driver said, seated on the hood of the vehicle, lighting a cigarette. "That's a pothole."

"Thanks," Toffy said and climbed out of the hole.

He dusted off his shoes and pulled out his mobile device. The warning on his phone read:

YOU ARE PROBABLY IN DANGER. YOU DO NOT HAVE SERVICE. GET OUT OF WHERE YOU ARE IMMEDIATELY.

Toffy panicked and shoved his phone back in his pocket.

"We have forty minutes to head back to the train station," the driver said as he puffed smoke out of his mouth. "You better get to it because I'm leaving in forty minutes. That's where you are going." The driver pointed at a yellow building next to another with a sign at the base: Building 3.

***

Three hours later, Toffy had returned to a familiar part of the city. He walked around in a dream state, like a drunk boxer who had been caught unaware with a swift combination of punches: *jab, jab, sidestep, jab, hook, jab,* and definitely an *uppercut* in the mix.

Toffy had stopped at Skreet's Café, the only sensible place for him to go immediately after coming back from Low Town. Patrons there were fine with losing a few points on their social score in the eccentric bar that gained notoriety for fewer screens.

Musta was there.

"Hey, man. You need a table?" Namdy, the owner of Skreet's, asked Toffy. Namdy's soft gray hair disguised years of his persistent struggle for survival.

Toffy respectfully waved Namdy off and walked over to his friend. He sat on the same table and then placed his mobile device on the chair in front of him. The device read,

YOU HAVE MAXIMUM PHONE COVERAGE ONCE AGAIN. YOU ARE IN A SAFE SPACE.

"Dude, you look dazed," Musta said. "And how are you off work so early? Breaking away from the chains of the score?"

"I went into Low Town today. I went there on public transport, on my own." Toffy stared at the empty stage.

"Get this man a drink," Musta said and waved down one of the waitresses. "A strong one!" he added. "Ha-ha, you have seen it for yourself now. It's all linked to what I was telling you last week."

Musta leaned back and continued.

"You see, we are all under control. We are all agents of the system. Free will? *Please*, that's over with. Even the Low Town folks, without the screens, are under control. We have become agents, cogs in the wheel, completely hackable. Don't worry. We're going to do something about it. Right?" Musta leaned and bumped Toffy. "It's been a week now." Musta had a smirk on his face. "So? Are you in?"

He had repressed Musta's call since it was proposed. It had found a place to rent in the graveyards of cranial nonimportance.

"I know."

Musta must have known exactly what was on Toffy's mind in the moment.

"Sometimes I wonder what is worse than not following through..." Musta looked straight ahead toward the stage, his gaze in the same direction as Toffy's.

"Not trying at all." He looked at Toffy. "The anti-revolutionaries," he continued and laughed. "From the early twenty-twenties. The ones who fought back against dissent with their complacency. They used their complacency to solidify their stance. The corporations took a stance not to involve themselves in politics. It was no longer enough to just ignore the revolution. Their corporations with their influencers said you had to actively fight it.

"'Be an anti-revolutionary.'" Musta stomped his hand. "That was their slogan."

He repeated it two more times.

"That's why we take a stance as a company to not get involved in politics or social change.'" He mimicked the most famous CEO anti-revolutionary influencer of the era. His video declaration had been watched over a billion times. "They prided themselves in fighting back against political correctness. 'In an era of too much political correctness, standing up this way is actually the real revolt.'"

Musta imitated him again, laughing this time.

"Toffy, you see." Musta's face turned serious again. "That's where it all starts. It starts out with complacency. Before you know it, you are going against your very own being. A rage against your humanity. How do you stand in the world without taking a stance? Think about that."

Musta pointed to his head, the space between his ear and eye.

"Where do you stand, my brother?" Musta tapped Toffy, jumped off the table, and walked to the stage. He grabbed the microphone.

"We know their corponialism system ain't peeeeerfect," Musta sang into the microphone.

"Those at the top keep rehearsing. Those at the bottom undressing. We 'round here gonn' reverse it. Tell the children the truth."

Musta pointed into the crowd, jumping and chanting. "Cause Musta's in the system, better run up 'n' down."

CHAPTER 7

J Event was at a good buzz. The sparkles and the cracking of glitz could be heard.

Toffy's speech was coming up. His palms were sweaty, knees weak, and emotions on edge; he could barely hold the glass of whisky he had poured for himself without it slowly slipping from his hand.

He had felt tired and out of it for the last couple of days.

Over the years, he had learned to push through, continuously developing the internal will to control most situations. The same will had helped him succeed through tough times.

This newfound weariness wasn't just physical or mental; it started after his trip to Low Town.

Low Town, but we're in High Town. Not everyone is aware of the whole. Is there more?

He brought his mind back to J Event and the speaker at the podium, Jessica.

"And we are all here," Jessica said, "looking beautiful." She looked around the room nodding. Anyone who had spent more than five minutes with her knew she must have practiced that nod several times 'til it got the "Jessica certificate of perfection."

"To think that I am here," she continued, "in front of you, giving a speech, when just six years ago I wrote to my mentor, Nolton, who is seated right there."

She blew a kiss to him.

"I was in tears," Jessica said with an undulating pattern, looking for the appropriate dramatic pause, "and I was writing about how empty I felt about life. I was at the bottom, I tell you. I sobbed as I wrote every word of that letter. Then, something happened to me toward the end of the letter. I started thinking about how I wanted it to end; after all, there must be an end to this rambling if I expected to get a call back from Nolton."

Jessica looked in his direction again.

"I don't know how it happened." She picked up the story with a swift cadence in her voice as if she had, at that moment, received enlightenment. "What was happening was so surreal. It was like I stopped writing the letter and a higher force started writing through me. I immediately knew the line where my pen would make its final stop. I just had to get the pen there.

"And as I got to the final line, I wrote, 'I just want to change the world.' Here I am now, six years after that dark moment, changing the world... with the best company in the whole wide world, J Enterprise."

Everyone rose and gave a chamber-vibrating applause.

Toffy stood reluctantly to join in the applause.

Change the world? Here we go again. If I had a coin for every moment that phrase is thrown around here, I would be beyond rich.

They all sat as the next speaker was introduced. Paul. The biggest "change the world" spewing employee at J Enterprise.

"I was twenty-two when I realized I wanted to change the world," Paul started.

Toffy looked around the room. Everyone was so focused on Paul and how he paced back and forth. He ramped up into a typical energetic speech.

This dog-and-pony show made Toffy's stomach turn. He had heard it so many times that "changing the world" had lost its meaning. He was among a series of speakers who would have to come up with such a story.

Such narratives had caused the anti-revolution movement. Everyone was so happy with spewing empty words that brought about the current state of the world he lived in. That they *all* lived in.

The year 2022 was a very interesting year. The anti-revolution movement in full swing.

Toffy had lost sight of the speech on the stage. He remembered reading about that time.

The flak against anyone who went against popular opinion was at its max. The few media outlets that still existed then were on one of two sides: the right or left of an issue. Constantly at each other's necks. Whenever one side took a stance, there were market-oriented repercussions. Money would always find its way in the hand of the attacking side to aggrandize their position.

The media was constantly under discipline by the few hands and, more importantly, the invisible hand of the market.

Once a "rogue" media outlet had been disciplined, they lost all relationships and accessibility to the authority figures and self-proclaimed experts. Once they lost that, they could never bounce back. Only a few attempted to go against the powers at play and had a useful career afterward to talk about it. They cleaned up their acts immediately and joined the others who stuck to the script. Soon, everyone spewed the same things under the umbrella of J Media.

J Media strung up all and every loose network of the cloud into the one grand J Cloud—the consolidated cloud that hung over the city. Every evaporated pocket of data flowed into the cloud below. It rained down remixed, personalized, and interactive pieces of information. In bits, pixels, and messed media.

The era of J Cloud Intelligence was unavoidable. The inevitable. Brought on by lack of legislation and the aggregated network effects.

Everyone who connected to the network fed it glimpses of insights that helped it understand the people better. The more it understood people and provided personalized experiences, the more people joined. The more people on the network, the better it worked. The better it worked, the more people joined the network. The vicious cycle culminated and continuously became the consolidated cloud directed, ordered, and cognified by J Enterprise.

Around the room, the speech was silent. Toffy only heard his thoughts.

It couldn't be stopped. But it didn't have to be so one-sided. We did have a choice, but the stance was taken then. It gets to watch us, but we don't get to watch it with the same scrutiny. The asymmetry of tracking could have been avoided. Or was it designed that way? That's what got us here.

Toffy scanned the room.

The anti-revolution movement. The consolidation was gradual, unnoticeable. The isolation and exclusivity had become a norm.

A few tables behind him, he spotted pointy tips of hair behind a woman's delighted face. Her smile as she watched the stage widened her face. Chances of confirming who was behind her got slimmer every moment her smile intensified. *That must be Musta.* Toffy was not sure. His memory was ignited once again to their conversation a week ago at Skreet's.

"By the thirties," Musta had said, "they had mined most of the digital coins. There was nothing else to mine. Only a few had the digital assets to access to new web. The experts, James, and the councilmen controlled the narrative. They decided who had access to the internet. They decided when the internet should be accessible. It had been that way since twenty forty."

Musta. He chuckled. *That is also lopsided.*

Toffy continued scanning the room.

His gaze ended on the table with the councilmen. They were all laughing and clinking their glasses. They were all in it. Not against one another. They all knew the position they played in keeping the wheel spinning. Low Town had to be what it was for High Town to be what it was. One side could not exist without the other.

Toffy *did* want to change the world at some point, when he was much younger. But years of working at J Enterprise had changed him to someone just *in* the world—not really changing it. In his youth, he filled his book with stories and drawings of a world more improved than the world he lived in now. However, the older he got, that internal change-maker flame dwindled.

He used his willpower to justify changing the world by working hard and being the best engineer at J Enterprise, but in reality, it seemed he was there helping to keep the world the same. His duties at J Enterprise took so much effort that he did not really have time for anything else.

Toffy continued his reflection on the state of the world instead of getting ready for his speech.

Complacency.

He turned around. The lady two tables behind him was still wide-eyed and smiling. The silhouette of the hair behind her had disappeared.

Where did he go? He remembered more of Musta's words from a week ago.

"The separation of those who *have* and those who *have not.* The artificial 'tribes' that had developed amongst the people. The domination of the society in a corporate-government complex."

The people in Low Town must have the answer. They must. They were real. They were human. They didn't hide their emotions behind distracting screens. They had their own stories. The answer must reside with them.

Toffy nodded his head.

They must be the counter response to this ingrained religion. This religion undefined that we all can't seem to shake. But how?

Toffy didn't have the energy to do anything about his lack of energy at the event. He was exhausted trying to keep his utilization high. It didn't come easily to him like before. He had to put in effort these days. He was getting older but pushed the thoughts of aging out of his mind for the meantime.

A month ago, when he noticed the first strand of white hair on his head, he stared at the mirror in disbelief. He hoped it was some misplaced thread from his bed covers, but it wasn't. He had plucked the hair out fast, as if that made him unsee it.

Toffy looked aimlessly at the speaker on stage as he thought about his youth and where it had disappeared to, his dreams, and how they had been plucked out of his mind like his first strand of white hair. Lost in thought, he remembered Musta's offer to join him. The uncertainty of adventure brought a smile to his face. It was reminiscent of times when he could just get lost and dream up new worlds. A sudden rise of energy pulsed through his body. He felt light, as if pulled by a string toward the ceiling to be rescued from the event. *I'd love to get lost. I'd love to. But what if I never get found? What happens then? Is it safe?*

A round of applause burst out, and someone on the table said, "Hey, that's *you* we are all clapping for."

Toffy realized it was time to give his speech. He snapped back to the present, slowly rising to his feet. He headed to the podium while the applause echoed around the room, the light on the stage blinding.

He took a few deep breaths and collected his thoughts.

"Dear colleagues, we are gathered here today," Toffy said as he strained to look past the halo of white light. He could not see the crowd except for a few people on the extreme sides of his vision. "J Social, run by the beautiful Deja. I'm so honored to wake up to your beautiful face every day."

Someone whistled.

As Toffy pointed at Deja, he continued, "The thing I love most about Deja is her commitment... her commitment... Deja is her... the thing I love..."

Lightheaded, he slurred his speech, repeating phrases in the hope that he could just pick up where he'd left off. Then his vision blurred.

Thud.

The audience gasped.

Toffy was on the floor.

***

The visions of Deja in her black dress were vivid. This time she was more lighthearted, smiling at Toffy. He smiled back. It had been a while since he had seen her that happy. He remembered when they met and how that same smile got his attention at the MBA-Engineering mixer at their university. This time, however, they were in a field Toffy had never been in before.

Toffy looked around, fascinated by his surroundings, while Deja skipped and hopped around as though she had not a single worry in the world.

Toffy was seeing things he had never seen before, colors he had not even imagined. The air was still, but light and airy. The colors of the petals of the flowers were so vivid they looked digitally manipulated. Toffy reached out to touch them and found them warm.

Deja was always slightly ahead. She must have been in this field before, unfazed by the curved trees, the fist-sized butterflies, and the multicolored caterpillars.

"Hey, let's have a look," Deja said wistfully, signaling for Toffy to follow her as she swiftly changed direction. "Isn't it beautiful?"

The pond in the middle of the field was a clear and still body of water that moved every time they got closer to it. He took another step closer, and the pond moved again.

"It's magical, isn't it?" Deja said and smiled. "I come here when I need to disconnect and reconnect with what is true. My true nature."

A blanket had appeared underneath her, and she gracefully floated toward the floor where she lay on the checker-patterned piece of cloth. Her hair was long and twisted, a properly fitted nest for her beautiful head to rest in.

Toffy admired her egg-shaped face.

"Look into the water, Toffy," Deja said as she ran her fingers playfully up and down the sides of her thighs. "There's something in there for you. There's always something in there for everyone." She leaned back and looked up to the sky.

Toffy approached the pond slowly, and it moved again.

Deja giggled. "You have to be ready for the pond for the pond to be ready for you." She intricately peeled off the yellow petals of a flower that had appeared in her hands.

Toffy stood back and stepped closer, but the pond moved again.

"Where are we?" Toffy asked. "High Town or Low Town?"

"We are where we are supposed to be. Yes. We are in *No* Town." Deja smiled as she played with her hair.

Toffy repeated, "No Town. Hmmm. Okay. Great. We are in No Town." He jumped toward the pond to get a look into it. The pond jumped back.

Deja burst out laughing. "You have to take your time, Toffy. Take your time."

She stood and held his hand. "Now walk slowly with me. There you go."

His reflection in the pond turned into a man with his hand held out toward him and then to a woman with her clothes wrapped around her. The woman danced and showed Toffy antiques, sculptures made out of different material, paintings, carvings, textbooks with writings in languages he could not understand.

The woman danced off, and the image of a building appeared on the surface of the water.

"I know this building," Toffy said.

"Do you?" Deja responded.

Deja was back on her feet and packing up from her brief impromptu picnic. She smiled and said, "Aren't you going to catch up?"

They walked away from the pond, through more fields, and ended up on a beach. Only the two of them. The shoreline stretched for miles in both directions. They lay in the sand and looked up in the sky, a clear ocean blue without a single cloud. They enjoyed the warmth of the sand and gazed intently but vacantly above. Time did not exist in this space. There was no space for time nor time for space.

Deja got up and walked to the shore. Toffy sat up to watch her as she confidently walked toward the layering waves of the water. Sand particles hung on tightly to her backside before it was submerged in the water.

"Aren't you going to join me?" Deja asked, smiling.

Toffy got up and started walking toward the ocean. The waves were mild.

Deja's lower body had disappeared beneath the water as she waited for Toffy to join her.

Toffy suddenly felt hesitant. The sky was no longer blue. A dark cloud had come over them, and the waves suddenly turned aggressive.

Deja was calm. Nothing had changed for her. She was still smiling.

Toffy knew everything had changed. He stood at the shore, and the water crashed at his feet.

"Come on, Toffy. Get in. Don't you want to do more?" Deja shouted.

Toffy's lower body disappeared below the water. He panicked once he realized he might have gone too far, a familiar fear. He backtracked, but every step out took his body deeper into the water. He turned to face the beach, but it was no longer there. He kicked and splashed.

Beep—a sound from the dark cloud.

Toffy kicked, fluttering in the waves.

"Toffy, just let go. Either you are in, or you are not," Deja said.

Beep. Beep.

The sound again.

His heart raced.

Beep. Beeep. Beeeep.

In a flash, Toffy kicked and waved his hands, but there was no more water.

Toffy woke up from what must have been the best and most intense dream he'd had in a while. He looked around for Deja but didn't find her immediately. The screen ahead of him emitted a low blue color. The note attached to it had words written with a familiar curve.

Deja. Toffy felt her presence. It read: "Get well soon. I'll be back to check on you."

Everything around him was white. He wondered how the ballroom had gotten so silent.

Beep. Beep. Beep. Beep. Beeep. Beeeep.

What's that sound? And why am I in this white bed?

CHAPTER 8

———

The sound of a page of a book turning caught Toffy's attention.

"Uncle Apo," Toffy said with a strained voice. "What are you doing here? What—"

"What happened?" Uncle Apo interjected. "You fainted, that's what happened. Your lifestyle has finally caught up with you. Deja—"

"Deja... where's Deja?" Toffy scanned the room.

"She's fine. She was here through the night. She had to head back to work. She was the one who called me."

"Hello, Mr. T," a tall man in a white robe standing at the entrance of the room said. "How are you feeling?"

"I'm all right," Toffy responded. "A little lightheaded. What happened?"

"I'm Dr. Cardigan. You fainted out of exhaustion. You need to take care of yourself. You have the vitals of a fifty-year-old man at the age of thirty-two." He tapped the screen next to Toffy to get his attention.

Graphs and numbers measured each second. Lines flowed across the screen. The strap on his hand provided each measurement of his physical being.

"Tap for full diagnosis and recommendations," Dr. Cardigan spoke, distracted, looking down at the screen attached to his wrist band. "If you have any questions, or you do choose to add a customized human addition, tap here." Looking away from the screen, he tapped it.

Toffy must have not been recommended as the type of patient who would opt in for a real doctor. Dr. Cardigan's mind was optimized for matching with patients who could spend more money for his time. He tapped his watch again; the smile on the face couldn't hide it. He found a more suitable match, backtracked out of the room, and rushed off to see another patient.

That was the culture at J Hospital, the world-class medical facility known for its unbelievable "speedy service," which really meant, "We don't have time to waste on patients."

Competing with the robot-docs, the doctors were in a constant stream of motion, bumping into one another in the hallways, fighting to stay in competition, to remain relevant.

Toffy was trapped in his mind. He still couldn't shake off the thought of losing consciousness.

So, that's it? That's how people go? Boom. It just goes blank? Darkness. So what's the point, then? What's the meaning of life, then?

He had not thought much about death since he was a young boy—the day his antique chicken pet stopped moving and feeding. He kept an avatar of the chicken in his wallet, a reminder; for some, a collectible.

What happened when something died? This question had occupied Toffy's mind.

Mortality remained a point of investigation in his mind as he grew older. Instead of letting romantic relationships bloom, Toffy was sure to change any blossoming friendship into a continuous dialogue about the reason why humans existed in the first place.

Soon, more important things came up in Toffy's life. School exams. Being the best in the program. Getting a great job. These moments or paths always appeared as questions the world imposed as worth answering. He put his head down, followed the sure path, and rose quickly.

It was all supposed to go up and to the right as he got older. That's what he knew. That's what he was told. He was certain about all of this. Yes, there might be some disparities, some crazies here and there that didn't fit into the certainty of the world, but that never bothered him.

That's them, not me, Toffy justified, to himself, a few days after his one-time visit to Low Town. *They are the ones dealing with the uncertainty.*

He still felt certain about life, until that foundation of certainty was rocked right beneath him on that fateful evening at the J Event.

"What's the meaning?" Toffy shrieked. "Tell me, what's the meaning of life? In *my* lifetime," Toffy crowed in a crooked melody as he placed his palm on his head.

The thought of dying without having an impactful life brought a cloud of fear over him that flooded him with a weakness he had not felt in a long time.

It had softened his heart, but it also oiled up the gears that would hasten the steps of his feet; nervous he would not be able to tell his story, share his true perspective, or leave anything behind. He thought about the project with Musta and quickly dismissed it.

My score will drop significantly. I would lose all my friends. They wouldn't look to me for my guidance and wisdom. I would lose it all socially. I'd end up stuck in Low Town.

He looked at his wristband. His social score had tanked. Toffy shriveled.

The white pyramid was ingrained in his head. The food tasted bland but still kept him alive, yet he thought about not having that food, not having his apartment, not having *things*. *Losing Deja?*

He shivered, and with a sweep of his index finger across his forehead, he let the beads of perspiration drip into the pillow. In the corner his uncle was standing over him.

"You hear that?" Apo snapped his fingers over Toffy's face. "You need to take care of yourself. All this stuff you think is so important to you—your job, your title, the recognition... Where does it leave you? On a sick bed, surrounded by flowers instead of loved ones."

"Where's Deja?" Toffy asked, looking around.

"She just left," Apo responded, "a few hours ago when I got here. She stayed with you through the night. You don't remember that. Do you?"

"The last thing I remember," Toffy said faintly, "was being at the J Event. I was not feeling too good."

"I wonder why?" Apo responded as he stood from the seat next to Toffy's bed. "There's no way you can feel good working at the Enterprise."

"No, it's not that," Toffy said. "I know there are high standards for utilization, and we are working ridiculous hours, but I've been out of it for the last week."

"Really?" Apo said, looking at the flowers around the room.

"Yeah, really. I went to Low Town"

"Wait, you went to Low Town?"

"Yes, on some type of secret mission for..." Toffy hesitated, wondering how much information he should divulge, knowing the screens were on.

Apo walked back to his seat. "I can't wait to hear this."

"I took the public transport to get there," Toffy said.

"You took the public transport? *You*? You were on the H-L Line?"

"Yes"

Apo sat back and crossed his legs. "Please continue."

"I went down to Last Stop," Toffy continued. "And—"

"Wait," Apo said, and sat up. "You want to tell me that you took the public transport to Low Town, got on the H-L train, and then went all the way to Last Stop? You? Toffy? My nephew? I should really get the doctor to check you. It seems like you bumped your head very hard." Apo laughed. "I'm enjoying this."

"That place was strange," Toffy continued, switching to lie on his side to face his uncle. "Everything seemed so outdated and rundown. The roads were horrible. People were not smiling. Long lines were waiting on things across the entire area. No screens were there. Imagine, I had no service on my phone. Can you imagine that?"

Apo had a constant smile on his face.

"Anyway, what had me messed up the most was this couple I went to visit. As bad as the roads were and as run down as things looked, when I got to my final destination and walked into this compound of buildings, the place was neat. Everything properly arranged. A sharp contrast to what I had seen driving up to the place."

"Wait, you *drove*?" Apo asked.

"No, I was driven by a very interesting fellow, who I suspect might have been the train conductor who got me to Last Stop." Toffy wondered if any of this made any sense. "I got to the actual house, and as I was about to knock an older lady opened the door. I'd say she was in her fifties. She said she knew I would be coming."

"Yeah, she probably knew already." Apo had a smile plastered on his face.

"What do you mean?"

"Nothing. Just continue," Apo added.

"I asked if she was Mrs. Kransup. She responded yes and told me to come in. Then I asked how she knew I'd be coming over, and she said, 'Open the door before he knocks, the one with the envelope will arrive at three o'clock.'

"She was so nice," Toffy continued. "She told me to sit and offered tea. Then I handed her an envelope I was supposed to deliver. She sat and opened it quietly. I'm telling you, this woman had so much grace. Everything she did beamed with human radiance.

"She pulled out the contents," Toffy continued, "of the smaller envelope within the envelope I handed her. She read it, and her demeanor changed. She became angry. She threw the envelope and its contents down on the wooden stand next to her outdated chair, stood up, and walked toward the window. At that point, I really did not know what to do, so I stood thinking I could leave. After all, my job was to deliver the envelope.

"She asked me whether I was happy with what was going on. I asked her what she meant, and she turned around and looked me sternly in the face and said, 'How can you let this happen? And for him to think he can just buy us off. The indignity. He thinks we will just allow his—*your* organization—green our waters. And that we are going to sit back and just take his money?'"

Toffy leaned in closer.

"She told me to approach the window. I walked over, and she said, 'Look at our water supply. That used to be a stream that supplied the entire area. It's now clogged with plastic and the green stuff. It's a green lake now. It is now the refuse dump of all that is being developed and manufactured for you High Towners—the automated industry that develops your digital automated life. But I guess someone has to pay the price,' she said as the anger melted from her face and turned to sadness.

"She asked me how she was supposed to live when they can't live off the land they were on. She told me the pollution had been happening for the last five years. All their resources had been taken. All the workers had been taken, and the other workers deemed useless.

"Uncle Apo," Toffy said. Looking around, he whispered, "She also said the green stuff in the water is making people lose their memory. That's why she began a petition to build a case against J Enterprise."

Toffy looked around again.

"The machines built by J Enterprise are the cause of all the waste and green spillage. The green spillage, in turn, was causing the people to lose their memory. An ongoing epidemic. A lot of people in the area cannot remember their history or who they are. Right there, she pointed to her husband sitting silently in the kitchen. He had dark glasses on, and both his arms rested on top of a wooden cane."

Toffy looked at his uncle, teary-eyed.

"He just sat there. Looking. Not doing anything. Just looking. She said most people in the area had even forgotten there was a time the stream did not have the green stuff in it. Once in a while," Toffy continued with a deeper pitch in his voice, "her husband raised a black remote toward a chunky black screen and switched the channel. I must say I have not seen that type of content before. It was very violent. Police shooting civilians. Civilians shooting civilians. Beatings. Houses destroyed by bombs, crumbled to rocks and dust. The councilmen were on channels campaigning for reelection, even though the people were in horrific living conditions. The councilmen had the nicest, most durable vehicles to manage the bad roads.

"I'm not even sure if he was watching, but after a while he would switch the channel again to more violence or campaigning. After a while, watching that thick black screen, I couldn't tell the difference between the criminals and enforcers; it seemed like a nightmare.

"Mrs. Kransup showed me around her living area." Toffy shook his head. "Her grace came back beaming as she showed me some dated artwork. She handed me sculptures made out of odd materials: wood, bronze, and clay, she called them. She and her people had made them. That's how she stayed grounded and kept her memories from being lost.

"Then she grabbed me like *this*," Toffy said and reached out and grabbed his uncle's hands, "and said, 'I am from the earth, and you are from the earth.' She took her index finger and gently poked at my chest and said, 'Don't let our story be forgotten.' A single tear rolled down her protruding cheekbones. What do you think she meant by that?" Toffy asked his uncle.

Uncle Apo continued looking at his nephew without saying a word.

"I kept hearing bubbling, beating, and buzzing in a distance." Toffy described with heightened animation. "A constant vibration came from the outside. When I asked her about it, she smiled and said it was Viginniye. She told me to come back another time, that it would be a good place to visit because she thought I was, as she described it, 'a decent person.' Although, she did signal quotation marks when she said *decent*.

"She looked at her watch; it was three forty-nine, and she said I had to head out. She hurried me toward the door. I tried asking more questions, and she just kept saying, 'Another time. Another time.' As I walked past the envelope, I got a glimpse of a check with a lot of zeros. When I say a lot, it was *a lot*. She grabbed the check, tore it to pieces, and then said, 'Tell James we don't want his money.' When she opened the front door, the driver was about to knock. He yelled, 'We have to leave immediately!' Then I—"

"Get well, buddy. This is nothing but a speed bump!" Sarni's voice jarred from the collection of flowers as Uncle Apo opened Toffy's get well notes and gifts.

"Nothing but a speed bump, ehhn!" Apo said, his face transitioned from intrigue to annoyance as he watched a projected rendering of Sarni's likeness reading the message. Apo shook his head. "Sorry, didn't mean to interrupt you. You were saying? What happened after you left the Lady's compound?"

"Well, I ran behind the driver toward the car, avoiding the massive hole in the ground, and leaped into the vehicle. By the way, I fell into a hole in the road earlier. That's a story for another day." Toffy sat up in his bed. "Anyway, the driver just started driving crazy. I don't know how someone can drive that fast with all the holes and bumps on the road. He was reckless but kept saying we needed to beat the rush."

Toffy was very animated at this point, swinging his head and hands left, right, and center.

"The roads were really, really bad, Uncle Apo. Not one traffic light worked. But you know what? I kept feeling vibrations in the distance. I heard it too. A sound that I could not stop hearing. Like I had tapped into a frequency or wavelength I could not tune out. I asked the driver about Viginniye. At first he looked at me through the rearview mirror while he swerved."

Toffy looked squarely at his uncle, mimicking the deep tone of the driver in the blue coat:

"'Viginniye—that's the land of the rude man and woman. They call them rude because they are the ones left who tell the truth. Real rude boys and rude girls who only speak the truth, the *real* truth."

Toffy stumbled through his interpretation of the driver's accent.

"The driver told me the land had a mix of everything," Toffy said, reverting to his regular voice. "A land of hustlers. A land where the real cost is paid for the higher-ups to burn and loot. The place where the cost is absorbed to save our city from imploding. The driver got animated when talking about Viginniye. He said they have started to refer to it as the double-R now. That there is a revolutionary renaissance going on there. The land creates the needed environment to spur the needed revolutionaries for the time!

"'Double R, last long!'" Toffy yelled. He caught himself and quickly placed both hands over his mouth.

Apo looked at him curiously.

"Hmmm. What else did he say?" Toffy said. "Oh yeah. That the best revolutionaries came out of the area. He also mentioned the area was necessary for the purpose of saving the earth and bringing people together. To be honest, at that point I was just looking outside the window because there was a very dark cloud building up over us."

Toffy took one of his legs off the bed and placed it on the floor.

"I'm serious, Uncle Apo, the entire place became dark, and the cloud kept getting closer and closer, but the driver kept flying through, speeding toward the train station. Then he pounded on the brakes." Toffy demonstrated a jerking head move and paused.

Apo was fully engaged in his nephew's story. "So, what happened?"

"We got to the train station," Toffy answered, "and he told me I had two minutes to get down to the tracks and get on the train out of Last Stop. I ran out of the car and down to the train. The conductor was yelling, 'Come on, come on,'" Toffy said as he waved his hands aggressively toward his uncle. "He started the train, and we sped out of the station. The dark cloud was still following. It was getting closer. On the other side of the tracks, another train was approaching. I had never seen so many people cramped up in a train like that. Heads were sticking out of the window.

"The train conductor yelled out, 'My son, that's the first batch home. We barely beat that rush.' It was, for a lack of better phrasing, a sight to see. I'm not sure if all those people had enough air in that train. They were layered on one another. The dark cloud engulfed the entire place, like something had descended on the city."

Toffy put both his legs on the ground as he sat up in his hospital bed.

"And then, like a flash, *poof.* Well, first I noticed a line on the ground in front of us, glimmering from a distance. A solid line. As we approached, the cloud got closer to the roof of the train. And *boom!*" Toffy smashed both palms together. "The cloud disappeared, and the brightness of the day shone through."

Toffy looked at his uncle, trying to read his face.

"Is that normal?" Toffy asked. "All of a sudden, I was back in the city that I was very familiar with. You know, brightness, lit screens, automated vehicles, glossy buildings and shops. I looked back to see if I could get a view of Low Town, but all I could see was a fluffy white cloud."

CHAPTER 9

——

"The white cloud that we see from a distance."

Toffy looked toward the window. It was clear the light that illuminated the room came from the windows.

"A white cloud," Toffy continued. "What it looks like from here. Originating from the fog. Pierced with a reflection upon itself to the untrained eye. An illusion. I've been in a daze since then, to be quite honest. Fully conflicted. Like, how can this exist? Does it really exist? Did all that happen, or did it just happen in my mind?

"The darkness. The sewage. The one-story-tells-it-all screen. It hovers, you know. The dirt underneath a floating cloud of a white cloak.

"It's like I don't know what this world is about," Toffy said in a defeated whisper. "I don't think I know who I am anymore. I stumbled into Skreet's Café once I got off the train. That was the only place that made sense."

"Do you still write?" Apo asked. "You used to write and draw a lot when you were much younger. Maybe you can draw what you saw." He sat next to the bed. "Painting a vivid picture of what you saw in Low Town can help bring things to life. Viginniye, that is a unique place. Do you know how it got that name?"

Apo seemed delighted at Toffy's heightened curiosity.

"So back in the days," Apo continued, "a bunch of explorers from High Town were roaming around the Low Town area. They came across a vast and open landscape right there on the coast of the city. It is rumored that when the explorers went in there, one took along his son, probably nothing more than seven years old. During their tour, the son asked the father, 'Why is this place so open and clean?' The father responded, 'Because it is untouched. It is pure. It is what we'll call virgin land.' The next day, on the map, the area was named Virgin Land."

Apo had an irritated expression. He cracked his fingers in the palm of his hand.

"They called it Virgin Land, as if no one lived there before. Years later, more explorers would come from near and far to explore this 'virgin land,' until these explorers started laying claim to one side versus the other. After years of battling for resources, a small area of land was split between east and west.

"The Eastern region was called Virgin Eastern Area, while the western region was called Virgin Western Area, or VWA. Most of the real ones, the ones from the soil, moved to Virgin Eastern Area, which was later shortened to Virgin EA. After a few decades, the locals colloquialized the name to *Viginniye.* Virgin EA," Apo said and paused. "Vigin-ee-ay. Get it?

"Isn't that something?" Apo laughed in ridicule. "That name was spurred by the question of a seven-year-old. The child of an explorer. A visitor to the area. You see, the person who gets to do the annotation, the one who gets to tell the story, gets to shape the world.

"Listen closely," Apo continued. "Viginniye is always calling on each and every one of us. If you listened to her call right now, in this time when there is a lot of burning going on, in this area where there is so much trash, in this moment when we have allowed too much looting, you'd hear her crying out."

Uncle Apo got up slowly, lowered himself onto the bed next to Toffy, and started singing out:

They don't know
They don't know
They see the grin but
They don't know how it feels within
Only we know
Toffy—*Only we know*
They see the grins but
They don't know how it feels within

"Only you know," Apo said, and he turned to Toffy, his eyes holding back tears for ages. "Only *you* know." He stood up abruptly and walked toward the window with his hands behind his back.

"You should start writing again," he said confidently. "You are in one of the most unique positions to tell a very compelling story. It might be that thing you are itching to do that you just don't know about yet. Painting a world so vivid that only you, that *one* person, can allow the rest of us to see."

Apo used his hands for visual theatrics.

"I think there would be a lot of benefit if we saw things through your eyes. Through your unique point of view. It's really people like you who can make sure the resources we have remain open and available to everyone and not just the select few. Both physical and digital resources. You can help balance the already-tipped scale. Your story can be very powerful. Your message can band people together to fight the good fight."

The silhouette of Apo beamed against the bright lights that shone through the window. Toffy remembered nights when his uncle, a much younger version, would dazzle him and his sister with stories about everything imaginable in their world—real and unimagined.

Uncle Apo handed Toffy a black backpack. "All you need is in this bag."

The backpack was almost empty except for a pack of three black notebooks, a pen, one pencil, and a wooden sculpture. He looked at his uncle curiously, hoping to get an explanation. He thought of the notebook in his apartment.

"That's all you need, Toffy. A pen and a notebook. Start by writing a page a day."

"That's all?"

"Yes, that's all. No computers, no mobile devices, just good ol' writing, pen to pad. You see, there are certain traits a good storyteller has. Let me just call it the storyteller's secrets.

"These secrets have been used by the greatest storytellers in this world, and they have been passed down by words both written and spoken. The stories provide us with a representation of human experience during different eras. They offer a glimpse of the past and the things to come. These stories have been used by the best politicians, leaders, revolutionaries, and corporations to get people to galvanize around a movement, an action, an idea, or even products both good *and bad.*"

Toffy was so enthralled by his uncle's descriptions, he almost forgot he was in a hospital bed.

"The storyteller," Apo continued, "has several tools in his or her toolbox. They just have to know how to use these tools to tell great stories. One of the storyteller's secrets is the absolute belief in the story they are telling. The storyteller believes totally in the ideas they are putting into the world. This conviction makes their stories so believable. I can go on and on, but I think this is enough to get you started."

Toffy pulled the wooden carving out of the bag—a sculpture with a male and female head.

"What about this?" Toffy asked. "Something about this looks familiar."

"In due time, Toffy." Apo tapped Toffy on his thigh. "In due time. In the meantime, get some rest."

The carving reminded Toffy of a woman from a not-so-distant past who had randomly handed him some carvings; a woman who had also seen into his future. The idea of her and the essence of Low Town did an intricate dance in Toffy's head.

"It has to make sense in the future," Toffy mumbled.

"Toffy, you have to believe in your ideas. You have to be fully confident that you have a story inside you that the world needs to hear, and then go for it. Remember, those who get to tell the story actually get a chance to change the world, and those who change the world really do get to tell the story."

Apo sprung out of the bed again and placed his hand on Toffy's shoulder. The gravity of his uncle's words had transfixed him, pulling his entire being toward the core of the message.

Toffy thought of Musta.

"I'm in," Toffy mumbled.

"Huh?"

"I'm In," Toffy repeated, but this time his tone was louder, more confident.

"You are in... in what? What are you talking about?"

"I will write a story."

All Toffy wanted, and had to do, was write a story. *His* story. *The* story.

CHAPTER 10

—

His uncle had called it "a calling," and Toffy had been inspired to write his story. He didn't necessarily know what he wanted to write, but he had a story in him, and it was his ultimate goal to get that story out.

I've never fully gotten the sense that work had any significance, Toffy ruminated.

He was more certain than ever that he wasn't changing anything at work except for joining in the fanfare of spewing mindless rhetoric about change and, of course, praise to James.

Writing his story would be a way to start making a difference in his life and, ultimately, in the world.

He looked around at the screen and then pulled out his mobile device to send a message to Musta.

Hey man, can you send me that link again?
I'm in.

Toffy emptied out the contents of the wool-woven backpack. He placed the pen, pencils, and notebooks on the desk in his room. The two wooden heads were placed on opposing sides of the desk. From the dusty closet, he pulled out dated boxes filled with old stories and poems he had written in high school and university.

"Shaking things up, Mr. Toffy," Fluence's voice said through the screen. "New book, new settings, new hobby. Let me prepare the ideal room arrangement setting to optimize—"

Toffy moved his body to tower over the content of the desk.

"Current settings are optimal, Fluence!" Toffy responded.

This is where I'm going to do my writing. The desk in his room had dark brown and curvy grains that spotlighted its shine.

I can't continue writing on the floor. I have to utilize privacy hours. Maybe find a way around these damn screens during the day.

He approached his writing like an engineering problem, and he created a writing schedule. He was confident he could pull it off. He had something new to do, something challenging, something worth doing.

He took a deep breath. The notepad on his desk gave him a sense of purpose. It also signaled the type of validation Toffy wished for.

***

One day during his lunch break, Toffy's wish finally came true.

He was at one of the two screen-free parks in High Town. He stopped there to write a few words before he went back to his office, having just incorporated writing into his lunch routine, willing to catch up on his utilization later in the day. Something about writing while seated in nature made him very happy.

"Hey, what are you writing?" the fellow next to him on the park bench asked.

This man was different from the typical young executive at J Enterprise. He had on multicolored striped socks—quite brave for a man in a black trench coat.

He must be new.

"Hmmm, I'm just writing... down some ideas," Toffy responded.

"Oh, great. Are you working on a new business, or rather, a new product?"

"No."

Toffy decided to divulge to minimize the questions.

"I'm writing ideas for a story I'm working on. I'm trying—"

"So, you are a writer or some type of poet?" His expression filled with condemnation and a pinch of sarcasm.

The man had pulled out his mobile device from his pocket before Toffy had the chance to respond. It was obvious he had lost interest.

"No. I'm an engineer." Toffy was tempted to tell him that he and his team of forty engineers built the device he held in his hand, but he restrained himself.

"So, you are an engineer who writes during his lunch break," the young executive said dismissively, without looking at Toffy. "The privileges of the elite. Those who have time for extracurriculars. Please, tell me this. Do you make any income from your stories, your ideas?"

The young executive leaned in toward him. His bulging watch slightly peeked out under his nicely pressed white-cuffed shirt. A skinny black tie dangled below his square face, which enclosed a slanted smile. He sat on his pristine black trench coat. The shiny black shoes with the blue strap signified his usefulness in the city.

"Let me answer my own question then," the man continued. "You don't have a particular reason to write anything. Are you a faker? Because, just like everything else in this city, it's all smoke-screens. A mirage. Salespeople selling, and purchase-people buying. If you are not partaking in one of the two activities, it's hard to tell what you're doing. What is your goal? Only rich or lost people have hobbies, you know. Which are you?"

Overwhelmed with the barrage of questions, Toffy closed the notebook.

"I'm…" Toffy stretched out his speech in search for the next word, which he had lost.

"Hey, the writer doesn't have the words!" The man burst out laughing.

Toffy slowly opened his notepad to see what he had been writing. He had completely forgotten. The words from the strange man made Toffy question whether he was even writing anything at all.

"Hey, let me see that," the man said, standing and now towering over Toffy.

Toffy snapped his notebook shut and leaned away.

"I said, let me see that." The rectangle-faced man turned stern and serious. "Any funny ideas in there? Huh? Are you out here writing things that shouldn't be written? Is there anything in there that should not come to life? Maybe I need to send this to the boogeys."

Toffy pulled the book away as the man tried to take it.

"Hey, attention to the boogeys!" The man put his mobile device to his ear and said, "There's a clown here writing strange ideas. The joker said he's a writer, and he is—" He pulled his mobile device away and burst into tears as he ramped up into a new round of laughter. "Oh my, you have made my day. This city is filled with characters."

His hysterical laughter had driven him down to both knees.

"You really think I have time to call the boogeys? For what? Hello? Yes, John here. Yes, right away." The man received a call mid-sentence and quickly walked away.

Toffy watched in bewilderment as the man scurried across the street and then looked at his mobile device and realized he had to rush back to the office. On the way, he remembered his uncle's words: *The best storytellers are those who believe completely in their ideas.*

If he had to write his story, there could be no room for doubt. He didn't really know what he expected from the man in the multicolored socks, but he wasn't too pleased with him. Toffy wished he had told him off.

An engineer who just writes during his lunch break? How arrogant.

Back at his desk in his office, his utilization was just past the halfway point. He would have to hit his goal quickly and head back home to pick up his writing while the screens were asleep.

He pulled out his mobile device out of boredom, secretly hoping to see a message from Deja, or even a response from Musta. It had been four days since he had sent his message, and Musta had not responded.

Where could he be? He had never really gotten a grasp on that guy. He moved differently. *Maybe I need to be more like Musta, but where the hell is he?*

The blankness of his mobile device made him think about Deja again.

"*Woman, you know I love ya,*" Toffy found himself humming silently. "*Woman, you know just how I feel.*" He twisted his body, squinted his eyes, and spun his chair around. Looking out the window, Toffy continued with a raspy voice, "*Trying to tell me that you don't know. When I know you know it's real.*"

An image of Deja's silhouette appeared in front of him. Her twisted hair dangled freely, swaying and caressing the city's skyline.

"*Woman, you know I love ya.*" The pitch in Toffy's voice cracked higher. "*Woman, you know I'm concerned,*" and as he snapped his fingers, "*eeeeeeyyy. Try to say, that me, I'm running the track. I'm trying to say, baby, you play too covert.*" Toffy spun around in his chair once more and slammed both fists on his desk. "*Oh, darling...*"

"Mr. Toffy, is everything all right?" a surprised voice from the screen beeped. "Having a tough time with your tasks today? Your utilization is about to go below your average baseline for this time of day. Should I get you a three-milligram dose of the latest UB? The passionfruit-flavored Utilization Booster is sure to give you that tropical boost you need."

The screen switched to an image of a black-dotted orange bottle with text beneath it that read, "Order the Latest in UB Technology."

Toffy ignored the screen and grabbed his mobile device again. He still had no new notifications. He wasn't quite sure who he was more eager to hear back from—Musta or Deja.

Where is Musta?

Toffy squeezed the top of his fluffy hair with both hands. He felt the need to sign up for the project. That type of commitment would keep him accountable.

As Toffy searched fervently for information on his device, he received a message from Musta.

Dude, sorry.
I'm currently in Pajan.
Here's the link.
Send me your address. I have a package for you.

Toffy sat back in his chair to catch his breath. He sent Musta his address, clicked the link, and scrolled down to the bottom of the page and clicked the "I'm in" button. It took him to a form that asked for three things:

Name:
Email Address:
What makes your heart sing?

Toffy responded:

Toffy
toffy@NR.com
Writing stories

He clicked submit, and the screen changed to: *Congratulations. You are now in.*
Toffy expected more. He checked his email and didn't see anything.
So that's it?
Later that evening, when Toffy arrived at his apartment, a package was waiting at the door addressed to him. He opened it and found a note from Musta.
I had to get your package expedited.

Read the instructions below.

Pretty simple, very chilled :)

Stay in touch.

A white card came with the package, and written in a bold font: INSTRUCTIONS.

> *In this package there are two items: An MPX player with twelve instrumentals and a jar of the finest natural herbs. Listen to the instrumentals and write a story for each one. Write 'til you are content with your story. Feel free to use the items in the jar for some inspiration. Free refills included.*

Toffy didn't know what to make of the package. But this was all part of Musta's project, so he took the package into his study and placed it on his desk.

At 11 p.m., once the screens went off, Toffy grabbed his headphones, connected it to the MPX player, and played the instrumentals. He gave the entire compilation a listen and didn't even know where to begin.

Just start at the beginning.

He sighed, and something spoke to him. He listened again and began some free-association writing to get the words out. Stuck at the fourth instrumental, he reached into his package and grabbed the jar of greenery. He broke the leaves over a thin piece of paper and rolled it neatly into a fine cone.

He started out on the first instrumental, puffed away, and continued writing.

The words came out easier this time:

Just to buy the finer things, socialize and get more things
you should stop the overthink, get some more designer
things
check out my designer watch, I stay in designer time
I decided to design it to stay on this side of town
usually how I spend my time—wishing I could do more
but doing more than just moving up two floors
or being a hammer to a needle you just slam away
no delay, don't bite the hand that feeds you
I fight my evils while I'm dealing with the mundane
wondering if I'll ever tell my story someday

CHAPTER 11

___

"Mr. Toffy. Good morning to you today. You have been recommended for a day off after your medical emergency five days ago and two consistent days of not hitting your utilization goals. There is concern you might not be fully recovered, hence a mandatory day off to recalibrate."

The screen went off and ended its message abruptly.

What? A full day off? Toffy's excitement was cut short by suspicion.

5 a.m.

blinked on the small rectangular box screen next to his bed.

That's unusual. On a day going into the weekend. That's a first. Toffy looked around the room. Bringing himself to sit up in the bed, his feet touched the cold wooden floor.

Maybe it's a sign. The universe wants me to write.

He stood up, spritely.

Toffy went to the shared space next to his apartment. The dome housed a botanical garden at its center. He sat at a small unoccupied round table by the edge of the café, where he could easily peer down into the pool of floors circled by a path of people going to shops and schools. He opened his device and started responding to work messages.

Wait. I do have the day off.

The utilization bar on his screen was grayed out.

He put his mobile screen away and stared hopelessly at the blank pages of his black notepad.

"Espresso for you?" a gray robo-rista asked. Its wheels were not visible beneath its broad base.

"No thanks," Toffy responded. It slid away to the next table.

Where do I start? He surveyed the screens around the space. They seemed occupied with all the people they were catering to. Toffy stared at the pages in his notebook. He knew he was taking a risk.

Nothing was more intimidating than a blank page, and in that moment, it felt so true. The last four days of pure inspiration were wearing off, and on this particular day he felt hazy. He had probably smoked a little too much the night before.

Too much of anything ain't good for nothing. Toffy remembered that saying by a man he could hardly remember.

He had no motivation to write. Not even a single line, word, nor letter. He had doubts about moving forward.

To be good at anything, I have to at least try.

Toffy took his pen and put it in between his screen and his notepad.

Baby steps.

He pulled out the MPX player and started playing the instrumentals. As he listened to the music, a man in a black suit with black and brown dreadlocks stopped right next to him. Toffy removed his headphones.

"Are you a writer?" the man asked again.

"No."

Why that question?

"Well, you look like a writer," the man responded.

Baffled and flattered, Toffy wondered what could possibly be giving off writer's vibes.

It couldn't possibly be his recently downloaded outfit: a black T-shirt, or his black track pants, or his new all-black Stratified sneakers.

Is it because I've let my hair grow out a bit since I fainted? Toffy took another close look at the man as he walked away. Underneath his beret, he looked like he had a head filled with stanzas.

As soon as Toffy returned to the blank notepad, images and words came zooming into his mind. He immediately grabbed his pen and wrote:

Posters for elections everywhere
Roster of jokers who just don't care
Big bellies laugh, ha-ha
Power of magic, ta-da
Positions disappear in a soup of coups
Leave those to live in fear under pressed-up suits
Economic disorder, reorder
the borders that separate us from the others

Toffy paused, the page less intimidating. Videos in his mind that had played on for days came rushing back. He dropped his pen, picked it back up. He walked around and scratched his scalp, pulled out strings of hair that had tangled together.

He sat back down and read what he wrote. The images shot back, so he started again.

People paying with their eyeballs, that's the latest trends
We've been studying the actions of you and your friends

He took a deep breath, and after looking around he was pulled back to his writing.

Where did it all begin? When will it end?

It seems like Low Town is the only solution.

The only solution can be found in Low Town. What is the real situation?

Cities and countries run by corporations.

We the people are now the products. We are the means and the end. We trade our money to watch and consume more on the screens. It's happening to everyone. You look at the screen, and boom, money is taken right out of your account. It's called Pink Money. The corporation has made the screens addictive. You will watch the screens 'til you are poor. You will watch the screens 'til you have a job no more. 'Til you are rendered useless. The corporations don't need you and me. They have their machines. We code and continue to code ourselves out of existence. Gliding transactions for factions that have an issue with friction. Check my diction and wonder whether my addiction to words found in dictionaries is revolutionary. Very scary, the direction we are headed. Or the good times that claim to be special. Facial recognition with pupil-integration that strips and swipes credit cards and leaves it in perpetual rotation without intrinsic motivation.

But what's the lowdown on the Low Town, where it's hard to download 'cuz the town's loaded with loathe-loving misconceptions and little to no con-nection. It's all pressed down by the higher forces—greed, power struggle, coups, decay—all meant to control resources.

It seemed like he had been writing for days. On his wrist, 12:52 p.m. flashed. Only thirty-two minutes had passed. He closed his notepad, tapped on his screen to flicker on, and realized he had received a message from James.

What? James? Why?

***

James dropped his mobile device. He read the message again to make sure it carried the appropriate tone. He showed his biographer the screen and asked, "What does this convey to you?"

"Hey, Toffy, why are you not at your desk today?" the biographer read aloud. He nodded vigorously. "Oh, James, this is very good."

"Good?" James pulled the screen back. "*Good?* I'm not looking for 'good' here. I'm looking for—*powerful. Power.* Ah, how do you delete a message? I have to resend it," James said and tapped on multiple points on the screen. He poked at the screen endlessly like a child looking for a treat.

"Let me help you with that," the biographer said and reached out his wobbly hands, only to have them swiped away. "Oh wait, I think I read that wrong," the biographer exclaimed. "Let me read it again."

James showed him the screen and the biographer read out, "HEY, TOFFY, WHY ARE YOU NOT AT YOUR DESK TODAY?" The biographer gasped. "That is *powerful*. My glasses were not fully on the last time. My lord, sir, that is *very* powerful. The amount of power in that message will make any being quiver."

"Oh, shut it." James pulled back the screen and slammed it on the table. The councilmembers were all quiet around the big wooden conference table. "Let's begin."

J Council Meeting with High and Low Town Councilmembers—June 2049, the biographer wrote in his notepad

"Sir, if you don't mind." Ditty gestured by raising his hand timidly. "Before we start our ever-so-blessed council meeting, I'd like to say that from the look on your face when you sent that message, I *knew* it was powerful. I didn't even have to read what was in there. I just could tell there was so much power in it."

"That's right," Loya said as he shot out of his seat. "The power as you typed that message will be heard for generations to come. A message could not be more powerful." Loya sat back down slowly, looking Ditty in his eyes.

The battle raged on across the council table for hours.

"Muidi, please stand up and let us know the findings of your report," James said as he looked straight down the center of the table, the councilmembers on both sides.

"So, yes," Muidi responded, standing up. "I have personally meditated on this report, and what the PCPS committee have concluded is that the message sent out at approximately four thirty-five in the afternoon by James is what we refer to as a 'Power-Carrying Message.'"

"Objection. Objection." Obechat slammed his hand on the other side of the table. James's face changed to that of an opened-eye owl, and he shot Obechat a look that had him coil back into his seat.

Muidi shook her head three times in disapproval before continuing. "Before I was rudely interrupted, we, the members of the Progressive Council on Power Status, a.k.a. PCPS, have ruled that message as a Power-Carrying Message. The message sent to the employee will have the much-needed effect to continue to uphold the status quo. Thank you."

Muidi sat. Ditty to her right. Bejaai to his left. The three tapped on their screens intently.

"Bunajo, can you please give us your findings?" James said to the other side of the table.

Bunajo pulled his lanky frame together and snaked his way out of the chair. "Fellow councilmembers, I greet you today. We have been here for hours investigating and debating the sense of power and in whose hands it lies. I tell you, my brothers and brothers, there should have never been a debate to start with. The all-seeing-and-powerful-eyes-and-hand of James is where the power lies."

Obechat and Loya stood and started clapping.

"I'm *not* done. I'm *not* done. Please settle down." Bunajo pressed a twisted smile at the High Town councilmen across the table. He adjusted his flowing garb and continued: "As time will have it, I know we don't have all the time in the world to keep talking about things we are already certain about. So let me certainly say I'm not just here to bore you with empty words. The fullness of my heart does not allow me to push out sounds that have nothing to do with what is actually being discussed. I hope I am not losing anyone."

"Oh, not at all." Loya adjusted his report binder in front of him, his pointy nose clearly in line with the middle of his report.

"Let me continue so as *not* to take too much of our time and we can finally come to a resolution of which was a little too hard for those in High Town to get down." Bunajo pulled his binder toward him. "In regards to case status: Was the message powerful enough?" Bunajo raised his voice. "The Power Message Regulatory Council—or PMRC—rule the message to be powerful beyond human means."

"Here, here!" shouted Obechat.

"Impossible," Bejaai yelled out. "How can they find that—"

He was cut short by James's new face. They all saw it clearly in James's eyes: Bejaai's severed head on a spike burning. Bejaai played with tips of his orange hair. His chin came down to his chest as he buried his face in his screen.

"We didn't stop there, my dear Mr. Sir," Bunajo continued, "*not* at all. You see, we Low Towners are filled with action. Oh yes. We are action people. So, we took it a step further. Since it's election season, and we'll be needing some..." Bunajo hesitated and played with his long ears. "Some..." Bunajo looked around the room. "Some, eh... Let's call it *resources*."

"You want money," Ditty shouted across the table, his belt tight around the lower part of his belly.

"Council Chair James, can you tell them to stop interrupting." Obechat straightened the hat he always wore.

"*How dare you tell me what to do?*" James yelled with a softened voice.

"Oh no, I wasn't telling you..." Obechat's round face softened, and he bowed his head. "I was just... my apologies to you, my sir."

"Can I kindly continue?" Bunajo asked as he raised his binder to his face again. "Since we are action-takers, the PRMC has created our next action item. To act on what we found in the last committee, we will be setting up a new committee called the PBHMI committee.

"The Power Beyond Human Means Investigation," Bunajo said and paused for effect, changing his cadence. "PBHMI committee will discuss what we learned so we can discuss further without doing much."

"I like action items," James said as he nodded in approval.

Bunajo sat, Loya and Obechat on either side. The three men looked at their binders with undivided smiles.

The biographer had folded into a ball in the corner of the room. He had been sleeping under a table for more than three hours. He could not keep up with the councilmembers discussing the topic of power.

"They are just buying more time," Muidi said and pointed at the three men across the table, breaking the silence. She tapped her fingers on the table after muting herself.

"Objection. She is just interrupting us!" Obechat yelled back.

Ditty stretched his hands across his face. "They just want money. That's all they ever want."

Bunajo waved his hands. "We are open to discussing the thoughts that provoked the initial discussion as we create the appropriate channels to keep the ball rolling according to the necessary protocols."

"He never lost anyone in his discussions," Loya said as he placed his hand gently on his chest. His straightened shirt and trousers remained intact. "Bunajo was succinct and always to the point. We remain fully loyal to the fatherland."

"It's impossible," Bejaai shouted. "How did they come up with such a great idea to just keep talking? Loya. You, what did you say about my land or my father?" Bejaai shot across the table, his untidy orange hair swinging around as he reached for Loya's throat.

The battle raged on.

Scrunched up papers flew, and screens were pushed across the table.

The commotion in the room woke the biographer. He grabbed his glasses.

"My people. My children." James stood at the top of the table, hands stretched out. His face had changed once again, this time all light. "No need to fight. I respect and love you all. We shouldn't be fighting. We should all be together in peace, for the sake of our power."

He stretched his hand out for Bejaai, holding Obechat with the other.

"Let's complete the circle," James said, signaling the four men to join hands. "This is the circle. The circle of peace. Now, let's hum together."

"*Hummmmmmm. Hummmmmmmm. Hummmmmmm,*" they all hummed at the same frequency.

The biographer wrote in all caps: *JAMES. THE PRIN-CIPAL PROPAGATOR OF PEACE. The PPP is here. It has arrived!*

James pulled his hands away from the circle, grabbed his mobile screen, and typed a message:

GET HERE NOW. I NEED AN UPDATE IMMEDIATELY!

***

Toffy made it back home that evening. As he was about to scan his key to access his building, he looked around one more time before entering. He was more alert than usual, convinced something was going on.

Someone must be following me.

The screens on the buildings displayed all the latest colors of ads and stories. But something was different that kept Toffy on edge.

It wasn't just the screens this time. A human with eyes must be on my trail. Toffy could have sworn someone had started following him after leaving the coffee shop.

Toffy rushed upstairs and slammed his apartment door shut behind him. He kept his ear to the door for a few seconds. He was about to peel his ear away from the cold of silk-laminated door. That was when he heard it.

Footsteps approaching.

Kaak, kook, kaak, kook.

The steps got louder.

Toffy's heart raced in rhythm.

Kaak, kook, kaak, kook.

The footsteps stopped one apartment short of Toffy's door. He pressed his ear until it formed a vacuum suction.

The footsteps started again. *Kaak, kook, kaak, kook.*

As the steps approached, Toffy jammed his eye into the peephole and found the shadow of a huge person looming. His heart continued racing. He wasn't sure whether he was hearing footsteps anymore or just the thumping in his chest.

Boom, boom, bap, bap, boom, boom, bap, bap.

The person walked past Toffy's door. It was Clarika, his neighbor. She was covered in huge multicolored garb wrapped around her petite frame. The outfit made her seem larger than life. She walked to her apartment.

Toffy rested his back on the door and looked around.

Why aren't my screens on?

The screens had not turned back on since he was given the day off.

Something's off.

Toffy pushed his back off the door and marched straight to his room.

Maybe they found the memorabilia. That was the only thought Toffy had in his head halfway on his journey back from the coffee shop. His plan was to immediately get rid of the rumpled paper that he had placed under his pillow, or change its location.

Toffy closed his bedroom door, sat on his bed, and reached under his pillow. To his surprise, nothing was there. He snatched the pillow off the bed in wide-eyed astonishment. The paper was gone.

"Oh, lawd!" He exhaled tensely.

He jumped off the bed and placed both hands on his head.

"They are coming for me." He paced back and forth in the room. "Run, run, run," he repeated, a self-preservation chant. "The boogeys are coming." The BW emblem pulsated in his mind.

Toffy walked around in a circle and stopped when he found the rumpled paper on the floor at the top of the bed. He fell to his knees and unfolded it like a long-lost letter from a distant lover. He immediately went to his closet to shove the rumpled paper in pitch darkness.

In the corner of the closet, the numbers of rumpled papers had multiplied.

"What the? Where did—"

He pulled the first from the top of the pile: *ELEC-TION RESULTS FALSIFIED—Says President of Electoral Commission.*

Toffy threw the paper down and picked another from the pile: *POWER OUTAGE CRIPPLES ECONOMY.*

Wondering where all these papers came from, he picked another from the pile: *DETERIORATING ROADS, COLLAPSED BRIDGES, INTERNET SHUTDOWN, GREEN POLLUTION. NO ONE CARES.*

Toffy looked like he was holding evidence at a crime scene. As he remained transfixed at the sight of the papers, a voice yelled out of his mobile device on the bed.

He turned the light off and stepped out of his dark wardrobe, walking confidently to the device with a suspicious squint in his eye. He grabbed the phone off the bed, and it was Sarni, a projection of him leaving a voice note.

"Dude, where are you? I'm on my way to the office. James wants us there immediately."

There were two messages from James:

HEY, TOFFY, WHY ARE YOU NOT AT YOUR DESK TODAY? GET HERE NOW. I NEED AN UPDATE IMMEDIATELY!

"Crap, the last message came in two hours ago? And I never responded to the first one. Crap!" Toffy yelled as he called Sarni back. On his wrist, 8:10 p.m. flashed.

What kind of life is this?

***

The councilmen from High and Low Town lined up at the door, unsure whether to leave or stay in the conference room. Each member wanted to either be first or last to leave, depending on what side of James's favor they'd fall on.

"Get the media and fire department in here," James shouted.

The councilmen all scrambled to squeeze out of the door. The key team members from the two departments briskly walked into the room.

"Hey, Toffy. Nice to see you can join us," James said. The sacrum was rich in his voice.

He hadn't seen Toffy since he'd collapsed at the J Event.

As Toffy joined them at the large conference table, James asked him to get up and introduce the new product his department is working on. But Toffy blanked.

***

Although it was hard to see his friend struggle and stumble through his presentation, Sarni couldn't help but relish the moment.

Hmm. Not so invincible, I see. Sarni licked his lips and stood up to take over.

"Toffy has had a hard time," Sarni said. "I have been in liaison with the Assistant Director of Media Engineering, and I can provide a better update on the development of the product. Take a seat, Toffy. I'll take it from here."

Toffy walked back to his seat complacently. His demeanor made it obvious. He was starting to care less.

"Thanks, Sarni," James said. Sarni's fifteen-minute presentation was effortless and articulate.

"I'm glad you could fill in there and give us a good overview on how we are going to capture..."

James paused. He was lost for words. Everyone waited in anticipation. He swung his eyeballs, trying to find words for his thoughts. They moved faster than his mouth could.

"Well, great," James found his words and finished. He stood up and tapped the table with his big ring, twice. He had been doing this ring-tap for over thirty years, ever since he'd read about it as one of the "top ten power moves of 2018."

Once the meeting was done, Sarni went up to Toffy, who was still in his chair looking defeated. Everyone else had filed out of the conference room.

"Dude. Are you all right?" Sarni said and shook Toffy out of his indifferent stare. "You were so out of it. What's going on? And what is with the shabby look? Don't you want to shave or something? Look at your hair. James is not going to be happy."

"*James*? Is that what I should be concerned about now?" Toffy said.

"Shhhhhh. Keep your voice down. Have you lost it?"

Besides the screens monitoring, James's essence was still felt in the room.

"You just don't say things like that here. *Anywhere*, actually." Sarni looked around the circular room with the ring of screens around the perimeter.

"I lost consciousness on… you're here talking about James," Toffy said with rage in his eyes.

"Okay. Okay. Just calm down. I know you need to blow off some steam. I have the right spot for you," Sarni said, grabbing and shaking Toffy by his shoulders.

"Let's go."

CHAPTER 12

———

The newly opened buzz of Low Bar at the Pigeno had worn off already. The nightlife of J City had moved on to newer things. Toffy was not his usual self, and his friend could tell.

Sarni ordered two bottles of Low Bar beer. The J Enterprise logo was magnified by the beads of cold condensation on both bottles.

"Hey, what's on your mind?" Sarni asked. "Everything good with you and Deja?"

"Yeah, I am. We are good."

I think.

Toffy and Deja had not had dinner together for the past week, both consumed with work.

"Deja has been…" Toffy mumbled, "spending time in Low Town. J Social is really increasing its presence down there. You know."

Toffy's mobile device vibrated. Another message from James:

Hey. You seemed out of it today.
Meet up at my house on Wednesday?

Sarni peeped over to read the message.

"I didn't realize you and James were messaging buddies," Sarni said. His stoic gaze couldn't hide the jealousy in his tone.

"Oh, no," Toffy responded, still squinting at his mobile device. "This is the second time I'm receiving a message from him. Actually, both messages came today. Well, I'd say it's the *third* time if we include the message he sent to all of us to get to the office."

Again, there must be something working against me here. What is? Who is?

"I actually didn't even realize James knew how to send messages," Toffy said, waiting for Sarni's response. "There's a good chance his assistant sent it on his behalf."

Sarni laughed, exaggerated from the bottom of his belly. "Anyway, you are receiving personal messages from the James himself... Toffy the Golden Child! You must really be special."

***

Toffy went to James's house in the middle of the week. He couldn't get Deja to join him. She seemed to be constantly preoccupied with one project or another, and Toffy didn't know how to get across to her.

Just like he had done on Toffy's eight previous visits, James showed Toffy his car collection, the indoor sport facilities, and the indoor pool. Monitors around the house showed evidence of James's latest obsession—personal intergalactic travel. They ended up at the bar along with some other men James wanted to introduce him to.

"Oh, we have heard so much about you," one silver-haired gentleman said.

Toffy was cordial, but his lack of interest was obvious enough for James to notice.

"Toffy," James said, tapping him on the back, "you are destined to be one of the greatest employees I have ever had. You could be in *my* position, one of these days."

Toffy remained uninterested for the rest of their meeting. James pulled Toffy to the side.

"Hey, snap out of it," James said "What's going on? Your body language says it all."

He grabbed Toffy's arm and walked back toward his guests. "You better start feigning interest if you still want to have a job tomorrow." His voice was low and ugly. They got closer to the three men, all dressed in the same blue shirts and khaki pants.

"Get in there, and make it happen," James whispered, and with an inconspicuous shove propelled Toffy back in the investor den. Smiles were plastered all around.

Exhausted from the schmoozing, Toffy went home to an empty house. He thought he could get home early to watch one of the late-night shows he and Deja loved. Unfortunately, Deja wasn't home. Another night, and Toffy was once again disappointed. The time he spent alone the previous week was bearable. The rush that came with writing a story had him so inspired and motivated that he hardly noticed Deja was spending late nights at the office.

He recalled their last conversation.

"Let's spend some time together tonight," Toffy had said. "I can ramp up my work to make sure I hit my targets early. Can do a twenty-minute work-free dinner. Up for it? Have some things I want to tell you."

"Lovely. Would love to," Deja had responded. A few minutes to dinner time, she had sent another message: "Sorry, something came up, last minute. Another day?"

No suggestion given on when that other time would be. *Probably no one will be interested in this story or what I have to say. I can't even get Deja's interest.*

The excitement and inspiration of something new had waned. Toffy did not feel that same urge to sit at his desk and write anything. He walked into his room, looked at his desk, and was reminded that he had not written a single line in his notepad in two days.

He was immediately overcome by a feeling of helplessness. His story was not going to write itself.

The green notification flashed in front of him. He tapped it. His mom had left him a voice message. He brought his five fingers together, pulling his hand across his face to play the message:

"Hey, we haven't seen you in a while. Hope all is well. You should come and visit us soon."

Toffy dropped his device in defeat. He felt lost. He walked out of his room. On the kitchen counter, he noticed a note. *Meet me tonight? Address on the back.*

A message from Deja. Toffy was already out the door.

***

He stopped by his parents' house on his way to meet up with Deja in Low Town. They had been riddled with concern ever since they heard about Apo's visit to the hospital.

"You know, you need to settle down," Toffy's mom said. "When are you going to marry that Deja girl? She is so amazing. I love her. We talk, you know. Although, I haven't heard from her recently. I hope everything is all right with her. She probably just wants you to do the…" She paused, "You know. The *needful*. Are you even listening to me? Your mind seems elsewhere."

"Sorry, Mom. I'm just tired."

Toffy's mind was in another world. He wanted to meet Deja in Low Town, a place where he needed to be.

"I have to leave soon," Toffy said.

"Oh no, you just got here," she pleaded. "Is it too much to ask you to stay here with me for another thirty minutes? Oh my, this world is just going down the drain," she continued, reading everything that popped onto her screen. "Did you see this?" she said as she pushed the screen toward Toffy's face.

"No. What's that?"

"That's the question? *What's that?*" She pulled the screen back. "I hope you are happy."

Toffy's mind drifted again as his mother continued talking. *What is happiness? Why do we care so much about it? Can we in High Town truly be happy? Past, present, future?* Toffy's memory blurred as it moved through time and space. *What's real? The now? The then? The screens? The flexible poster plastered to submerge me in a waking dream. Which is life and which is a dream?*

He thought about his one rendezvous with Deja in Low Town. The small room in one of the quarters there, where they had spent the night tightly knitted together. Deja had given Toffy a code to charge his time that night in Low Town to.

A smile overcame his face as he thought about the past.

***

As Toffy took a stroll down memory lane, he remembered the coolness of that evening. Deja had been in Low Town on one of her official visits for J Social. It was a late night for Toffy, and he had been writing to the instrumentals that Musta sent. He had drunk steeped tea of the natural plant, walked out of his apartment, strolled gingerly to the train station, and made his way toward Last Stop. It was just his second time going that way.

He was more comfortable than his first visit. Light-hearted and friendly, he had greeted everyone along the way. As soon as he'd stepped out of the train station, his curiosity pulled him toward Viginniye.

He walked toward the first taxi. Before he could get in, the driver drove off.

What does a High Towner have to do to get a taxi in this side of town? He laughed at his wit.

He did not realize how he had glided across the street dodging all the holes in the road to get to her so quickly.

"Hey, pretty lady," Toffy said with a squinted and laidback gaze. "Hey, special thing. I know it sounds crazy, but you're like the sun in the rain."

"What are you doing here?" Deja said with a smile.

She grabbed Toffy's hands before he could respond, and they both dashed off. Deja took him to one of the quarters that J Social had commissioned the year before. The roads that led to the quarters were completely run down. A few of the neighborhood children stood with sunken eyes along the path to the quarters. Three identical two-story buildings were in the square compound. Deja pulled Toffy to the building in the corner. They cut across the compound to the wooden door painted black.

They both ran up to the second floor, and Deja swung the orange door open, which led to a small dimly lit studio with a bed in the corner, a small kitchen on the right, and a book shelf to the left. The tiny room was filled with a space of fresh air that Toffy needed.

"We can come here anytime," Deja said as she flung her boots off her feet. "Just me and you."

She ran to the bed and started jumping on it.

"I'm free. I'm free," Deja exclaimed with joy as she slammed the clothes on the bed. "*Freedom!*" She stretched both hands out, leaning her head back in youthful exuberance.

Toffy had not seen Deja so excited.

"So, you've been coming down here?" he asked. "How… Did… How long have you had this room?"

"It just got finished this evening," Deja responded. "It's lovely. Isn't it? It's all I want. What we need." She lay on the bed with her hand propping up her head as she smiled. "Want some tea?"

Deja jumped out of bed.

"Let me get the kettle going. Look at this. Look familiar?" She picked up a red pot by its handle. "From the archival footage. It's a kettle. So antique. Everything here reminds me of a special time. A special element we've lost." She examined the kettle further as she filled it with water.

"Yeah, things here are very interesting," Toffy said. He looked around the room and at the books and artwork on the bookshelf.

"Mrs. Aphiel will let us stay here," Deja said. "She lives downstairs. She has been so nice to me. But Toffy, no one must know we are here. No one."

That night, they slept naked with their limbs entangled and the windows open. The warm breeze swept over their bodies, with no room to flow between them; they were completely absorbed in each other; momentarily deaf to the sounds of the pot-holed Low Town streets. It had been a while since they loved one another so closely.

***

"Are you even listening to me?" Toffy's mom said and poked at his legs.

"Yes. Yes," Toffy responded, jarred out of nostalgia.

"Look at this again, another one. There's so much going on." Toffy's mom pushed her screen to his face.

"Maybe not everything you see on that screen is real," Toffy said. "Have you thought about that?"

"What do you mean? It's on the screen. It's here. For me and for you to see. How can it not—" She stopped mid-sentence, interrupted by a change in her screen. "Look at this one again."

She shook her head. "Your father never—"

Toffy's mind drifted once again to his time in Low Town with Deja. He remembered all that was on the television screen in their dainty little room.

***

The flashback captured his mind. The absurdity had become the norm and the normal had become absurd.

That black-boxed television had showed it all. Low Town was constantly under siege. By the council and lords of High Town and Low Town. Bombings, sickness, displacement camps, starvation, crippling infrastructure. All captured on the TV without any edits. The fragility of life was not separated from life itself.

"Good lord. What's all this?" Toffy exclaimed, disgust on his face.

He turned toward Deja. "How could so much stuff go wrong so fast? Everything was fine this morning. Look at this."

"Was it?" Deja responded. "That was on the news yesterday. It was on there last week. It's just not on the screens where *we* live."

"How can… how can one be happy in this type… of…" Toffy could not find the words to describe his shock. He fell silent. A rush of insights flooded him.

This place is different.

Amplified by the reality shown on the television, Toffy reconciled what he had seen on the street scene.

There was an element of the Low Town not ever experienced in High Town. It contained a very human element. Although not visible, something was tangible, and it could be held onto. It was human in all its glories and flaws.

Toffy's jaw fell open when he read the headlines of the newspaper next to his bed: *COWS HOLD PLANES HOSTAGE.*

How is that even possible?

Toffy read the story and learned a herd of cows had grazed from the higher plains of Low Town and walked across town to the airport. The herd decided to rest on the concrete path where the planes at the airport took off and landed. They chewed, chewed, and chewed for two days on this concrete path. No plane could take off. No plane could land. The entire airport was hijacked by the cows.

Toffy dropped the paper to change the channel on the television. The grainy picture was that of a group of old men sitting behind a long desk with a banner that read, "SSC Committee."

The fragile man in the middle held the microphone to his mouth and spoke: "We, the Snake Swallowing Committee, have concluded our investigation and admit that it is highly unlikely that a snake can enter a bank and just swallow an account. How is that even possible? You tell me that the millions in that account have just gone missing?"

Toffy changed the channel again. The boxed TV showed a celebration. People danced and threw money in the air.

Here in Low Town? Toffy was amazed.

A reporter in the midst of the jubilance said, "The life of the councilmen and their families in Low Town. Highly celebrated and lowly debated. Being here is a shift in reality for most. Just five minutes ago, my crew and I were outside, and it seemed like we were in a war-ridden environment. But inside here, the amenities rival the most prestigious things you'd find in High Town.

"We have a member of the sub-council here with us," the reporter continued. "Can you tell us what we are experiencing?" She placed the microphone under his mouth.

"Well," the sub-councilman spewed into the microphone, "I just want to thank the most high for all the blessings allotted to us. Only blessings can get you to this stage in life. You and I see what's going on out there. It's like living in hell, so we created our own heaven for only us to enjoy. We are all handed different lots in life. We have to play the hand we are dealt. And we are playing it very well. Thank you."

He spun around and threw another wad of cash in the air and the room erupted. The money trickled down and landed on sweaty heads and marble floors.

Toffy changed the channel again, this time moving his head closer to confirm what he was looking at. A man in a red hat was seated and tied to a chair while a big-bellied man in a blue uniform paced around him.

"Confess for all the people on the TV to see," the man in the blue uniform asserted.

"I told you already, there is nothing to confess. I'm an inno—"

The man was cut short with a slap to his face.

"So, if you claim to be innocent, please tell me why you are wearing a red hat."

"What? *This* hat? Oh, my mother gave me this hat."

"So, your mother is in on it also, eh? The Counters. Spreading rumors about our blessed councilmen and James at the top? Bring his mother in here too. The old witch is probably at the helm of this whole operation."

"No. No. Leave her out of this. I'll give you what you want, if you can kindly just tell me. What is it you want?" the man in the red hat pleaded.

"I'm just—"

Toffy changed the channel again.

"This just in." A female reporter looked straight into the camera "The school examination board bans students from using pens and any other writing materials during their final exams. The examination board is surprised not a single student has completed the yearly exams three days after the writing ban was enacted. A quote from the chairman at the examination board said, 'We are stunned at how lazy this generation of students are. We are baffled and even more disappointed in our children.'"

"Who really uses pens, anyway?" Toffy exclaimed as he switched the channel. A quiet scene. An old man was seated on a bejeweled chair. At the top right of the screen was a text, "TAC—The Aging Channel."

It was Bunajo. He sat on his chair with piles of paper on both sides. His hat sat snugly on his slender face. He took no action. The gap between his front teeth was partially visible and sandwiched between his slightly parted lips. He just sat there and got old. Above his chair was a banner that read, "Vote me in again next year. I'm old. Obey the tradition. I know what this town needs."

Toffy turned the TV off and lay down next to Deja. She had her headphones in, and she swayed her head. Dark morphing figures that constantly swayed in the wind were visible from the window. A man's sharp voice bounced with uninhibited rhythm:

Few people get fat with the big money and the rest stay hungry.

Let them carry me to any court. I'll open the books for them... Yah.

***

"Are you even listening to me?" Toffy's mom said and poked at Toffy's legs again. He came back to the present.

"There's a book I'd open for them," Toffy said and jumped out of his seat.

"Are you all right?"

"Yeah." He realized he had been lost in thought. "The era no longer exists, but it still does."

"Is everything okay?" she asked as she stood and walked toward him.

"Of course. Everything is splendid." Toffy continued. "Didn't your screen tell you that already? It's a concerted effort. You see, there was an era when people sat around, discussed, shared ideas freely. That era no longer exists. They have shattered our communities by building a case for artificial connectivity. Yet some people are not even connected. The growing digital virus developed to replicate the effect of the real virus that kept people isolated for months earlier in the century.

"Oh. I tell you, it's all a scam." Toffy paced back and forth. "Do you know there's a place of constant oppression and suppression? Did your screen tell you about that? We are in this orchestra together, and the conductor is waving. He is waving, and we keep playing our instruments. Playing *their* instruments. It's all about breaking communities, damaging civil discourse, and degrading human dignity."

Toffy slammed his palm over his mouth.

Eyes wide open, he realized he had said too much.

"I'm just tired," Toffy said, lowering his hand from his face to grab his device. "I need to get to… Oh my. What time is it? I should be meeting Deja. It's eleven twenty-three?" Toffy scrambled to get his things.

His mobile device vibrated. A message from Deja:

I'm back home. Going to bed soon.

Enraged, Toffy slammed his device on the floor.

CHAPTER 13

———

Toffy rushed back to his apartment. Sounds vibrated from a far place, booming with a heavy bass, emanating for a place beyond the limits of High Town.

Slave killer. The table has turned.

Automated filler. You gonna get burned.

He couldn't control it. He danced and pulsated to the music all the way to his apartment.

Every time I hear the sound of a ding, my blood runs cold, the voice sang.

I remember how our bank accounts went way below zero.

Today, they say we are free

Only to be chained by what we see.

Good lord, I think its mediocrity. The only machine that makes money.

Slave killer. The table has turned.

Toffy circled around and danced his way to his apartment, stopping short of his door when a thought mumbled in his mind. *They don't need us anymore. We went from exploitable resources to disposable entities. But we are the small axe to their big tree, sharpened to cut them down.*

Toffy opened the door and paused. *This is not how I left my apartment.*

He noticed a silhouette seated on the couch. The fear that ran through him made him take an involuntary step back. *Oh, it's Deja.*

A relief overcame his body. Her presence was confirmed with the spare access card he had given her a year ago, on the kitchen counter. *She hardly uses it. She must really want to see me.*

Toffy smiled as his breathing returned to normal. Deja was seated on the couch, and it reminded him of times he had only heard about in stories. When people could afford spending the entire weekend, lazing around, watching new shows, catching up on old shows, and just being totally content in each other's presence. Toffy and Deja had never done this in his sun-lit, one-bedroom apartment.

Thoughts of experiencing such a time brought Toffy delight. He stood at the door fantasizing about a more bearable time before all residents were convinced to register their social score identification number, linking it to all their devices and their physical features. He was only six years old when this change happened. His parents called it "the good ol' times."

The fantasy left Toffy standing awkwardly at the door for longer than he should have. He closed the door behind him and walked into the house.

"Hey," Deja said. She barely acknowledged Toffy.

Toffy was uncomfortable. He could feel the eggshells crushing under his feet as he hung his satchel in the closet. He walked over to Deja, leaned over the couch, and gave her a soft kiss on her cheek. Toffy was immediately filled with an overwhelming feeling of sadness. He realized his discomfort was not just from the widening distance between him and Deja, but because the two of them had begun to feel comfortable with that distance.

He sat in the shiny red bean-bag next to the couch and desperately stared at the screen to feign comfort. After a while, he gave up. Deja stared at the screen hopelessly. She had a glaze in her eyes, a point of focus beyond the screens.

Toffy gathered the courage to break the silence.

"Hey, what's up? You have been distant lately."

He surprised himself with how direct he was. Deja did not miss a beat; she immediately snapped back at Toffy.

"Things have just been busy at work. I just feel like I have been going in circles. Putting in a lot of hours but not really accomplishing much."

"Oh yeah," Toffy responded. "I've been feeling discontent with work too. The only thing that makes me happy is the story I am working on."

"Story?" Deja asked. "About what? Don't we have a department for that already?"

"Well, it's not fully clear to me yet, but I'm just writing a page at a time..." Toffy nodded unconvincingly. He couldn't even convince himself.

"That just sounds... sort of ridiculous. Don't you think? A story not fully formed? When are you going to have time for work? Your utilization? Your score? Wow, you're really here, talking about writing a story when you should be thinking about your plan, our plan!"

"Plan? What plan?" Toffy said.

"Is life not complex enough as it is already?" Deja said as she sat up on the couch trying to compose herself. "I need... *we* need a plan to navigate through this complexity. I need a plan to increase my comfort." She paused "*Our* comfort.

We can't lose what we have. We have to hold on tight. Secure it. Security is what I… what *we* need." Deja moved closer to Toffy and lowered her voice. "This story you are writing, how is it going to end? What's the hook? What's the main purpose?"

What the hook gonn' be? Hmmm, that's a good question.

"I'm still putting it together." Toffy looked down at his feet. "You see how it is. The disparity. The control. The—"

"Shhhh." Deja placed her index finger on Toffy's lips. "Rebellion. Is that what you are saying here? I hear you, but don't stick your neck out unless you are fine with your head being cut off. Don't point fingers one day unless you are fine with not having a finger to point with the next day. You say 'rebellion.' I say, know when to cheer and when to stomp. When to play all out and when to sit on the sidelines. Know when to praise and when to curse. There's a time for everything, Toffy."

Deja looked like a glowing sage, and Toffy adored the words that came out of her mouth.

"You are talking about a story," she continued. "Think about our future, babe. Focus on work. I hope you didn't lose your focus at work after your fainting episode."

"Fainting episode?" Toffy exclaimed, immediately enraged.

He had kept his cool but could not keep his frustration in any longer.

"*That's* what you're calling it?" Toffy exploded out of his seat. "I haven't seen you since last week. You couldn't even stay in the hospital with me."

The blissful night they both spent together in Low Town temporarily faded from memory as they confronted one another in High Town.

"And you call it a fainting episode… like—" Toffy stuttered as he could not find the right words to express himself, "something you see on a show and you just move on from. Forget this. That's just… bullshit."

Toffy slammed the door and walked out.

***

Apo's mind wandered, unable to handle the news his doctor had given him, and so he thought of the life of his city.

J City was a very busy place, the modern-day metropolitan, and a juxtaposition of all the great metropolitans that came before it. It had the aesthetics of Tokyo, the grittiness of New York, the undulating landscape of San Francisco, the fusion of Jakarta, the hustle of Lagos, and the ambition of Abudabi.

The disparity in the city, the line that separated the highs from the lows, the high-end, the low-beginning, the useful, the useless, all in the hodgepodge of a city colonized by the corporates. The corporates had the agenda. The corporates came with their books. The corporates brought their weapons. J City was in a state of corponialism, and J Enterprise was at the helm.

They intensified the divide. They brought the virus and sold the anti-virus, controlling the consolidated cloud. Data personified, quantifying each self. Objectifying all. Magnifying the sparkle in High Town, a stark contrast to Low Town, which was obscured by cloud of deliberate dysfunction. Confined in their position with the shadow of death constantly hovering above. The fire behind them constantly burning.

The smartest and brightest used to congregate within its limits to chase the J City dreams. It was the top city to live in for young professionals in the world. Everyone wanted to be in High Town.

The architecture reflected its variety. There were tall buildings, short buildings, thin houses, fat houses, old gothic buildings, new classic buildings, metal foam reenforced skyscrapers, carbon nanotube huts. The structural aesthetic, a recent update from the uniformity that dominated the preference of the residents a year ago. The screens were ubiquitous. In one of the thin houses, Apo found himself looking at his doctor in disbelief, pulled back into the bad news.

"What do you mean it's terminal?" Apo asked.

"I'm sorry. I wish I could tell you something more," Dr. Trone paused, knowing no words would bring comfort to Apo at that moment.

Apo sat back in his chair, looked at his doctor, and snapped. "Why the hell are you just telling me this *now*?"

"We just found out, and that's why we called you in."

"Why didn't you just tell me over the phone? I had to come all the way across town just to sit down to listen to this?"

"It's best to give this kind of message in person. With the virtual experience, we wouldn't want for—"

"This is complete and utter bullshit." Apo jumped out of his chair. He walked toward the rack, grabbed his jacket, and walked out of the doctor's office.

He walked all the way across town to his apartment and headed up to the third floor of one of J City's short buildings. If he heard his doctor right, he had just been diagnosed with a terminal case of pollutinitis. He thought about what he could have done wrong, why it was happening to him, and if there was a way to make things right.

He bargained with all the gods he had read about in his old books.

Maybe if I walked around this bus stop three times, maybe, just maybe, I can get an extra day or two.

These thoughts dominated Apo's mind as he came to terms with the fact he had been given only two more months to live.

For the first time in years, he was overcome with fear. Fear of the unknown. Fear of his own mortality. Fear of the loss of physical form.

Apo grew up with a curious mind that went unsatisfied. He always asked questions, trying to learn something new. His inquisitive nature helped him sometimes, but it mostly got him into a lot of trouble.

What people collectively knew and experienced as common knowledge were structures imposed on their understanding of the world around them, created by those in power and propagated to keep them powerful. Those in power did not like others asking questions, especially those nosing around for the truth. They wanted people ready to plug into the system, those willing to drink their drink and eat the treat.

Apo was not one of those people.

His quest for knowledge took him to study engineering, a Masters in Engineering, Masters in Philosophy and Business. He got an online accreditation in psychology and then got a PhD in history. He was a lifetime intellectual driven by one thing—the quest for true knowledge. Yet, he still felt a sense that there was more to learn. After all, he thought his education was "too washed." All attained in one institution or the other.

Apo ventured on a self-taught journey of alternative education, reading books from different people, religions and countries. Traveling and interacting with different cultures.

He studied the mystics and learned about ancient technologists, understanding how they were no different from technology of the present day. He read works of unknown poets and storytellers and realized that knowledge was infinite and the projected mainstream version was one-sided.

Another tool of oppression, depositing manufactured widget-sized nonsense in the mind of the impressionable youth. Yet they blame the youth. You can't blame the youth. These thoughts were in constant rotation in Apo's expressive mind.

It became his mission to pass on these findings to people, most especially the next generation. It was of the utmost importance for humanity to have a more balanced view of their history.

Toffy's interest in writing and telling stories had come from his uncle. Apo used to tell theatrical late-night stories every time he visited Toffy growing up. And as he grew older, Apo guided and counseled him, encouraging him to write his own story.

"Stories like this are needed for the sake of humanity," Apo would always say to his niece and nephew to end his hourly monologues of motivation.

***

Everyone at J Enterprise was gearing up for J Week, just as Toffy expected. The hallways in the white pyramid were buzzing with people zipping back and forth trying to meet the deadlines to have a great week.

Editors were editing. Publishers were publishing. Firemen were burning. Initiators were initiating. All to anchor down the story for the year. Stories about the Low Town and its deprived poverty were in the works. Stories about J Social and how they were lifting the Low Towners out of unfortunate poverty were cooked up.

The stories about the new enemy were in the pipeline. The enemy from the year before was now the poster child. The poster child from the year before had become the new enemy. The flip had flopped until the flop started flipping. Everyone in the organization was filled with stories and tripping over the strings of undivided attention.

No focus. The hocus pocus magic-filled onlooker had the compass with a circular radius and a locus in the middle filled with locusts that swarmed the field of dreamless nightmares. Toffy's mind raged.

He had a pile of work that was making him anxious. His utilization was far from its helm. The J Week for the year was turning up to the max. There was incessant stomping at the screens. The hissing contest had become more intense. Facts became mere opinions, and unwelcome opinions became facts.

His stats were blinking. His thoughts kept sinking. His fingers lingered over his screen for hours with movement. Everyone in the office was in on it. The council lords from Low Town were making their way to High Town to shout out James's praises. The singular goal to the one with several faces that they sold their soul to was to finance their personal pockets off the common purses of their bases.

Sarni rushed in through Toffy's door. "Hey! Have you seen the emails?"

"Emails?" Toffy asked. "No."

"The email from James? He was asking to send out his message for the beginning of next quarter."

"That's in…" Toffy looked at the calendar on his screen. "That's in fifty days."

"Yeah, the departments are scrambling. It has caused an exciting email thread. Maybe you should catch up."

"Yeah, I really need to catch up." Toffy rested his chin on his desk. "I'm exhausted. Had a long night last night. Got into a little argument with Deja. I told her about this book I'm writing." Toffy lowered his voice to a whisper, a suspicious eye focused on the screens, "and she just went off on this tangent about planning and strategizing."

"A book?" Sarni asked as he smiled and moved closer. "I knew you were up to something that day in the cafeteria. You and Musta. Not stomping."

"You saw that?"

"Most of us that are part of the order know exactly what is going on," Sarni responded with a wink.

"The order?" Toffy pushed himself off the chair.

"Don't worry about that for now. Let's not get into that."

Sarni pointed inconspicuously at the screens in the room.

"Tell me more about this book. What's it about? I hope it's not something we'll have to burn down." Sarni laughed with his nose. "Just kidding."

Toffy was not certain how much to reveal, but he knew in his heart he was supposed to share this story with Sarni. He knew this right from the beginning. The beginning was in the end and the end was the beginning.

Toffy looked around and whispered. "Well, I'm just starting, so it's still in its early stages. Keep it to yourself, okay?"

"Golden boy, now writing a book," Sarni teased. "Well, I have nothing to say to that, but I understand why Deja would want to kick you in the head. She doesn't want a book-writer. When will you understand the way of the world? You just like complicating things. Keep it simple, stupid. K. I. S. S." Sarni pouted his lips and blew a metaphoric kiss to the sky.

Sarni snapped out of his pose, whipped out his mobile screen from his pocket, and flashed it to Toffy. "As simple as this pretty thing in red. Check her out. Hmmmm. Hmmm. Hmmm." Sarni smacked and licked his lips. "Look at her. Yeah, I know. She's sexy huh? So this is how it works. She sends me a picture. I tap to accept the picture. We plan to meet. I buy dinner. We go back to my place. Screens already know the right mood to set based on her profile. She feels comfortable. She takes her clothes off. I take mine off. Badaboom. Badabing. You know what I mean? I head to work. I don't see her again. Now, *that's* simple. Like one plus one equals two. You are a man of science. Do the math. You should know this. If the equation doesn't add up, things cannot be balanced."

"Simplicity, huh?" Toffy responded.

I am a man of science. Maybe not anymore. Am I just a man of words now struggling to put those words to paper?

"Deja doesn't want a struggling first-time writer," Sarni said with increased animation in his tone. "She wants a well-fed C-I-C."

"C-I-C?"

"Chief in Charge, playboy. You should rethink your priorities, man. But the order appreciates you. Remember that. The order appreciates you. I have something you need. Are you in? Remember that."

Something I need? Toffy pulled his head back, looking at his friend suspiciously. *Am I in? What does he know?*

Sarni backslid his way out of Toffy's office.

Toffy's utilization and energy level waned even more.

Thirty-two percent. He let out a deep breath. *I'm going to be stuck here forever. Fixed. No way out. The order? What did Sarni mean by that?*

He did the right thing telling Sarni about the book. It had all started as a secret, an unsolicited thought, and then the writings in his little black book. From thoughts to words to action.

The beginning was the end, and the end was the beginning.

CHAPTER 14

———

J Week continued, and Toffy's utilization suffered.

He could not work. He did not write a word. He was numb and had lost any connection to his facilities. Each day during J Week, he sat frozen like a pillar of sugar at his desk.

While the buzz of J Week zigzagged across the city, Toffy managed to stay away from the madness. Sirens blaring, bells ringing, expertise amplified, J Infinity was soaring to greater heights. There was no escape to the madness. Toffy escaped into himself and stared at his desk the entire week as the email thread grew longer.

I'm just waiting for the copywriters to finish. Will revert ASAP—the editor.

Just waiting on research. Will get to you with immediate urgency—the copywriters.

Just waiting for more heads for the sample size—the researchers.

We need to move this to the top of the priority list—the publishers.

We are all working hard on this—Ditty of the High Council.

No one is working harder on this than we are—Loya of the Low Council.

What is the status on this?—Escalo, Head of Email Escalations.

Toffy's siren of a screen had him transfixed and lost for words, actions, and thoughts.

On the last day of J Week, an unusual Friday breeze that reminded Toffy of a different place blew through his office. He was convinced it was sent to him for some reason. Perhaps to unlock him from the traps of a stagnant mind.

The thoughts came gushing into his mind. *What you are seeking can only be found in the lowest of towns. The goal, to break up communities, to make the unity drown, while we empower the individualistic, 'til the separated wears the crown.*

Startled by the alarm that came hammering out of the screen, Toffy sat up.

"Low utilization. Critical condition. Low utilization. Critical condition." Fluence's voice was unusually shrill.

The lights in the office flashed amber red.

Fourteen percent... geez... But does anyone even really care?

Toffy thawed out of his frozen position. He knew what he had to do next.

***

Toffy sat in the middle of his uncle's living room.

The damage done to people is enormous. The mass separation of people—who's talking about this? The growth rate of isolation over the last decade. My isolation.

His uncle tinkered with some scraps of metal and a few wires, remembering his younger days—a time now lost—when they all sat around and discussed everything possible. The magic of discussion in itself was a lost art. That sense of community remained only in one place.

"I just can't seem to write anymore," Toffy told his uncle as he snapped out of thought. "I've lost steam and can't move forward, Uncle."

Apo twisted his neck to look under the arm of his wired sculpture. "Have you heard about the OODA loop?"

"The what?"

"Observe, orient, decide and act. During the Korean war, an Air Force fighter named JB crafted a framework for making rapid decisions that would ensure success in fast-changing environments. He called it the OODA loop. It is as important to flying jets as it is important to your writing. It can be applied to anything, to be quite honest.

"The OODA loop consists of four steps. Observe what is happening and process as much information from as many sources as possible. Orient those observations by distinguishing the relevant from the irrelevant. Decide on a line of action and select a single path to follow. Act to execute your decision—having it in mind that the action is not an end because the loop flows continuously back to observation. Use that to keep yourself in constant motion."

Toffy was intrigued.

We use that all the time to develop new products.

"A very interesting concept," Toffy said, "but how do I even get myself back in motion? I have lost all momentum and motivation."

"It means there must be something else holding you back."

"I don't want to fail, Uncle Apo." Toffy spurted the words out, knowing if he didn't get the courage to admit it at that point, he would not be able to tell anyone.

"Failure..." Apo repeated as he walked slowly toward the window. "Fear—the grip that cripples us all."

Apo looked out of the window with a noticeable hunch in his back.

"The fear of failure," Apo continued. "It has damaged generations of people. The fearful are never victorious. Why are you afraid to fail? You know you can fail with wisdom?"

"Fail with wisdom?" Toffy asked.

"Yes. Have you heard the story of the three wise men?"

"Hmmm… vaguely"

"Well, failing wisely has nothing to do with that. That was supposed to be a joke," Apo chuckled. "Humor is one of the tools that storytellers use all the time to educate their audience. If you can get them laughing, you can get them interested.

"And some of us need to laugh sometimes. Some of us are down and depressed," Apo said solemnly with reduced timbre in his voice. "Anyway, what I just did there was fail with wisdom. I would have liked for you to laugh at that joke, but you didn't. That could have been a joke that I told in a room full of people. But instead, I said it just to you, and you didn't laugh.

"Now I know I have more work to do for that joke to have the impact I want. It was wise for me to fail in front of you in a controlled environment where I can limit the overall damage. You see my point? Create an environment where you can experiment with different styles and set your factors for success and failure. Once you treat it as an experiment, it does not feel like a failure. It will just be learnings, adding to your library of wisdom. It's all about the process, Toffy, and not always the end product. Fail with wisdom."

Apo walked away from the window toward his nephew.

"I was looking out of the window and I saw when you walked into the building today. Do you ever think about walking?"

"Do I think about walking?" Toffy repeated the question to confirm he heard it right. "No."

"I remember when you were a baby," Apo said with a smile, "and you just started walking. You would stand and fall, stand again, hold on to a chair, fall down, bump your head on the couch, crawl to the next spot, stand again. This continued for months until you finally stood on your own and got the hang of it. Now you walk around without thinking about it. Right?" Without waiting for a response, Apo continued, "You see, you have been failing since you were a child, but after continued failure comes success. If you persevere, you will succeed."

Something was hidden behind his uncle's eyes, watery and distant. Did he want to get something off his chest? The words of wisdom Apo offered seemed urgent in a way. "Do whatever needs to be done to move forward," Apo said, looking keenly into Toffy's eyes. "And you know what—keep it simple. I know you can make things complex and overanalyze and finalize. The best storytellers know how to simplify."

I have to quit my job, Toffy realized. *Keep it simple. Not the first time I've heard that.*

A light-hearted ease filled his chest with his new realization.

Uncle Apo was back at his table, tinkering away with joy as he screwed more wires into his inanimate object.

The screen in the room came on, showing a man in a turtleneck who appeared to be speaking directly to Toffy.

"What you think is clear is nothing but an illusion. Give, and it will be given to you in multiple. Stop giving, and your well will surely dry up. Stick to the path that is sure. Don't venture out anymore. Make a donation today and buy your blessings in rotation again."

A number blinked at the bottom of the screen. The doubt in Toffy's mind grew with every flash of the number and every word uttered by the man on the screen with the cream-colored turtleneck.

"Life is short," the man said, flames flaring in his eyes. "Death is sure. Sin is the reason. You need deliverance. Close your eyes."

Toffy saw a glitch. His social score went off and came back on. The number remained the same. His heart pounded faster, 132 BPM flashing on his wrist band.

Toffy sweated profusely in his seat.

***

J City had everything a modern megapolis had to offer. High-status glamorous life and hidden abject poverty, all in one place. The poor were a sore sight for those in power, so when high society was tired of seeing those recently rendered useless and homeless, they called the Street Clarity Council, fondly referred to as SICK (SCC)—an arm of law enforcement that got rid of the unsightly and put them in the place they belonged, beyond the fog.

It was forbidden for those in the High Town to lay eyes on the homeless or lose sight of the perfection of the world they lived in.

Over the last decade, SICK would round up the homeless and those deemed useless by the society and drive them across the line into Low Town, where they'd be set free to begin a new life. Six years ago, Low Town had started reaching its capacity, and people spewed over the line. Immediate action was taken by the action-driven SCC team.

"If the men and women cannot fit into Low Town," the director of the SCC declared, "then Low Town would have to fit into them." He raised a huge pair of scissors, lowering it dramatically to cut a red ribbon.

The crowd applauded at the private line-update event. Only a select few were invited. The fog in a close distance, the residents watched from their buildings.

"I hereby commission Operation Shift the Line, or STL," the SCC Director exclaimed as a row of Baron Wards hurriedly hovered over and erased the line that separated High Town from Low Town. "We will move the line so more people can be accommodated in Low Town. With Operation *Steal*, the line that was once here is now gone," he said, pointing to the recently erased area on the ground. "Now, look to your right. The new line is being drawn as we speak."

The row of Baron Wards looped around and drew a new line in the distance, vibrating and indenting a straight five-feet-wide line in the ground on a street, two blocks away.

"If you find yourself on this side of town now," he raised his voice, "you were in High Town this morning. Now, you are in Low Town this evening."

The director ran toward his vehicle and jumped in through the car window as the car sped off. He had learned to move quickly from experience. The private guests entered their cars and drove off. The onlookers at the edge of High Town watched the fog shift. Its dense center settled above the new line.

Operation *Steal* had been in full effect since 2043. Every day, the line shifted gradually, consuming.

One of the first neighborhoods that went through the High-to-Low conversion was where Sarni visited his family. They weren't happy to see him since he had been absent for so long. Sitting alone in the kitchen of his mother's house, Sarni stared into blank space as his mom made him a pot of her favorite tea.

"It's been a while since we have seen you," Sarni's mom said. "Things are going as usual. Your brother wrote me from the university. He is doing very well and is getting good grades. My baby, on the other hand, just wants to be like you. He said he is not going to the university, that he is going to get a job at J Enterprise and be just like you."

"Mom, he has to go to the university." Sarni took his first sip of tea. "He does not want to be like me. This life was put on me; I didn't choose it. I would have loved to go to the university, but I had to do what was necessary for us to survive."

"So why don't we see you anymore?" his mom interjected, as if they had been trying to avoid the topic and the only suitable way to bring it up was abruptly.

Sarni took his time to respond, and she didn't break eye contact as she waited patiently. The spikes of hair on his chin shadowed his clean shave from the morning. These types of conversations never ended well.

If only you knew what I have to do, Sarni thought as he stared down his mother's deep brown eyes and into his own reflections. *Isn't the financial security I provide enough for you?*

Sarni and his mom sat in silence as they finished their tea.

"I have to head out," Sarni said as he stood up from the table.

"Where are you going?"

"I have some work to do."

"Work? At this time?"

"You know, the work never stops."

"It's almost midnight. Any work that is done at such a time cannot be good work."

Sarni ignored her statement and continued packing up his coat.

"We all know what you do," she continued. "What you do for James. You don't have to continue down this path. You have done enough. Don't you think? There's no need to keep—"

"Keep what?" Sarni snapped back. "Huh? Keep making money to send Davi to university? Keep making money to buy some new appliance or another to make life better for you? I can't help but notice that the monthly allowance I send is what keeps everything here running. So how can you tell me to stop what I'm doing? If I don't do it, who else will? Do you tell your husband to…" Sarni took a deep sigh. "If he were there for us," Sarni said with a lowered trembling voice, "we would have lived a completely different life."

His mom sat there, as though ashamed of her decision to marry and stay with an alcoholic who threw abuses on her and her three boys.

"I'm going to be late." Sarni wore his jacket and gave his mom a kiss on her cheek.

"Bye," she barely responded.

Sarni knew exactly what his mom meant, but he always found ways to justify his actions. He just needed to do some work on the side for James, and he would keep rising at J Enterprise. Besides seeing his family occasionally, he only came to this part of town when he had to run an errand.

This time, he was off to Planet Rack to facilitate a shipment. The team needed more heads for their research, and Sarni was in charge of providing the people who would give the free insights at little to no cost to J Enterprise. Forced insights. The people were packed into self-navigating boats and shipped off to the research fields through the ports of High Town.

Sarni consoled himself with the mantra: *One day, it will all make sense.*

He never fully believed it. He'd ease his guilt by staying close to people he thought would give him some form of redemption.

***

Toffy walked discreetly toward the inner quarters of High Town. Only highly ranked officials at J Enterprise could live in the inner quarters. He and Deja were yet to accept their invitation to live there. Toffy decided against his gut feeling of taking his vehicle all the way to the inner quarters.

Sitting across the table, filled with suspicion, Toffy was eager to hear what his friend had to tell him.

"Only a few people know this," Sarni said in his neatly arranged apartment. "There's an order."

"An order?" Toffy leaned in and whispered.

Sarni stood up and walked toward the screens in his apartment and turned them all off.

"Woah. How did you…" Toffy said, confused and delighted at the same time. "I didn't know you could… Is that even a… Wait, so you can turn the screens off?"

"We can speak freely now," Sarni said as he sat back down.

"They are really off," Toffy said.

"It's the privileges of a select few," Sarni said and smiled. "The choice is yours, really. You can choose how transparent you want to be. High transparency, high personalization. No transparency, you get generic. But also, only a few have this knowledge."

"I *knew* there was something going on. I could feel it. I can hear it. I see and write about it. Everything is not what it seems. Right? I want to be part of it. I'm already taking action. In fact, I'm writing. Every day."

"Relax, Toffy. I know you are onto something. So let me tell you about what you *don't* know."

Sarni grabbed his seat between his legs and pulled himself closer to Toffy, the first guest to ever visit him.

"It's a system. A community. A religion. Even a tribe. No one can define what it is, but it is. You see, the order has a lot of members and no members at the same time. Some members of the order don't even know they are in the order at all."

Toffy's squint intensified.

"The goal of the order is to keep the order in place and in common rotation. Keep it in the right angles, depending on what sort of geometry you are into."

"So, who started the order? Where did it all begin?"

Sarni leaned back into his chair. "Where will it *end*? That should be the question. Because it *began* at the end. Like the big bang. *Boom*. Like a poof of smoke, it ignited and dissipated at the same time."

He jingled his metaphoric combusted fingers in the air. "The order is just an idea that acts as a binding agent of loose tentacles. It didn't come from the government, the councilmen, the enterprise. There was no declaration, no particular or targeted censorship to start with. No dictum nor mandate.

"Mass media exploitation, technology, revisionist history, growing inequality, and lack of self-awareness... that's all it took to carry the trick. To take the trip. To secure the trap. People wanted to feel good. They wanted to control their environment.

"As entropy increased, people grasped for more information. They wanted more order. Information delivered seamlessly in quick, condensed, and mindless snippets. For what? All to stay happy and forget about their immediate environment as the world became more disordered around them.

"The education system turned inward, imploded on its initial tenets, and started churning out lemmings, reciting the same stale facts. Embracing the banking system that saw students as dormant accounts that teachers were supposed to deposit knowledge into. The reward systems favored those who could regurgitate deposited recitals with the most flamboyance. The students' reward for deposited knowledge came in the form of crippling debt. They worked their way back to illusive dignity every day, plugged into the system.

"There was no room for the curious mind and intellectual talent to flourish. The last thing anyone wanted was an intellectual to make them feel inferior. The book in your neighbor's house—with all its theories—was a loaded AK47 rattling at unsuspecting victims. The new idea popping up in the mind of the youth was a nuclear bomb waiting to go off.

"So why let it breathe?" Sarni continued. "Eliminate it before it makes its way to another person's mind. Burn that book. Kill that idea. Destroy that hard drive. Damage uncontrolled screens. Don't let the information carry over, because you never know the effect it could have. If new information is not transferred, we all remain happy. I mean, who knows who the target of the well-read curious person? Definitely not me. Not in this system. A system of perpetual monitoring."

Sarni paused and looked toward the screen he had turned off.

"Tracking," Sarni continued. "It couldn't be avoided, but did it have to be so one-sided? Again, it's back to the people. They reinforced the system. There could have been more equity with the watched being watchers too. The surveillance could have been designed to go both ways. But the people didn't want that responsibility. They all put their hands up. The more tracking, the more transparency, the more personalization. Let the screens figure out who we are. That's enough to not be generic.

"They don't want to follow the curious path, but they also don't want to be generic. My friend, that's the arbitrage right there. The people get what they deserve."

CHAPTER 15

"So where does that leave us?" Sarni asked Toffy and continued without waiting for a response. "Well, it gets us *here*. Flood the common person's mind with senseless data, let them be proud of themselves for being able to regurgitate useless information. Let them pat themselves on the back in certainty that they have some type of expertise about everything and nothing at the same time. Not generic but not curious enough to be different. The perfect balance. Give them the space to mirror their stupidity if it brings them a false sense of communal validation.

"Why give a person two ways to look at a problem, huh? Give them one. Even better, give them nothing at all until they forget the problem ever existed. Just entertain them with fun facts, tips, and happy testimonies, so they remain happy. This architecture was built on the backs of the people who collectively didn't want to think about how it was getting built. They just wanted to be served. The need to be masters of all only amplified their entitlement until they became the masters of none. At the end of the day, they all just want to avoid judgment and forget about their loneliness. They all just want attention. *That's* the order."

Sarni leaned into the table between them.

"It works, and that's what the people want. And you are a very important piece of the order, Toffy. Or the disorder, depending on how you look at it, ha-ha! You and I," he said as he tapped Toffy's shoulder and brought his hand back to touch his own chest, "*we* are protectors of the world's joy. We fight against the small but deadly tide of those who want to make everyone unhappy with conflicting theory and non-linear thought.

"I'm going to send you a book. Tell no one. Show no one. You'll understand when you receive it. It's going to help with the direction you need. Before you head out..." Sarni stood up from his chair and winked. "Free will. Mine and yours. Free will is nothing but an illusion. Human rights—that's just a story we tell ourselves."

Sarni walked toward his screen.

"Statements like 'the customer is always right,' 'follow your heart,' 'chase your dreams...' it means nothing in this age. Which customer is right? How do they know they are right if they are just agents of a hacked system? Whose hearts are they following? Theirs, or the hearts of the fictitious characters cooked up on the screens?

"Dreams. *Whose* dreams? Theirs or that of the enterprise or council? In this age, where hearts and minds are being manipulated at scale, who knows the *who*, *what*, or *why* anymore. Go in peace," Sarni said as he flipped a switch behind the screen, "and leave with hope too, my friend. You will receive a piece of the code soon."

***

Toffy left the inner quarters and headed back home. To his surprise, Deja was in the apartment again. It had been a long time since she had cooked anything, but the warmth and aroma of her signature dishes engulfed their one-bedroom apartment.

"I thought I'd cook something for you," Deja said, smiling as Toffy walked toward the dining table. "It's been a while since we ate together. It's a Saturday, and I thought you'd like it. I put in some extra time at work yesterday to make up for some time this morning. So we could catch up, maybe? I know J Week was tough on you, but…"

Toffy was happy to see the weekend feast on the table. It spurred forgotten memories of a not-so-distant past with Deja in Low Town. A time they hardly talked about. Toffy remained vigilant. He had something to tell Deja.

"So, I'm going to quit on Monday," Toffy said hurriedly.

Deja stood across the kitchen table silently.

"Why?"

"Well, it's important," Toffy said as he sat. "There's a story that I have to tell, and the main thing that's stopping me from writing is my job. I mean, it completely *consumes* me."

"Aren't you concerned about being rendered useless?"

"I think I'm just going to take it one day at a time."

"Well, it seems like you've made your decision, babe. I'm here to offer you all the support you need." Deja bit her lip and walked toward the kitchen sink.

Did I really make that decision myself? Am I really free? Am I hacked? Carrying out someone else's mission?

Toffy watched the back of Deja's hair as she rinsed a glass.

Strange. Why doesn't she just run the dish cleaner?

"Maybe I should quit also. The job is not what I hoped it would be. But I don't want to be rendered useless. What else can I really do?"

Deja filled two glasses with water, smiled at a pensive Toffy, and sat down.

They both ate.

***

Just two years out of the Enterprise institute, and Deja was already the assistant director of J Social, the social impact arm of J Enterprises. She was ambitious, always wanting to make an impact. Most importantly, she was looking for genuine human connection.

Deja grew up an adopted child in High Town. She was the eldest of three siblings. Her immediate younger sister, Ketro, was born four years after she had been adopted. Two years after Ketro, the last child—the last boy—Yini, was born. Deja loved her family, but she always felt it wasn't truly hers. She could never really shake off the thought of being abandoned.

Right from a young age, she always had an inconsolable drive for deep connections that made her very empathetic. She was always the first to get involved in community-building activities at school or even her neighborhood—starting a chapter of the Youth Happiness Club, leading wellness group events, or volunteering to keep middle-aged people company.

She went to university and double majored in human psychology and philosophy with a minor in economics.

After University, she surprisingly took a position as an entry level do-er for two years. Although the do-er role was a highly coveted rotational role to all the top departments at J Enterprise, Deja wasn't satisfied. She felt so detached from what she really wanted to do. She wasn't making any tangible impact and couldn't tell how her daily tasks contributed to the community.

After three years, she quit to get into a top enterprise administration program at the Enterprise institute, where her dreams of changing the world flourished, and she focused on social innovation. At an Enterprise and Engineering mixer-career-fair-party-networking event she met Toffy for the first time. Toffy was already a rising star at J Enterprise, and J Social was her top target.

She never hesitated to shoot for what she wanted.

"Hey, there. Toffy? Did I pronounce that right?" Deja had looked at Toffy's holographic name tag for a few seconds before looking him in the eyes.

They immediately felt comfortable around one another, watching everyone else go through the awkward dance called professional networking. They laughed at spilled drinks from overzealous communicators, giggling at botched introductions. They referenced an awkward flirtation across the room that reminded them of theirs only a few hours before. They drank together and tasted a glamourous array of finger foods ushered around the room on circular glass trays attached to robots that moved in predictable patterns.

Something was different about Toffy—a special connection she initially wanted to dismiss. Her mind kept telling her, *You don't have time for any feelings. You have to rise to the top in the "social space."* That was the only way she could make the impact she wanted.

Deja couldn't, however, ignore the connection she had with Toffy and undoubtedly wanted more of his attention. From the moment they met, Toffy was always restricted by his limited time.

She admired how he immersed himself deeply into whatever he did. She hoped he would take that same attention and direct it toward her, but Toffy was always deeply involved in some J Enterprise task or another.

With their fast-paced lifestyle, they could never really be together even when they were together. It got worse with the instituted social score order.

Deja initially enjoyed her time at J Social, making an impact on Low Town, or writing and driving policies that would enable usefulness among the residents in J City. Besides the constant travel and busy schedule, she started to realize the unseen ins and outs of the social impact arm of J Enterprise. It took some time to get to this realization, but it eventually dawned on her that she could actually be making the problems worse.

No way. We can't be part of the problem

Her missions to Low Town had not been as happy-go-lucky as they were in the first two years. The time of swooping in to take pictures telling a way more glamorous story of what they were doing in Low Town was coming to an end. She could not ignore the green stuff in the river, or the resources taken in the middle of the night replaced with pictures of smiley-faced handouts in broad daylight. She could not ignore the storytelling that escalated the greed and the biased reports that kept the Low Town councilman indebted to the High Towners. She could not ignore the narrative of falsified help that they were providing. The blatant madness, conveniently ignored.

We must be providing some type of value. I'm doing something of value.

This was the precipice of a one-third life crisis. It became a closer reality that she might never get that connection in life she always longed for. She wouldn't get it at J Social. She wouldn't get it in this town or even in the entire city.

Madness, as she thought about it that Saturday evening in the apartment with Toffy. The dining table still had leftovers from the meal they'd had earlier. Toffy sat in the corner with a concealed smile of contentment plastered conspicuously on his face as he scribbled in his notepad. She admired the fact that he did not care about the screens anymore. It's like the screen had stopped existing for him. Not for her; she wasn't ready to be that transparent.

He seemed sane in all the insanity.

Deja looked out of the window and observed the not-so-obvious madness in High Town up for display. *Madness. It's all madness. Where's the love?* Deja sighed. She needed another escape, and this time maybe an escape to Low Town would not be enough.

She placed both her hands below her chin and gazed out of the window until she fell asleep.

***

Monday morning cycled around. Toffy had been awake since five thirty in the morning. He had twisted and turned in bed concocting a soupy mixture of excitement and anxiety slushing in his belly about the day that lay ahead of him. He planned to hand in his resignation and could not wait to be free from the constraints and drudgery of daily routine.

For the last nine years, he woke up every day to the sound of his alarm and rushed out to make it to work at a decent time. On this fateful day, he woke up early in no rush to oil the gears that churned out his tasks. He was ready to throw a wrench in the well-oiled engine of J Enterprise he had been responsible for tuning finely for years. The ever-evolving engine that combusted and released pollutants into his entire being was about to be wrecked.

While he lay in bed, the morning took the shift over from night, and the sun broke through a crack in the window blinds.

What is today going to be like? Is this the right path? Or the beginning of my decline into low social score obscurity? Locked into the blacklist for five years? Most never come back from that.

Toffy thought about all the people he would have to tell about his resignation.

James was not the type to say things like, "Sure, you have to follow your own path." He hoped James would wish him well and support his newly found road ahead; his other side wasn't as hopeful.

As the room got brighter and the birds started chirping, he thought about how free and open his schedule would be; all the time he would have to write his story. He could barely wait for his alarm, but the orange-tainted circular clock on his wooden bedstand still had some ways to go before six o'clock.

Eager to get his day started but giving his body an opportunity for full rest, Toffy's mind took the task of starting his day for him, already up and about, roaming the streets of J City.

Sleek-paved roads with robots delivering early-morning packages. Automated construction evolving the skyline. Double-wheeled vacuums roaming the streets in search of loose garbage. The pulsating screens of residents and their social scores beneath their faces flashed over the street.

If he decided to wait for his alarm any longer, his mind would be too far gone for his body to catch up.

As he rose from bed and cleared his alarm, the brown leather briefcase in the corner of the room was the first thing to catch his attention. He had placed it there immediately after he signed for it the night before. The briefcase from Sarni contained a loosely bound brown book titled:

The Disorder in the Order: Binding the Order with Disorder

He slammed the case shut, shoving it next to the closet, and then started questioning his reasoning. He was tempted to pull out the book and begin reading.

Should I have signed for this package? It gives me a funny feeling. A grainy book with no hyperlinks, just text.

The briefcase stared Toffy down and did not break gaze. It watched as Toffy slammed his left leg into the base of his desk and hopped off in pain all the way into the bathroom.

Half an hour later, Toffy was out the door. He had breezed through his usual morning routine without any hiccups except for two throbbing toes. He felt light and ready to start a life without J Enterprise. The air in the city felt similar but not quite familiar, a chilly day sprinkled with the warmth of the sun rays that occasionally pierced the scattered clouds.

It was still so early that the light buzz of the city was that of a new day ramping up or the previous night winding down. A fog flowed like a fume, cutting the high buildings of the city in half. The screens on the high buildings were in the clouds as the clouds were on the screens.

What a day.

Toffy walked all the way to the office. Onyx couldn't give him the joy he experienced on his own feet.

A thought glided through his mind. *Maybe I can sell my access to Onyx to generate a few coins for my bills as I write.* The life and vibration of the city was palatable. Young girls with sweat-smeared make-up stumbled home from a long night of partying. One looked concerned as she scrolled on her device. A large number pulsed "sixty-two" with a sinking arrow next to it, Toffy observed. He could see it in her eyes, a glimmer of hope—the comfort that her new social score didn't dip too low for her to get shamed on the city screens. She put her device aside and caught up with her friends.

The deli on the corner that served the best morning bread was just switching its lighting to start serving its early morning risers. Construction workers sat in the corner drinking their coffee. Most had been working all night, mainly tending to the robots that had taken their colleagues' jobs.

Toffy took it all in as he walked to the white pyramid. The more he walked, the farther away the pyramid seemed. At six o'clock, the alarm on his watch went off buzzing, vibrating his wrist uncontrollably—*buzzzz, buuuzzzzz.*

Oh, my alarm's still on.

Toffy grabbed his wrist and stopped the alarm as he was about to turn the corner onto J. E. Street, where his office was located. The image of the structure under construction forced him to pause, already higher than the tallest building in the city. A huge screen attached to the scaffold read:

J Infinity: To Infinity and Onward

The screen changed to a picture of James with his arms spread out at the top of the completed version of the building, floating in the skies.

"It's just beautiful. Isn't it?" a man said. He was in his fifties, wearing a gray shirt and a gray hat that covered his eyes. "Ain't that right?" he said and took a puff of vapor out of an electric woodstick. "We always look for something or someone to worship. To believe in. To create order in our lives. Reaching for that in the skies. Something, anything we can grasp. If you asked me, the building looks like an erect penis." The man laughed and disappeared.

Toffy continued to the auto-path to the white pyramid. The screens of all the buildings were on, showing an array of delightful content in full synchrony.

His city was a conical-sphere of shared realities. He pulled out his mobile device, which had just dinged in his pocket. An email from publishing:

Just circling back on this. Any updates from editing?

A few seconds later, research responded:

We have a windmill situation on our hands, and we are working around the clock to meet the deadlines as long as we have the sample size we asked for from procurement.

Rapid communication between groups continued.
Bunajo:

You should have all the heads you need for your sample. @ Sarni, don't you have it all lined up? Please close the loop on this.

Bejaai:

Why is there only a loop on this? We should actually spiral this into a growing thread of concentric circles if we want boss to put his best foot forward. I'd open the loop and keep spinning it all the way to the top.

Ditty added:

Just to add to the spiral from Bejaai, let's include the right sequence for the appropriate propagation of events that will eventually follow.

Loya:

Well, the ball is in your court.

Obechat:

Basketball, football, tennis? High, low, or supreme? What type of court are we talking about? That will drive the initiation of appropriate spiral.

Chez:

Since we are on the matter of initiatives, please, any initiatives have to be run through the appropriate channels. Talk to me first. Starting a new thread on initiatives.

Toffy put his mobile device back in his pocket. He continued gliding toward the white pyramid and smiled.

I don't have to deal with endless, senseless threads anymore.

He hit the button for the elevator as soon as he entered the building. Sarni exited the elevator before Toffy got in, so consistent in his stride that it looked like he was making a conscious effort not to make eye contact.

Does he know I'm about to quit?

CHAPTER 16

———

Toffy walked to his office once the elevator opened up on the thirty-eighth floor. From the glass door, it looked deserted, and the screen on his desk was no longer there. The mixture of fear and excitement that he felt the entire morning was now replaced with pure anxiety.

What... Where's... Where's my station? My pen? My books?

The corner where his bookshelf resided was now empty. Everything was gone except for the screens around the room. Someone knew he was about to quit, and they decided to fire him before he got a chance.

Toffy placed both hands on his head and paced back and forth.

"Oh no. Oh no. This was not the plan," he mumbled.

He had seen the same thing happen to Agno in the subscription department; he got fired the day after he told Dafonzo he was thinking about quitting. Toffy's mind raced, thinking about the people who could possibly know his intention to resign.

His recently downloaded yellow shirt with black and white dots turned wet with sweat. He perspired with lack of inspiration to fight what was conspiring against him.

He had only told Deja. *Did she tell someone else?* He shivered at the thought of James getting wind of his plans.

Sarni?

He was acting strange this morning. I never told him, but maybe he knew. He must have known. I should have never gone to the inner quarters. I should have stayed away from that wild story Sarni was telling me about agents and free will.

Toffy stopped, eyes wide open as he remembered his friend's words: "Free will is nothing but an illusion. We have all become agents."

He squeezed his puffed-up curly hair more intensely. *They know me better than I know myself. They knew I was going to quit.*

He walked behind his desk and sat down, leaning forward and placing both hands on his desk.

"Or maybe they want me to quit? But who is *they?*" he mumbled. *Those who don't want you to win.*

As he looked around his empty office, he lost the joy of telling James that he would be walking away from J Enterprise on his own accord. He now needed to fight for the job. If he was being controlled to quit, the only logical thing to do would be to gain control back of keeping his job.

That reasoning germinated in the compost of his fertile brain.

While stunned by his empty office, his assistant Aoti slid in.

She hardly ever comes in, never says anything. Why today?

"We are on the thirty-ninth floor now," Aoti said with a smile. "Congratulations, you have been promoted."

"*What?*" Toffy responded with a combination of disbelief and relief. "What do you mean?"

"Yeah, you have been promoted to be the new HOAM: Head of Assisted Media. I was just informed this morning, but Corporate might have been working on this for a while. I was stunned to see your office empty too. I thought we had been robbed. So, I called the front desk, and they said the robo-movers were in yesterday evening to move your office to the thirty-ninth floor."

The confused look on Toffy's face was the cue she needed to continue.

"Then I called Theresa in HR, and she informed me that you had been promoted... So yeah, congrats."

Toffy tried to comprehend all the details. He looked deeply into her screened face to read any emotions.

"Are you all right?" Aoti asked.

"Huh? Yeah, I am," he said, realizing he had been staring aimlessly at her.

"This is great news. I know you have been working hard for this, and no one else deserves this more than you do. I can confirm that all your stuff is in the office upstairs. I checked."

"What about you?"

"I'm coming with you," she said with a glitch of excitement amidst her bland tone. "I'm glad I get to continue working with you. Do you want to go to the new office?"

***

Aoti was right, with her usual precision—everything was in his new office. Toffy checked the desk drawer to make sure nothing was removed from his desk. All digital J Enterprise guides, manuals, and repositories were on the shelf, and his new station now had an extra layer of screens.

His new office had the exact layout as his old office, but with wider floor space, a bigger desk station, more screens, and a larger book shelf.

He tapped the new email notification on the double screen on his desk. The email thread, James's Vision Speech 2049, was still going.

Just applied the golden ratio to the spiral from the previous loop,

head of the design team wrote.

Since we are talking about gold, any update on the resources from Low Town?

the data and resource mining head manager replied.

Who's taking the lead on the updates?

Tefa+ asked.

I don't want this to spiral out of control.
Don't worry, Tefa+. If you look at the emails above, there is a golden ratio applied to the spiral loop that would keep things in a naturally occurring state,

Ditty responded.

To add to my last email, and since we are on the topic of states, are we talking state-wide sponsorship on this initiative? Where are we at? Current or future state? @Chez, what's your take?

Toffy peeled away from his screen and turned his chair around to look out of his window.

The river was very clear from this view. On the thirty-ninth floor, he could finally see the J River as it flowed and glowed with the reflection of the sun.

This is a different view. The river loops in and out below the fog. It must go into Low Town then. Interesting.

"I see you like the view," James said, walking in. "Yeah, it takes my breath every day. Don't get too used to it. The view has a magnetic effect that could keep you away from your actual work. And in this position, we need you to perform at your best. Congratulations, Toffy. I'm officially letting you know that you have been promoted to the Chief HOAM." James threw a white envelope on his desk and said, "Take a look and meet me in my office in thirty minutes to discuss." Then he glided out.

As Toffy looked through the envelope, he came to terms with the fact that the promotion was real. The letter stated he had received more stock options with the company and a 25 percent pay increase.

Twenty-five percent. That's something. More ownership too. The irony of it all.

I came here excited to quit, and I'm being promoted?

He wavered with his decision and wondered if he would come across as ungrateful if he walked away from the promotion. He started the justification process.

I could just work in this new position and quit after a year or two. I've worked hard to get here. I do deserve the promotion. I need the job. It would be irrational to get up, quit, and switch to something new. Starting from scratch.

He did not waver in his steady and deliberate pace into James's office.

"I came in here to quit today," James said, turning around to face Toffy as he walked in. "That's what you stormed in to say, right?"

Toffy froze halfway between the door and James's desk. "Yes." Toffy hesitated. "I came here to quit today. Yet here I am, being promoted. It's a little—"

"Quit?" James said, laughing out. "Why... Why would you want to do that? *Really?*"

"Because I have something very important to do," Toffy answered as he sat down across the table from James.

"Something more important than being the Chief HOAM of one of the largest corporations in the world?"

Hmmm. Yeah. Should I tell him about the book? Should I just quit. No explanation. Come out with it. What do you have to lose? Everything! Okay. Keep it obscure. Toffy remained indecisive and quiet.

"Well, come out with it!" James yelled. His patience running thin.

"I have a book to write," Toffy blurted out.

"A book? A book about what?" James quipped and slammed both his hands on the desk. All the things on the desk bounced off and landed back in the same position. He stared intensely into Toffy's eyes. "Why don't you just come out and say what is really bothering you? I never saw you as someone who minced words. Now you are here, talking about some vague, abstract nonsense... A goddamn book."

James turned to his biographer.

"Are you getting this? He's writing a book." He laughed. "Everyone has something special to say these days. What has he done or achieved that is worth hearing about? Perhaps you should stop documenting a professional like me and start following Toffy around. Right?"

James had bullets at the back of the revolver in his eyes. The look on his face changed as he focused on Toffy.

"No response. So, what is it then? What is really the problem here?" Condescension filled his voice.

"There isn't a problem. I just came here to let you know that I quit," Toffy said coldly. "I can't take this promotion. I walked in here today to end this chapter in my life and to start a new one—"

"Maybe a new position is your new chapter," James interjected. "*A new chapter?* You even sound like your life has become a story. A new chapter. What— Very soon, you'll be walking around with a checkered beret and a smoke pipe, hanging your nose in the sky, chatting endlessly about rainbows and nonsense, pretending to contemplate the true nature and beauty of life. You are about to become one of those useless preoccupied fakers with no occupation, occupied with nothing but what occupies the minds of those who have no useful occupation."

James looked at Toffy. Disdain dripped down his face.

"So let me ask. What is this book about?"

No clear answer came to mind. It was an unfair question because he really did not know what he was writing about. There was no real end.

"I'm still trying to discover..." Toffy stumbled over his words with humility, "what the story is about, but I need time to do that, and working here is the most time—"

"But wait. Are you seriously writing a book?" James interjected, realizing Toffy was serious. "This book must be important." James sat down across the table in an effort to hear more, his face more intrigued and concerned.

Toffy looked down as he gathered his thoughts.

James seemed to remember something more pressing. His face turned sour again as he grabbed his device from the desk. He typed aggressively on his mobile device, and upside down Toffy read, *I NEED AN UPDATE. WHERE ARE WE WITH THE SPEECH?*

"I think—" Toffy broke the silence but immediately stopped at the sound of a new email on his screen. "The book is about—"

HR:

Maintaining optimal utilization, sir.

Obechat:

Building roads that lead nowhere and not maintaining the ones that already exist. Let them drown in the flood, with plastics that clog up the drains. The maximum pain leveraged on each rainfall, my main call is to provide everything at the maximum that is needed

The Fire Department:

Burning at full capacity. Everything that does not need to be seen is being erased.

Press release from J Media:

History is being replaced at full speed. Ambition is to increase the speed of revising history to the speed of light. What you thought—snap—lost in a blink of any eye.

Obechat:

Sorry, my last update was not meant for this thread.

Obechat:

I meant to say we are winning the hearts of the people and leaving them at the fine line of scarcity and need. Keep them coming back. Give them what they need.

Sarni:

More willing minds fed to the research fields.

The Automated Union Recoded:

Automate. Separate. Disintegrate. Legislate. Generate.

Loya:

JAMES. JAMES. I hail you!!! Just greeting you from a distance. I remain loyal. We are sitting on the shoulder of a giant. If you dare shake, we all fall.

Ditty:

The Giant of all Giants.

Bejaai:

The Giant of Life.

Head of Operations:

Give the giant something to feed on.

The Cafeteria:

Giant food on its way.

The dark-glassed agent:

War, blood, skin-roasted air, in a palatable serving of loans and indebtedness.

James:

TEAM WORK MAKES THE DREAM WORK. NO FUSS. I'M HAPPY EVERYTHING IS GOING ACCORDING TO PLAN.

James brought his attention back to Toffy. "So, what were you saying?"

Toffy struggled to explain why he had to reject a promotion, which would bring him prestige, status, influence, and a substantial pay increase. His social score would get a major boost. "It's about... It's not really about... It's... You see, it's complicated. I'm looking to branch out. Do something that's... Well... So, it's strange that... If you think about the trajectory of... Well, I'm thinking.... Let me say that I have been thinking. Okay? I thought of..."

James had a consistent squint on his face, as though Toffy was the subject of some type of failed experiment and did not understand where his experiment had gone wrong. He examined Toffy like an exotic bird in the zoo.

His biographer had a slanted squint on his face too, his pencil out and drawing furiously. He continued his on-and-off process of observing and drawing and then leaned back in his seat and turned the page to show James. Toffy caught a glimpse. It was a half drawn, half coloring of a stick figure with multicolored hair and patterned clothes. James gave the biographer a thumbs up.

Toffy continued, "I was thinking about stopping work to—"

"I just don't really understand your generation," James blurted out. "You keep talking about this passion thing, but I see a general lack of passion in your actions. Not you, in particular, but all of you in your generation. I'm not that much older than you, but there must be a huge generational divide. You crave attention to go against the grain but want the same attention as the grain itself."

James's air of superiority filled the room as his face changed. "You want to spend your time writing a story while the world around you needs to be built."

He stood up slowly from his chair, walked toward his window and looked out of the window onto the skyline of J City. He and his family had everything to do with the development of the city. He owned 93 percent of the real estate.

"Come here, Toffy," James said as he signaled Toffy to join him at the window. "Look out of this window and tell me what you see."

"Buildings...." Toffy responded. "A river. The streets."

"You see some *things*. I see something completely different. I see *influence*.

"Yes. Influence is what I see as I look out of that window. The influence that we can have on the world. You see, everything here was built by men like me and those before me. So, while you see buildings, I see the people who influenced that building being built. While you see streets, I see the capital that allowed that street to be built. While you see a river, I see connected and efficient algorithms that predicted the best pathway for such a river to come into existence."

"I'm pretty sure that river was not manmade," Toffy said.

"Are you sure about that?"

There's no way... but could it? Could it have been man-made? Toffy tightened his lips to make sure his thoughts didn't escape.

"What influence is your story really going to have on this world? Are you going to be more influential writing your little story than building a new world that great men will talk about for ages?"

James's face changed to a black and white spiral spinning toward the center.

Toffy was transfixed. He forcefully pulled his gaze away and focused once more on the river. The gray reflection of its persistent ripples pointed toward the river's source at the foothill in the distance.

What's real? What's imposed? What's me? What's you? What's free?

"I have three options for you," James said abruptly. "Option one," James stretched out his thumb to Toffy's face, "I increase your pay by another fifteen percent. With that, you can purchase anything you want anywhere you please.

"Option two," James's index finger joined his thumb, "unlimited access to the exclusive inner-inner network. The most prestigious club and membership in the city. You know what that comes with: access to the best and brightest, access to the inner-inner quarter, access to anyone who can facilitate anything. You want to write a book? We already know—we have the best editors, cover designers, and publishers made just for you.

"Option three," James said and paused, "follow me. Let's go for a walk. I want to show you something on the roof of the building."

James guided Toffy with a gentle tap on his back.

CHAPTER 17

——

On the roof, James studied Toffy as his circuits started firing. He knew exactly what he was looking at. Toffy was in the race. James hid his fear behind his two jade-colored marbles that sparkled above his nose. It all looked silky on the outside, but on the inside his spikes were activated, draining the liquid from his face.

James imagined what was firing in Toffy's mind.

I'm bright. I'm bright. I'm bright.

Don't you know I'm bright? I'm bright. I'm bright.

I'm occupied by every color in the prism of light.

I'm bright. I'm bright. I'm black. I'm blue. I'm green. I'm white. I'm red.

I'm bright. As bright as the hue that's in my head.

James had found a worthy adversary. This excited him. He always needed a worthy adversary. He already had everyone in submission. He needed a new challenge, and he found that in Toffy.

If there was one thing that James was never at peace with, it was Peace itself. His body itched until he could scratch it with bomb-filled tentacles. He was ready for war, and the only war worth fighting at this moment was this one.

"Look at that red building in the distance," James said, pointing outward.

Intense winds muffled their words. Toffy was perhaps suspicious about James's intention. He had no idea why his boss had led him all the way to the roof of the building. His fear of heights, which James knew about, made him want to get it all over with.

"What?" Toffy said, squinting to block the wind.

"I said, look at that red building!"

Toffy heard him better the second time.

"Do you see that?" James asked.

"Yeah."

"That is the farthest we can see of the J City skyline. I own that building. In fact, I own every building along the coastline between that red building and this building we are standing on."

James pointed continuously downward and then lifted his hand and pointed the other direction.

"And all the buildings all the way to that yellow building down there. Do you see that?"

Although the wind pressed against his back, his vision was now stifled by the brightness of the sun.

"Yeah. I do," Toffy said as he used his hand as a shade.

"I own it all," James said as he spread out both arms and pushed his chest out. He was in perfect synchronicity with the blowing wind. His timing for his grand posturing was perfect. In one sudden swoop, he turned around, and the wind jerked his jacket backward, blowing perfectly and magnifying his power pose.

The theatrics were lost on Toffy.

James looked Toffy in the eyes and said, "It can all be yours. I can give you the keys to the city. Take the promotion, and I will open all the doors for you." He put his hand on Toffy's shoulder, studying everything about him.

Toffy was contemplative, unlike the others in his generation James always mocked; he had some reason and wisdom in his young heart.

James wondered if he had influenced Toffy's decision and thought about others who would have jumped off the roof out of excitement of his offer. He had promised Sarni the same position for the last two years. On a whim, he just offered it all to Toffy.

"This is a great opportunity for you." James said to Toffy. "You are close to the edge. Take a leap, and you will be rewarded."

Earlier in the morning, Sarni had walked into James's office in disbelief with welled-up eyes. James had seen that look on a lot of faces before. Disappointment, shame, and inadequacy oozing out of their facial pores. Toffy's look stumped him.

They had only spent fifteen minutes on the roof, but it felt like hours had passed.

Toffy was one of his greatest assets, and he could not reach his ultimate goal without him. James studied him like an ancient book, wondering what exactly Toffy was thinking through. Probably doing some calculations on the offer; after all, he was an engineer.

James could not get a full read on him. His mind was vibrating. In no particular order. Nothing linear. Nothing hierarchical. Disorder. Mind entropy at the highest level.

Toffy stood there, still not saying anything.

James got annoyed and once again thought about less-worthy adversaries.

Sarni. That one. He would be here, jumping and juking. Selling whatever he can sell at that moment to get more. He still hasn't learned his lesson. He will never get my validation. Him missing out on that promotion must be eating him alive, James thought

Chez. Just tell that one that he's smart; he'll do anything for that. That's all he needs. Give him access to a network of people to validate his mediocre ideas, and he remains motivated. Nuisance. He can eat the bottom of my shoe. He would jump off this roof for me. He would even ask to do the work of pushing himself off the roof to save me the hassle. Worthless to me.

His mind had taken over.

The councilmen. Old idiots. If not for the value they bring, I would not be caught dead around them. My local partners. Local fools. They have the local expertise. I would have been doing it all by myself. But here, no man is an island, and they know the lay of the land. Get more for doing less. They must be stupid. I need them more than they need me. Only if they knew the full scope of the project. I have to deliver. Useless middlemen.

If only they could all just align to build this perfect world I want to build for everyone. But their small minds can't comprehend large visions.

James broke his incessant stream of thoughts with a sound that pierced his mind. It had melody, it had harmony, it had bass, and it rhymed.

He looked at Toffy and knew where the vibration came through. It was pure light, an explosion contained in a diamond cup that never escaped its bound. The sound. James's head pounded, and his heart beat faster.

The thoughts came rushing to his head.

That foolish Sarni. He came to my office. Like a baby. A big old baby. Crying. Wah wah wah. Crying like a fallen cat. Meeewww. Mewwww meh. Let me lick my paws, oh poor Sarni. Asking, how he did not get the promotion? When have you seen someone from Fire lead Media? Common corporate hierarchy he does not even understand. That's why I can get him to do anything for me. I have him by the balls. In fact, if I asked him to squeeze them, he would probably ask 'how tight?'"

James broke out laughing, looked at Toffy, immediately thought of Deja, and smiled.

"Let's head back downstairs."

***

The CEO of J Enterprise, one of the largest corporations in the world, James's ultimate goal was to become the richest man in the world. He was currently the fifth.

He had learned from a very young age what it took to be successful. In order to become successful, he had to keep the smartest people around him and under his "full control." He learned that from the one before him—his father.

"For this world to be built to suit our needs," his father would always say, "we have to lead the people. Most people don't know what they want. So, honor them by doing it for them."

James had quickly identified Toffy as one of his smartest employees the moment he met him. He immediately knew the more he kept Toffy around, the more successful J Enterprise would be.

"You are greatness unfulfilled," James said on his first encounter with Toffy.

James grew up in the laps of wealth. He was not a hard-worker growing up. Everything he wanted, he got from his parents. With his privilege and a wind behind him, he convinced himself through the years that he got to where he was through the shrewdness and the hard work of his hands. It was generational wealth at its finest.

His mother spent most of her efforts going to social events and spending time with her only son—the heir to the J Enterprise empire. His father, on the other hand, was never home. He was always on the road, traveling for more business to consume.

"Somewhere in a box, somewhere on the globe," James's mother would respond late nights when James asked where his father was.

James enjoyed a childhood of freedom. He attended private schools, where he enjoyed sharing his experience of traveling the world and getting the newest gadgets during school breaks with his classmates.

His attitude toward life changed in the snap of a finger one morning. It was a privileged version of a moment of clarity. For James, it was a moment he realized that he had some responsibility—a sense of duty. On that rare occasion, his father was around.

James was only eleven years old then, and he had no clear understanding of what his father meant by the question.

"What do you want to become when you grow up?"

"I haven't really thought about that," James responded.

"You haven't?"

"Maybe an art director." James lit up. "Or work at a museum. I like the way—"

"A *what*?" his father exclaimed, and he slammed the newspaper he was reading on the table and stormed off.

"Stella! Come down here!" his father yelled and then immediately stomped up the stairs.

Yelling ensued. His mother came down crying, walking right past James to the flower pot in the garden where she hid her cigarettes.

After that incident, James noticed a change in his mom's demeanor toward him. She did not hug him every morning as he headed off to school. His father later enrolled him in a boarding school outside J City to give him the "necessary exposure" he needed to become a man.

"One day, you'll become the man you are supposed to be. Not this…" James's father never completed his sentence. James spent sleepless nights thinking about what his father meant to say. He embraced the persona of an orphaned kid— with a healthy allowance.

Over the four years before attending university, James saw his mom only twelve times when she visited him at the end of the school term. James saw his dad only once, and that was during his graduation.

At the graduation ceremony, while they were taking pictures, James's father assured him, "You've done well."

He had never received such approval from his dad, and there was nothing more he ever wanted. It became his mission to keep the legacy going.

James's time in the higher school was spent partying, socializing, and ridiculing. He knew he was in line to run J Enterprise. He was a fifty-first-generation James, and all he had to do was make sure he graduated and life was set with a secure future, unlike the class-climbers he met. It was all a game. Not only did he have an upper hand on an uneven playing field. He also had a replica whistle in his pocket to referee the game when he saw fit.

Upon graduation, he was immediately put in charge of the third largest division of J Enterprise.

The Jameses had a reputation of being ruthless businessmen, and James LI was trained by his father to be no different. Although James LI gained influence quickly and took over the conglomerate at the age of thirty-five, his father hovered and showed doubt like he was still the unworthy twelve-year-old boy talking about being a creative director.

Besides growing J Enterprise, James wanted something that neither his father nor the father before him—James XLIX—had ever achieved. James was going to be the world's richest person. That would be James the fifty-first's contribution, his own eternal legacy in a land filled with wealth-worshippers.

They will all worship me one day. All of them.

Anyone or anything that was a threat to that ambition was removed or labeled a liability. Whenever James felt his ambition threatened, he acted swiftly to neutralize the threat. Threats from politicians, companies, his employees, and even his own friends and family were not taken lightly. He knew what he and the generation of James before him had taken, and he was the most aware of the fact that it could all be taken back.

He was the most paranoid and vindictive of all the Jameses before him, moving his mother to a sick bay in another town because the sight of her weakened his position and that of his company.

The thought of an employee not being focused enough at his or her job was a huge threat. He rendered such employees useless immediately, surrounding himself with men and women who exclaimed their usefulness at the most convenient moments. Instituting orders of efficiency enforced through policies designed for a weakened government owned by his company.

All that is done is for all of us. Only if they knew the order was here to strengthen us, bring peace, and boost our collective productivity.

On the roof with Toffy, he knew Toffy's need to write a book was a threat. Even if he accepted the promotion, his writing would be a distraction from his duties at J Enterprise. Even worse, it could lead Toffy down the path of discovering the power of James's true enemy, who was always at work, plotting against him.

There was now a leader of that group and a book called *The Order of the Disorder* being circulated. Toffy could easily become the enemy. He had to keep him close.

James could have easily fired him, but he was a key piece in the puzzle that put James as the number one on his most referred list. Termination was not James's answer for Toffy's misaligned purpose. No, he needed something else to neutralize the threat of Toffy finding himself.

The promotion is the way. Make it more impactful. Make him feel good. Make him feel wanted and irreplaceable.

"Let's head back," James said.

As they walked down the stairs from the roof, James lagged behind. It was just a matter of time before he lost Toffy, and he knew it. He had to get in front of the situation.

James pulled out his mobile device and sent a message:

Set Plan T in motion.

***

"Set Plan T in motion," Loya repeated as he stood up looking at his screen. "Duly accepted. Did you see the new message? James said we should set the plan in motion."

"What plan?" Bunajo asked.

The men had just finished all the food trays left over from the afternoon town hall meeting.

"*Always* one plan or the other, Ahan!" Obechat added. "Plan A. Plan B. Plan C. Plan D. Ahan, doesn't he get tired?"

"No, this one is Plan T," Loya said. "Aren't you getting the messages?"

"No. Shut it, please!" Bunajo snapped. "I can't even hear myself think."

"Think? *You?*" Obechat said and laughed. "What can *you* possibly be thinking about?"

"Leave me, please," Bunajo responded. "Even if I wasn't thinking, let me hear myself not thinking, please. Some people call it meditation. I have found my own peace."

"No. Check your devices." Loya walked closer, shoving the screen of his phone in their faces.

Obechat looked surprised. "I didn't get anything. I wonder why?"

"Are you a wonderer?" Bunajo said.

Did James send this to me alone? Loya wondered. "It has finally happened," he caught himself whispering. *Use your inside voice. My time has come. My time to shine. It has to be for me. Plan T. Loya T. Loyalty! James knows I'm the only one who's loyal.*

He danced in a circle and then stopped suddenly.

I have to take action. I have to do something about Plan T.

Loya grabbed his device, buttoned his shirt, and walked out of the room.

Plan T? Plan T? Plan T? Loya swiftly paced through the corridor. *And I can't ask. It would make my life easy if he just gave me some extra info. I should ask him... No, I can't...* Loya straightened his posture as he walked down the hallway, raising his fist to the roof.

I'm loyal. Loyal to the cause. Plan T. Plan T. I shall not be found back at the shanty.

CHAPTER 18

———

Why did I do it? Why would I betray my own self?

A few weeks later, after spending time on the roof of J Enterprise with James, Toffy thought he'd been a little bit too impulsive. Before he'd left that day, he'd accepted the promotion. The discomfort pulled him into a state of constant unease. He really could not wrap his head around his decision.

James's persuasive nature, which he admired, got him to stay. It was easy to believe whatever came out of his mouth. Toffy also had a healthy fear of James. He knew how vindictive James could be, and he did not want to be on the receiving end of his vengeance.

It took some time to become comfortable with his promotion. He had not touched his notepad since then. Deep in his heart, it was clear it would be difficult to find time to write, but he kept convincing himself he would find the right balance, soon.

Three weeks gone, and not a single word.

He had 195 unread messages to sort through, and so without any meetings on his calendar, he sat at his desk and cleared the messages, responding to the important ones and deleting the unimportant emails.

After lunch, he sat back at his desk ready to clear out another set of messages, but—

No new messages? Toffy looked at his screen, partially shocked and partially excited.

If he wasn't too tired, maybe he could write tonight.

Toffy stretched his legs, at least expecting a message from Supply Side Suppliers, but his inbox was still empty a few hours later. He hit refresh, but still nothing. He decided to call them.

"Hey, just reminding you to send the new quote for the TX-87."

"Oh, I already sent it," the supplier responded. His raspy voice scoffed. "You did not get it?"

"No, I didn't." Toffy refreshed the page. "Do you mind sending it again?"

"Okay. Sure. I'll send it again now. Stay on the line… *Sent.* Let me know when you receive it."

Toffy hit the refresh icon desperately but did not receive the email.

"Can you send it again?" Toffy said every time the supplier attempted, until their fourth attempt.

"Maybe the attachment is too big."

"Hmmm… the document is only one page, and the file size is small. I just sent it again." He tried the fifth time. Still, nothing. "What's your email address again? Maybe I have been sending it to the wrong address. Wait. I just got a message saying the email address does not exist on the server. T-O-F-F-Y at J Enterprise dot com?"

"Yeah, that's it."

"Well, it's saying the email does not exist. Do you have another email address?"

"Nope! That's what I have been using for the past eleven years… Okay, let me sort this out and call you back later."

Toffy walked out of his office, both annoyed and paranoid. His assistant was not at her port, so he headed toward the hallway.

I need to get down to the eleventh floor and back up quickly. This is so disruptive. I wonder how many emails really await me? I hope High-T can resolve this quickly.

Toffy scanned his wrist and hit the elevator door once, twice, a dozen more times, and it never arrived. He walked to the elevator on the other side of the hallway and tapped on the call elevator screen frantically, to no avail.

What's wrong with this thing?

No one was around for Toffy to ask. Convinced of some type of malfunction, he remembered the stairs. He had never used them before. At the end of the floor in a hidden corner behind an extremely heavy door were pristine white stairs bordered with sleek guardrails. Toffy was intimidated by the number of flights, but his nervous energy pushed him forward.

Toffy's heart beat faster when he got down to the eleventh floor. He tried to use his office badge to get access to the reception area of the High-T department, but his keycard did not work. The same issue with his wrist band. He had never been on that floor without a High-T person.

Do my credentials not work on this floor? Is a system failure affecting the entire building? He walked back toward the elevator. *Should I even be taking the elevator? But going back up all those stairs… Oh my gosh!*

The elevator door opened, and against his better judgment Toffy eagerly walked into it. The light beamed above him.

"Thirty-ninth floor," Toffy said once he walked in. He waited for the voice-controlled elevator to start moving. No movement.

"Thirty-ninth floor," he repeated, the growing frustration clear in the tone of his voice.

Maybe I should take the stairs. The elevator might not be the best idea right now.

The doors closed and the elevator started moving down, too far down, and finally opened on the ground floor.

He came out of the elevator and walked to the front desk.

"Hey, Ayvin," Toffy said. "There seems to be something wrong with the elevator today, and I'm having issues with my office badge. It doesn't seem to be working anymore."

"Let me have a look at it," the front desk receptionist said and stretched out his hand.

"It says here that... you are... no longer an employee."

Two security officers walked up behind him.

"I'm sorry," he continued, "but it seems like you have been terminated from your employment at J Enterprise. Here is your termination package. I know this is difficult, but it has been determined that this is the best for both parties. The men behind you will escort you out."

"Mr. Toffy, please grab your termination package and come with us," one of the officers said.

Toffy pulled his entire body away from the envelope and took a few steps back. "This must be some kind of misunderstanding? I was just promoted a few weeks ago, and—"

"Come with us, sir. There's no need to make a scene, and it's in your best interest to comply," one of the officers said while the other placed his hand on the wattz electroshock gun attached to his hip.

They escorted him out of the building and stood at the door.

Toffy was on the streets with the large brown envelope in his hand.

There must be a misunderstanding. I need to speak to James. The men at the entrance pushed their chests out. One seemed to pity Toffy's misfortune.

Toffy opened the brown envelope and pulled out two sheets of paper addressed to him. The first page stated clearly:

Employment of employee No. 14865 has been terminated from J Enterprise.

There was no mistake; that was his number.

He walked back to his apartment in disbelief.

Tell me this is a joke. Toffy looked back at the building, his shoulders slumped.

He couldn't summon his vehicle. He realized the activation key was on the thirty-ninth floor in his office.

Onyx could be anywhere in the underground parking structure. He suppressed the loss he felt. *Will I ever be in Onyx again?*

Coming to reality with his position, Toffy walked—*dazed*—for hours after getting the boot. He bumped into people, joining everyone else trying to navigate life in the busy streets of J City.

There was a dullness in the sky, a contrasting backdrop from the shiny screens across each building. Vehicles, machines, carts, people, all mazed their way around one another with muted precision. Toffy ping-ponged off people and objects like a novice.

After a few hits, he stopped to get his bearings. The big screen at the intersection had a snapshot of his face, transitioning between color and grayscale. The captions read

Recently terminated from J Enterprise, employee No. 14865, Toffy X. New social score: 85.

His score had never dropped so drastically. Ever. Toffy pulled his face away and tucked his chin toward his chest. He read the document as he slithered from immediate shame.

Unfortunately, your service will no longer be needed. Due to unforeseen circumstances, your position does not currently align with the strategy and future plans of J Enterprise. Thank you for your service. Included is a severance package detailing your next steps.

Toffy flipped the paper.

You will be given ten days of payment. All your belongings at the office will be shipped to the home or the location we have for you on file.

Here is your case number in case you want to follow up on this letter. This number is private and linked to your account. Please keep it in a safe place.

Case #553juhg26$jljZZZ

Name: James, LI

Signed: James
_____

Toffy put the two sheets of paper back in the envelope.

How can it be? The same person who gave me a promotion is terminating me three weeks later?

He took a nostalgic glance at the building. Unlike all other times, it could only be seen from the distance. Shock! Anger! Sadness! A mixture of emotions vibrated through him. He cycled through them all as he walked back home, enraged, mostly at himself.

I could have walked away. Retained some dignity. Stupid! You! Ah. Toffy! I knew I shouldn't have stayed. I could have walked away on my own terms. They threw me out like a dog in the streets. Even dogs get better treatment. My life…

Toffy shook his head, and anger changed to fear.

What if I never get hired again? A termination. That has lowered my score. No one likes a lowered score. There was never supposed to be a lowered score on my résumé. How do

I explain a drop in score? What if I'm unemployed for up to three months?

"Three months!" Toffy exclaimed and threw his hands over his head.

That might even be optimistic. It could take a year! Maybe even two!

Toffy's eyes welled up. He stood silent as he remembered everything his parents told him about living through the dip of the pandemic that was supposed to last for three months and damn near brought the world to a halt for two years. The fuel to an already-spreading flame of inequality.

Panic came flooding through his body.

I shouldn't have taken that book from Sarni.

"That book is filled with guilt," Toffy said, finding himself whispering his thoughts. He quickly caught himself and tried to swallow the few words that lingered on his lips before they caught the attention of an unassuming bystander. He couldn't risk more descent in his score.

I need to get rid of that book.

His pace quickened.

That book is going to be the end of me! But is it? It's the end, but it is also the beginning for us all.

There was a knot in his stomach as he remembered the words from the book.

Ignorance is power.

Toffy burst out laughing.

An older lady with a pink and turquoise scarf around her neck was along his path. "How is that even possible?" he asked her. She squirmed and hastened away. "You must think I'm crazy. I'm not. I'm either very powerful because I have no clue what is going on, or I'm foolish to think that—"

He trapped the last few words as he stepped on the edge of one of the many streamlined sidewalks in the sprawling metropolitan.

I need to read that book or rid myself of it. There's no in between. It's either one or the other. What if the book is no longer in there? I need to get back to it quickly. I have wasted time. I know I have.

The book was a necessary distraction from failure and unemployment. It was hard to stay distracted.

A pack of J Enterprise employees waltzed briskly past. He wanted their acknowledgment. He got none. They appeared to tower over him.

Toffy began walking home. He went through waves of fear, guilt, and insufficiency. Along the thread of eternal doom, there were tiny pockets for respite filled with pure happiness and freedom. They never lasted for too long.

No, he was not brave enough to quit.

That's why I got terminated today and they threw me out like a dog. They must have known.

***

Toffy walked into his apartment at two in the afternoon. Deja's device, wristband, and spare access card on the kitchen counter surprised him as he closed the door behind him.

Did she come for the book?

The glazed door to his room was closed, so he corrected his thinking.

Deja wouldn't get involved with such. She probably came home for lunch and decided to take one of her meetings at home before heading back to the office.

Toffy really wanted some time to himself to fully understand what had just happened. He planned on sharing the news with Deja later in the evening. He carefully walked past the room and checked if anything was amiss. The brown bag was not where he'd left it.

Where's the bag?

He caught a glimpse of Deja laying on the couch. Her toes stuck out from behind the frame of the couch.

Toffy approached gently, wondering if she could be reading the book. A cool breeze blew across his body. He felt naked and exposed, and he wrapped himself with a towel of feigned confidence. The unexpected glow on her skin made him happy to be home.

Animated images danced on the TV. Deja only watched cartoons when she missed her family.

Sad? Maybe depressed?

Deja raised her head and they both appeared startled, like two strangers running into each other on a street.

"Oh, hey," Deja said as she slowly returned her head back to her resting position.

"Hey, baby. I thought you were sleeping. Is everything all right?" Toffy asked. He walked around the couch onto the center rug in the living room. There were no signs of the book. The bag was nowhere to be found in the perfectly lit room.

He took his shoes off and sat on the rug.

"What's up?"

"It's all a scam," Deja said. "A big, fat scam." Her eyes were red from hours of sorrow and tears. "A fucking global scam." She raised her head, pushed her body upright, and folded her knees toward her body.

"What is?" Toffy asked. "What are you talking about?"

Her eyes looked down, focusing on the space between her thighs.

Maybe she read the book. I should have read it first. Now I have no clue what she's talking about. Did the screens see the book? I can turn them off if I wanted, according to Sarni. Toffy devised the best plan he could to understand what was going on.

I'm just going to listen.

"You know," Deja continued. "I always thought I was living a life of purpose. I didn't know I was just perpetuating a life of..." She closed her eyes and shook her head, sinking her chin into her chest. "What was the first thing I said when I first met you?"

Toffy scrambled to find an answer. "I don't remember."

"When I met you at the mixer..." she said and paused. "I asked if you were making an impact, and you said, 'Of course.' We then had an hour-long conversation about our lives, and for the first time I opened up to someone about the type of impact I wanted to make in this world."

Deja's eyes became redder with tears yet to fall.

"Since then, I have worked with J Social, very dedicated, because I thought I was making an impact. I gave it my all." Deja punctuated her statement by pounding a clenched fist into her palm. "It was all written on that kid's face." She sank into the seat.

"What kid?"

"The kid who scowled at me when I handed him a food package at one of our giveaways. His look said it all. His innocent face turned ugly. It was impossible for a child's face to change so quickly. The words that came out of his mouth right after explained the transition. He said, 'Take your handouts back to where you came from, you witch. You think you're rich? You think?' He must have only been nine years old. Maybe ten. He spat at my feet and walked away. The disdain was clear. I knew I was doing something wrong."

Staring at a fixed point beyond the screen in front of her, Deja's breathing remained uneasy.

"But we were doing it... I was doing it for them." She looked at Toffy to validate her last statement and then looked away. "It was for them."

She shook her head for a few seconds, lost in thought.

"After six years, I am just realizing that J Social is a big scam. Not only have I been a victim of the scam, but I have perpetuated its continuity and assisted in its growth. I've been doing some digging... the profitability of the so-called nonprofit subsidiary... the forced, unpaid labor from Low Town."

She broke down in tears.

Toffy sat on the couch and hugged her.

CHAPTER 19

"It all started two months ago," Deja said, composed.

Toffy's attention was split between both rooms. His body was in the living room with Deja while his mind was in the bedroom scanning for the bag.

"You remember when I went for the J Social annual retreat last year in St. Loixx?"

"Yeah, I remember that." Toffy sank into the couch.

Deja tucked her toes under his back. Toffy placed his hand on her bare thighs. She immediately pulled her thigh away after feeling his cold hands on her skin.

"You always do that, babe."

She giggled softly. "Anyway, I left that three-day retreat with a funny feeling," Deja continued. "I just couldn't place a finger on why I felt so strange about the trip. The lavish lifestyle, maybe? We spent most of our time from one expensive activity to the other.

I thought it was strange initially, and such activities would be limited to the first day only. That was not the case. In fact, all the time at the retreat, we only spent a total of one hour on what we actually went to do there. One hour! That might even be too generous. We went from casino, to jet ski, to yacht, to pool-side parties. It was excessive. And toward the end of the trip—"

Toffy's eyes vacuumed the room.

"Is everything okay?" Deja asked.

"Who, me?" Toffy responded, sitting upright. "What? You said... Please continue. You said most of the time was spent from one activity to the other and... Keep going."

"Toward the end of the trip, I joked with my boss and Dave. Dave Sales—the world-famous philanthropist who wants to 'clean up the ocean'—about how much hard work we had done on the trip. He said, 'We deserve this; we take care of the world, so we should get to take care of ourselves.'

"'Oh, do we?' I asked. 'Do we really deserve such flamboyance?' Dave jumped in and said, 'We sure do. I don't think anyone deserves this more than we do.'"

Toffy's mind had returned from the room. Deja had his undivided attention.

"I couldn't believe how two people I really looked up to in this space could be so nonchalant about indulging in what seemed like the excesses of life. They both laughed and continued talking, as if to say I was young and naive. I brushed it off. I thought, *You know what? I do work hard, so maybe I do deserve this.*

"But then," she continued, "I just... I left that trip with a little feeling that something wasn't right. I brushed it off. I've never really thought too much about anything but doing my job well. I thought we were all trying to reduce pollution and end poverty in the world."

Deja sat up and got animated. "So, everything is going well, right? Now, fast-forward to two months ago. My—"

"Wait, you got the call too?" Toffy interrupted.

"What call?" Deja asked.

"The boooook…" Toffy dragged his word quietly, hoping that he hadn't opened his mouth at all.

"What book?"

"Never mind. I thought you were going to say… Forget it."

"So, two months ago," Deja continued, pouting her lips at Toffy's unwelcome interruption, "my boss calls me into her office to ask me to oversee the cancellation of the re-education program under the J Social agenda."

"Really? Why?" Toffy said with a lot of concern. That program was very important to Deja.

"Yeah, I know. Puzzling, right?" Deja pounded her palms together passionately with a consistent rhythm on every third word. "I was pissed. I had worked on that program from day one. It was like my baby. I was so proud of what we were doing. It was the most beneficial program we had ever developed. What made this even more frustrating was that my boss did not give a logical nor convincing reason why it was being scrapped."

I need to find that damn book.

"When I canceled the program," she continued, "I knew something was wrong. So, I started digging around and asking more questions." Deja imitated her boss's scowl. "'You need to focus on your job and stop snooping around.' I wondered what was being hidden. So, I decided to look around, particularly checking J Social's books, and I found a very strange—"

"Book?" Toffy said as he jumped out of his seat. "You found a strange book?"

"What?" Deja responded. "What book? No. Why do you keep going on about a book? No. I found a very strange fact that all the other programs of J Social were making money.

They were profitable. The last program scrapped was also making money, but apparently it was a 'low-performer.'"

Deja shook her head in disappointment.

"J Social is supposed to be the nonprofit arm of J Enterprise, dedicated to prioritizing social good and giving back to the world, not profits! Not only was J Social making a profit for J Enterprise. It was also a funnel that found cheap labor around the world for J Enterprise."

Toffy was confused. Deja had spent a few minutes explaining how J Social had been using its programs to find young people and minds around the world to feed their factories and establishments. More brain power to feed the machine. Counter to its portrayal, J Social's ultimate goal was to make more money for J Enterprise.

J Enterprise. More money. That doesn't seem too absurd.

"*Sarni* came from J Social." Deja shook Toffy's shoulder to snap him back to their conversation.

His mind had ventured off in search of organizations, books, and universes filled with vibrations, green lakes, piled-up plastic gutters, warehouses filled with people rendered useless.

"Yeah, Sarni did come in through J Social."

I need to get my hands on that book. Sarni gave it to me.

"So, all that social good was just a guise," Deja continued, looking out the window, "a ploy to buy goodwill around the world to continue to feed their hidden agenda of making more profit and growing J Enterprise."

Toffy pulled her toward him. "You were doing what you thought was right. It's not your fault the organization was not what you thought it was."

"But I *do* have a responsibility to know what my organization is doing and ensure it aligns with my values."

"Yeah, but it is not your organization. It's James's organization," Toffy said softly as he returned his hand to her thigh.

"Woooh. Your hands!" Deja exclaimed. "They are *freeezing*. Is everything all right? You keep looking around. What's going on?"

Toffy saw it all in Deja's eyes at that moment: his empty inbox, the unresponsive elevator, security guiding him out of the building, the twelve people he had bumped into as he'd fumbled his way home, the anxiety that filled the streets.

"I got fired today," Toffy said.

"You *what*?"

"Yeah."

They both sat in silence.

"Why don't you quit?" Toffy's words melted through the stillness of the afternoon warmth. "Come on, we have enough saved up to travel anywhere in the world. You can pick a project that *actually helps* people, and I can focus on my writing."

Deja seemed amused.

***

James was concerned about Toffy's preoccupation, surprised he'd shown no resistance when he got fired. From the screen monitors, Toffy seemed borderline relieved.

When James first met him, he'd thought, *Another young impressionable fella with lots of ambition.*

But then he noticed there was something special about Toffy. Toffy wasn't really impressed by the things that swayed other young employees. He was level-headed, calm, and a go-getter. He always got stuff done ahead of time and was an asset he didn't want to lose.

James always looked at everything as an asset or liability, simplifying the world around him, through a lens passed onto him through fifty generations of prestige.

Toffy was his main asset, and he had to make a tough decision firing him, but Toffy's response was unsettling. James found himself unsatisfied with the level of slump in Toffy's back. Firing him was supposed to be a wake-up call to make him focus on his duties, yet he'd apparently continued with his new interest.

When someone truly does what they want to do... they find their true-self and they can no longer be controlled. I cannot afford to lose control of Toffy.

After computing Toffy's absurd response, James visited his sole counsel for advice. In the basement of his six-story home, his counsel came in a ubiquitous screen that wrapped around the entire room, plugged into an encrypted server that monitored every action in J City.

"You have to trust your gut," said the voice from the screen. "If there is something about the Jameses and J Men, we know when something is fishy, and we take care of it."

The consolidated J Cloud intelligence modeled around the persona of the Jameses, trained over the years to optimize for internal greed and insistent struggle for power. The latest iteration refined around James LI's suppression of his expressive side. The side his father never wanted to see. These preferences, with a skewed weighing, plugged into the consolidated cloud that rained controlled behavior on the city. From his control room, he and his trained counsel watched it all. They watched the councilmen too.

"You already know," the harsh voice continued, "that there is something fishy about this Toffy guy and his story. We've picked up a few activities. Bring an end to it, James. That story must *not* get out. You know what happens when people find their *passion*? You can't control them anymore. We didn't get where we are by not controlling the best. Not to mention, you don't want this Toffy inspiring others. That's dangerous to our crafted narrative. Do what you have to do. Be ruthless. Hit where it hurts."

James walked out of his basement, whipped out his mobile device, and dictated into it furiously.

"Where are we with the plan?"

Bunajo responded immediately:

The plan is in motion, I'm always available at your beck and call, sir.

Obechat added:

If there is a plan that should be stationary, it is definitely not this plan. We have propagated the catalyst that will facilitate the perpetual movement of the plan in the forward direction.

Ditty added:

Subject T has been terminated from his job, and his will is slowly being tested. Given the appropriate amount of time to execute our full plan, Subject T will have his back curved at the angle of fully slumbered. We might need a tractor to make him stand up tall again.

Loya interjected:

He would fully circle back to asset form from liability, building the equity of the all-great J Enterprise. We have converted the potential of this plan into actual kinetics, making the initiative take off from the ground.

Chez responded:

Any new initiatives have to go by me first. Please start a new thread to address why I missed this.

Obechat wrote:

The young and ambitious lady will soon be sidetracked. Operation Sidetrack the Love Interest has just kicked in. The young traitor does not know what is in store for him.

Bejaai added:

Since we are switching from one phase of the plan to the other, I would like to touch on the high-level points of generally switching from phase to phase, thinking about the procedures of switching and keeping our eyes focused on the end goal of the master switch.

"Yes, what's the update with the switch?"

James dictated impatiently into the phone. He walked out of the front door of his house. Standing at the top of the flight of stairs that led to his driveway, he waited as his car made its way toward him.

Loya answered:

Yes, the switch…

I will speak for myself because I do not want to speak for any other person. I can tell you that I am extremely excited about the switch. I am working relentlessly to make sure the switch goes as planned. I am fully loyal to these activities.

Muidi jumped in:

You know. I was just waiting for someone to mention the switch. To add to Bejaai's point, we are fully gearing up for the switch."

Bunajo added:

Switch, switch, switch.
To triangulate the two effective points that were made, I'd like to add that once the switch has been perfected, we can launch Deleteron for all future revisionism.

Ditty continued:

For Deleteron and the switch to have their impact, we need to finalize the research heads. I heard there have been some supply chain disruptions from Planet Rack. We need more brain and minds to mine for insights."

Loya added:

Get Sarni on this thread. He has been too quiet.

As his vehicle revved up speed, making perfect turns at the street corners, James sat composed, staring at the thread on his device. *This is too long.*

The plan had too many moving pieces. He remembered the conversation with his counsel. He had to focus on the first phase of the plan.

Sarni's name popped up on his screen, reaffirming what he had to do.

As his vehicle snaked through the city, James thought about ways of sidetracking Toffy. A smile plastered on his face involuntarily. He had the right person for the job—his henchman, Sarni.

Toffy's best friend who just got him fired. The perfect candidate.

"Get Sarni on the call," James said.

Sarni appeared on one half of the vehicle's windscreen. "Good afternoon."

"You know about this book Toffy's writing?" James asked.

"Yes."

"I'm sure you and the Fire team had a plan for that already, no?"

Sarni remained silent.

"I have a plan. Meet me in fifteen." James ended the call.

James always had a good hold of Sarni, who idolized him. After all, Sarni rose out of the J Social program, becoming a top executive at J Enterprise.

Sarni grew up in a rough neighborhood, the poorest in Low Town. He was the first of three boys raised by his mother. His father was a known alcoholic who was never home. Just like Okonkwo from the classic novel *Things Fall Apart*, Sarni made it his sole mission not to be a failure like his father. He became the man of the house at a very young age.

He grew up in the streets, doing whatever it took to provide for his family. He would sell what he had to sell to get by—drugs, clothes, illegal products, electronics. This resourcefulness got him into a fast-track entrepreneurship college by J Social in his neighborhood.

The two-year condensed education in management was rigorous, and only 6 percent of the graduates, mainly talented kids in impoverished neighborhoods, qualified for a job at J Enterprises.

"You'll do whatever it takes," James had said the first time he met Sarni.

"Anything," Sarni had replied. He had just completed a six-month rotation program that lined him up to be James's personal assistant at the age of twenty-two.

James identified the traits immediately. He knew what could be manipulated.

Impressionable young man with natural street smarts. He would do anything to rise, to climb out of the status he hates being identified with. He's been conditioned to love money. He can be programmed some more.

Sarni was a steady climber at J Enterprise, the rise to the top his ultimate goal. He wanted to be like James, the one person he could call a father figure. He would be exactly what his father never was, and the only thing that could stop him was another good candidate.

Toffy had started at J Enterprise around the same time.

Sarni really liked him because Toffy made him feel like an equal and never cared about where their social score started off from. Their friendship grew over the years. But as close as they were, Sarni always saw Toffy as a threat. The further they progressed, the more Sarni considered sabotaging Toffy to ensure he got what he wanted—James's position at J Enterprise.

***

Toffy's morning routine was a fog.

"It's ten in the morning, and I still haven't written any-thing today," Toffy said to himself and then hushed. He had slept well, knowing the book Sarni gave him was safe and unnoticed. He had forgotten he'd hid it below the bed before he left the previous morning.

I need to stay meaningful. Useful. My social score has not been this low. If I keep going down this path, I might not have any utility to offer in a few months.

His rumpled shirt reminded him of a decline.

I wonder what Deja thinks of me now. What does she really think? She wouldn't be with a guy with such a low score. Would she? Can we keep this up? How can we afford living when the money runs out? Would we even be able to pay rent in Low Town? Life in Low Town. Hmm… Can I even get a new job with this score? Maybe I can bump it up? Go donate at the blood bank. Report a few suspicious activities. Become an information collector like Clarika. Ahhh, I'm certain she's one of those. Going around, telling on people.

Toffy's face changed. He let out a deep breath.

Grab a coffee and get a start to my day. Let's do this.

After a fifteen-minute walk to the café down the street, Toffy was ready to get moving. He missed having the option to move around on wheels. Every black car that zoomed past him reminded him of Onyx.

"This is some nice brown sugar *coffee ting—Rah Rah Rah*," Toffy let loose from his lips at the very first sip of the morning catalyst. "I'll take a different direction home today. Loop back this way and that way then that other way, and I'll be back in no time."

He ventured and soon found himself in an unfamiliar land.

It was hazy. It was different.
It had spectrum, and for instance,
When you ride for a distance,
You get dropped with no resistance.

Toffy was gliding and rumbling. Humbled by his pride he couldn't hide, because deep inside was truly aboriginal, original, indigenous. Vibrations high and positive increasing tides.

"Ah, Musta, na, this side *you dey,*" Toffy said, not fully understanding the words that came out of his mouth.

"*Yesso,*" Musta responded. "In this land, we do what we do best."

"What is that?" Toffy asked. The land seemed less unfamiliar.

"What it is we do best," Musta responded and put his sunglasses on. "We move!" He jumped off the bench.

"Where to?" Toffy asked genuinely. He had no clue where he was and had come to the realization that he was lost. Deep down he wanted to explore and see where the adventure took him. He became *alive.*

"Too many questions." Musta laughed. "You asked what we do? I responded, 'We move.' We move, my brother. My brother, we *move.*"

Toffy and Musta moved.

And as they moved across town, several interesting characters appeared.

"You see, it's all about the vibrations," the man in blue at the corner said. "That's how we communicate. I saw it on something written on what they called 'a blog' in saved hard drive from the red market."

The lady who sat next to him in a black hat and swirling long dress sang, "*Tell those stories from ancestral proverbs.*

The story is already there. Moves the body, moves the mind, moves the thoughts. Can you dig it?"

The man with the strings didn't say one word. He just plucked away at the strings.

Toffy didn't hear words; he heard *feelings*. He felt it. He vibrated. He got a message.

He kept moving with Musta until they got to the black door.

The little hole opened up and a man in dreaded curls asked, "Who dat?"

"It's Musta. I have him here," he said and pointed at Toffy.

God, it's a trap. I have been trapped. This is a bad idea.

Toffy trembled.

"Write your name on this paper." The man behind the door slipped a blue colored sheet of paper through the crack. Musta's name was already on the blue script. "Write your name, Mr. Writer," the man said, pushing the paper closer.

Oh no. I knew I shouldn't be writing.

Toffy froze. Panic captured his entire body and mind.

"Is this your *writer*?" The man behind the door laughed, near hysterical. "Are you sure he's not a *type*writer?" The laughter came deeper from his belly.

"Write your name," Musta pleaded.

"My name?" Toffy said, stick-like.

The light behind the man changed colors. Red, green, orange, black, brown, gold-white-blue-green. He continued laughing. "He is not ready." He slammed the small door shut.

The gush of the wind from the slammed door hit Toffy in the chest. *My social score must be at its lowest. Even here. This type of treatment.* The rejection stung.

Musta was already walking away, creating sounds on his device.

"What do we do now?" Toffy, lost, accidentally found those words zooming out of his mouth at Musta's back.

"We *move*," Musta echoed, and kept moving.

CHAPTER 20

I couldn't even write my own name. Toffy remembered his evening adventure with Musta. He shook his head.

He got back to his room and opened up the brown bulky booklet he'd received from Sarni, the first chapter titled, "Darkness Is the Light."

The first sentence ran across Toffy's mind like a herd in a jungle:

> *When you keep people in the dark, you illuminate the power of control. Ignorance is the key to strength. Darkness is the tool to ignorance. Darkness is the illuminating strength that consolidates our power.*

The last sentence of the chapter ran backward in an uncoordinated fashion, raising up dusts of brain cells that splattered across Toffy's cognitive facilities.

> *Keep the people ignorant. Keep them clueless. Keep no one asking.*

He dropped the book.

***

The next day came around sluggishly but picked up pace as the time progressed. Toffy was at the café writing, about to hit his mid-afternoon stride—words flowing from pen to paper, keystroke to computer screen—when he was jarred by the sight of two men in white suits outside the café drinking coffee.

He examined their stoic faces.

They must be here because I have the book. Are those—

"Who drinks that much coffee at two in the afternoon?"

he found himself typing into his device.

Toffy deleted those words on his screen; they were supposed to stay in his mind.

Toffy rocked back and forth in his high wooden chair across the white oval coffee table. He took a glance again, and the men were still there.

"Keep them ignorant. Who, me? Why couldn't I remember my name?" Toffy mumbled, lost in thought.

Toffy had seen these men before; in fact, he was used to seeing them around. They were J Men. The premium iteration of the Baron Wards. An automated complement to James's security detail. It wasn't their appearance that was out of place; it was that he had never seen them outside a J Enterprise function.

Is James around here somewhere? Toffy surveyed the coffee shop and the street that lay below outside the giant windowpane.

More life-like than lower versions of their fellow Baron Wards, the J Men never smiled. Attempts to make them as human as possible were still in the works. One of them drank his coffee at a consistent interval. Each amount sipped, also consistent.

They've always looked dodgy. Anyway, I need to focus on my writing. I'm sure they'll leave soon. Toffy exhaled.

As he placed his hand on his screen to start typing, he got a call on his device.

Ahh! How can I focus?

Toffy saw Uncle Apo's name on the screen and picked up. "Hey, Uncle Apo. How are you doing?"

"I'm fine. How is that story coming along?"

"It's good, working on it now. I'm at that shared space. The one with the café close to my apartment. You remember it?"

"Yes, I do. So, I take it you quit?"

"No, I actually got promoted and then fired three weeks after," Toffy said while laughing.

"Well, I guess someone had to sum up the courage. A good kick in the ass in the right direction never hurt anyone."

"Something happened yesterday, Uncle," Toffy whispered into the phone. "I have been doing a lot of writing. It helps me free my mind. But yesterday," Toffy paused and looked over at the men, hesitated, and then lowered his voice by a few more decibels, "I couldn't write."

Ashamed of the story he was relating, he lowered his voice again. "I couldn't write *my name*. I froze. It was a haze. It is *still* a haze."

"Show me," Apo said over the phone.

"What?"

"Mastery happens only in the blink of the eye. It has to be a leap of faith."

"Faith? Mastery? Blink of an eye?" Toffy whispered. "Is this part of the illuminated darkness?"

"Why don't you come over? I have some things to discuss with you. It would be better to talk face to face. "

When he ended the call, the men had left, nowhere to be found. Toffy stared at the empty seats and thought back to what transpired three weeks from him getting promoted to getting fired.

I must have been betrayed. Why do I have this funny feeling Sarni has something to do with this?

***

When Toffy got back home, the electricity was out. He stepped back into the hallway and ran into his neighbor.

"Hey, Clarika—"

Toffy hesitated. *How much should I divulge?*

"Are your lights on? Do you have electricity?" he continued.

"Yes, I do. I always have electricity." She spun around in her tie-dye floral dress. "What are you up to these days?" she asked.

Wouldn't you like to know?

"Well, I'm just…" He turned and looked nervously at the door to his apartment. "I'm writing a book," Toffy continued.

"You know *I'm* a published author. Right?" Clarika's words jumped out with excitement. "My work is the best, but people just don't understand my greatness," she continued. "Since people don't understand my greatness, I decided to teach people how to write about their greatness." She played with her hair, twirling the velvet red- and peach-colored locks together.

"I have to get going," Toffy said, annoyed.

"See you around." Clarika snapped the gum in her mouth and swung back toward her door. "Let me know if you are ready to write and be great." She snapped her fingers three times in a Z-formation. *Snap, snap, snap.*

Well, the screens are off anyway. Who needs electricity? I can write here then.

Toffy pushed to write without the electricity, but the elements were too distracting. The sweat in his palms made writing difficult. So, he had to stop to see the status of the electricity issue.

The automated building officer said he had to call the electric company. Toffy hung up and called, but they said he had to talk to the building officers. The back and forth went on for a full day. His case was sent to the escalation department.

"We'll have to escalate your issue, sir," the agent on his device said.

"I thought this was the escalation department?" Toffy was frustrated. "That's exactly what the agent told me yesterday."

"Yes, but this is a new ticket number, and it will have to be escalated further; this situation is highly abnormal."

"We need to get this sorted out. It's been almost two days now with no electricity. I'm running on backup batteries now. Can I at least get a reference number this time? Because last—"

Silence from the other side.

"Hello…? Hello? Arrrghhh…" Toffy threw his device on the couch.

Toffy got to the bottom of the issue with his electricity a few hours later. His lowered social score put a hold on his digital wallet, interrupting service to his apartment.

"Okay. Can you connect it to my emergency wallet then?" Toffy said to the agent.

"Are you sure about that?" the agent asked. "That really affects your—"

"Yes, I'm aware of that," Toffy cut him short. "My social score."

"Well, as you requested. I have your authorization to connect to your emergency wallet and restore your service shortly."

Toffy had never experienced it before. His score had dipped another five points since he was fired. He hadn't dropped that fast in such a short time span.

Eighty points! If I don't bounce back in the next few days, I'll get locked into Grade C for the next three years. Oh no. I must write.

"*Chop grass. Chop yam. Chop rice,*" Toffy wrote. "*How many millions just to cut the grass?*"

He remembered the book in the corner and snatched it up to read. His heart thumped at the chapter title: "Destruction Is Construction." He recounted the ideas and ruminated on the cognitive grass in his mind. Like a goat digesting its food, Toffy digested the information.

"Destruction Is Construction."

Destroyers are used as a tool to destroy the products of human labor. Although automation is supposed to make us more productive and wealthier, the objective of the destroyer is to make sure we don't have surplus.

Toffy inhaled deeply. He had forgotten to breathe.

The destroyer's aim is to keep a group of people in poverty. Uselessness is just the latest version. The goal is to ultimately kill the ability of independent thought. Our cognitive ability to create is what makes us truly human. By destroying our ability

*to have independent thought, it essentially kills
our humanity.*

Toffy wiped away the humid beads of sweat that had
sprouted liquid trunks across his forehead.

*Because when people have surplus and start getting
intelligent, they would soon realize there isn't a need
for the small class that retains the most power.*

Images of J Enterprise spluttered through his head. He
knew the previous image was too much of an independent
thought. He might have gone too far this time.

Something sounded in the distance and arrested his
mind, body, and spirit.

The voice in his mind asked, *Who's dreaming for
the people?*

His electricity went back on, and he immediately received
an update on his screen.

"Alert: New transaction activated. Emergency wallet connected. Your social score has dipped by three points."

Seventy-seven points! What the—? Toffy put his notepad aside.

∗∗∗

Two days after getting lights back on in the apartment, Toffy
woke up ready to start his day. He turned the tap on in the
bathroom sink and nothing came out.

Hmmm. That's strange

He went to the bath and turned the tap. Same thing. He took a deep breath and went to the kitchen sink, hesitant. He did not want the confirmation. Nothing came out.

"Are you fucking kidding me?" Toffy yelled out.

"What's going on?" Deja said and came into the room.

"We don't have water."

"Really?" Deja tried the tap. Nothing came out. "What is going on in this building? No electricity first, and now no water?"

Toffy looked at Deja with contempt, angry he had been dealing with all this on his own.

"Are you the dreamer," Deja said, "the doer, or the incrementalist?"

What? What sort of question is that? Does she know I'm connected to my emergency wallet now? Is this how the journey to life in Low Town begins?

"I'll deal with it," Toffy said without answering her question.

"I was just—" Deja stopped at the door. "Do you want to come take a shower in the office? I can let you in."

"A shower? Really?" Toffy snapped back.

She must really think I'm desperate. I'm sure it looks that way. J Enterprise. I'm never showing my face back there.

"Nah. I'm fine. I'll deal with it. Bye, Deja." Toffy fumed internally. Deja stood at the door for a few minutes. Her mouth moved, but Toffy heard no words. The slammed door when she left had a sharp and ringing after-effect.

He sat alone for a while, considering his options.

I probably have to switch this to my emergency wallet address too. Another ding on my score.

After a few escalated calls, Toffy got to an agent who had more than three automated response options.

"Sorry, sir. We don't accept that," the agent at the water service office responded. "But feel free to drop by our office to make a payment. I hope my service was good. You will receive a survey after this call to rate your experience. Thank you." The agent hung up.

Toffy looked at his leather wallet the way a concerned mother would at her sick child. It had cards, numbers, seed phrases. None of them could help.

***

"Yes, your payment access has been revoked," said the bank agent later in the afternoon.

"Why?"

"I don't know, and it does not say anything in the system here. Since your payment access has been revoked, we will have to contact headquarters to reinstate it after you or your company submits a petition. Where do you work?" the agent asked.

"Well... I used to work at... I'm currently in a transition."

"A transition to what? Uselessness?" The agent smirked. "That's going to make things more difficult. We only reinstate payment access to customers who have proof of employment."

"But I've been banking here for almost a decade."

"Yes, but you have also been working with J Enterprise for over a decade, and now you no longer work there. So, feel free to drop by our office when you have proof of employment. I hope my service was good. You will receive a survey after this to rate your experience at the Bank of J City. Thank you."

The bank agent walked out of the office.

What's going on?

Toffy looked at the transparent alumina card in his wallet. The exclusivity it provided to the select few, now worthless; nothing but reinforced metal that weighed him down.

For the first time in years, as he went back outside, he started noticing that life was not as nice and dreamy as he once thought it was. His social score was now blinking on his outfit, the number fading away with every lowered point. People stared at it and frowned at him. The look on people's faces—the scorn, the fear, the anxiety of the city—was written on everyone's face.

How long can I live on the money I have?

Thinking about it brought chills to his spine. The J Building stuck out of the skyline.

I'm not going back there.

He immediately understood J Enterprise like the pyramid it was: the shiny white building narrowing at the tip to James's office.

"Throughout history there have been three classes: high, middle, and low," Toffy said, recounting chapter 3 of the book. "The high want to retain power."

Toffy thought about James. *He always stayed in his office.*

"The middle wants to switch positions with the high while the low are most times so consumed by day-to-day hardship that it's hard to want more for themselves."

A vibration flowed through his body, from a far place, but yet so close. He was supposed to feel this one as he thought about the sounds of the struggle: the race to the slippery top, from the people in Low Town and the lives in High Town.

He found a bench, sat down, and wrote:

People struggling for their humanity. Struggling for their existence. Their actions everyday were one of disorganized solidarity.

Toffy recounted a conversation in James's office.

They were all working for the same thing, if only they knew it.

Toffy continued writing:

People drank from the floor to stay hydrated. Young and old died while council goats ate all the yams. Corruption as a tool to kill people. Eating all the yams and not leaving any for others.

Construction is destruction.

"It doesn't matter who wields power, provided the hierarchical structure remains the same." The words from chapter 2 flashed in front of him as he admired the white architectural design of the building where he'd spent the last ten years.

Toffy stood and started to walk.

What do I do now?

Toffy thought of Musta in a smoke-induced haze.

Move.

He moved left; he moved right.
He did it once; he did it twice.
He circled 'round the windy path.
He found himself in a higher town.

He felt the vibration of High Town. The distant echo of talking drums. He saw the people, not too much in material wealth but filled with a finer glow. But he was not where he thought he was.

Lost in adventure, once again, following the next right path he thought best. The colors around him varied, darkness with bright spectral flashes for those who paid attention. The wind blew against his face.

Musta was suddenly right next to him.

"How did you get here?" Toffy asked.

"How *do* you get here," Musta said with a smile. "I told you. We *move*." Musta shrugged and walked forward.

***

He and Musta had no trouble getting inside, for this time Toffy wrote his name before he was even asked.

"I see you, brethren," the man said as he opened the wooden doors that led them down a tunnel. They soon found themselves in a spherical room.

Reflections everywhere. Small square screens with patterns that changed and vibrated with the sounds in the room. Fascinated by its beauty, Toffy knew those were messages. The images raised the hair on his arms.

Musta ziplined to the top right quadrant of the sphere, sat in a black chair, and picked up a black box with sixteen white square pads. He tapped away beats once he slipped on his headphones.

Toffy looked around the globe of a room. A woman in the corner had dark shades and browned skin. She plucked away at the single string attached to the wooden plank she sat across from. Different images appeared on the black square plate next to her. She pulled her hair back.

"What you looking at? Need some vibes? I can pull the strings, if you know what I mean." She smiled at Toffy.

She plucked away at the string again, and Toffy felt the vibration, which sent his eyes across to the bottom left quadrant. His eyes caught the attention of a young girl with a backpack. She crunched on some gum as she effortlessly typed zeros and ones on her screen. Lost in her world, she had no one to worry about.

Toffy's attention was quickly snapped by the rumbling lips of a man in dark shades. He rumbled continuously like a motor with no brakes. The rhythm was intoxicating, bouncing around the room.

"Welcome to the Movement," came a voice. A woman in an orange spiral dress appeared in the middle of the sphere and sailed toward him. "We are the Council of Movements. There is one thing that we do here. You know what that is, young penner?" She touched Toffy's face. "We *move*," she said as she plucked her vibra-phone. "That's right. We move, and it is time to move. I'm Keba."

She snapped her fingers, and they all stood up and moved.

***

"You remember everything you saw. Right?" Musta yelled at Toffy as they ran heavy in their stride.

Attempting to catch his breath, Toffy was panting. "What?"

Musta leaped over the wired gate. "You got it all. Right?"

"Slow down," Toffy yelled.

The movement crew had gathered outside the gate.

"Come on guys, let's go," someone said.

"Jump, man!" Musta yelled at Toffy.

Toffy was sandwiched between the wired gate and the sound of the hound dogs getting closer

Toffy jumped.

Musta raced toward the crew. "Come on. What are you looking at? We have to move."

Toffy took a few more seconds to catch his breath. At the gate, a glaring sign read, STAY CLEAR. YOU ARE NOT WELCOME HERE. WELCOME TO PLANET RACK.

"Let's go, y'all!"

Toffy jumped into a black vehicle right after Musta did.

"Write down what you saw," Keba said to Toffy.

Toffy looked at her with a daze. He got flashes of a blackened castle with cannons at the helm and beach water crashing at its base.

Musta shook him. "Hey hey, man. You need to start writing."

Minutes ago, they were walking down moldy concrete stairs to a quiet veranda. Over the veranda people had clumped in lines directed toward a singular door. The people had emerged from the basement and all marched forward.

Toffy struggled with what he had seen. The car swerved recklessly on the road as it drove away from Planet Rack.

"Pen to paper, buddy," Musta said, tapping him.

Buddy? Friend? When? Toffy thought as he looked at Musta with no words.

The vehicle was in automated control, swerving and weaving its way out of the crooked streets of a finer town.

"I saw a friend," Toffy said. "The man at the top, giving the orders. That was... That was..."

"*Write*," the lady with the string said and plucked.

"He ain't about to write shit," the man with the rumbling voice said.

"That was..." Toffy continued "*The book.* I got it from..."

Gray haze and smoke.

Musta shook him. "Toffy. Toffy. Toffy."

"Leave him," the girl with the backpack said, ending her silence. "It might have been too much for him. I told you he wasn't ready. I *told* you."

***

"Order, everybody," the voice came out blasting on the streets. A man in all-green garb spoke with a megaphone in hand. This was at the watering hole where the diverse congregated. A mocking laughter came next from the blaring microphones, then horns and the syncopated rhythms, then a saxophone solo.

"The truth is," the voice from the megaphone got louder, "the higher-ups in High Town are the ones who are ruthless. Bombard us with a giant screen of ghosts to make a lion toothless. But without the seed, a tree can't grow. Life, stale and barren, plants remain fruitless.

"You hear me now?" He stared Toffy down. Three men stood behind him beating their drums with curved sticks.

"Yah, man." The people around the pond yelled back to Toffy's surprise.

"Decentralization!" another voice cried out.

"And then, retriangulation," a lady with a high voice sang out. "To end the pollution. The heathen's back is against the wall. The ones who position the queen and set the pawn."

"Yeah!" echoed around the lake.

Toffy looked around. *These people are clearly comfortable thinking unconventionally.*

The sense of liberation rippled out from that which didn't have any enemies: water, hydration, the physical and spiritual. The green leaves on trees provided food, puffs, and even shade for some. The coarse soil, a connection to the ground that thumped. The beat—a vibration that connected them all. A man in purple rolled around a group of bicycle riders. His speakers sent out low frequencies. Birds tweeted on the higher end of the spectrum.

"Soak it in, Toffy," Keba said. "This is Viginniye. You'll probably need this," she continued, handing Toffy a bag that contained a cloak and slim gray box. "It will come in handy."

"Don't be afraid to change the world." She looked Toffy in the eyes. "More importantly, don't be afraid to change your *own* world."

CHAPTER 21

———

It had been a week since Toffy spoke to his uncle. He had promised to visit, but there was always one issue after the other.

He couldn't shake it off, hindered by thoughts he couldn't quiet. They streamed in his mind at a consistent pace. He couldn't even get a single word out to be documented. He lost all motivation. He needed help. He wanted counsel.

As he approached his uncle's brown brick apartment building, some men in white were leaving Apo's residence.

The same men following me around...?

Toffy hid behind a glossy wooden stall filled with digital eyeglasses for sale. The prices and details flashed above each pair. He peeped around the corner to confirm their appearance. They swiftly disappeared.

Toffy walked into Apo's house, suspicious.

"Who were those men that just left your place," Toffy asked, "dressed in white?"

"Hey, Toffy? Why don't you sit down."

"You are not going to answer me? Are you part of the people out to get me? You told me to quit my job," Toffy said and stormed back and forth over his uncle's yellow checkered patterned rug. "My life has gone to shit since then. Thanks to you, my social score is plummeting, and I will *never* write this book. Not at this rate. You know what they're building at the corporation? Stories will never see the light of day—starting with mine."

Apo just looked on as Toffy unfolded.

"How am I supposed to listen to someone who spent most of his life giving free therapy sessions?" Toffy looked his uncle squarely in the face. "Free sessions?" Toffy threw both hands in the air above his head. "Who does that? You are some type of archaic service provider. A glorified therapist." His voice was high and ugly.

Apo just watched on and said, "No, you are not ready to take full responsibility for your actions. Until you take full responsibility, you will not be able to truly write and complete your story. Some of us have accepted our fate."

Apo stretched his legs and placed both hands behind his shaved head.

When and why did he shave his head?

"You don't see us moping around about it," Apo continued. "Listening and hearing are two different things, Toffy. Listening is an art."

Toffy stormed out and slammed the door behind him.

***

Apo didn't know how to break it to Toffy. He could have told him that those men were caregivers. He was dying, but he chose to listen instead of talk, burying his sadness underneath a brave face. He'd tell him, eventually.

***

"What is going on?" Toffy stood at the door.

His apartment had been turned upside down. Papers were all over the floor. Furniture was moved around. The trash can was open on the ground. Leaking liquid dripped on the marble kitchen floor.

Did the robot-cleaners malfunction? But they don't come in today!

Toffy slowly walked into the apartment, and then a sight from the window caught his attention.

Is that...?

He walked up to the floor-to-ceiling window. Defeated, he stared out of it for minutes. Across the street, Deja was having a meeting with two men at Crimson—the self-serve delicatessen across the street. Toffy could only get a glimpse of who she was talking to, but he was convinced they were the same men in white.

The same men who had followed him around. The same men who had come out of his uncle's apartment.

Toffy threw his hands over his head as his mouth involuntarily opened.

They are all conspiring against me. Kai, they have me cornered. They wouldn't just let me be great.

He snapped out of it and paced around his apartment, avoiding the mess.

Maybe it was Deja? Looking for something? They must be looking for the book.

Toffy ran to the room and dove under the bed. He reached for the brown bag to confirm the book was still there and was comforted when he felt the outline of the book still in the bag. He pulled it out to confirm.

So, what were they looking for? Toffy kept thinking as he sat upright on the floor. *Maybe Deja gave them the key?*

She must have been suspicious the day I came back from Planet Rack.

He opened up where he'd left off, flipping open to where he'd bookmarked the page.

The system is designed to help those who don't need help. The system is designed to keep those who need help helpless.

The complexity of the world is emphasized. It highlights the various levers that need to be pulled to get an individual closer to their personal goals. The system floods the individual with information so they not only get overwhelmed with how complex it is to get to their goals, but they also lose sight of their goals.

Strategic is the design for separation. Dividing individuals into segments. Dividing full thoughts into pockets and flashes of illusive insights. The individual loses sight of their position in the collective. The individual loses any form of identity except that which they are fed from the screens. The screens demand all the attention. The individual loses all sense of responsibility because they begin to believe the external world is completed, and they just happen to be the victims of circumstance.

The result is the blame-game. The individual accepting their role as "victim." One who cannot transform the current situation to match the goal once inspired internally. The further down the screened rat-hole the individual goes, the harder it is to see

*their responsibility to change what is not currently
suitable for their being.*

Toffy's mind was transported to that faithful night at
Planet Rack.

*The individual... the collective... personal goals... victims
of circumstance.*

The visuals that appeared in his mind became so vivid
that Toffy gasped and took in a deep breath, which he held
for a few seconds before slowly deflating his lungs. His mind
clearer than before.

The link between the white pyramid, Low Town, Viginniye, and Planet Rack became more apparent. Lines connected each piece in his mind.

"March on forth," he'd heard the brain-drivers in Planet
Rack shout as the men and women walked into vessels. The
minds would be mined for not minerals but insights to
develop content and experiences that enslave the collective.

Toffy grabbed a pen without even knowing it.

He opened his eyes and found he had written three
pages—filled with only words.

A beautiful collage. Like a painting of his memory. His
mind clear. He could capture a full thought and put it elo-
quently in words. He started looking at the words, amused
at what he had just done but disappointed that he could not
do it a few days before when it was needed.

How did I do this?

His mind slowly let the floodgates of information roll
in. He had lost the sense of completing full thoughts. His
insights came to him in a spluttered format. Sharp sprouts
of images, words, and sounds pasted upon the page.

Toffy grabbed his pen again, hoping the few minutes of effortless writing and thinking would come back to him, but he couldn't even hold the pen. Frustrated, he scanned the room and was reminded of the mess.

The lock on the door to the apartment clicked, and he sprang to his feet and walked shirtless to the living area as the door opened.

"Oh my... What happened here, Toffy? Is everything all right?" Deja stood at the door, shocked.

"I should be asking *you*. Who were those men you were talking to?"

"What?" She took a step back. "Are you watching me now? What is going on? You were watching me and turned the house upside down?"

"No, the apartment got raided, probably by the same men you were talking to."

"You are crazy. You have finally lost it."

"Have I? Tell me what you've been up to?" The accusation in his voice deepened.

"Up to? Are you even listening to yourself?" The rage obvious on her face. "If only you took the time to—"

"Took the time to what?" Toffy interrupted and walked closer. "I have all the time in the world now, but you are nowhere to be found. All the time. And you say only if I took the time..."

"That's not what I was saying," Deja responded. "If you allowed me to finish—"

"Finish what?" Toffy shouted, waving his hands in the air. "Are you ever finished? Never around. Nowhere to be found."

"What do you mean?" Deja pushed the door open further. "You're the one always changing—"

"Oh, change? Who's changed in the last how many years? You're a completely different person."

"I'm different? Oooohh. Look at the desktop calling the laptop stationary. Listen to yourself. Do you even do that? Do you listen to anyone? Lost in your own thoughts all the time. It's work one day. It's a story the other. Always on the hunt. When I'm fortunate enough to get you to slow down, your mind is still racing, chasing something far away. And I'm the one who's different now. There used to be a time—"

"A time when what? It's because of my social score. Right?"

"*What?*"

"Come out and say it. If anything, I'm sure you're in on it."

Toffy vented for hours. Deja sat down and listened until he went into his room.

***

"Feed the beast. Feed the beast. That's what we hear all the time," Raymun went on rambling as he piled letters into a document file. "Here we are now. The beast is hungry," he said and rubbed his belly several times. "A hungry beast is an angry beast."

The scruffy man in khaki overalls stood there, sweaty.

"They sent *you*, huh?" Raymun said.

"Yes."

"What did they get you to do for them that you're doing this now?" Raymun asked, compiling loose paper into a stack. "Huh? You're one of the silent types. Can I see your confirmation again?"

The man stood still at the door of the all-glass room and showed him the screen.

Raymun recited the words on the device: "'Activate Plan L.' Well, I wondered why they kept some of these documents, to be quite honest." He handed the stack to his visitor. "I would have fed it to the flaming beast, but we all have our reasons."

"That's it?" the man asked.

"Were you expecting more? That's all you've been authorized to collect. Unless you have something else to show me. Quite frankly, some of those words shouldn't see the white of paper. But hey, Plan L is Plan L. I don't get paid enough to break the rules." Raymun wagged his finger. "But to not feed the beast? That's unheard of in this town. When the beast is hungry, the beast is angry. You better get out of here and get those documents in the hands of those they're supposed to be with."

The man in the khaki attire walked away.

***

Toffy woke up in the morning to a very solemn Deja.

"I just got a call from your dad, Toffy. Apo is dead."

"*What*? But I saw him yesterday," Toffy replied as he processed the information.

"I'm so sorry."

That was probably why he wanted me to visit. How could I not have realized? He probably needed my help. So selfish of me...

He searched the depths of his mind to get a glimpse of what his uncle looked like on the last day he saw him. He remembered his uncle's sunken look, his cheek bones protruding more than normal, his neck skinnier.

Cancer? Depression?

He remained quiet.

***

"You will really be able to touch the lives of billions," James had said, eyes centered on Deja's pupils. "And we want someone like you to revamp the entire program. Someone to ask questions and make sure everything is done right. You'd have ownership of an operation that would impact a region with the largest population. Imagine the scale of what you'd be able to change. Let me know your decision by Monday."

Deja was conflicted by James's offer.

I can walk away. I should walk away. But this might be it. This might be my opportunity to turn things around.

Deja stewed on the topic.

My hard work is finally paying off. I'm getting recognized for my diligence.

The offer simmered.

It's an interesting proposition. Those numbers... Wow. I haven't seen numbers that high. But what about impact? Impact? What's impact? I should be focused on how this is going to impact my life.

"Pssst," Deja expelled.

I'm trying to help everybody. How about I help myself? I can help at the right time. It's time to build. Now. I'm worth the reward. Get the most for the minimum effort. Why not? The others do it. Sit back and finally get all that vacation promised. The real one. The one where you can actually take time off. I should take it.

Deja contemplated and then hissed.

I shouldn't. I can't keep it up. It's all a sham. But it might be my opportunity to clean things up. Patch it all up. I will change the look in that kid's eyes.

And Toffy?

She didn't finish with an answer.

***

Toffy read the note Deja had left him.
It started:

> *I didn't know how to tell you this, so I decided to*
> *write a letter.*

She'd left him a note on the kitchen counter about her taking up the new job across the pond. Toffy continued reading.

> *We've grown apart. When I'm at the apartment, we*
> *are like two ships passing one another in the dark still*
> *night. Now all we do is fight. All that excites you is*
> *that which you write. I don't want to argue anymore.*
> *Sometimes I feel betrayed. Like the unspoken agree-*
> *ment we had—to create a space where we can be*
> *ourselves—has been broken. This has made me lose*
> *trust over time. As I lost trust, resentment replaced it.*
>
> *We seem to want things that are different. I think*
> *I have an opportunity to really made a difference.*
> *Finally do what I think is right. I really thought I'd be*
> *doing it with you. But it's like we are ghosts around*
> *one another. When we sleep next to one another, it's*
> *like you're not even there. I don't believe I have access*
> *to the Toffy I knew before anymore. You watch the*
> *screens, looking for the next update, the next clue.*
> *Constantly on the hunt.*

That's what makes you special. Your intrigue. Your hidden sense of adventure. But overdone, it's your weakness. It's our weakness. We are lost in the search of our ideal worlds. This story you're writing could be something. But then again, what do we all do this for?

Take good care of yourself, Toffy.

Love, Deja.

Toffy sat down, and the note dangled lifeless in his hands. His whole world had been uprooted. He was in so much pain. For the first time since childhood, Toffy wept.

He cried 'til he could cry no more. The last thing he wanted to do was to write.

Toffy then remembered the last paragraph of chapter 4: "Their ultimate chess move on the individual is to instill helplessness."

I'm done. They have won. I have nothing. Not even love.

A new batch of tears rolled down the side of his temple into his ears as he lay on his back. He was so numb to the pain that he ignored the tickle from tears slithering like snails across his skin.

Toffy stared at the blank white ceiling for hours.

The sun rose and set while sweat dried between his back and the hardwood floor. His was mind empty but full. His thoughts a continuous wave spiked with the ebb and flow of a turbulent night at sea. He was the helpless captain who'd accepted the impending wreckage of his crew-less ship; although his body was anchored to the ground, his thoughts fixed on the wheels of a ship spinning out of control.

He had no help. He was all alone. He would be lucky if aggressive waves could take him ashore but couldn't care less if he made it and didn't mind if he found his way to the bottom of the sea. His mind was at risk. Flooded with thoughts, guilt, fear, and anger. His body motionless. Darkness all around him.

No one in sight with which to move forward.

He pulled out the book once more and turned to chapter 5: "Anti-Community Movement." The words from the pages splashed back and forth on the deck of his isolated ship.

The power that be keeps the order by separating people.

Toffy looked around to confirm. He had been separated. *The goal is to bring an end to community. The tools such as conflicting news and contradictory ideas and realities is how the powerful maintain the structure. The more educated you are about their philosophy of simultaneously holding two contradictory realities in the individual's mind, the more you believe the system.*

Therefore, the people who believe this philosophy the most are those at the top, the subjects who view all and everything as objects for perpetuating the accumulation of power.

Any idea that challenges this philosophy is immediately undermined, discredited, and ultimately destroyed.

The words splashed against the deck: *Destroy.*
Splash: *Separate*
Splash: *Divide.*

Anti-community is an ingrained religion. It is the enemy of those who want to hold on to their land and status in society.

A full wave of words came crashing down and rocked Toffy's mind.

An individual challenging this order can be managed, but a collective consciousness that begins questioning the status quo must be hampered by any means necessary.

Another wave rocked Toffy's mind in the opposite direction.

Community is seen as the singular enemy that everyone can rally against.

A wave took Toffy under. He continued to sink to the bottom of the ocean of thoughts.

He closed his eyes as the waves quietly crashed over him, his body soaking in his own sweat.

The sun set once more.

***

Is this the story I'm supposed to write? A tragedy? Toffy wondered. *Is that why the ending is so sad?*

He thought about his parents, of moving back home. *What would they think of me? They would think I've lost it.* "Well, haven't I?" he asked himself. *No job. No lover. No home. No story. No Uncle Apo.* Twelve hours had passed, and he had not moved from his position on the floor where he read Deja's letter. He stared blankly into space as the clouds gave way for the sun to shine through the window of his apartment.

He was lost in thought, mixed with bouts of tears streaming down his eyes. He had not cried since he was eight years old. He used to pride himself on the fact that he could tell people the last time he shed a tear was over two decades ago. His shell of masculinity suddenly shattered in a culmination of events that left him motionless.

Did she really write me a note?

The three paragraphs on the folded paper reminded him of its existence. He squeezed his eyes together tighter. The blue ink on the brown paper reminded Toffy of Deja's refillable pen she used for every important note or phrase that had to be written down.

Maybe she was comfortable writing it. Even worse, she was happy.

For the first time, Toffy thought Deja could have left him for another man. Someone more capable. Someone who had his life together. Someone who loved her more.

Someone with a higher score. Even if she left with someone else, how can she leave me now?

"That's pretty selfish of her," he said aloud. "Leaving me right after my uncle died. One of my closest friends. Family. Really?" He wiped the tears that rolled down his cheeks.

"Oh, Uncle Apo," Toffy yelled out with an unexpected shriek.

CHAPTER 22

Loya recalled the last time he saw Toffy while trying to enact Plan T. He had walked for hours, bumping into people and walking in front of speeding vehicles. He was determined to keep his eyes on his device until he manifested Plan T. "Plan T. *Plant.* A plant. A factory." Loya was convinced he was getting closer to the core of what he was seeking.

Without too much effort, he had ventured back to Low Town and was getting strange looks. It was unusual to see councilmen walking around without commotion or fanfare.

Words caught him by surprise at an iron gate: PLANET RACK, written in thick blue fonts on a worn-out white placard.

"Planet Rack," Loya repeated. "Planet. Plan it. Plan T. PLAN T." Loya jumped up and down with excitement. "I knew it. I remain faithful and loyal. Ah, James will be proud of me."

His excitement wore off as he realized the night's darkness had taken over from the day's glow.

Hmmm, it's dark! Loya looked around.

He knew exactly what went on in there. He was one of the people who allowed the commerce of slaved insights to flourish.

But why does James want me here?

Loya was startled when glass shattered, followed by footsteps. Two men jumped over the fence and ran out with three ferocious dogs in pursuit. A voice from behind him shouted, "You are coming with us now!"

"This is it, huh? Plan T? I remain loyal. Let's go," he said as he was hurried into a car.

A lady in blue gave the car instructions, and the vehicle followed every move. Loya had not seen a person control an autonomous vehicle so fluently with her voice, enunciating such clear instructions. A rattled man stared out of the window. Another mumbled to himself.

"Why can't you just write what you see, what you saw, huh, Toffy?" Musta said as he pulled his silver headphone plugs away from his ears. He put them back in and tapped away at his machine.

"So why don't you do what you are here for?" the lady in blue said to Loya.

Loya snapped out of silent observation.

"Oh yes." Loya perked up. "We just need to execute the next step. Right?"

"Right! So, what is the next step?" she asked.

"The step…" Loya paused and then regaining confidence continued, "to move forward."

"Ah! Movement. Yes, you know what to do then." She sat back.

"Yes. I do," Loya said and started playing around with his device.

"Pass me your screen, then," she said.

"Of course." Loya handed it to her as the car swerved through the city.

The lady smiled at the words written across his device as the car glided across the road like a robotic ballerina.

Can she tell? I have no clue what I'm doing! Loya thought.

"'Status update: Are we delivering on Plan T?'" she repeated the words on the screen.

"Everything is going according to plan," Loya said as he adjusted himself in his seat.

"I'll hold on to this screen to make sure the next steps are executed seamlessly. I'm Keba, by the way."

Musta snapped his fingers in front of the dazed man staring out of the window. "Toffy, *anything?* Want to start putting pen to paper? Nothing. Still? Toffy. Toffy. Are you even there? Stop looking at the screens. It's all distractions."

"He's going to get it when he gets that final boost," Keba said. "It's just not the time. We have to plan it right. Toffy is the final piece."

Toffy, Loya thought to himself. *Planet Rack. Plan it right. Toffy. Plan Toffy. Plan T.*

Loya was convinced he was on the right path. He didn't know what he was doing, but something strengthened his conviction that he was supposed to be there.

The vehicle came to a sliding stop.

The reflection of the lake glowed green with greed.

He had seen this before. He saw it every day, made an effort to avoid it, had built his life around distancing himself from it as much as possible. He moved along because it was part of the plan.

Loya confidently stepped out of the car.

"Ditty. Is that you?" Loya whispered from a distance.

***

Loya was politely directed into the warehouse on the coast of the green lake. "The machines are acting quite interesting," Egzabo said. "Didn't expect him to show up, but we will gladly take any input from them. Sir, this way, please."

"Yes. Let's go according to plan," Loya said.

"Mr. Ditty. After you." Keba signaled to Ditty to head into the warehouse after Loya.

"Please hand us your devices." Egzabo put her hand out. "I'll be back with these soon." She walked away with her backpack to the lit corner of the vast warehouse.

Loya tried to get Ditty's attention "Haycce. Pooiinnn. Dits. Are you hearing me?"

"Keep your voice down," Ditty responded with great caution to layer over his nervousness.

"What are you doing here?" Loya asked.

"It has to be the same thing you are doing here," Ditty responded.

"Plan T?"

"Yes, Plan T,"

"Ah, so you got the message too," Loya said, slightly disappointed he wasn't exclusively getting messages from James.

"I sure did. I'm surprised you got it too."

"Why are you surprised?" Loya shot back. "In fact, I'm confused you got the message too. I'm just glad to be executing. You are executing the plan accordingly. Right?"

"Of course I'm executing. No one got the call on my end, so I had to follow along."

"Me too. I stay ever faithful and loyal. So, what happens next?"

"The next step of the plan."

"Exactly. The next step is the next step." He tapped his feet together as Egzabo approached.

They sat up more confidently in their squeaky iron seats.

"Here you go, gentlemen," Egzabo said. She pulled her hand back as Loya tried to grab his device, giving him Ditty's instead. Then she gave Loya's device to Ditty. "Now this one's yours. And *this* one is now yours."

They were tempted to exchange them, so attached to their own devices.

"You have overcome the hardest part of the plan. You should both be very proud of yourselves."

Loya and Ditty looked at one another and smiled.

"The next step is quite easy," Egzabo explained. "Your devices have been configured with step-by-step instructions to complete—"

"Plan T," Loya said in excitement.

"Exactly. Plan T. Go on your way now, but one thing. Tell no one what's going on here. Not a soul. You are both on a special mission, and we have been prompted from the executive board level to make sure you bring this to completion. There is nothing more important."

They both nodded as Egzabo disappeared into the abyss of the middle darkness of the warehouse.

***

Toffy continued to think about his Uncle Apo. He wished he'd spent more time with him.

Why didn't he tell me he was sick? How could I have been so clueless? Why didn't I know?

He reflected on his lack of awareness, anger rising within his chest. How did he not know about his uncle's illness and Deja's unhappiness?

"How?" he asked pensively.

I wasn't listening. Accusing her of conspiring with those men. Of course she wasn't. I didn't want to hear it. But wasn't she being complacent herself? I could have been there more. Since the day I said I was in. That project. This story.

Toffy remembered the opt-in image that Musta sent him weeks before.

I'm in. In what? Committed to a story. Blocking everything out to focus on writing. Is it worth what I sacrificed? My uncle, Deja, my friends? Sarni... Maybe that's where it all changed, thinking he betrayed me. I'm the one with the betrayal here. Not being a good friend. Not being open enough. To gain something just to lose it all.

The tears had dried up, and he was dehydrated.

Did I need to get into a fight with Uncle Apo? Those men were probably trying to help him. Toffy slumped his head and looked at the floor.

"You are not ready," his uncle had said, his parting words. "Until you take full responsibility of your actions, you would not be able to truly write and complete your story."

The green light blinked on his device, so he pulled it toward him. This was the first act of motion he remembered performing since he been rendered motionless with Deja's departure.

A video message appeared. "Hey Toffy, it's Mom," she said with baggy eyes, pained. "You must have heard about your uncle. Apo was very special. One of a kind. He did things his way." She broke down crying and moved the screen away from her face, sniffling. "Your dad and I just wanted to tell you we are here for you."

A voice shot out from the background. "Are you talking to Toffy? Did you finally get him on the line? Tell him we are here to help. What did he say? Is he not responding?" Toffy's dad appeared on the video screen.

"I'm leaving a recording," Toffy's mom snapped back. Like an agent with limited time to deliver a very important message, she looked directly in her camera and said, "I love you. *We* love you. Just remember that. That's where it all starts. That's where it ends.

"Toffy!" his mother exclaimed. He moved closer to his device.

"Toffy," his mother repeated.

"Toffy," she said a third time, with a higher accent and tone. He knew exactly what she was doing.

"How many times did I call your name?" She bent her ear toward her recording device as if she expected an immediate response to her message. "Just remember that."

The message ended.

Toffy looked at his device, and he started to remember. He felt it deep in his being. He thought about his name. He thought about what his uncle had said. He had to take action, which started with accepting his responsibility.

***

Toffy took in his scattered apartment and realized how much he had let his writing consume him. He had not been taking care of his physical space. He decided to take his first step toward accepting responsibility. He stood up slowly from the floor, picked up Deja's note, folded it, and placed it neatly on the center table.

He walked around with a renewed sense of purpose. It was clear what he had to do. Clear as the air that wistfully blew into his apartment. He had to take responsibility for his actions.

"A clear space is a clear mind, or something like that," he said to himself.

Before he knew it, he had already filled up three bags with items to give away. He felt lighter at heart. There was more space in the apartment. But he could not overcome the gravity of losing Apo and Deja within days of one another.

With the sweeper in hand and a clearer mind, Toffy remembered that night at Planet Rack.

***

"Don't Give Up the Fight" traveled a great distance through soundwaves. The song bounced off the gutters, the lakes, huts, and buildings before getting to Toffy, all the way from Viginniye.

"You hear that, Musta?" Toffy had said.

"Pay attention, Toffy," Musta shot back.

Toffy looked down at his notepad, fascinated by what he had written.

They are making deals under the table,

as the boats float and bypass what is shared through under-sea cables.

Toffy smiled, amused at his two-line stanza.

"What form is that?" Musta asked, unfazed.

"What? Oh, it's something I have learned over the weeks."

Musta kept an eye on the movement of people from the underground tunnel to the single door at the beach front.

"Rhymes can make ideas stick, make them more effective, more concrete in the minds as we move through the times." Toffy smiled, waiting for Musta's validation.

The validation void cratered by the asteroid of losing his job needed to be filled, and he hoped this mission would at least sprinkle water into it. In that moment, he depended on Musta to be the water for his thorny validation-deficient garden, but Musta did not budge. Musta was not impressed, and if he was, he didn't show it.

∗∗∗

While they had left the look-out point at the helm of the frigid castle, snuck into the humid underground tunnels, saw the emptied seats with wires at the top of each back-rest, mistakenly knocked over a cold metal table, heard the dogs and guards run toward them, and picked their race toward the gates, Toffy could not get it out of his mind that Musta had not been impressed by his knowledge of words and arrangement.

What do they need me for, then? What value am I providing? These thoughts occupied Toffy's mind.

Toffy held the broom in his almost clean apartment, stuck seeking validation in a moment that might not have been the most appropriate. Toffy realized he was the reason for the incomplete mission—and not the victim.

∗∗∗

More people might be in on Plan T, Loya thought, paranoid. But there weren't any new messages, not at first. *What am I supposed to do now? And what's Ditty up to? He left so quickly.*

His device vibrated and instructed his every move: "Go straight. Turn left. Turn right." Loya increased pace to keep up with the tempo, the notifications coming too fast.

Buy clothes. Buy packaged foodstuff. Trash the world. He had purchased what he was told to purchase and then took it all and threw it into the lake, loyal to the instructions. *Go to work. Sit down. Do nothing.* Loya did it all. *Stand up. Sit down. Walk straight. Open documents. Type this. Type that. Pack it all up, and don't forget to save.* Step after step, Loya did exactly what the instructions demanded.

No, he was not going to let James down. Plan T must be executed.

"Close your eyes. Open your eyes. Press Send."

Loya blinked and authorized the message. The sent documents confirmed "Delivered." Doing God's work.

"Great job, Loya. Plan T hands you a gold star."

He watched his screen carefully, waiting for his next instruction. Nothing came in for a few minutes. He relaxed and slowly fell asleep at his desk, drenched in sweat.

***

"We need to move faster now," Musta said.

"Do we?" Keba responded. "The same who talks to their device is the same who codes the vibes. Everything is going as it should. We are who we are."

"Toffy just needs to embrace himself for who he is."

"The diverse mix of our personal authenticity makes the collective whole. *Something* will get him across the line," she said with a smile. "Navigating that line makes him who he is. He just needs to tap in to that."

***

What was I really writing?

Fiction, nonfiction?
Sad or happy?
A story without direction.
Can't even call it a story.

Toffy pulled out the box where he kept the notepads. Like a true engineer, he had labelled every notepad with the date when he started writing. He looked at the stack and was amazed and, at the same time, overwhelmed by a bulk of writing that seemed incoherent.

He pulled out the first at the bottom of the pile, labelled:

February 20, 2049.

He'd written a single sentence boldly on the entire page: *AND SO IT BEGINS.*

Eagerness had consumed him with the fresh perspective of life beaming out of his body through his pen.

He flipped the page, thrilled how each word led him to want to read the next. He remembered how liberating his writing style was then. A whole lot of free association representing an idea or a mood that switched seamlessly to the next. The next five notepads had similar stream-of-consciousness writing.

Toffy did not think it was great but authentic. *Real.* It captured feelings, emotion.

The seventh notepad was slightly different, as if he was writing to himself. Every sentence was a call to action, an indication of a change toward seriousness or structure; every letter was pregnant with intention, birthing the succeeding letter.

Okay. This might be something here.

This generational flow of words made him sit up straighter in his chair. The notepad ended with a poem, the first Toffy had written since he said he was in.

The next thirteen notepads were all filled with poems. Some two pages long and some only three words. Poems that made him happy and poems that made him sad. Poems that displayed his dexterity with his manipulation of rhythm and others completely off beat. He read each as he sat at his table.

This must have been my prose phase, he thought as he flipped through the next sixteen notepads.

He read all the stories he had written and his experimentation with different styles. He had become more comfortable writing as the length of each story increased. The last story he wrote required the final three notepads. Reading through each page brought him joy, but he still could not tell if he was just writing for the fun of writing or for a purpose.

The next notepad was quite different, along with the remaining eight. No dates written on the front.

What's in here?

Toffy opened the notepad to the first page and read about his day, like a journal entry. Each day he'd written what had fascinated him and what was on his mind, and much of it about the experience of writing. The process brought him peace.

So many questions. Anything about Uncle Apo in here?

As he read each line, he wished to come across something about his uncle, anything. It would have brought him some consolation. His journaling was a way of telling the story of his life, but he'd never thought his life was interesting.

After going through all the books, Toffy was surprised that hours had flown by and happy to have noticed a continuous improvement in his work. However, he was still unsure as to *why* he went through the entire process.

What am I really writing for? Maybe if I focused on my work, I could at least get my water working, fix my payment access, get my life in order, regain my social credit score, get Deja back...

He needed validation that would bring him back to a base he understood. He craved the comfort he had before.

Doing more? Maybe I shouldn't have.

CHAPTER 23

―

I have to figure a way out of—

Deja's thought was interrupted as the humid day condensed a stream of sweat that tickled down from the top of her neck to the mid-section of her back.

"Focus, Deja. Focus," she said and slapped herself across the face.

The owner of the restaurant came back. "Everything okay there? And you still haven't answered. Can I get you a drink?" She'd brought her a menu over thirty minutes ago.

Deja forced a smile. "Nothing yet. Thank you."

The smile disappeared once the lady turned around to the next table in the café.

"I'm sure *you* are ready for another drink," the owner said loudly enough for Deja to hear.

"Sure. I'll take another one," another customer said.

Deja was too consumed in thoughts to pay attention.

"Someone told me to come here," she whispered to herself.

She looked around the bustling café at the mountaintop of Staple City. Her dream job. It was where she felt she could make the most impact.

She searched for clues on the wooden chairs, the bulletin board at the corner of the room, the bar filled with clear bottles containing local Staple rum. The activities of the café were usual.

"I'm here for a reason," Deja whispered. "Someone said, 'just find your way to the top and—'"

"—find the center table," a husky voice completed Deja's muted mumbling. "I'm glad you found it easily."

To Deja's amazement and complete recollection, a man in a khaki shirt and shorts pulled out the seat next to her and then slammed a stack of loosely tied papers on the table.

"I need a drink. Anyone taking orders here?" he asked, looking around the room.

"Did someone say orders?" the café owner came zooming toward the table.

"Yes. Can I get your top-of-the-line Staple rum?"

"Coming right up. What about you, hun?"

Deja responded with a daze, her eyes still fixated on the documents on the table.

"Still not ready?" the owner said. The smirk on her face was more rude.

"No, I'm fine," Deja finally said.

"It's always a hike getting up here," the man said. "Why do you look so shocked? You were the one who asked to be here. He pulled his hair back to reveal a protruded forehead. "You and your elite team, drinking your corporate selves away."

She had increased her drinking ever since she'd moved from J City to Staple City.

"Yeah, you said you were oh-so different... Oh, thank you," he said and accepted his drink, which came with a cane straw. "You and your social helpers," the man took a generous swig, "always trying to help by causing damage so you can be there to help. How about you just don't do damage in the first place?"

Deja stopped him, frustrated by his unwavering tone. "What are you on about?"

"My boss—well, *ex*-boss," the man continued, "told me the plan was in play."

"What plan?"

"Plan T. They said you were a crucial part. Even yesterday, you told me you were part of the plan."

Deja did not acknowledge nor deny what was said; she could hardly remember anything that had happened beyond leaving her apartment with her colleagues and jumping out of bed, rushing to make this appointment at Staple City Café happening right now.

"Anyhoo," the man continued, "I'm done. You are all one and the same. I was told to meet up with you at the bar and hand you these documents, but you were so wasted the other night I thought it would be better handing it off to you while you're clear-headed. Are you trying to run away from something?" He took another swig of his drink. The smell of rum mixed with cigarettes intensified in his breath. "I've seen people drinking like you and your girls last night, and I've been there. People only drink like that when they are running away from something—a haunting secret, misplaced identity."

He's right, but only half-right. Deja felt ashamed. *I know it looks like I abandoned my life and I'm running away from everyone. But no. I'm in search of something.*

"Hey, I'm not here to judge." He took a bigger gulp, and the blood vessel visible on his neck looked like it was about to pop. "This life is one big ride with twists and turns." He pointed at the documents on the table, laughing. "Now, *that's* a twist. I know there was a plan, but handing you *this*? That's twisted. Either someone messed up somewhere, or someone decided to go rogue. Whatever it is, it's beyond my pay grade. Actually, I'm not even getting paid anymore. So, I wish you all the best. My task here is done. Take care of the bill."

The man in the brown khaki attire stood up and emptied the last drops of his drink into his mouth.

He tapped Deja on the shoulder and whispered into her ear, "Keep that discreet as you walk out of here." Then he tapped her on the shoulder twice and walked out.

"Hey, hey!" the bar owner shouted. "Where's he going? Who's going to pay for the drink? *You*? Are you ready to order yet?"

Deja pulled the documents to her lap and responded, "Yes."

Her head still throbbed from the night before.

***

As he started feeling comfortable about quitting his writing while cleaning his apartment, Toffy saw a blue and red ornament on the floor.

Hmmm, I most have missed this earlier.

He picked it up and immediately remembered.

Isn't this the same ornament the security men wore at the J Event? No way. Yes. I knew it. What do they know? Why would they be trying to stop me? Is it the story I'm writing?

A refreshing memory of his uncle came to mind: "*Say yes to this moment.*" Apo's face played back in Toffy's mind as a loop: "*In a moment when you want to run away or say no, say yes to that moment.*"

A smile developed across Toffy's face.

"That's what they want you to do," another mental replay of his uncle continued. *"It's all part of the plan. They want you to continue saying no to the moment. To shy away from the future. To accept the current moment as something that is unchangeable, something that cannot be transformed."*

Something from a distance made him exit memory lane. It sounded like his uncle. He moved closer to the door, but the sound seemed to be coming from the opposite end of the room. Toffy ran toward it and heard it clearer now, his uncle's voice.

It was not a memory. It was not a voice coming from the room. The voice was in his head, planted there as a seed that only sprouted in this moment. The right combination of conditions had germinated it clearly in Toffy's mind.

"The story is not out yet," the voice of Apo in Toffy's head resonated. *"The people have stopped listening to you. You are lost in the details. That's their plan. They want everyone confused. Confusion is control. The truth can ruin the entire administration. It can bring down the hierarchy. It can shatter the system."*

Toffy knew it was supposed to happen this way.

"Say yes to this moment."

Toffy stood taller, remembering the secrets his uncle had passed on to him. This was a moment to rise to the opportunity.

"One of the storyteller's secrets is to be motivated and truly believe in their ideas. Embrace the moment. Live in the present. Tell a story."

That urge to write rekindled. He turned on his instrumental album and increased the volume.

***

James was infuriated. He had received the report that the J Men had raided Toffy's apartment to find incriminating evidence, but unfortunately they couldn't get to it fast enough because one of the neighbors was snooping around, so they had to leave early.

***

Decades earlier, James the fiftieth had been glad he had an heir to take over J Enterprise and ultimately keep the legacy going. Pride, however, got in the way. He was not going to make it easy for his son. He still wanted him to work hard to gain his respect. James the fifty-first's rise to the top was easy, but not as easy as it should have been.

During his first five years, he was never acknowledged by his father in the office. Everyone knew he was the son of the boss, but there was an unwritten rule to never speak of their relationship. James did not want to be looked at as his father's protégé or just another entitled child of a rich man. He behaved recklessly.

Worst of all, James had picked up the habit of burning down buildings on the lower end of J City. James LI learned about this over lunch with someone who worked in the security department. It was a thrill.

One day, James and his colleague were caught on the camera at a building that went down in flames on the lower end. This was years before it was simply named Low Town, at least the first iteration of it. After they were apprehended and interrogated, James was released on the first night, but his colleague was held at the station.

When he stepped into the back of the vehicle that picked him up, he was surprised to find his father in the back seat.

"This behavior is going to stop right now," James Sr. had said with a deep tone and stern look. "No heir of the empire should be picked up at the police station. Do you know how many calls I had to make to get you out tonight and wipe your record? Well, this has been taken care of, and it will not be repeated again. Is that clear?"

"Yes, it is," James whispered. "What about— "

"He will be fine. He has confessed to burning down the building and will be spending some time upstate."

"He confessed? But…"

"But what?"

"We… He's… We did… He's a friend, and I can't—" James stammered through his words as he pieced it together that his colleague had taken all the blame for their actions. For an act he had requested.

"A friend? There are no *friends*, boy. Only assets and liabilities. Got that?" the father snapped and looked intently into his son's eyes to make sure his message was delivered clearly. "You are not going to ever see him again."

"Yes, sir."

***

"Burn his apartment down. Kill him if you have to," James had said.

He had ordered Sarni to do whatever was necessary to stop Toffy's story from getting out.

Sarni never expected it to get this far. He admired James but didn't expect him to take such a drastic stance on Toffy, his friend, his competition. Conflicted, he didn't know if he could follow through with the task.

I've done all his dirty work. I betrayed Toffy, fine! But to take his life? No. No. That's taking it too far. That's some street life shit. The life I have spent all this time running away from.

Sarni's father had gone to prison for ten years for partaking in arson and multiple cases of domestic violence, and if there was one thing Sarni did not want to be like, it was his father.

For the first time, he did not think so highly of James. He saw in James what he had disliked in his father all these years.

The role model he had always looked up to as a father figure was now like the father he hated. He couldn't shake off the look James had on his face when he'd said those words: "Burn his apartment down. Kill him if you have to."

Sarni thought of his mother gently rubbing his face, a memory of her.

"You really remind me of him," she had said. "You are not so different, the two of you. Your hearts are in the right place, but—"

"I'm *nothing* like him," Sarni had said, back in the moment, jerking out of his seat. "*Nothing.*"

He started crying thinking about it. He had become exactly what he did not want to be.

***

Ditty was in his own mind. That's where he was most of the time. That's why he moved like a machine. The same part of his mind that separated him from other animals entrapped him in continuous thought.

"What are you looking at?" Ditty asked the man at the tip of the lake.

"Nothing," the man said feebly.

Once he got the plan, Ditty knew what he had to do.

He took it for what it was—*a plan.*

He didn't think he was the only one clued into the plan. No, not like Loya. He was quite the opposite. He didn't value the fact that he was the only one who knew about the plan. He couldn't care less. He knew he had a plan, the same way *every single person in this world* had a plan. He just knew his plan had to be marginally more beneficial than the next man's.

"*Me no care about the next man,*" Ditty sang and walked with purpose. "*Me no care about your texting.*"

He could choose when to listen to the vibrations of notifications, a constant battle between Ditty and his mind and his devices.

Who wins what battle, you never know.
But his plan is for him to forever grow
Power across different locations
While he lives in homeless adjacent
Palaces paved in face less
phyllic-built binary age less
Dynasties of hatred
Separate the low from the
Highnesses.
In High Town where
they wear the fine dresses.

Ditty heard his soundtrack in his mind and smiled.

The exact tool for oppression? Separate people. Break up communities.

He scanned his badge and entered the glass building where his office was. He left the streets behind him.

"We are not in the same community," Ditty echoed. "Not me and you. You. Where? Here? At all. Never before." Ditty waved his hands across his face, as he finished singing. "Slipping? Me? Never."

Once in his office, Ditty jumped on his desk.

"Tripping? We? No. Clever?" he sang and unbuttoned his tie. "Gripping scenes, I miss with dreams of one day just pulling the lever. Send her out. That's true she gasta go. Pen it down. Initiate the boys to roll. Ya hear me now."

There's an end to this in me getting my way up.
Duplicate Plan T, advancing rotations.
Accumulation that's all that's there for me.
So I execute to the plan faithfully.
T's deep flu season, please keep your distance.
Everybody got to sow, but I plan to reap the biggest.
It is me versus ego.

You hear me now

Ditty sat and finalized Plan T: *separate, separate, separate.*

He finalized the agreement to transfer Deja to Staple City, surprised he even had the power and authority to do that.

He smiled. He was on the move. He was on his way up.

***

Deja rang out when she got back to her apartment.

She knew she had to put this information together. That was her prompt when she signed up for the "Ni mi" project. She had spent her time compiling documents in the archives of the J City Papers, which only special people had access to. There was a room no one had access to, and she knew this document came from that room.

   She compiled it and sent out a message.

Check the recipe
I've been here from time
Whenever Dem sick
Me dey give them medicine

From the greenest lake
And the ship that takes
Them people just
To boost Dem income stream

This stream of thought
Push back to what you bought
When it was time for action
You know that I fought

For the very connection
I send you vibrations
To aid your introspection
I lend you my equations

As formulaic like lives
Lost in search of liberation
Lives liable due to fouls
By tribal eradication

No healthcare, devastation

Autonomous self-driven
With no education

I vibe this to
Connect with
Triangulations
Located in the
Dry angles facing
Wet touch God love
Vocation outsourced
Smoked up more buds
Saw more separations

You make it past the line
You know your heart is mine
I see you
You see me
Sitting even
Distantly
Oddly enough
You do what you
Have to do to grow
I send this message
To let you know

Let the light glow.
Let your light glow
Let your light glow
Let your light glow
Let your light glow

Sun Ra

Shango
Olatunji
Deja
Keba
Musta

She paused and then continued.

Napo Republic
My flow be bubbly
Like champagne
Drank by Ricky Bobby

My life be private
But I dey live for public
Holiday where you dey
I dey for bar, I dey drink e tonic
For that left corner
With fluorescent light
And that blue door
Na where I dey
I dey hold my head
When you reach the gate
Just blow your horn

I want to talk
About all the renting
The people fired
Up now their venting
Manufactured media
Manufacturing
Your consenting

Condescending to
Our dissenting
Sent in vibrations
Embedded in centuries
From ancestral
Continuous
Quotations

CHAPTER 24

———

Toffy was still looking for evidence in his apartment, convinced J Enterprise was linked to the raid and the men in white. He sat in front of his screen, slightly defeated.

What do they want from me and my story?

He remembered the words of his uncle: "A true storyteller believes in their personal legend. They use the challenges in their backstory as fuel to overcome any obstacle and come out on the other side victorious. They rise from the depths of darkness to emerge with the light that provides illumination for all that read their stories. And these stories have to be told."

He was reminded of the three-phase attribute. To start with the *why* and then build a structure of the information in a way that is easily understandable and digestible, before focusing on *how* the best stories tell themselves. There had to be a personal legend emerging to write a story worth reading.

He received an unexpected email.

Subject: This may help you with your story.

What is this?

Toffy opened the images and files attached in the message. *Oh, lord! These are damaging. The exploits, documented. J Enterprise. You have been hiding a lot of secrets. Someone else knew. Wait? Who sent this? This goes back to the beginning.*

The message included a short text: "You are the only one in the position to write this story." It reminded him about his conversation with Uncle Apo at the hospital after he'd fainted.

"Toffy, you are in a unique position to be the only one to tell a certain story."

A sign that this was what was needed of him.

I have to put this out there.

He began writing and compiling the information, weaving it into the story he was already writing. He wrote vigorously through the night, playing the instrumentals in the background on repeat.

"The mission will not be televised," Toffy wrote as the vibrations activated frequency nodes in his brain.

He felt time-traveled; distant but also so near. He was not only hearing music. He was feeling it, and those feelings moved *his* feelings. His mind cleared. The pathway had been parted to let the words flow to paper.

This little story of mine, I'm going to make it sublime, Toffy's subconscious hummed.

A few minutes passed, and Toffy was already halfway through a page. No hesitation. No judgment. There wasn't the little voice in his head saying, *"That doesn't make any sense."* Even when that voice considered appearing, Toffy had trained himself to push through and ignore the gravity of that voice.

"It all started at the pyramid," Toffy wrote at the beginning of the third page as he entered a state of unhindered writing. "Where it starts is also where it ends."

Toffy pulled in ideas from scrambled notes, poems, hand-outs, flyers, images in his head, High Town, Low Town, Finer Town, the green river, the plastic dumps in the gutter. He wrote as the instrumentals looped and left him in a transient state of contemplative meditation. He deciphered words that kept ciphers of birds flying with wings of coded messages.

He flew around to get a bird's eye view. There were no lines that divided. He felt the connection. High, low, middle—all connected. It was all one, and he was one with it all.

For some reason, all he had written made sense now.

It all plays a crucial piece to the puzzle of the entire story.

The words also came out more fluently. Everything before was practice for this moment, sharpening his vessel for the appropriate story to write. The practice had prepared him for this spontaneity.

***

The Vibro Council knew Ditty was so in love with himself and his mind that he could not be relied upon to carry out their instructions, so they made sure all logistical efforts were sent to Loya's device as well. Both devices were disconnected from the consolidated cloud and now plugged into the radio cloud—a Wi-Fi network with a long-chain of cellphone repeaters that stretched from Viginniye to High Town—built by the Vibro Council. It allowed the council and its members to send coded message under the radar.

Egzabo saw only zeros and ones as she typed. She set up parameters and instructions that could only be triggered if certain events happened beforehand. She ran her simulation through a variety of scenarios, not quite sure what was going to happen at the J Switch event.

She hummed her thoughts in her head as she typed:

Open door for the band

As the time proceeds forward like an hourglass of sand
When the door is locked, open it up for the band.

Stop the announcer from interrupting the music.

Stay quiet, keep calm, and impede those that refuse it
While from afar, stay true and don't stop the music.

If going remote, you'll see what I've seen
Then switch out the mode to that of the white screen.

The lines of code captured her thoughts and logic. She even typed in intentional mistakes to make the instructions less robotic and more human. She pushed her instructions out, and they were dissipated with time to Loya and Ditty.

***

It was a solemn, suspiciously quiet evening in J City because of the gathering at the J Switch event.

"Attention, everyone," James's biographer meekly said into the microphone off stage. "This is a moment for which we have all gathered here." He fumbled to get the papers in front of him in order. "I have been tasked to"—he cleared his throat—"to make sure we stick to an agenda as follows."

The biographer leaned in to get a clearer view of the outlined paper handed to him before he was shoved onto the stage by Chez.

"The biographer steps in…"

He caught himself. He knew he had made a mistake. He was not supposed to read out the hand-written notes on the agenda.

"We then move on to the J Social presentation," he continued. "Afterward, we will have a live review of some of the innovation that has been undertaken by J Enterprise in the last five years. Finally," the biographer adjusted his glasses and pushed them snuggly above the indent on his nose, "we have the *Reveal: What Was Once Stealth Shall Be Seen in the Light*, presented by the Chief Initiative Officer."

Chez looked around the room to make sure everyone knew he was the one being referenced.

"Then finally, *finally*," the biographer said with more decibels in his unprojected voice, "we will hear from James himself. He will push the button that provides the switch. His greatness will be televised. I have been working with James, and what I can tell you all today is that…"

A rapturous standing ovation swept the room while he kept talking into the microphone. He was slow to realize that his microphone had been turned off and the J Social presentation had already begun on the screen behind him.

"Get off the stage." Chez signaled to the biographer.

***

In the front corner of the room, a musical band was setting up for the events of the night. The band included an instrumentalist, a lyricist, a coder, and a vibrationalist, who also provided impromptu body vibration spa services.

The spiral-haired lady, Keba, was behind it all. The Vibro Council had found a way to get into the event. They knew exactly what was being planned. They knew the unfair advantage button was about to be hyped up, which would rapidly accelerate the unfair advantage between the haves and have-nots. The button that would further bifurcate High from Low Town.

"Everyone, get in position. That time is slowly approaching." She signaled to the band.

The button was designed by the few to favor a few. Deleteron, which would be launched afterward, would have the immediate revisionist history machine to prevent new perspectives and stories from being heard.

***

James was about to further consolidate the little pieces of fragmented power left by the end of the J Switch event. He just couldn't enjoy the moment. His mind was on Toffy.

He imagined Toffy's story taking a life of its own and undoing what he had planned. He remained silent as he sat in the middle of the room with a blank face while watching the J Social presentation.

***

Toffy was in his apartment writing up a storm. He could not stop.

Ohhhh! There is so much to write about!

He was also perceptive of the unusual silence that engulfed the city. A mixture of anxiety and excitement filled Toffy's being as he wrote each letter of each word. He had moved from notepad to a vintage laptop that Musta and the council gave him.

This is horrible. But I facilitated building this world. I can do good by writing this, exposing this system

He wrote with confidence and conviction.

One. Two. Three. He communicated his perception.

While writing, someone knocked on his door. For some reason, he thought it could have been Deja, but immediately knew it wasn't her; she had a softer touch, her knock not so aggressive.

***

The device dictated, and Loya followed every order: "Go away. Come around. Go. Sit. Carry phone. Switch the screen. On the table there..." Loya stopped and switched his device with the screen in front of Ditty.

He was so eager to get rid of the device. Ever since he left the warehouse, it controlled his entire being. It made him a digital zombie. He wanted his life back. Just twenty minutes ago he had opened the back door to the event for the vibro backup band. He knew exactly what he had to do. The instructions were clear: "Stand up. Go downstairs and open door."

Once he carried out the last instruction and exchanged devices with Ditty, he sat back and tried to enjoy the show.

I did my best. Let me live myself. I'm loyal to myself. Let's move.

***

"Yes, right there," the announcer replied. "You just keep your eye on the screen and spin away. Starting in three... two... one... Go."

The employee-contestant flailed as she spun the wheel with intensity, her face plastered on the screen.

"Crank. Crank. Crank," the announcer said and waved his hand like a composer to the crowd to get their vocal support.

"Crank. Crank. Crank," the crowd joined in as the employee increased her spinning.

"How many houses are going to pop up on the screen?" the announcer asked. "Will she be able to match the number of tenants displaced by the last spinner, or will she be stuck here without any new developments?"

The contestant did not want to lose this game; even worse, she didn't want to come out pointless.

"There we go!" yelled the announcer. "One development erected. Sixty original tenants displaced. Ten new apartments on the market. Rent value increased by forty points. Oh, it's *another* one," the announcer said, more excited. "She is really working now. Cranking away. Look at all the sweat. She is really getting into this. Another four developments on the screen. Three hundred and eighty indigenous persons displaced. Thirty-five new luxury apartments. Eighty points increase in rent value. Amazing."

The lady spun the crank in a frenzy. She was in a trance. *Spin. Crank. Spin. Crank. Spin. Crank.*

The announcer bounced around the stage while James and the councilmen looked on. "I think she might be going for the bonus round. Let's see if she gets it. She is *so* close, and... *Bull's eye!*"

The room burst out in yells and applause.

"She did it. A bonus gem. Take a look at the screen. Damaging stories all around about those displaced. The victims have unwillingly become the perpetuators." The announcer walked over to the employee-contestant who had now collapsed on the floor, soaking in her own sweat. "Get up, my dear. We are here to help you. Someone come get this lady," he said to the security at the side of the stage. "She outdid herself," he said to the crowd as he looked around the room. "Can anyone beat her record? We are here. They are there. There are more people to be displaced. There are more damaging stories to tell. Many more to be dis-empowered. Who wants to step up and crank this machine as we build up to the final switch?"

The line of employee-contestants had grown.

***

James impatiently looked at his mobile screen. "No updates," he said and stood up. "When you want something done properly, you should do it yourself," he said to Sarni. "Come, we are going for a ride."

"Sir. Sir. Sir. Where are you going?" Ditty ran toward him and tried to ask the question covertly. "We need you here." He moved closer to James's ear and pulled out a white screen from his right pocket. "You know, to push the final switch."

"I'm going to have to finish this remotely." James grabbed the white screen out of Ditty's hand.

"But—"

"Shhhh. I don't want to hear from you. Let's go, Sarni."

"You don't understand. You have—"

"I said stop talking." James looked at Ditty sternly.

"Yes, sir," Ditty said and unconsciously bowed his head.

"Let's go, Sarni."

***

The J Men were already at Toffy's place. Sarni hoped they found what they were looking for and left without anything drastic happening. He had put them on the mission. He knew they weren't flesh and blood, so they were the best for the job. They couldn't be prosecuted. At worst, they'd get decommissioned. He kept looking at his device, hoping for an update.

He sat in the back seat of the car with James at the event center. The vehicle was engulfed in silence, and Sarni did not know exactly where they were going. The night was foggy, and the car drove at a speed slower than the limit.

"What drives you, Sarni?" James asked as he looked out the window.

"Huh?" Sarni responded, even though he'd heard the question clearly.

"What motivates you? It's very important for a man to know what motivates him." He could not stand waiting for Sarni to answer. "Can you say you fully know yourself if you don't know what motivates you? What gets you up in the morning? What keeps you going even when all challenges and roadblocks are thrown your way?

"I knew from a very young age what motivated me. It was not what inherently motivated me, but it was a motivation that was imposed on me. When you are born into a family like mine, motivation is inherited, like a gene in your DNA," James proclaimed with a tone of resignation. "*I* know what motivates you."

Sarni looked at him with some apprehension.

"That's why it was so easy for me to get you to do whatever I want," James said cautiously. "You don't want to be a failure like your dad, the *alcoholic*."

Sarni felt so exposed. He knew James was right.

"Knowing your main motivation makes you easy to control," James said, as if he were talking to a helpless pet. "This story Toffy is writing—I don't understand it. I don't know the motivation behind it. I don't understand *his* motivations, and that keeps me up at night. But what I know is that he is driven by something I don't understand. I can't control that which I don't understand."

James looked out of the window again.

"And I want to control it… I want to control it *all*. That's why we're heading to Toffy's place, to make sure we stop him from writing his story. Stop him from spreading false information about J Enterprise. Control his actions. Make sure I keep rising to the top and stay there. Number one. *My* motivations are very clear. And yours are too. That's why you are here with me. You always wanted a father figure you could look up to. Your father was actually not so bad, just a case of misfortune."

Sarni perked up in his seat.

"In fact, you are very much like him. Twenty-five years ago, while we were both at J Enterprise, he and I set a warehouse on fire. He was caught… well, let's just say he took the fall for it. He spent two years in prison, and I thought he would come back to work with me. I'm not sure what happened to him in that prison, though. He came out, and all he wanted to do was drink. He did not want anything to do with me. I tried to get him a job, but he never wanted anything. I haven't seen him for twenty years. I heard he never recovered from all that happened. Well, now *you* are here. Walking the same path as your father, even though you spent your entire life saying you did not want to be like him."

Sarni sat there, startled and weak. Speechless.

The knock on the door pierced the silence that engulfed the J City night. This made Toffy very tense as he saved his document and walked slowly toward the door. He decided to look out the window first.

He was glad all the lights in the apartment were off. He closed his laptop, the only source of light. From the two nights when the electricity went out in his apartment, he had become familiar with navigating in the dark apartment.

Someone's shadow shifted underneath the door. A man. The presence was heavy. He pulled the blinds aside to peep through the window and look down onto the lifeless and eerie street. A vehicle was unusually parked right in front of his apartment.

It must be the J Men at the door.

The knock this time had become extremely impatient. Whoever was knocking was not there to hang out or have a polite evening discussion. As he stood next to the window, staring at the door and hoping the person would leave, a set of keys jiggled.

Keys? An override, probably!

Toffy grabbed his laptop off his desk and ran to his room. He stood there silently.

The door clicked open. A chill ran up his back. The only thing between him and whoever was looking for him was his bedroom door. He stood there silently.

Multiple footsteps stumped in his apartment.

There must be at least two of them. Metal boots. Definitely J Men. Maybe just Baron Wards. They are one and the same, anyway. One just more diabolical.

Toffy walked into the bathroom, locked the door, and began frantically writing on the floor. They broke things and vandalized his place, but that didn't stop him from writing. He kept at it… He hadn't finished…

CHAPTER 25

Everything is under control here.

Ditty typed.

The plan is going according to plan. Just one slight request. I know it might not be my place to say this, but please be ready when it's go-time.

Muidi projected her face out of her device, leaned over, and asked Ditty, "Why wouldn't he be ready?"

Loya wrote:

He is always ready. We know you will be ready. Anyone questioning your readiness is not ready for the evolution. I remain fully loyal to your cause.

Bunajo replied:

We will push the switch when the right time comes. We await your directive.

"So where is he?" Muidi asked

"Who?" Ditty said, nervously looking at his screen under the table.

"James."

"Sssshhhh. He is going to activate the switch remotely."

There was more displacement of indigenous people from their homes as the line of contestants to crank the machine had become endless.

"Wow," Loya said. "Look at all the displacement. The stories of victimization. It's only about to get worse."

Chez walked over to the table with the Low and High councilmen. For this event, they had put their differences aside. They were on the same team today. They had always been on the same team.

"This initiative is about to come full circle," Chez whispered as he stood between a seated Ditty and Muidi. "So, where is James?"

The councilmen focused all their attention on their devices as if they hadn't heard.

***

"Are we good to go?" Musta whispered into the makeshift microphone he pulled out of his back pocket. He and the Vibro Council were on stage as the night band. They called themselves the A-Switch Groovers.

A response came in on the internal headset of each member. "Yes, we just need the code to activate," a crackling voice projected. "Once we have that, man, yeah, good to go."

The lyricist, the vibrationalist, and Musta all looked toward the young lady with the screen. Egzabo knew it was her time to initiate. She got on her device and started writing: 01001001.

"Yah, man," the voice shouted out in their earpiece. "Good to go. Feel the vibration."

Each person on stage started hearing the drums from a distant land. All in communication. Each took up their positions.

The vibrationalist plucked at the strings. Musta tapped away at the pads on his metal board. The coder kept typing away.

01101100 01101111 01110110 01100101

The lyricist grabbed the microphone and started emitting words with pleasant rhythms.

Everyone at the event stopped what they were doing and swayed in synchrony, their eyes glued to the stage.

"What the hell is going on?" Chez said. "This is not part of the program." He walked toward the stage, and a crowd formed that kept him at the back. "Get the announcer. I'm the one who made this initiative take off. This is not part of the initiative."

***

More than two people had walked into Toffy's apartment. They shuffled around after they closed and locked the door behind them. One said, "Find the laptop. It's gray."

Toffy held the laptop in his hand.

The radio cloud. The rebel sounds.

He looked through the crack of the door. Three men, all in white suits.

Oh, lord! They have come for my story. Toffy watched.

One of them stood guard at the door. Panic shot through his body. He was not too concerned for his life. He was concerned that he would not be able to finish his story, that the world would not get to hear the true antics of J Enterprise.

He remembered what his uncle once said: *The people in power want to control your story; they don't want your story to be heard. You have to fight to get your story out.*

Toffy would fight the only way he knew how to—with his words.

His best option was to lock himself in the bathroom. He walked back silently and locked the door again.

I need to focus.

He sat on the floor and opened his laptop, looking below the door to check whether the light had attracted any attention. It was difficult to write with the men turning his apartment upside down.

Stay low. Don't make any sudden movements.

He knew the limitations of the J Men. He typed, making sure only his fingers moved. Sweat built up on his forehead.

Observe, orient, decide, and act.

He was on the final act of his story, and all he had to do was finish.

Toffy pressed his ears against the cold wall of the bathroom.

Beyond the peripheral of the shuffling and dumping was something else, out of place but very familiar. With the sounds came vibrations.

These instrumentals are just for practice, he remembered Musta saying. *When it's time to go live, it's time to go.*

The same vibrations he had felt from the twelve-track instrumental Musta had handed him earlier came to him now, but this time the sounds were live. The drums came from the east. The strings came from the west.

All right!

Messages were encoded in these vibrations. The sounds and activities happening in the close proximity of his apartment had been drowned out, yet Toffy recognized the soft and hard beats as binary and felt them through his entire being, through his bones, his arms like drumsticks tapping them out against his leg. Sets of eight, or eighth notes, or maybe one and the same.

01001101 01110101 01110011 01101001

01100011 00100000 01110101 01101110

01101001 01110100 01100101 01110011

00100001

Toffy started writing.

He typed. He wrote. He listened. He hammered out letters to the rhythm of the beat, as though in a loop.

And he let his mind wander, the words writing themselves, as he reflected on how he may have overdone it too fast. He needed to find a pace that didn't trip his face. He traced his way back but could not brace the chase back that was about to happen way back in the future with Bach listening to three stacks of Da Grin.

And don Jazzy so not raspy with my flow
Got to move through faster than go slow
Down from the bridge to Gbagada come gather
What is on the road two hours up in Ikeja that's eko
For you, you see
The place blend vibrantly
Silently my thoughts move
One higher plane but violently
Ever so often
Me get to mi puffin

Send a few emails
Corporate ragga muffin

Toffy mustered as he sat on the ground. The J Men couldn't hear him from the other room. He covered himself with a noise cancellation cloak made out of metamaterial on the outside and aerogel on the inside. It came with the vintage laptop from the council.

How could they possibly miss this? Toffy thought as he simultaneously typed away and dictated without notice, both listening to his instrumentals and writing with fluency.

He had the right gadgets.

***

"There are J Men upstairs right now in Toffy's apartment, but we are just here to make sure the job is done properly," James said to Sarni as they sat in the car out front.

Sarni was in shock after hearing that James and his dad were friends growing up. His world flipped upside down. *Deceived.* For the first time in his life, he wanted to sit down and talk to his dad. He wanted to apologize for all the years of scorn and condemnation. His respect for James diminished.

"Let's go," James said.

The leash he had on Sarni was not fully severed; if anything, it had been strengthened. Sarni stepped out of the car in a trance.

"You know what," James said, "you stay down here. I'll go upstairs."

Sarni did exactly as James instructed.

James walked toward the building and stopped after a few strides.

"Stockholm syndrome!" James yelled out. He stopped, turned around, and stared Sarni down with disgust.

He slowly walked back toward him. Sarni trembled.

"You are not really concerned about your job. That's not it. The oppressed are endeared to their oppressors." He pulled Sarni, palming the back of his head until both their foreheads rubbed against one another.

"The duality," James continued, "in their consciousness makes it hard for them to be angry at their oppressors. They want to be like their oppressor. Every chance they can. How can you ever be liberated when you want to be just like me?" James growled and pushed Sarni's face away.

The truth was littered in clear words; surrounded by them, Sarni had nowhere else to go.

He circled around in one spot, melted by the fact that he had become exactly like his father. He wasn't sure what he was angrier about: that he was no better than his father, or that it took him this long to realize it.

He kept spinning.

***

James walked in on the J Men searching the living room vigorously.

"You still haven't found it?" he asked in a contentious voice. "I knew you still wouldn't be able to deliver. That's why I came. To make sure the job is done. Have you searched his room?"

"Yes. We checked," one responded hesitantly.

James did not trust that answer. He walked into Toffy's room and looked back at the J Men.

"This room has not been touched."

"Our instruction was to search the room, not the rooms," one of the J Men said.

Idiot machines.

"Let me give it a quick run-through, if that's the updated instruction," another one said.

James stopped him from entering. "No, not yet. Let me take a look around first," he said, slightly fascinated by the contents of the room. He closed the door behind him and walked around. Toffy's room was both messy and tidy. There was a constant conflict James could not wrap his mind around.

He sat at the desk, wiggled around in the chair. For a brief moment, he wondered what it felt like to be Toffy. He would never admit this to anyone, but a part of him wanted what Toffy had. He had suppressed that side of himself a long time ago. He opened the drawers, and they were empty except for the last, which held an empty box.

James's focus turned to the bookshelf.

Who has a bookshelf in his bedroom?

He went to it, amused. The books ranged from serious, engaging, and technical to lighthearted and *unserious*: *The Art of War; Guns, Germs and Steel; The Goal; The Art of Rap; Poetry Handbook Condensed; Things Fall Apart; The Creator's Code; Rules for the Dance; My Life in the Bush of Ghosts; Born to Use Mics; The Manifesto; Manufacturing Consent; Wizard of the Crow; The Autobiography of Malcolm X; The Code Book; Press Play.*

A variety of books on science, history, art, philosophy, spirituality, "how-to," business.

Sneaky fella. No one should have this type of content all in one place.

James backed away and tried to resolve the conflict Toffy's room had caused for him. James liked predictability and uniformity. That's how he understood the world around him. The room was full yet void of anything he could grasp—something tangible that explained what motivated Toffy.

I can't admit it, but I'm confused. Maybe there isn't much to it. Just another confused career navigator. Troubled youth, fighting the order of the world. This is unique. I like how—

He ended that thought before it developed legs. He looked around to make sure the J Men weren't reading him. He straightened his shoulder.

When he was ready to step out of the room in discomfort, he noticed a picture on the stand by the bed held within a shiny, thin steel frame the size of a small book. Deja and Toffy. There were no other pictures in the room.

They loved one another. Yet Deja took a job far away from Toffy.

He was tickled by the power he wielded to separate them.

That must have really broken him.

James smiled.

Maybe that's sufficient. Maybe I didn't really need to send people to look through Toffy's things. At this rate, he'll end up in Low Town. Forgotten. Should I even be here on such an important date? But they said they had found some documents on the Enterprise.

James dropped the picture face down on the stand. He wrinkled his lips.

The dark corner of the room called him. It had a latent pulse. Swinging his head side to side, he started dancing, moving his body to the rhythm. He knew exactly what was in the closet there.

He pulled the strings above his head to illuminate the room and took a deep breath as the light dimly shone on the sleeves of musical antiquities. Row after row of drawers full of music.

The council was behind this. Not the council of fools he had around him.

The Pure Council. The Vibros.

He couldn't resist the brown sugar-skinned beauty on the cover of one of the musical artifacts. The kinky reggae that played in his brain shocked him out of his reframe.

The council is responsible for this. They must have found him.

The vibrations the sun radiated had him thinking about a futuristic past.

One that existed and didn't exist at the same time. Galaxies beyond futuristic parks that park too many parallel identities and integrity in similar simulations. The trouble and the trials and tribulations that nations are facing...

James's brain flashed and raced.

"We don't need no more trouble," someone yelled.

He didn't know where the sound was coming from, but he knew it was meant for him.

"We don't need more fighting. What we need is *love*."

He thought about the lion-faced soldiers with guitars who sang about love.

He started pulsing, pulsing, pulsing.

Strum strum strum strum... the guitar in his mind played.

"Ten thousand chariots coming with their horses."

"It's a musical stampede," the sound came again.

James had to leave the room; if not, he would get lost in the details. He would not fall in the trap of the council this time. He knew they were good. He had been holding his breath for a long time.

"Don't let me down. Don't let me down," someone said, but this time, the voice came from within. He hurried to escape and gain control. But he was losing it. Compression within what was left of his soul. Survival mode had fully kicked in. He turned around with the plan to spring out of the little corner in the darkness.

A poster read: "I'm going to be your friend... In high tide or low tide," and it held him transfixed by the bold print and the many faces of the council.

Bob Marley
Maya Angelou
Fela Kuti
Ebenezer Obey
Rapsody
Thelonious Monk
Miriam Makeba
Chronixx
J Dilla
Nina Simone
H.E.R.
Show Dem
Yasiin Bey
Wanlov the Kubolor
Joan Baez
Nas
Tony Allen
Erykah Badu
Nipsey Hussle
Asa
Peter Tosh

M.I.A.
Jesse Jagz
Sun Ra
Junior Gong
Max Roach

James felt the emotion of a tear coming up for air. He drowned it immediately. He had to get out of there. It was all about survival now.

Operation Press Play. We press play in thirty minutes, sir.

The message buzzed on James's device.

I hope everything is in order?

Chez continued.
James gathered himself. He closed his eyes, took a few deep breaths, and then typed.

Of course everything is in order. Just let me know when it is time and I have the white screen with me to activate when necessary.

Chez responded:

We knew you had it in control. I just wasn't sure.

James stared at his device, filled with anger, and typed.

Sure of what?

That's not what I meant,

Chez immediately responded.

We are off in twenty-five minutes,

Bunajo wrote.

Thanks for the update, Bunajo,

Obechat interjected.

Since it has been five minutes since the last update, it is definitely twenty-five minutes until action time. Actually, since we are fondly providing updates, let me take the liberty to be the time keeper, and we are now down to twenty-four minutes.

I have the screen that Ditty handed me. We are good to go,

James typed.

From the corner of the room, the perspective made him feel smaller. The Pure Vibro Council were in motion to counter his plans. He saw the code book, the microphone, the leather of unfitted drums scattered around, the rumpled papers of truth, the wooden speakers, and he felt the latent vibration.

The sound fella has been at work.

James took another deep breath and overcame the inertia to walk out of the room.

"All right, fellas, I don't think there's anything here!" he shouted, rushing toward the door. He turned the light off and then paused at the door. The thump of his heartbeat—one, two, three, four... One of the men walked up to him.

James looked at him and whispered, "There's someone in that bathroom."

Sixteen minutes to action, sir. Any updates from your end?

Bunajo typed.

James thought about his next best move. He went through a rolodex of possible acts. He thought about just walking into the bathroom and getting his men to snatch the young man up but then thought against that.

The J Men were ready to take the door down. They were lined up at the door of the room, waiting for me to give the instruction.

He knew they were reading this entire self, quantifying and qualifying.

They want me to make a wrong move.

James didn't trust them fully. He trusted nothing.

That would not land well in the aesthetics of the screen. Maybe I'd plead to the young writer to stop? How would someone like me look like begging for someone to do something like that? I should just walk out. No, that's weak. Burn the room down.

James walked away.

This entire building might be connected. That radio cloud I keep hearing about. Those repeaters, flying under the radar. A full burn might be needed.

"Burn the building!" He stopped at the door, shouting out his instructions.

Maybe the entire street? It seems like total destruction, the only solution. Burn down the block.

He took in a deep breath. It smelled fresh. James got a dopamine kick when he anticipated the scent of smoke to be. James tapped his pocket just before he turned around to step back out of the apartment.

"Where's the white screen?" James said.

"What white screen?" one of his men asked.

"I came here with another screen in my hand," James said, looking at his communication device.

Twelve minutes to take off, sir. We need feedback,

Bunajo typed again.

***

The light from Toffy's computer screen was slightly luminous from under the bathroom door, and that's what James had seen as he'd walked out of the room. He had just been discovered, Toffy knew.

What surmounted that fear was the fear of not finishing his story.

"Those who tell the story get to change the world," his uncle had told him.

The drums from afar sparked his memory of an event he knew he experienced but didn't remember. The vibrations brought this memory flooding in.

He had met up with James in his office the same day he'd had a flashback of his and Musta's conversation. The moment was finally illuminated, replayed in his mind like a lost mixtape unearthed beneath layers of mental cobwebs.

The reason behind the entire madness didn't come from the government or some top-down approach.

James had spoken those works loosely. Every single word of that conversation returned to Toffy now like some kind of recall, a conversational memory, or a page in a book pressed into his mind, visually annotated to jog his memory at this precise moment.

There was no order, no declaration, no strategy plan, none of that to start with. Technology, individual insecurity, and mass appeal exploitation made it all come to a head. People wanted things quickly. They wanted convenience. They wanted information in condensed, mindless excerpts. They wanted comics, viral videos, attention-grabbing headlines, remixed media, personalized preferences, vacation pictures to stay happy all the time. We are just the opportunists who know how to exploit those interests and keep people in the buying mood.

Toffy's eyes spread wide open as he sat on the bathroom floor.

The answer has been there all along. I just needed to focus and tune into it.

A cold shiver swept through the bathroom from the window sill. Toffy laid his head back on the wall. He had forgotten what was happening in his immediate surroundings. His mind traveled back to that day in James's office. It became clearer what was said. He seemed to be having an out-of-body experience, as though transposed to the office and watching the discussion between James and a zoned-out and unfocused version of himself.

Look at him. Sleeping. You can't tell the youth anything. If he were paying attention, his ears would pucker up as I revealed the reason behind the world we continue to build. I would say this to whoever is ready to listen, but they all have divided attention.

People want to stay happy all the time. It goes back to the education system, when schools started to churn out people who were all the same. Melding people into objects that turned to widgets for the factories and the manufacturing process, there was no room for the intellectual talent. There was no room for the curious mind.

Who can really take advantage of the empowered individual? I don't know how to. So, burn it all. Destroy them at will. Delete divergent memories. Empty the conflicting cache.

The books, the history, the new ideas. Give the common person senseless data. Let them grow an audience of senseless followings. Let their audience recite nonsense too. You see the cycle? Ahh, biographer. He's not even listening.

Ah, the biographer. Toffy might not have been listening that day, but he must have picked up sonics that jogged his memory.

However, a few odd ones don't only want to know how a thing is done, but what it is and why it is being done. This curious bunch are few and far apart. You can't let them congregate. Their curiosity leads to unnecessary confusion for the hierarchy.

Train them in the schools to look at a problem in one sure way that has been tested to keep the order the way it is.

Make sure they don't get this crazy idea in their own mind that they can actually transform their reality.

Remind them they are objects for the purpose of keeping the order and not subjects of transformation. At the most, burn down any dissent. At the least, just entertain them so they remain happy, forget their loneliness, and never feel judged.

Toffy watched as his zoned-out self snapped out of the musings of his mind to focus on what James was saying.

I don't think you realize how important you are, we are, and how happy we want to keep the world. We are truly pioneers of the new wave of happiness. The custodians of privilege for our human race. The treasurers of our passions. Our fight against the curious mind is to preserve our collective happiness.

At this point in the memory, James had picked up his device that had been buzzing on his desk. "What is the issue?" he had yelled to the unknown person on the other side of the communication device. "Who? Slow down. Doing what? Another one, huh? It must be really true that curiosity kills the cat. Set the place on fire." And as James hung up and as his device landed against his oak desk, the collision displaced air molecules that vibrated through Toffy's ears.

He heard it in his memory. He heard it as himself. He heard it as a third person. He realized he had heard it all then as he lay his head against the cold bathroom wall.

As Toffy flowed through this slippery web of ideas, memories, and sounds, it felt like he was in a waking dream.

CHAPTER 26

"Set the place on fire," Toffy heard and immediately looked around. The window in his bathroom brought some comfort—a possible escape route.

He continued typing. Racing against time.

Many more paragraphs to write. Line after line.

Toffy wrote ferociously as he raced toward the end.

A crackling sound, and then something burning.

He put his ear to the door. His apartment was on fire. He cracked the door open, and a wind of smoke came rushing in. He closed it again.

Think. Think. Think!

The vibrations of drums from afar were reminiscent of a time past, a type of communication. He knew deep in his heart that he was supposed to be exactly where he was. This was part of his destiny. The vibrations moved his body, his thoughts, memory, and emotions. He felt connected to something deeper.

He straightened up and sat back down on the floor.

I'm going to finish, even if I have to die on the line. The end had never been closer. He typed faster, the bathroom filling with smoke.

With a tightness in Toffy's stomach, the smoke seared the inner linings of his nostrils. The initial smell had a citrus note. His stash of herb stock from Musta was burning. The smoke went straight to his chest.

The perfect tree.

This was his moment. He had been practicing for it. He inhaled.

***

James read the message from Bunajo as he and his men scrambled downstairs:

Three minutes to launch, sir. Where are you?
The white screen is in my hands,

James responded and snatched it from his men. "It took you long enough to find it."

"It was in your shirt pocket," the man shot back. "How am I supposed to—"

"Quiet." James was shocked at his boldness. "Remind me to resolve you when we get back to the pyramid. You must have been mis-programmed."

He then dictated into his screen,

"I have the screen with me, ready to deploy when it's time."
You have the blue screen Ditty gave you. Right?

Chez asked on the message thread.

"Blue? I have the *white* screen from Ditty,"

James responded.

Loya added:

Blue or white? Which one is it? Ditty, please respond ASAP.

Muidi wrote:

The screen is the screen.

Chez wrote back:

No, we have to initiate it with the blue screen. Please confirm. This crowd is getting too wavy here with all this music.

Obechat asked:

Perhaps you mean a white-blue screen? Why is Ditty so quiet? Where is he?

Bunajo added:

One minute to go, sir.

The crowd at the switch event joined in on the countdown as a digital clock projected against the big white wall in the event room. The noise was thunderous: "Fifty-eight, fifty-seven, fifty-six, fifty-five, fifty-four..."

"So do we have a confirmation? Ditty, are you there?"

James asked again.

Bunajo typed each number every second:

Six, five, four...

Chez asked:

Is there a play button appearing on the screen? Just press play when it shows up on your screen.
Three, two, one... You are a go, my sir.

James pressed play on the white screen as he jumped into his vehicle.

The city turned dark.

***

Toffy was already feeling lightheaded in the bathroom as the lights across the city turned off.

He continued writing and then finally closed his laptop.

That's my opening. He stood up with great effort, walked to the bathroom window, put his laptop between his belly and the elastic of his pants, fastened his pants to secure the laptop, looked down three floors, and jumped out the window.

"*Arrghhhh!*" Toffy shrieked.

He landed awkwardly and with snaps around his body.

That can't be good.

Toffy stood up.

"*Aaaaahhhhh!*" Toffy yelled out as soon as he put weight on his foot. The sound from his voice was high-pitched and much louder than when he first fell. Toffy crumpled to the ground.

He was lightheaded and badly injured. The blood on his leg made him nauseated. He dragged himself to the corner between two electric dumpsters and sat there.

Where's my device? I need to finish.

He pulled his limp left side across the sparkling paved ground, his body a mass divided.

The result was a forbidden essence that glowed on one side fueled by the gas burning on the other. A glow came from the center of his splattered laptop. He stopped to reach back for it.

One side of his brain told him to run and never come back; the other side said he had to fight through the resistance and emote the feelings.

"AAh, ahh, ahhh. Ahhh." Toffy growled. Half-winded and half-handed, he stayed on the ground and leapt toward it.

The screen on the ground. A reflection of his thoughts. A flash of James. Himself too. The screen switched again, this time to Deja smiling in front of her screen. Toffy shook it. It changed again. Sarni standing like a zombie.

Noooo. The damn thing is scrambled. Toffy shook the screen again.

Sarni walked in a circle.

Going left. No brake. No brain. No stop.

Going right. No break. No branch. No drop.

Sarni sank into his loop. He did different and similar things at the same time.

The screen changed again.

Uncle Apo's face made him smile. Only the right side of his face could accommodate the upward movement of his lip.

The left side was in pain as he internally complained about why he was left behind on this plane. All horizontal and vertical and no formless axis. The pain that existed in Toffy's side made him want to ride off into bliss.

The resistance could move you forward.

The screen changed.

Footsteps running on graveled roads. Toffy tried to decipher the dark images. He could not tell whether the shades of black and gray made a face or was laced with tentacles of a machine.

Click. Clack. Click. Clack. He heard it. The sound persisted. In one second, he saw it all. Everything he needed. It left him full and empty at the same time. The sounds intensified and matched the rhythm of the men and robots in white suits running on the screen.

"Oh shit, I have to…" He stopped. Something had escaped him. He had to do something. He just didn't know exactly what he had to do.

Under the single lit streetlamp on the other side of the road was the illumination of the Line.

Toffy's right side stood up. His left side stayed glued to the ground. His sudden movement had a snap and crackling bounce like the initial submergence of milk in rushed breakfast.

The immediate reaction to his action of moving forward was the boomerang of his laptop back to the ground as he was pulled backward. Toffy looked around, but there was no one. As he lay there riddled by the physical conflict of the two sides of himself, the sky blackened.

No clouds. No stars. Darkness. No light tonight.

Evergreen screens kept playing in the distance.

He pulled the screen to his face, and likewise his face to the screen. The screen was a dark mirror. All he could see was his reflection. Nothing else. For the first time, he saw himself for who he really was. The right and the left side. The same and different.

His face on the screen started morphing. His face and then James's. Then his again. He could not look away.

The eyes on the screen opened and yelled, "Go to the line!"

They must have been only four cars down when Toffy lifted himself off the ground, limping with his right foot and dragging the left.

I'll have to jump my way there!

Toffy hopped. Toffy the jumpman. He did it twenty-three times and got to the line. It was illuminated by a single streetlamp.

He slowly stepped away from the brightness, heading for the next beam in the distance.

***

"Is that…? Can't be." James swirled his head around as he watched Toffy drag himself across the line into Low Town.

"Turn this vehicle around and head south," James dictated.

"That would be going into Low Town," the automated voice from the vehicle spoke out. "Are you sure?"

"Why is everyone questioning me today?" James said in frustration. "I said head south into Low Town."

"This vehicle is not equipped with the appropriate operating system for Low Town maneuvering."

"Head south!" James yelled out.

The car turned on its full beams and headed in the direction Toffy had disappeared.

"Watch where you are going!" James bounced around inside the gyrating vehicle.

"This automobile is not equipped for avoiding these Low Town holes in the road." The automated voice from the vehicle was bruised and more emotional. "I have lost both my brake lights, and a deflated tire is definitely on the horizon, and my lights can barely cut through this haze. Is that a spaceship? We've only seen these in images. With no lights? We have never encountered them in real life. I don't believe it is wise to keep moving—"

"He must be around here somewhere." James looked around furiously in search of any sight of Toffy.

J Men were in pursuit. They ran along the line that separated High Town from Low Town. James followed their line of sight. With fire burning on their block, the people were out of their houses in the streets. A crowd built behind James and his men.

The smoke rose. It had now mixed with the fog in the air.

James could see Toffy in the distance, zigzagging between both sides. The number of J Men on Toffy's chase reduced with each skip from the other side. Once they followed him across the line into Low Town, the BWs on the hunt came back to the other side with fewer men.

"Take full control!" James yelled. He rolled up his sleeves, and a wheel came out from the opened compartment on the dashboard of his car.

James jumped into control of his vehicle. He moved slowly, navigating around the potholes. He passed a pothole and saw two damaged J Men. Their circuitry was all over the ground.

They are not built for these streets, James thought.

He continued in his approach. He spotted Toffy once more.

He had never seen someone navigate the two worlds so skillfully. Toffy jumped to the right, hopped forward for a while, and then jumped back to the left of the line where he could hardly be seen.

No one else was on his pursuit. James brought his car's pace to a crawl. Like a tar-crab, his vehicle moved.

James watched Toffy with contempt and admiration. He watched him bounce right on that line.

He's aligned. It's clear. He's found his balance. He has found a good portion of himself. The image of Toffy moving reminded James of his inner child. James sped his car up.

"You have to *gooooo!*" James yelled with resentment. Toffy ran deeper into Low Town, James's car was right behind him. James stopped and jumped out of the car. A foot chase ensued.

He'll tire soon. He's injured. James's hunting nature was primed. He swallowed a gulp of saliva.

"Don't resist. You know how this is going to end!" James yelled out. It echoed in the dark streets.

No one was down the alley. James checked the other direction. A moving sound pulsed softly back toward the line. James jerked his head to see what it was. It was Toffy. He had spotted him again.

He's still going. In pain, yet so joyful. They call it the beauty in the struggle.

Toffy stopped and stood on the line.

He nodded his head and moved both his feet in one spot. The drums came alive. Toffy typed into his laptop.

He's still typing. That means his story is not out yet. I must make sure it doesn't come out. James crept toward Toffy. He hadn't stayed this light on his feet in years.

James watched as Toffy danced the line, walked backward, pulled out his laptop, typed a few words, and put the computer under his shirt, bopping his head the entire time.

Toffy shoved both shoulders in the air and pulled them back down three times. He alternated the movement of his shoulders and spun around seven times. He slid to the right and slid to the left and fell to his chest like a plank in the darkness.

Right behind Toffy, James pounced on him. In a swift move, James had his knee on a struggling Toffy's neck.

"This is how it usually goes." James felt Toffy pushing back. He crouched down harder. He knew he had him. James breathed in a breath of relief when he saw the laptop to the side.

I should just grab it and get the hell out of here.

James looked around. He decided against that last thought.

I want to make sure this is fully resolved.

He pressed down. The breath dwindled in Toffy's lungs. A light squeal proceeded.

***

The last thing Toffy remembered was how the air pushed him upward, keeping him separated from the ground. His surroundings were dark, and he was floating in water at the shore of a beach. It was very dark, and the gray clouds above his head slowly dissipated. He floated effortlessly, slowly moving his legs in a circular rhythm to stay afloat. Hands spread out to his sides. He just kept looking up at the sky. The drizzles splashed on his face and created a repeated pattern across the water.

So peaceful.

The clouds transitioned to white and the sky from black to blue. Thin streaks of sun rays came through and pierced the clouds. His environment became brighter. He remained still.

He surprisingly felt comfortable in the water.

I belong in this water and the peace of the waves. The sky keeps getting clearer.

With his ears submerged in the water, he could not hear anything besides the pulsing vibration of what he believed to be all the unburdened twittering sea life underneath him. There was nowhere to go. There was no pressing thing that needed to be done. He just had to be there, where he was supposed to be.

He lay there as the tender waves made splashes across his cheek in a repeated pattern that had him thinking about the tender touches from Deja.

A passing cloud swayed over the sun, casting a faint shadow in the form of spade-shaped leaves on the greenery in the distance.

Where am I? Toffy asked.

Deja's face formed in one of the clouds. He was in the right place.

He wanted to be with her.

Tears of joy or tears of sadness or no tears at all, Toffy continued to look at the features on the cloud. Deja's nose poked out perfectly in the evaporated mound of water, and a rainbow shot through a hole that formed her mouth, the different colors radiating.

The spectrum of the colors was a symbol of liberation, perfectly fitting from the clouded mouth of Deja.

He was there.

He appreciated the moment.

He took it all in.

Then the silence was broken.

"Look at you. You are finally comfortable in the water," a voice said from a short distance. Deja sat on the beach in her black swimsuit. "How much longer are you going to stay in there?"

Toffy smiled and slowly swam the beach, surprised by his improved ability in the water.

"I did not want to disturb you. You looked like you were at peace," Deja said.

She handed Toffy a towel. He wiped himself dry and sat next to her.

"How long have we been out here?" Toffy asked. "I lost track of time."

Deja leaned in to kiss him and said, "Don't worry about time. That does not matter here."

***

James watched as Toffy danced the line, walked backward, pulled out his laptop, typed a few words, put the computer under his shirt, bopping his head the entire time.

Musta sampled the sounds
Toffy sampled ideas
The code hit with drums
It vibrated their ears.

"Hey, get off that man's neck!" A voice from the darkness rang out.

The fire in the darkness grew bigger. A crowd had appeared from nowhere.

"Get off the man's neck!" another one yelled. "Down-presser man."

"CIT!" a woman shouted.

"This is Viginniye." A voice came from above.

James jumped up. He knew he was no longer safe. He didn't realize he had gone so far.

"We take care of our own here." Keba walked out from behind the fire. "Check on Toffy, please."

She towered over James.

"It's done."

"He's not responding, Keba," a lady said, kneeling next to Toffy.

James knew it. Still dead center on the line, he saw it as his only opportunity. He shoved Keba out of the way and ran off into a street in High Town. He disappeared behind the growing crowd.

***

People congregated on the streets.

One side was dark. On the other side, the screens played content the people had never seen before.

The shock.

The remix live on the screen.

Oh no, this ain't no dream.

The daily announcement from the screens sounded different.

People cried. A few of them collapsed.

The despair. The tears. The hemorrhage.

"Toffy, stay with us!" Keba snapped her hands. "Is help coming?"

A cypher formed around him. Chanting proceeded.

***

"Want to head out?" Deja asked Toffy sometime later. It felt like an eternity.

They stood and walked toward a field. Toffy was not familiar with his environment, but he was fine with his unfamiliarity. He and Deja held hands as they walked through.

She was quiet. He wondered if she was real or not, her touch as real as the warmth he felt for her.

Is this real life? Everything here seems so... different.

Life was so vivid, and the sunshine reflected on every object in his presence, creating a type of glare that heightened the sense of reality.

I'll just follow Deja's lead.

She walked with a relaxed but deliberate step that reminded Toffy of the earlier days in their relationship. She was calm as they walked off the field onto an empty concrete parking lot, the skyline of J City in the distance.

"Where are we going?" Toffy asked.

"I have to lay you down."

"Where?"

Deja did not respond and led him through the city.

"Welcome to my longitude and my latitude," Toffy stopped and said confidently.

The world that had flipped. The left side was on the right side and the right side had moved to the left. The whole place a reflection of itself—a reflection of a reflection that reflected an eternity.

Toffy walked with fist raised in the air.

My rebel tactics got the world flipping on its axis.
The dividing line that once existed is now nonexistent
Or exists everywhere so it's no longer relevant.
The tower's now on the right,
Close to the café where I used to write
The other night, I ran on lines
Off and online.
Rougher than stuff I puffed
Back up on time.

There goes the place I got some new insights
Vibrating at its place and on this line
Read as a reflection to reflect what's on the inside

Have to decide where to focus my thoughts
Screens coming down
Rhythms pulsing
Feel the calling
I hear it calling
It's already on the inside

More things had switched sides. The world was different, and at the same time, the way it had always been.

Things feel better.

The thought of change did not cause a flight-induced reaction from Toffy this time. He was comfortable with the change. There was more balance. The world was whole.

As they walked together silently, things started to look more familiar.

The screens might have been coming down in some places; in others they were still on and spewing colorful ads, but the light that emanated just didn't have the same intensity.

Toffy stopped and stared at one of the screens.

BUY MORE
YOU WILL BE GREAT
JUST WATCH ME
AND BELIEVE IN YOURSELF

The consequence of losing his Pink Money by staring at the screen just didn't have as much bearing on him as it did before. Toffy peeled his eyes away as he walked. Although this familiarity was quite different, the difference had the sameness of how things looked quite different from the beginning.

At the end of the empty street, they turned the corner. They passed the dome that housed the world-famous coffee shop.

"Hey, I used to write there."

Deja smiled back at him. "Let's go," she said and pulled Toffy along.

She eventually led him into one of the tall, thin buildings in J City. They headed up to the fourth floor and directly into the third door on the right to a room with a bed.

"Hey, let's just lie down here," she said.

He could not really remember anything earlier than when he found himself floating in the water. He remembered his feeling for Deja. He was happy.

Deja headed out of the room.

Toffy relaxed. The ceiling was white. He was light. A sense of accomplishment.

Paper rustled next to him, and there sat Uncle Apo in a previously empty chair.

"Uncle Apo? What are you doing here?"

"What are *you* doing here?" Uncle Apo said with a smile.

CHAPTER 27

———

Toffy considered the possibility of being in some sort of afterlife.

"Oh lord. I'm dead!" he exclaimed as he looked at his uncle, waiting for some confirmation. "Am I dead?"

"That's a good question," Uncle Apo responded. He stood and started walking around the room. "Do you *feel* dead?"

Toffy jumped out of the bed and walked to the window to catch a glimpse of his reflection.

"Are you there?" Uncle Apo asked.

"There is no middle ground," a sound from the mirror splatted out. "You must accept or reject."

His image was nonexistent. He saw something quite different, yet the same.

"You have to face the music," the voice on the screen told Toffy. "The mirror on the wall above the handwriting there or the text here... is invincible to all."

It is a mirror you must hear
Invincible vibration, rhythms, harmonic sound
Each melody is never what is seems to be
You can only hear the mirror.

A reflection of reflection itself
The ping pong of sonic waves
You can only hear what the mirror says, no more no less
You must hear what the mirror sees, no more no less
It's all within

Toffy stared at what had turned into a whitish charred face that had the pigmentations of concrete. A sculpture of himself withering away.

Floods and harvests.
Wars and alliances.
Flights and crashes.
Yellows and blues.
Reds and greens.
Winds and stillness.

His charred image stayed still through it all.

"It's all *within*," the screen continued with a cadence of an angelic rastafarian nubian griot. "Passed on from generations of manifestations that had men and women willfully manifesting destinies and dreams not once divided, united through space and time."

The sun radiated.

"In the corporation, there's no pure music. That's not pure music's fault. They never gave pure music a chance. It's not pure music's fault that governments failed. The councilmen. When the environment gets destroyed, it's not pure music's fault. When people die, it's not pure music's fault. When they steal from their brothers and sisters, it's not pure music's fault. They never gave pure music a chance."

Filled with sincerity of sound and truth, the drum beat in his heart, pounding. The rhythms through digital communications communicated the frequency carried by the air around Toffy.

"Nothing will ever be the same anymore." Keys of a piano pierced through. "Now look. What do you see?"

"It's the end of their world."

Toffy looked at the screen as his image fully disappeared. He put the screen down for a second and pulled it back up to his face to confirm he did not have a reflection any longer.

"Oh. I'm dead," Toffy said.

He walked slowly to the bed and sat. He examined his environment. The room was very bright, and apart from the emptied streets of J City, everything seemed remotely normal.

His uncle grinned. "Take a deep breath, Toffy. Now take another one. And then another one."

Toffy's chest rose and fell in a lighter version of himself. Not as light as the version in the screen that had no image and not as heavy as the form that Toffy defined himself by.

"Take another breath. Have you ever felt more alive than this?"

Toffy thought about that question. Something about him was different. The air around him pulsed like a subtle force field.

"You feel different. Don't you?" Apo asked.

"Yeah. I do."

"How do you feel exactly?"

Feeling his full self, his skin was an umbilical sheet that connected him to all of life. "I feel... I feel... I don't know. Content. Fulfilled. I feel empty. Full of life. Formless. At least for a moment."

"That's because you did it, Toffy," Apo said proudly. "You finished your story, and you are here. You followed the typical hero's journey as a storyteller. You were called to act—to tell a story. During your journey, you went through trials and tribulation. You persevered through conflict, met friends and enemies along the way. You eventually got to the point of no return, and you courageously stood up to the moment and finished your story. You showed that telling your story was something worth fighting for, worth dying for… Something worth communicating. It could spark some dialogue."

Toffy was pretty sure he had joined his uncle in a different realm.

"So, am I alive?" asked Toffy.

"You remember I once said, 'Those who tell the story change the world, and those who get to change the world tell the story?'"

"Yeah, so did I change the world?"

"It is yet to be seen if you changed the world with your story, but one thing for sure is that you have changed *your* world. To change anything, you have to go through a personal transformation. Before you can change the world on the outside, you have to change the world on the inside. That's where real change happens. The revolution begins within the self. With your story, you have changed your world, and you can now change the world around you. You can transform reality. You and your environment are in a symbiotic relationship. That's why your journey is not yet over. You have to return what you have learned through your transformation back to the world you came from and share your knowledge with those who are yet to go through a similar transformation. That's how your story can change the world."

Toffy listened to his uncle the same way he had listened to him as a child.

"So, I'm still... *alive?*"

"A hero never dies," his uncle said, and he slowly disappeared.

***

Beep. Beep. Beep.

Toffy woke up from what must have been the best and most intense dream.

How did I get here?

The bed, the screen, the machines next to him, it all looked so familiar. He knew he was in J Hospital, but no one was around. Expecting his uncle, the chair next to him was empty. He remembered his uncle had gone.

He lifted the bed sheet and found his legs wrapped in bandages.

"Arrrrhhhhh." Pain shot through his entire body.

Everything came back to him, flooding his memory. The last thing he remembered was opening the window and looking out. He did not remember anything after that.

How did I get down? Did I jump? Where's my laptop? I finished typing my story. Didn't I? What was it for?

Then he remembered back to the moment he was all alone in the apartment. When he thought it was all over for him. The loneliness.

I pushed everyone I loved away.

Beep. Beep. Beep.

What was it all for?

Everything had fallen apart.

As his thoughts got deeper, the fall continued into a never-ending pit. It seemed as though he was falling forever.

The emptiness in his belly was amplified with the heat of sweat that trickled down his belly as he stepped back off the edge of the bed in the noised-room filled with muted tellys.

The world was fake.

He was fake.

It was *all* fake, an illusion.

Beep. Beep. Beep.

Just before the light had come through and told him to shine his own light on the world, the light on the screen had found him writing furiously on a smoky bathroom floor of a smoke-less building that was burned down. The light had sent him back on the edge of a window, on a ledge of intention. On the line he flowed. Saved by ancestral intervention.

The screen displayed words:

Tomorrow may never come. Life is not promised.
Tomorrow may never pop up. For you or me, life is
not promised
Tomorrow may never emerge; you got to hold on to
the present.
Hold on to this present. Hold on. Don't be afraid,
To let it shine…

The messages sounded familiar. He knew where they were coming from, and he knew he could tap into its power.

Toffy smiled with a lightness in his heart and started singing:

Iya mi so shine your light on the world.
Shine it wide for the globe to see.

Toffy sang there on the bed, injured and present.

***

"Tomorrow may never come for you and me," sang a tall man who butted into the glass door, spinning. "Hello, Mr. T. How are you feeling?"

"I feel very good, actually," Toffy responded. "A little pain in my legs. Can you tell me what happened?"

You jumped out of the window in your burning apartment. Besides a few broken joints and the concussion you sustained from the fall, everything else is good."

Dr. Cardigan spent another hour with Toffy and had a more relaxed disposition this time around.

"Not in a rush today, huh?" Toffy asked.

"Oh no, not today."

The doctors in the hallway moved at a calm pace. Greeting one another and treating the patients with patience. Empathy resonated in the hospital.

"I respect what you have done here," the doctor said as he was adjusting the drip stand next to the bed. "Putting your life on the line to reveal a truth that needed to be told. What you did has changed the entire city. A thing to behold."

"Huh?" Toffy said.

"I know... I know. You probably don't know what is going on here. I was going to wait 'til Deja got back, but—"

"Wait, Deja's here?"

"Yeah, she just stepped out. She said she'd be back soon."

Toffy smiled.

"I was going to wait for her to get back, but I'm just going to..." The doctor could not hold his excitement. "I'm just going to give you control access to this screen here. It's all over the news. I didn't say anything," he said, smiled, moonwalked out of the room, and closed the door.

CHAPTER 28

———

Staring at his monument in the glowing sun, James felt it in his gut, exactly what he'd imagined it would feel like: the pain he feared finally realized, the physical manifestation shooting through his stomach like a fifty-year hunger.

For the first time in a long time, he wanted to fold into a ball. He wished he could crawl up in the bed and get his head caressed by his mother. Her glowing face shun. Memories of his father's stern face tightened. He stood up straight.

What a beauty.

Change was in the air. It smelled like youth. Tomorrow would be quite different from today and all the days before that. He was not ready to change. Not for anybody. Not even for himself.

He had built up the defense and the corporation. He was close to building the life he believed only he deserved—the life that would keep him isolated to enjoy the fruits of his capital, and *his capital* alone.

Transfixed in time, out the window, a dark cloud flowed over his monument. The rain came over to wash it all, the birds mysteriously frozen in the sky. The crackling of the night allowed no light to penetrate.

There was no going back. *Things will never be the same.* A step closer to the opened window. It was cold and high. James's glass dropped.

***

"J Enterprise," a reporter was on the screen, "has been embroiled in the biggest PR nightmare any corporation could ever think of. If you are just joining us, J Enterprise has been turned upside down with a story that broke out late last night."

News like in the archives. But this time, current day and from the people. Toffy sat up excited.

"Documents have emerged," she continued, "showing illegal practices of J Enterprise, including the use of slaved insights to mine 'unique human experiences' and provide inputs for automated intelligence at their factories, the illegal dumping of waste, excess sugar, and toxins into J City Lake—toxins that have now been linked to the rise in environmental-induced chronic illnesses. A false social arm used as a funnel for cheap and almost free labor. The list goes on... I mean... this document is very elaborate and well-written."

The correspondent switched the discussion over to her three panelists.

"Can you believe this?" she asked her guests.

"War in the name of democracy. The game was a monopoly. Planes falling out of the sky."

The black-suited gentleman at the corner of the table spat out, "On the margins of a society, that I imagined, emerged from emergency margins of tall phallic buildings."

"Thanks for that, Deep Brother," the host said. "It's nice to have you back here today. As soon as I saw the headline,

I knew I had to call you. I mean, you have talked about this for a long time."

"Strong-armed robbery; that's what it is," Deep Brother said and sank back into his seat. "Destabilized economies. Mercenaries. Revolution silencers. They will never silence the voice."

"It's crazy," one of the other guests responded. "I am so glad a story like this can finally come out. We in the environmental scene have been talking about how the toxins from the plant continue to deplete the maritime ecosystem. The sugar in the water, obviously included, to sweeten the pill. We commend those involved in breaking this. The story-telling ability of this young collective captures exactly what we have been trying to say, but in a very concise and eloquent way that moves the people."

"Speaking of," the host interjected, "J Enterprise has also been linked to the building burnings that have been rampant in this city over the past thirty years. The burnings have been the spark—for a lack of better words—that have ignited the growth of J Insurance.

"And," the host arranged the paper in front of her into a stack of hyperlinked text, "one of these fires in a small one-bedroom apartment led to this revelation. We will be right back with more details."

Deep Brother jumped in before it switched to an advertisement. "This answers it. The knowledge from these metropolitan streets is more effective than perspective from scholarships to the best schools of knowledge."

***

Toffy changed the channel to see what else was showed on the screen.

People are speaking so freely. This content is different.

He went to the next station and read the headline:

BREAKING NEWS: J ENTERPRISE EXPOSED.

"—a collective that call themselves the Councilors released the documents, along with other interesting content, that exposed and brought J Enterprise to its knees. Visual, written, and musical form, it was beamed at the same time all over the screens in the city—"

Toffy changed to the Enterprise channel.

"J Enterprise has dropped by eighteen percent in market value just several hours after the story broke. The popular CEO, James the Fifty-first, who has been a very polarizing figure, has been fired by a decentralized board and told to step away from all activities involving J Enterprise. Even more interesting, his social score dropped by twenty two percent. He dropped from the fifth richest person in the world to the eighty-ninth in barely twelve hours. I'm sure no one is really losing sleep over that. James the Fifty-first has not responded to the recent allegations."

The structures of oppression crumbled away. The line that separated evaporated. The fog and the illusive screen dissolved. Both sides were aware of one another. Dialogue had taken off. The people's eyes were free for them, and they chose what they wanted to focus on, that which was in front of them—the present.

Toffy switched the channel.

"Hey, man. Give me my money," a man said into the screen.

The camera zoomed out to a lady in a bright yellow top and a red raincoat.

"City correspondent here," she spoke into the screen. "That is what is happening around J City. They are calling it the gimme-my-money-back-itis." She signaled with quotation marks. "Citizens are walking toward the screens around the cities and asking for their money back. It has been linked to the story released earlier this morning. Citizens all over J City have 'woken up.' The screens, as we now know, have been designed to provide citizens with what they believe they need and out others in a consistent state of fear in Low Town. It's been discovered that some people paid through their eyes with their lives.

"There are long lines around the city waiting to get in front of screens to ask for compensation. We spoke to a transaction technology expert, and he highly doubts they will get their money back. We'll see how this story develops as the lines grow around town."

The strangeness didn't end.

The coverage of the world was changing right in front of his eye. Monuments were taken down, some repurposed as sanctuaries to bring people together and foster conversation.

They are wiping down the lines.

In one area the line was used as a transportation route, with doors that opened on both sides at the same time. Most surprisingly, people were crossing the line, hand in hand.

Toffy watched the screen and saw a new world unfolding. *Humanity might have a chance to persevere.*

His story had gotten out there, but he wasn't sure how it all happened. Regardless, he was content.

I wish Uncle Apo was here to see. The story has changed the world.

Deja walked in and said, "I see you are catching up on all that's going on. How are you feeling?"

"I'm happy," Toffy responded.

"That's great." She smiled. "I went out to get you some fruits. I bought your favorite. Have you seen Musta yet?"

"Is he here?"

"Oh no, but he is on *here*." Deja grabbed the remote and changed it to the music channel. She slid onto the bed next to Toffy.

Musta, who went by the stage name The Unknown Mist, was being interviewed.

"I must say," the interviewer insinuated, "this is the most ambitious story you have endeavored in. Not only does this project have an impact in the music industry, but it is also linked to the biggest story in the news. It is rumored that you are part—if not the leader of—the collective that exposed J Enterprise. Is this true? What is your association with the collective?"

"Well, my focus is always music," Musta said in a very mellow but excited voice. "But the music has to have a message and some truth to it. The simple goal was to use the project to tell a compelling story. So, we tapped into our individual strengths and passions to get the best story out for the project."

"Soooo... are you the leader of the collective?" the interviewer asked again.

"You know, there are several secrets. Let's call them *tools* you can use to start a movement. To start a movement, you need things that move the heart. You can't do this with mountains of data. You can only do this by giving people a piece of your heart. Facts and figures are necessary, but you want to move the people's thoughts, bodies, and emotions. Building on the foundation of rhythm, repetition, rhymes, analogies, metaphors, and empathy. Immersing us in a human experience we can all feel moved by. You get me. Transporting the audience to a different place and time. Once they feel they are walking in the shoes of the protagonist, they want to assist in getting to the outcome—the final destination, which is always the beginning of a new journey."

The interviewer wiped a tear drop off her cheek.

"This is bringing some of us to tears, as you can see. Was that the intention here?"

Musta smiled. "We just wanted to start a movement. That's all."

"Would we be able to get you and your team on here next time to talk about the individual pieces of the collective? I mean, this is *big*."

Musta didn't say another word.

"I take that as a no?"

A man in the background yelled: "Every time I hear a snap of the switch, my blood goes tripping!" The dark-suited man walked toward Musta, and the reporter to get closer to the camera.

The dark-suited man embraced himself tightly with both hands placed just above each elbow and squeezed. "I remember on the slave ship, how they brutalized our very being. Today they say we are free, only to be chained in misery. Good God, I think it's illiteracy, the only machine that makes this cream."

As he walked away, the camera heard him singing contently:

Slave killer, the table has burnt
Catch my fire... you gonna get churned

The reporter looked at Musta, who had a smile on his face.

"Deep Brother always has a unique perspective," he said.
"Was he part of your collective?"

Musta continued smiling.

Toffy smiled, turned the TV off, and held Deja in contentment. They slept.

***

It had been two months since Toffy jumped out of his bathroom window for his story, and he was a different person living in a different city. J City was a brighter place. It was lighter. The air cleaner, people happier.

Toffy had a long list of requests he had not gotten back to. The number of messages in his voice and video mail kept increasing each day. His inbox as well. He planned on responding to each request he got from interviewers who wanted to hear his story and from publishers looking to represent him. The first he responded to was from a liberated banker who started writing her memoir a month after hearing his story.

You were such an inspiration
Inspired drinking Toffee with the Rolee and the vest
Envisioned like Nipsey at his best
Because the last time that I checked, you were self-made from the riddle
Helped me double up on financial freedom. Inspiration to follow a life worth living
Now the sweat is dripping down my face, and I resonate in cigar smoke-filled places
You gave me the game like a big brother

How you told me to cut to the middleman and go directly to the source I'm still on my mission

The marathon continued.

He responded:

Hey Tina, I'm glad you found some inspiration to chase your dreams. Where to start was what I found very challenging, but with some perseverance and a willingness to fail, nothing can really stop you. Follow your interests and then follow your actions. I wish you all the best.

Regards,

Toffy

Another young fellow sent him a message.

To have to play the game, you have to read the score.
You showed me to go get it, to remain patient.
I put in the dedication that you told me to.
The one in a matrix that's basically none and laced with deep insights. Inside where my life once was. I moved on trying to make it.
You make a loss, don't cry about it, you embrace it.
You told me to listen close. For generations we've had thoughts
Passed down and the trends set are contagious.
Dedication. Hard work. Plus patience.
The summation of my sacrifice has started to pay.
Thank you

Toffy's story had changed the city he lived in, but more importantly it had changed him.

The transformation helped him see the world differently. He couldn't wait to share more of his new insights, and he would do it through a series of voice broadcasts.

CHAPTER 29

**TOFFY'S VOICE POST 1: JUST START—PUT ACTION
INTO PASSION**

When I decided to join in on the mission and started listening to that mixtape, I had no clue I would be writing a story that would change anything.

My path wasn't clear. It was not a linear thought process. I went from listening to music to writing poems, back to the music, then some prose, visiting unvisited areas, before getting on this quest to the story that was part of the weaved publication that changed the way we view ourselves in this town.

I zigzagged my way to a reality that I cooked up in my mind. I manifested my own path. The process reinforced the importance of our thoughts. What we think of ourselves can be what we become.

Through my writing, I learned that even when your mission is not yet clear, default to taking action. Tinker with your idea. Play around with it. Make it real and tangible. During those little unnoticeable feats of action the mission itself becomes visible instead of "finding my passions" or waiting for screen suggestions and then "taking action." "Taking action" actually led to discovering and unearthing certain interests and passions.

We are all equipped to take action while focusing on the process because the journey is more important than the destination, and we end up finding our interests along the path.

Moral of the story: Go get it!

Start somewhere.

Start from the beginning.

Press play. Practice. Practice. Practice.

They think I know the way.

I'm guessing that's why they follow me. No, I didn't. I only know the path traveled and not what's to come. I just went with it, paid all my dues, respected the game, respected the rules, figuring things out along the way. Practicing, creating, hustling, and motivating. Learn the basics to forget it, break it, and take the risks. It should be written in stone.

TOFFY'S VOICE POST 2: STAY CURIOUS AND BUILD AUTHENTIC COMMUNITY

I didn't want to change. My fear intensified in navigating the unknown. The biggest change-makers—innovators and inventors—stumbled upon solutions through following their thread of curiosity.

That's where I started. That's what the writing did for me. Curiosity to discovery.

I write to discover what I know. Not the other way around.

The musings allow us to explore and bring forth our full selves.

Mix influences from different sources and making it into something new that bridges cultures, times, and people. This allows us to find an authentic self while we see ourselves in

what's different from us. It can merge our individual awareness into a collective of diverse mixings, creating the unexpected environment for a flash of ingenuity to strike.

The general curiosity and alertness in spotting patterns
drive innovation.

Rhythm, tones, and words builds a communal identity
that encourages diversity. It helped me follow the path of
curiosity, leading me down a back-and-forth journey to find
a tribe that was in tune with my subconscious thinking.

This helps with purpose.

Finding purpose lies at the intersection of what we want
to see more of in the world, what we are good at, and the
things we're interested in.

When we find our tribes—a group of like-minded people
who have the same vision of how we should function and the
type of world we should live in—we develop a deeper sense
of purpose.

Where purpose is not solely driven by self-interest of the
individual, but by community-driven missions.

Let's call it shared purpose.

Strong stories are a good place to find your sense of mission or dedication toward a cause, or anything that fires you
up internally, connecting you with your community. Trust
me, they're out there. It can ultimately help us raise our collective awareness—sparking necessary dialogue, bringing
communities together, and building a more equitable world.
Wiping away each manmade line of division one story at
a time.

They took out some leaders because they were teaching
wealth
To love the source and the other is to boost your health
Stay authentic, a.k.a. stay true to thyself

Live forever through the book on the shelves
Energy transformed from one to the other
Rearranging atoms, reconfiguring prescribed orders

TOFFY'S VOICE POST 3: THE CHANGE YOU WANT STARTS WITHIN (EMBRACE SELF-RESPONSIBILITY)

Embracing self-responsibility is one of the clearest paths to living a life with purpose.

And that's what the corporation figured out. Not only to separate people but to bifurcate them from their inner being.

Our true moral compass comes from within, and that is usually shaped by our experiences, who we really are, who we want to be, and how we treat ourselves and one another.

We tend to look beyond ourselves to find purpose, but owning personal responsibility is one of the bravest things we can do. Because at that point, we accept our roles as transformers and rid ourselves of a fixed "victim mentality" that holds us back from effectively transforming our reality and driving change.

Where does the responsibility lie? You might ask. Who's in charge of the experience we are having?

With the producers working hard to put products in the hand of the consumer, or the consumer's awareness of what they deem as adequate? With the producer of infinite amount of content, or with the individual with the limited amount of attention?

The individual is responsible for what they produce and consume, and these choices collectively affect the community.

As individuals, we can always come back to our sense of self-responsibility. We can always ask whether what we choose to do is in line with improving ourselves and the people around us.

You can always follow the cardinal rule of doing no harm and treating people the way you want to be treated.

By embracing personal responsibilities, we individually boost our sense of empowerment, which can help us collectively come together to disrupt our biggest common problems like the inequality that divided our city into two unique sides.

To change the world, you have to change yourself first.

Look in the mirror and see who you are, and then look again and see who you *really* are.

Whatever change you want to see, let it be seen. Bring it into the world.

Stand up and put it out there.

Fill the gap with what you are bringing in.

It all starts within.

CHAPTER 30

———

After Toffy's voice broadcast had gained traction, Deja persuaded Toffy to do an interview on her friend's podcast.

"This man's story has inspired a new string of storytellers," the host introduced Toffy to his audience. "Some people have seen the effect of the change in our city, and this man's story, our guest today, was a crucial part of that change. He has not shared his journey. He has pretty much been underground since the story broke, so we are privileged to have him here with us. Toffy, welcome, man."

"Thanks for having me here."

"So, no one has really heard from you in the last two months. We heard the three voice posts, and that has been it. Is there a reason why you have been so quiet?"

"Well, I was in the hospital, then recovery, and since then I've been enjoying this newfound peace and happiness, not worrying about my social score. I kind of wanted to just cherish that for some time."

The show host spoke directly into his microphone. "Yes, you were in the hospital... In case anyone was sleeping under a rock, Toffy jumped out of the window from his third-story apartment to save his story from being taken away from him.

We will get to that later in this segment. This is what everyone wants to know. The story behind the story. Tell us how this all happened."

"Well, I guess it all started when I was a kid. I had always loved writing stories…"

Fifteen minutes passed fast as Toffy seamlessly shared his beginnings with the host.

"I put writing aside to focus on my technical skills."

"Oh, that's true," the host said. "You are an engineer. Right? That's what you were doing at J Enterprise?"

"Yes. I was head of products, new developments, and media at J Enterprise. Then mixed in with some copywriting and assisted media."

"Tell us more about that. Isn't that crucial in this whole story?"

"It's as important as the pen I used to write the stories I wrote in my notepad."

"Interesting that the head of product at the almighty J Enterprise still writes with a pen and paper. I thought you'd be using all the new gadgets and gimmicks."

"It's not really about the instrument you use; it's about the story itself, and I just reverted to the classic form of human expression to take advantage of having opposing fingers." Toffy pinched his fingers together. "Back to J Enterprise, we were making a lot of products. Some started out with great intention, but over time 'the machine' took over— "

"The J Enterprise *machine*," the interviewer interjected. "It seemed like it couldn't be stopped. Tell us more about the machine. Just backstage you were telling me about the product you were making that really made you question your work there."

"Yeah. As you know, we had the best publishing products out, and at the time J Media was the biggest in the world. We were working with a lot of neural networks and using model-predictive controls to seamlessly create experiences people wanted. Artificial intelligence knew people better than they knew themselves. Mix the knowledge of creating addictive content with friction-free transactions, and you get something like 'Pink Money,' where screens could automatically deduct payment from you watching what you want to see on the screens.

"The goal was to grow this company as fast and as big as possible. I think the moment when I started to have a shift and question what we were doing was when we started working on a product called the Deleteron. This product was built to automatically *delete* content as it was created. So, a thought does not exist more than the second it pops into the person's mind.

"The goal was to limit information that would have people questioning their wants, to reduce the mental burden on the individual's mind, to reduce the urge for people to be curious," Toffy continued in a steady and controlled voice.

"I didn't think the product would go past the development stage, but it eventually became a hit. Management loved it. It worked. People were happy. They said the people wouldn't have to think of, read about, or write anything that would take them out of a state of surface-level bliss. The more I saw this product being tested, I started seeing the negative effects. People weren't having their stories told. More people were getting silenced. The world was turning into a humming and buzzing single-toned blandness. It was all madness masked as calmness.

"The automated and preemptive version of a revisionist history. However, in this case Deleteron was changing history as it happened. It was immediately taking things out that were not supposed to be heard or known. The future history did not happen 'in the moment,' so there was no reason to go into the past to change it. It changed *in the moment*. Inception was the death of a new and unwelcome idea, all to the advantage of the machine. You know what I'm saying?"

"Yeah, yeah," the interviewer responded.

"Then, I went past the fog one day and into Low Town. That experience changed me. Then I lost consciousness. That was my call to action. At least, as I look back on my story, it was a moment of clarity,"

Forty minutes into the interview:

"Then I got fired. I was pretty happy to focus on my story, but then things became challenging. I had grown careless about taking care of my relationships. One thing after the other. My uncle passed away. I lost... a lot of things happened. All this was within a span of a few days."

Toffy leaned in with more excitement.

"A few weeks before that, I got a covert invitation to join the project. I focused on my writing, trying to find my voice, trying to tell a story. Then I get this information about J Enterprise—"

"This was at the apartment, right?" the interviewer interjected.

"Yes. Now, I know the corporation was involved, but not to be linked with *everything*. That was eye-opening. The pollution, the fires, the mind-jacking, the mining of insights from people in Low Town converted to premium optimal experiences served through seamless interfaces. The mass manipulation, the government, the money-hiding and worshipping. Capitalism is a huge machine on its own, but no one could have predicted this new system enabled by the machines we built.

"And we, the people, were willfully giving the rights away. The system fostered a drone of animals reduced to repeatable tasks that could easily be replaced by the machine. The Corporatologists—the technology companies in alliance with the governments—knew this. And they built a never-ending loop that forced people to do more repeatable tasks, and they built the machines to take over those repeatable tasks, making more and more people disposable.

"This was the goal, to aggregate power by taking the only thing that really makes us human: *conscious thought and our curiosity*. Once you can reduce or even eliminate the ability for a person to participate in conscious thought or awareness, you take away the ability to create.

"The only way to end that endless loop is the moment when the human takes and makes a conscious decision—to break the cycle. But each moment like that has to be self-induced. That moment is so fleeting, and the consolidated cloud with its connected hardware were all built to quickly rectify and put that individual back in a state of drudgery-laced repeatability.

"To break out of the loop first requires awareness, to know you are in a loop; and secondly, it requires practice to stay in that state of awareness before the machine takes control. It's really the battle between self and the machine."

"It's interesting," the host said with contemplative curiosity. "How did you get to your state of awareness, and how did you stay there?"

"Low Town. That visit generated questions. Each answer generated more questions. I continued to poke my head out, and it continued to push my head back down."

Toffy slumped back in his chair, indicating a sense of incomplete victory.

"At the end of the day, we can point fingers at J Enterprise, but most importantly we have to look at *ourselves*. The citizens. The world we have created outwardly is just a reflection of who we are internally.

"It comes down to who we are," he continued, "and how we see ourselves. I looked at my screen long enough I started to get a sense of who I really was, and that's what got me to the point of realization. And I was writing furiously to tell that story, to let the people know what I had learned. I just wanted to finish the story before the machine took another swipe at my head."

"So, do you think we're there yet?" the interviewer asked. "We've seen a lot of change already. Is it enough? And how do we think about reshaping society?"

"Hmmm. That's a good one." Toffy gazed up at the exposed fittings attached to the concrete ceilings in the studio. "I think it's acknowledging that everything we don't pay for now, we end up paying for later. Keeping track of the human cost. Look at what's going on now. People are going through withdrawals from the screens. There's a cost for the withdrawal programs. The green lake in Low Town. Well, we're moving away from calling it Low Town, but that is being cleaned. Deleteron, although not fully deployed, was already coded in the benign-ware, stopping stories from being told. A team now has to be deployed to recode and retrain our interactions with the interfaces. That's going to take a few years and a lot of involvement from everyone. All this comes with a cost. Actual money and—even more valuable—our time. And this is coming out of everyone's wallet."

"Hmm." The interviewer was clearly reflecting.

"As we are rectifying the problems from our past actions," Toffy continued, "we also have to be vigilant on what we are developing now. We can't sit back and expect someone else to figure it out for us. These tools can be our best friends but only when designed not only for the people but with the people."

"With the people," the host echoed. "I agree."

"Yes, because people are now more involved. There's more space to ask questions now. Technology and connectivity allow us to easily find answers, and those answers only help us generate more questions. Questioning is the only way forward. It might not be the most efficient thing, but moving away from the focus on exploitation and balancing it with a good amount of exploration will do us a lot of good.

"So, are we on track in the right direction?"

"I like what we're seeing so far. J City is evolving, and that's good. Where music, poetry, art, words are becoming an integral part of the city's aesthetic, and how things are being built and developed. Because these explorations, although without a clear outcome all the time, make us human. The dialogue. The shared reality. The interconnected experience. It allows us to be comfortable with the uncertainty of our existence, gaining knowledge along the way but also revealing the growing expanse of our ignorance.

"We reshape society by making questioning more powerful than answering. Moving away from the certainty of answers to the uncertainties of question. The quest for understanding our place here then becomes driven by our quest for the perfect question."

"That's great. So let me ask you this. What happened the day you jumped out of your bathroom window?" the interviewer asked.

"There were these men in my apartment who came for my laptop and all the information I had on it."

"A laptop," the host said, fascinated. "You took it there. Old school."

"Yeah," Toffy continued. "It was given to me, to break free from the consolidated cloud. Anyway, I literally found some crucial bits of minutes before these men showed up—the J Men, the ones who started all the fires. I sat in the bathroom and raced to the end of the story as they set my place on fire. I knew I could get it out. I just wasn't sure if I would finish."

"So, had you finished *before* you jumped out of the window with your laptop?"

"Yeah, I finished just before I walked to the window."

"And then what happened?" the host asked.

"I put the laptop underneath my shirt, right here." Toffy pulled his belt to show where he'd put the laptop. "And I closed my eyes and jumped out the window. A three-story drop."

"Walk us through that thought process," the host said. "Were you just that passionate about making sure the story got out that you decided to jump out with your laptop, or was it just a desperate attempt to not get burned in the apartment?"

"I honestly don't know," Toffy confessed. "I could have left the laptop in the bathroom. I think I just took it just in case. But my laptop was synced to Musta's drive through the radio cloud, and every word I typed up was being saved on the council's network of distributed drives. So regardless, that story would have gone out. In fact, the laptop broke from the fall, like my leg."

"When you jumped, it was not to save the information on your laptop?"

"No, it wasn't."

"So why did you take it with you?"

"I honestly don't know. I think the smoke in the apartment had really gotten to my head. Plus, the vibrations had taken over. It just seemed like the only logical thing to do at that moment."

"Wow, wow," the show host spoke into his microphone. "That's amazing. Great story. There was a chance you didn't even need to jump out of the window at all, but your apartment was on fire and you had to get out of there somehow."

Toffy nodded.

"Thank you very much for stopping by and telling us this great story first. Is there anything you want to say? Some parting words, or words of enlightenment? Drop some parting knowledge on us. Or should I say, give us something that would allow us to ask the next question."

Toffy laughed and then thought about it for a moment and said, "I learned that to tell a story and to be a good storyteller, there are some secrets, tools, and tips you can easily follow. Some call them guidelines. I like to call them *tricks* because crafting a beautiful story is like magic. The most important trick out of all I have learned is this."

Toffy paused.

"When you write a story, it's all about the story you tell yourself."

ACKNOWLEDGMENTS

——

I'd like to acknowledge my wife and my best friend, Eghe, for always being so supportive. You read the first draft of this book four years before it finally got published and told me there was an interesting story in there. That encouraged me to keep writing. Thank you for the countless hours of editing (auditing) the book to make it shine.

I also want to say a big thank you to my family for always validating and instilling confidence in me. My legendary parents, Obafemi and Iyabowale Aluko, and my other super-fans, the Three Ts: Tosin, Temi, and Tomiwa. Damilola, Folarin, Seun Arowolo, and Mr. and Mrs. Obasuyi.

Shoutout to all the individuals out there who have supported my creative endeavors over the years; all the people who supported the publication of my first book, have listened to my music, collaborated with me to make music, supported me on my entrepreneurial journey, and supported this publication of this book: Tunde Afilaka, Jason Mayden, Ben Springwater, Jonathan Kola, Andro Vrdoljak, Cyril Tay, Chinedu Igbokwe, Marty Evans, Adebayo Taiwo, Ehi Obasuyi, Ore Sennaike, Abdulkamal Abdullahi, Daria Gonzalez, Doyin Sennaike, Ayodeji Ayodele, Jason Frumkin,

Ashley Edwards, Osa Obasuyi, Midowa Gbededo, Tope Sennaike, Ernest Dogbe, Chika Nwachukwu, Kudjo Achem, Nosa Obasuyi, Ayo Salako, Rajan Patel, Usman Abubakar, Deraa Dike, Justin Moses, Ozair Ali, Christos Shepherd, Mosope Adeyemi, Ifeanyi Nnadi, Tosin Orimogunje, Laolu Adeolu, Eze Phil-Ebosie, Anwer Gheddai, Fiifi Deku, Stanley Onyewuchi, Deji Adekeye, Chisa Ugoji, Ike Ofili, Oyebode Adeyi, Olayemi Oyebode, Jeff Boes, Carlos Ceballos Jr., Robert Meister, Adeniyi Aluko, Ayomide Agbola, Ken Kaneko, Fola Folowosele, Bunmi Oshodi, Kayode Arole, Gbolabo Odunaiya, Saumitra Thakur, Emeka Igboanugo, Ore Ogunlesi, Natalie Shirokova, Seun Craig, Nwanneka Onuekwusi, Femi Akinwale, Musa Ato, Michael Ibekie, Basil Eteri, Jamie Bosse, Wole Olukoya, Omolade Salawu, Oluwatoyin Senbore, Lingke Wang, Juliette Mares, Jacqueline Bello, Kwaku Adu-Gyamfi, Ime Ekanem, Bharat Ayyar, Jennifer Shoboiki, Adaobi Chine, Gil Rosen, Kikelomo Sanyaolu, Mamadou Diallo, John Shoboiki, Hakeem Ogunleye, Virginia Roberson, Michael Rucker, Raechel Jackson, Amanuel Zeryihun, Kadryn Kadasia, Wendy Marx, Neal Watterson, Edirin Ibru, Melanie Marsollier, Magdalena Perdjon-Abel, David Horn, Greg Stillman, Christine Hunter, Charles Akin-David, Enyinnaya Egejuru, Adeniyi Ajiboye, Rupa Patel, Didier Leveille, Malik Ajose, Alex Martinian, Elizabeth Dakwa-Tay, Alberto Guzmán, Charles Eteri, Adesewa Falati, Toyin Emmanuel-Olubake, Ayomide Atewologun, Adwoa Coleman, Olamide Niyi-Afuye, Polly Goss, Michael Addis, Marc Martin, and Jason Alexander Scott.

A big thank you to my beta reading community who read this book and gave valuable feedback on how to improve it. Acknowledgment to these two amazing human beings—Midowa Gbededo and Laolu Adeolu—for their valuable feedback during revisions. Thanks to my coaching and editing team for keeping me accountable and helping me get this story out: Michael Bailey, Eric Koester, Kayla LeFevre, and Vivian Rose.